Roses are White

Lesley Lambert

Simcoe Publishing

Simcoe Publishing
100 Cedar Glade
Dunnington
York
YO19 5PJ

© Simcoe Publishing 2005

First published 2005

All rights reserved. Reproduction of this book by photocopying or electronic means for non-commercial purposes is permitted. Otherwise, no part of this book may be reproduced, adapted, stored in a retrieval system or transmitted by any means, electronic, mechanical, photocopying, or otherwise without the prior written permission of Simcoe Publishing.

ISBN   0 9551509 0 6

From 1 January 2007
ISBN   978 0 9551509 0 6

Cover design by BP Design, York

Prepared and printed by:
York Publishing Services Ltd
64 Hallfield Road
Layerthorpe
York
YO31 7ZQ
Tel: 01904 431213   Website: www.yps-publishing.co.uk

Contents

Author's Foreword	iv
Prologue	1
Part 1	5
Part 2	129
Part 3	265
Author's Notes	436

Author's Foreword

After seeing Lord Olivier in the title role of Shakespeare's play, *Richard III*, I became fascinated by the life of this fifteenth century King of England. I was twelve years old at the time. Fifty years and dozens of ancient and modern non-fiction books later, I am sadly of the opinion that historians will never agree on either the character of King Richard or on the solutions to the many mysteries that surround his life. The most famous debate concerns the fate of his nephews, the young sons of Edward IV, who disappeared from the Tower of London in July 1483.

Dispute has raged for over five hundred years and continues to inspire modern historians to retell the saga from endless new perspectives. Backed by hours of diligent research and presented with the professional integrity we have come to expect, each new book sheds minute flickers of light on the mysteries but still the full truth remains elusive.

Even the characters involved are distant and sketchy but digesting so many 'retellings' has developed an historical cast in my mind's eye, just as the characters in TV soaps evolve through numerous episodes. Fifty plus years of re-runs has left me with an intimate knowledge of my own personal cast, which I use in this book together with fictitious characters as part of an experiment. The fictitious characters interact with my historical cast and interrogate them from within the story as it develops.

To what degree this experiment provides plausible solutions is for the reader to judge.

Prologue

Tewkesbury 4th May 1471

The clouds parted and evidence of the day's battle rose out of the blackness in a wash of weak moonlight. From his position on the ridge top, the middle aged priest stared in disbelief at the mangled mounds of flesh, broken staves and trampled banners that stretched from beyond the Gloucester road to within an hundred paces of the great Abbey at Tewkesbury. At first light, the familiar sounds of adversaries preparing for battle had gladdened the priest's heart and made him proud of his long service to Lancaster, for in those early hours he had not contemplated a Yorkist victory, only the just and rightful crushing of the usurper, Edward of York.

The priest sighed and brushed the persisting tears from his face with the back of his chubby hand. How could this have happened? What was God's purpose in allowing this defeat? When the news of the Prince of Lancaster's death had been brought to the Abbey by mortally wounded noblemen, the priest had fled the Cathedral, unwilling to believe the words, even of dying men. But here on the battlefield itself he knew it to be true. In the distance he could hear the triumphant cries of celebration still emanating from the Yorkist camp at Tredlington but the Lancastrian camp south of Tewkesbury was dormant.

However, the ghostly tableau to his left was not entirely still nor indeed silent. The last vestiges of life shuddered and moaned amongst the glints of discarded metal; the final gasps of those not important enough to be carried from the field by the victors.

Sickened by the sight, the priest turned to make his way back to the Abbey when he was startled by a much closer groan rising from the hollow below the ridge. Carefully he peered over the edge whilst clinging precariously to a small hazel bush that was growing defiantly from the outcrop. At first all he could see was the carcass of a large destrier sprawled motionless across the beck, a spear sunk deep into his flank. Then, as the moon escaped the remaining wisps of cloud and increased in brightness, he spotted a man on his back, draped across a boulder next to the dead beast's head, his own head hanging over the edge of the huge stone and his left foot still in the stirrup. Even as the priest assessed the scene the man moaned again and tried in vain to raise himself from the boulder. Using the hazel bush to lower himself over the edge the priest slid and tumbled down the loose stones until the steep incline gave way to a gentler slope and he was able to make his way to the stricken man more easily.

The brook was reduced to a trickle where horse and rider lay and whilst the overweight cleric had no problem removing the trapped foot from the stirrup, pulling the half conscious man from the boulder required all his strength. He was forced to rest after such exertion and sat huffing and puffing whilst the rescued man lay moaning and writhing on the grass beside him. With a determined effort the priest forced himself upright, pulled a cloth from his sleeve, soaked it in the shallow water and tried to revive the man by pressing the wet cloth to his lips. The water seemed to calm him and gradually his breathing became less laboured until eventually he opened his eyes and with the priest's help managed to sit up. A cursory check convinced the priest that his patient had no broken bones and as there was no blood seeping through his clothes neither had he sustained any flesh wounds.

"A blow to the head seems to be your only injury," ventured the priest, dabbing gently at the egg shaped swelling on his left temple. The man winced but made no reply.

There was something incongruous about the appearance of this fallen rider. He wore no armour, yet a red mark around his head was evidence of a tightly fitting helmet, recently removed and he should be wearing a tabard displaying his lord's insignia. Had that also been discarded? And where was he going? He had been riding a valuable war horse away from the battlefield. The priest voiced his unease.

"Where were you going when your horse was felled?"

The man said nothing but held out a clenched fist in front of himself, staring at it as if it had some meaning he could not fathom. Tentatively the priest reached for the fist and gently prised open the fingers. In the man's opened palm lay a small brooch. It was a beautiful piece: the three plumbs of Wales encircled with a coronet depicted in pearls and diamonds and all set in gold with a remarkably fine pin.

The priest gasped, he had seen it before: he had been present when the Earl of Warwick had given this very brooch to the Prince of Lancaster as a wedding gift. He remembered it so well because it signified that the great Earl recognised the boy as the rightful Prince of Wales. The priest could hardly contain his excitement. Had the Prince given the brooch to this man to identify the bearer to a third party? It was common practise to use a recognisable item as identification and proof of trust.

"Who gave you the brooch?" demanded the Priest, "Was there a message? It could be important."

"I have no recollection of anything prior to you pulling me from the stream," stammered the man.

"Well no matter for now. The blow to your head must have taken your memory, but it will return given time." He folded the man's fingers back around the brooch. "Put it in your script and show it to no-one until you remember how it came into your possession." The priest watched the man stuff the jewel into his purse. "I shall take care of you until the matter is resolved. Now, can you walk?"

The man got to his feet, teetering as if drunk but with one hand on his saviour's shoulder he managed to stand. The priest looked up into the face that was at least three hands above his own. A noble face, probably of Mediterranean origin; a Frenchman perhaps? That would make sense as four weeks earlier the Prince of Lancaster had sailed from France with a thousand French soldiers provided by the King of France himself.

"We must leave this place, make for the coast and find a passage to France," said the priest, moving gingerly forward, the man leaning heavily on his shoulder. "You can call me Doctor John. I shall call you Lazarus until your memory returns."

PART 1

"Clarence is come, false, fleeting, perjur'd Clarence"
(Richard III – Wm Shakespeare)

CHAPTER 1

Clerkenwell 14th January 1478

The wind rattled the shutters and blew the snow into drapes of white, dressing the buildings and hedgerows in winter uniformity. It had snowed all day and the evening had brought the north wind and a sharp frost to intensify the season of human misery.

Giles Butler huddled deeper into the additional covers that had been piled onto his bed but nervous excitement was conspiring with the chill to keep him awake. Tomorrow was the birthday he had anticipated with both fear and longing since his mother's death ten years ago when she had left him a casket, to be opened on the day he reached his eighteenth year. Giles had not known his parents, his mother had entered a small Carmelite Priory somewhere in Norwich soon after his birth and the identity of his father was unknown, even to his guardian, Bishop Robert, in whose London house he now shivered.

Before retiring Giles had removed the crude wooden box from his private chest and placed it on the stool where he could just distinguish its outline in the fluttering light of the hour candle. He closed his eyes tightly and hugged his knees in an attempt to stem the panic. Every night for the last ten years he had included in his prayers a plea that his mother's box would reveal the identity of his father and tomorrow Bishop Robert would surrender the key and the waiting would be over.

There was neither warmth nor comfort in his bed and Giles reckoned the fire might still be alight in the great hall, where his friend, Mark Taylor, would be curled up with his hound Woof, along with the rest of the household's servants. So Giles pulled on his soft shoes, wrapped himself in the largest of his bed covers, pushed the box into his nightshirt and set out along the screened passage. It seemed as if his every step echoed on the short journey but whilst the numerous bundles that were sleeping servants, gently rose and fell to the accompaniment of snuffles and wheezes, nobody stirred, except for Woof, who padded up to welcome him. The shaggy haired black and white mongrel was unable to bark or even whimper and had been near to death when Mark had rescued him from a midden by the Thames two years ago. Wedged now between Mark and Woof, Giles soon began to feel warm and drowsy but his friend had been roused by the invasion of another body and woke to scold Woof, only to find it was Giles who had disturbed his sleep.

"Isn't mi lord's bed warm?" grumbled Mark, shuffling to one side to allow his young master better access to the remains of the fire. He was a large ungainly man whose hands and feet were too big, even for his long limbs, his movements being reminiscent of a marionette whose controller had not quite mastered his art. He was the son of the Bishop's housekeeper, Mary and three years older than Giles he had appointed himself squire to his young master.

"I couldn't sleep," whispered Giles, "Hell's teeth, this hound smells."

"No he doesn't, its Arthur," mumbled Mark from beneath his blanket and from where a long, disembodied finger appeared and pointed towards a large bellied, grubby man wheezing in the far corner. "Bishop Robert said he was to sleep indoors because of the cold." Mark turned his huge frame away from the offending Arthur to face Giles. "Only Bishop Robert don't have to smell him all night, does he?"

Giles wrapped the corner of his own cover over his nose and patted Woof's head by way of an apology. Bishop Robert was a good man even if his critics did accuse him of dereliction of duty. It was rumoured that he had received the mitre of Bath and Wells as a reward for some personal service performed for King Edward and that he had not been seen in the diocese since his enthronement nineteen years ago. Giles and Mark knew the Bishop to be a kindly man but he confined Giles to the manor at Clipberry, only allowing him to venture beyond the bailey under his personal supervision. True, Giles was small for his age and his fair hair and pale complexion gave the impression of a much younger man but he was strong for his size, demonstrating formidable skills in the tilt yard, so the Bishop's rigorous control of his movements, caused resentment and frustration for both young men.

"Have you opened that box yet?" whispered Mark, with mock innocence.

"You know I haven't. Bishop Robert still has the key and because of the snow, he's gone to Westminster today instead of at first light tomorrow, which means it will be tomorrow evening before I discover the contents of the stupid thing, " sulked Giles. "It's ludicrous. I should have prised it open ten years ago when I was first given it."

"Temper, temper," warned Mark, "you know you don't mean that."

"I do. I have built my life on the basis of what that box may contain. I swear to God Mark, after ten years of speculation nothing less than the deeds to my father's estates or the knowledge that he is some honourable knight, will satisfy me. And now, because of this ... this ... ridiculous wedding tomorrow, I must wait another full day."

"Calm yourself Giles. You will wake the whole house. It isn't the Bishop's fault that the royal wedding is the same day as your birthday."

Both young men lay in silence considering the royal event scheduled for the following day, when the Bishop was to attend King Edward on the occasion of his youngest son's marriage to Lady Anne Mowbray at the Abbey of Westminster. The little Duke of York was barely four years old and his bride just six. Giles contemplated what it would be like to grow up with your wife as a playmate and Mark wished such an arrangement could have been made for him, for he was shy and awkward with women. If he had known Alice Twynho from the age of four he would be spared the embarrassment he was currently experiencing in his attempts to woo her, or so he thought.

Giles pulled the box from inside his huddle of wrappings and ran his finger round the keyless lock.

"If this holds the secret to my father's identity, then I can join him and avoid going to Oxford or becoming a novice at that Abbey in Yorkshire as the Bishop suggested."

Mark sighed, he knew Giles did not want to go to university or take holy orders. The Bishop should have placed him in the service of a lord years ago and now Oxford was one of his remaining options.

"Alright, alright, keep the noise down. There is no point in tormenting yourself, you'll know the truth soon enough" said Mark, "but the box is no bigger than your hand Giles, I think it is unlikely to hold legal documents." Mark pulled his blanket over his head to signal the end of their discussion but before he fell asleep, he prayed that Giles would not be disappointed when he opened his box in the morning.

Giles woke the next morning coughing and spluttering into his blanket to find the rest of the household already up and about their business. Somehow Mark had raked the fire and added fresh logs without waking him but it was yesterday's muck being brushed from the floor of the great hall by smelly Arthur that attacked his lungs. Mary and most of the more presentable servants had been seconded to the Queen's household, to help organise accommodation for the numerous ladies' maids journeying with their mistresses to the royal wedding and so Arthur was replacing Mary in certain of her duties. Grimacing at the odour in the great hall, Giles strode out into the yard to relieve himself in the cess pit, to find the snow had covered the foul pit, as well as every trace of green slime that surrounded its approaches. He inhaled deeply, feeling energised by the cleansing frost but as he fastened his points, his wonderment gave way to the reality of the freezing cold. With sudden urgency, he picked his way back, stepping in his outward footprints as he tried to minimize the stinging wet sensation working its way beyond his feet to find the warm flesh of his ankles and calves. He stopped briefly at the wooden tub by the Buttery door to splash freezing cold water over his face before hurrying inside to find food with which to break his fast. Mary's absence had upset the smooth running of the household but Mark had received clear instructions from his mother and arrived from the bakery balancing a basket of fresh bread and a tub of goats cheese. He dropped them awkwardly onto the trestle table whilst Giles poured watered ale into two cups from a large jug.

"Congratulations on your birthday Giles," said Mark, smiling broadly. "Guess what? The Bishop has instructed me to accompany you to Westminster, so that we might join the crowds celebrating the royal wedding."

"Really, I'm allowed out without his Grace. I can't believe it. We can take refreshment at the Westminster tavern afterwards," enthused Giles, "and then you can introduce me to your beloved Alice."

Giles laughed whilst Mark fumbled clumsily with the bread basket.

"What's this?" said Giles, picking up a small key which appeared to have fallen from the basket. Mark feigned innocence but the colour in his face betrayed his guilt. "Bishop Robert gave you the key last night," cried Giles, " and you let me believe I should have to wait another full day. Mark how could you?"

"Oh very easily," said Mark with a grin. " Go on then, take it up to your chamber. And Giles, Good luck."

Within seconds Giles had retrieved his box from the great hall and pushed by Arthur, now sweeping the screen passage. Sensing the excitement Woof bounded after him, only to pull up short behind Giles' firmly closed bedchamber door. Sitting on his bed with the box in one hand and the key in the other, Giles tried to steady himself. Aloud, he prayed his special prayer for the last time and then inserting the key in the lock, he opened the box.

Nervously Giles removed a tiny silk drawstring pouch and two small scraps of folded parchment, both bound separately with cord and sealed with a daub of wax. With clumsy, shaking fingers he released the drawstring on the silk pouch and tipped a gold ring into the palm of his hand. It was the work of a master goldsmith. His mother's initials EB, entwined with tiny gold vine leaves were so exquisitely crafted and gracefully arranged about the band that they could have grown in that formation. The ring slid easily over Giles' largest finger but no matter, he would wear it suspended on a thong around his neck. He turned his attention to the pieces of parchment and could hear his own heart beating against his chest as he read the names scrawled on the outside. His own name was on one and on the other, written in the same hand, was the name 'Robert'. Giles broke the seal on his note and gasped in horror as he revealed three meagre lines of communication. For several moments all he could do was gape at the inadequacy of the script but when he finally made sense of the words he felt sick with anger.

Dearest Giles,
Please find it in your heart to forgive my not being there for you all these years. I want you to know that your father and I were married before your conception. Ask Bishop Robert, he knows the truth. God bless and keep you.
Eleanor.

"Ask Bishop Robert," he screamed at the note, "I have been asking Bishop Robert for ten years and he has always claimed to no nothing about my father."

Giles had been told that it was his uterine grandfather who had forced the unmarried Eleanor into a convent and employed the Bishop to raise her son and that the old man's continued support depended upon Giles making no attempt to contact him. Nobody knew the identity of his father and the Bishop had even hinted that Eleanor herself was unsure, leaving Giles feeling justifiably resentful of his mother and placing all his hope in a father he believed would be glad to know him if only he could be found.

The pulse on Giles' right temple throbbed painfully yet all he could contemplate was striking out at the Bishop until he hurt … and hurt … and hurt. He was thumping the bed so hard that the second note lifted into the air and came to rest against his avenging fist. Giles picked it up and tore off the seal. The second note was even briefer than the first.

Dearest Robert,
I beg you, ensure that Giles never encounters George, Duke of Cla[rence].
Tell the King! God bless and keep you.
Eleanor.

Giles read and reread the words. A knock on the door and Mark's head appeared.

"Well, does the box reveal the name of your father?"

"No," said Giles angrily, "but the Bishop knows who he is, look."

He pushed the two pieces of parchment into Mark's hand and waited in silence whilst his friend read them.

"Oh Giles I'm sorry. To think that Bishop Robert has known all along. But why must you never encounter the Duke of Clarence?"

"How should I know?" shrieked Giles, "unless ….unless *he* is my father. That must be it. King Edward's brother is *my* father."

"No Giles, that doesn't make sense. Why should your mother tell you to ask the Bishop to name your father and then instruct him to keep you from meeting the man?"

"I have no idea. I will ask Bishop Robert that question when I accuse him of keeping the truth from me all these years. Tell me what *you* know about George, Duke of Clarence. Start with why he is imprisoned in the Tower."

"I have no idea."

"Oh Mark, you visit Alice at the Westminster tavern. You must hear all the gossip."

Mark shrugged. He heard all kinds of gossip at the tavern.

"Two years ago, a distant cousin of my Alice, Mistress Twynho, was appointed midwife to the Clarence's wife Isobel. Both Isobel and her babe died soon after the birth and the Duke accused the midwife of poisoning them."

"Hell's teeth."

"It was untrue but never-the-less, Mistress Twynho was dragged from her bed by Clarence's retainers and hanged without the authority of the King's justices."

"Jesu! But would the King imprison his brother for injustice dispensed to a servant?"

"That isn't the point Giles. Clarence convened his own court and administered his own justice: he undermined King Edward's authority. Ask Matthew about it next Sunday."

Sir Matthew Pawson was a close friend of the Bishop and had spent every Sunday at his house in Clipberry Street for as long as Giles could remember. He was a kind, sensitive man who had made time to play when they were children, arranging fishing trips and practising for hours with Giles in the tilt yard. He was a member of the royal household, a knight of the wardrobe and he would certainly be privy to most events that took place at court and as Giles knew from bitter experience, he loved to gossip. He made a mental note to encourage the knight to talk about the Duke of Clarence on Sunday next.

"This cannot be right," said Mark, scrutinising the second note, "and it's addressed to the Bishop, you shouldn't have opened it."

"And he shouldn't have lied to me for the past ten years."

"Two wrongs…" began Mark, quoting the Bishop but he paused mid-sentence.

"What is it?"

"Eleanor wrote this note, warning the Bishop against you meeting the Duke of Clarence ten years before she intended it to be read. What threat does the Duke pose from today, that was not applicable over the last decade?"

"How should I know," replied Giles jumping off his bed and searching for his strongest boots and heaviest cloak. "If George Clarence is my father, then the King is my uncle and the little bridegroom my cousin. I want to take a look at my family. I'm not a bastard Mark, I'm one of them by right."

"I see, so does my lord require a shave before he meets his royal cousin?" mocked Mark, "and perhaps your highness should change out of your nightshirt before joining your royal kin?"

Chapter 2

Westminster 15th January 1478

The sky had turned an ominous pink but temporarily it served to enhance the winter scene, providing a fairytale backdrop for the marriage of prince to princess. Guests had been arriving at the Abbey since early morning but none had been able to travel by barge for fear of becoming trapped in the ice that was accumulating on the River Thames. However, their onerous journey by road, provided a longer and more spectacular parade for the crowds to enjoy. Richly clad noblemen struggled to steady and reassure their nervous steeds as they picked the safest path through the snow and ice. Grooms were walking the ladies' carriages but with less success as slipping and slithering horses staggered in their shafts threatening to upend the trailers.

Giles and Mark walked the mile and a half to Westminster, leaving the city by Newgate and joining in the general celebrations en route. A group of youths already under the influence of drink linked their arms as they passed, encouraging them to join in a tuneless rendering of a bawdy song. Younger children threw snowballs at Mark, laughing at his ungainly efforts to stave them off but Giles was quick to retaliate with accurately thrown icy missiles and they ran off tumbling and sliding as they tried to dodge his unexpected advance.

Turning into the road that led to the Abbey, they forced their way into the crowds of well wishers that lined the roadside, when a horn sounded in the distance. Folk appeared from nowhere, swelling the eager throng which pushed forward, expecting to see the King and the little Duke of York. They were still some way off but the herald at the front of the precession was just coming into view, so the crowd pressed forward again. This time Giles lost his balance, toppling heavily into the back of a large woman, who fortunately was able to stand her ground. Mark was to Giles' right and had remained anchored by his oversized feet but a high pitched scream on *his* right, drew the attention of those in the vicinity and the crowd swayed again to determine the cause of the outcry. Giles could just make out the figure of a man crumpled in a heap on the ground, when another stumbled in the sway and came down heavily on the fallen man's chest. The second faller managed to scramble to his feet, leaving the first man motionless and in danger of being trampled by others carried involuntarily forward. Reaching into his script, Giles pulled out a few coins which he threw into the back of the crowd. Immediately, folk turned around and tried to recover the coins from the slush, providing just enough space for Mark and Giles to haul the trampled man to his feet and drag him towards the comparative safety of a handcart abandoned in the deeper snow. Mark lifted the unconscious stranger aboard and climbed up alongside to examine the extent of his injuries. Giles was about to join him when he became aware of a young woman hanging onto his cloak and realised that she had been dragging behind him throughout their retreat.

"He needs his medicine," she wailed, "please help me get him to the tavern over there. I know the owners, they will help."

Without waiting for Giles and Mark she started to push her way through the back of the crowd towards the tavern. With some difficulty Mark and Giles hauled the limp body after her and by the time they reached the tavern the girl had alerted the landlord who was in the doorway waiting to receive the patient.

"Morning Ned," puffed Mark as they struggled through the narrow opening. In return the bemused landlord slapped Mark on the shoulder, causing him to stagger and nearly drop the head-end of the unconscious body. The landlord was small with square shoulders and well developed arms which he placed under the body and relieving the younger men of their load, he gently lifted the man onto the bench he had placed before the fire. Then, without taking his eyes from the patient he ordered Mark into the back room to find Alice and bring hot water and ignoring Giles completely, addressed the unconscious man's female companion.

"Mistress Margery, have you some of those salts master Luke takes for his condition?" he asked, trying to revive the man by rubbing his cold, elegant hands in his own warm, rough ones.

"In his purse I think," she replied in small voice, whilst wiping blood from her companion's forehead with her sleeve.

Giles felt at a loss, for he was the only stranger in the rescue party. From what he had heard, the tavern must be the one owned by Mark's Alice and her father, and it seemed that both the unconscious man and his female companion were known to the landlord.

The tavern was singularly unimpressive and Giles was surprised that two such well dressed young people frequented the place, although the floor had been swept clean and fresh rushes laid this morning and there were no dirty jugs or black jacks left by last nights drinkers. As Giles' eyes became accustomed to the weak light he could see that pots of fresh herbs had been placed on some of the far tables and that one side of the room had wooden screens that formed alcoves into which people could hide away from the general view.

He was about to ask the landlord the name of the injured man when Mark and Alice returned from the backroom, both rather flushed and carrying a jug of hot water and a pewter bowl. Whilst Mark quickly introduce Alice and her father to Giles and the landlord explained that Margery and the injured man were valued customers, the young woman rummaged in her companion's script and produced a small leather pouch from which she tipped a few green crystals into the bowl. Alice added hot water and a strange smell rose with the steam. Ned and Mark raised the head and shoulders of the unconscious man whilst the two women lifted the bowl to his mouth and attempted to force a few drops of the brew through his parted lips. Giles watched as they soothed and cooed over their patient. He estimated that Margery was about his own age, and perhaps five years younger than her companion but she had the confidence and poise of an older woman. She was dainty and bird like in her movements, with smooth pink hands, clean nails and the clearest blue eyes he had ever seen and although her hair was hidden beneath her wimple, Giles was sure it would be long and golden fair. Alice was about the same age but not nearly so appealing. Uncharitably Giles thought she had the makings of a typical alewife with broad hips, rough hands and weather chaffed lips but she had exceptionally beautiful hair: a cascade of bright auburn held carelessly in a large net that flopped about her neck and shoulders in defiance of her efforts to keep it bound.

The man on the bench was regaining consciousness and those administrating to him relaxed slightly, congratulating one another with exchanged smiles and words describing his gradual improvement.

"There, that's better Luke my love," breathed Margery softly, "you will be well again soon," and handing the pewter bowl to Ned she brushed the creases from her gown and adjusted her wimple. "Please take care of Luke until he has recovered fully," she begged earnestly, "I really must go now. Lady Stanley will be asking for me and with no good reason to have left her quarters, I shall be in dreadful trouble if I am missed."

She blew Luke a kiss and flitted passed Alice and Mark without a word but she stopped by Giles and placing a delicate kiss on both his cheeks she thanked him with such affection that even the most cynical of male hearts would have been captivated. Mesmerised in a cloud of her perfume and seduced by the closeness of her body, Giles was unable to reply but Margery, delighted by the affect she had on him, smiled the sweetest smile and pressed a second, fuller kiss onto his lips. Whilst she whispered farewell in his ear, Giles floated away someplace beyond reality. Then brushing her hand casually across the top of his thigh, she smiled coyly and departed.

Meanwhile out in the backyard an argument had erupted between two stable hands and Ned thrust the medicine bowl at Giles, forcing him to abandon his private heaven

"Watch you don't spill it lad," he growled and then rolling up his sleeves the landlord strode out into the yard mumbling something about, 'banging their bleeding heads together.'

Outside the sound of cheers from well wishers signalled the arrival of the wedding party but Giles had lost interest in gawping at his possible royal relatives as Luke was recovering quickly. He swung his long legs carefully onto the floor and stretched his back and neck in readiness to stand and then taking the bowl from Giles he drank the last drops of medicine, raised his body from the bench and stood.

"I'll be fine now thanks," he said, wiping his mouth on the back of his hand, "Margery ... where is Margery?"

"She had to go," said Giles, blushing deeply at the uncontrollable reaction that the mention of her name was inducing, "she ... she said something about, a Lady Stanley?"

Luke nodded his understanding. "The formidable Lady Stanley," he said, pulling a long face and observing Giles' discomfort added, "we are betrothed, Margery and I, but sometimes she tends to forget and gives the wrong impression." He laughed with a knowing sadness and whilst Giles recovered his composure, Alice picked up the empty jug and pointed to the bowl, for Mark to collect and follow her into the back kitchen.

"You appear unconcerned about your attack," said Giles, when the two lovers had scuttled off, "have you always been so afflicted?"

Luke flexed his shoulder blades and stretched his neck again.

"For as long as I can remember but that's only back to '71, after the battle of Tewkesbury when I sustained a head injury during combat which took my memory and gave me these seizures in return."

Giles could imagine that Luke had been a soldier, he had a scar above his right eye and another very deep one on his left hand. "Don't you even know who you are?"

"No, I have no idea. Not that I haven't tried to find out and before you ask, nobody has been looking for me either."

Giles stared in disbelief at Luke who began to laugh but stopped instantly, gripping the sides of his head as the pain reminded him to keep calm for the next few hours.

"I've been very lucky," he continued more soberly, "I was rescued from the battlefield by a priest and I have prospered under his tutorage for the last seven years. I sometimes think it might be best now to forget my earlier life." He winked and nudged Giles with his elbow, "who knows what awful crimes I might have committed."

I wish I could be so philosophical about my own problem," said Giles wearily, "this morning I expected to learn the identity of my father but instead I find my guardian has been deceiving me for the past ten years."

"Really," said Luke, immediately empathising with the younger man's dilemma, "why is your father's identity not known to you?"

Giles was eager to share his disappointment with someone. Mark would have been his preference but he was occupied with Alice and so Giles unburdened himself on Luke, starting with his mother's death and her leaving him the casket and ending by pulling the notes from his script and handing them to his new acquaintance.

"Let's sit over there behind those screens," whispered Luke, "away from the fire," which was where most customers were beginning to congregate now that the procession had passed by. He hailed Ned and ordered food for them both, ale for Giles and some more boiled water for himself and in response to the query on Giles' face he explained, that he must not drink alcohol for some hours after taking his medicine or he would suffer agonising head aches for several days. As Luke began to move, Giles stepped forward to assist him but he appeared completely recovered, walking easily to the screened alcoves. Giles joined him at the opposite side of the table and was struck for the first time by his new friend's Mediterranean appearance, recalling an Italian cleric that Matthew Pawson had brought to Clipberry Manor last year. His skin was the same olive colour as Luke's and he had a high bridged long nose, dark eyes and blue black hair. Was Luke Italian?

Ned reappeared from the back kitchen with their drinks, two bowls of steaming rabbit stew and cakes of freshly baked bread which he set before them with obvious pride. Luke made exaggerated noises of approval and the landlord shuffled away, satisfied that his efforts had been recognised.

Whilst Giles ate his stew, Luke reread the notes.

"What do they mean?" he eventually asked.

"Well ... I am not a bastard and the Bishop knows the identity of my father," replied Giles, "but when I first read them, I concluded that George Clarence was my sire but now I am not so sure."

"Why did your mother wait ten years before warning the Bishop not to allow you to meet the Duke? I mean, what possibly difference can your birthday make to whatever threat he poses?"

Giles stopped eating for a moment and considered the question. Mark had made the same observation this morning.

"Unless it was just a reminder of an earlier agreement she had made with the Bishop," continued Luke, answering himself, "that is, if he *is* your father. Perhaps the real message lies in what it is the Bishop should tell the King."

"That he has a legitimate nephew" suggested Giles, "but why now, why not years ago?"

"I agree it's odd" said Luke thoughtfully, "but the only way to find out if Clarence is your father is to confront the Bishop with both notes."

"I intend to," Giles said tersely, "but I doubt he will change his story now."

"Then you must confront George Clarence himself."

"How can I? he's locked away in the Bowyer Tower."

"But not chained to a cell wall." Luke sipped his water and pulled a face at the brackish taste. "He lives in comparative luxury, attended by his own squires and receiving visitors without scrutiny. Your Bishop Robert calls every day."

Giles' mouth dropped open. "He does what?"

"Bishop Robert is the Duke of Clarence's legal advisor and long-time friend ... you didn't know? How could you not know?"

Giles' face turned white with rage and he brought his fist down on the table with such force that Luke instinctively lifted his bowl. The drink filled blackjacks bounced up and spilled but he was so beside himself that even the silence that fell on the rest of the tavern failed to embarrass or quiet him.

"How do you know so much about the Bishop?" he shouted

and all the customers in the tavern awaited the reply.

"Sit down and control yourself, do you want all Westminster to know your business?"

With enormous effort Giles resumed his seat and waited whilst Luke continued his meal. Nothing more was said until the audience gave up straining their ears.

"Well?" urged Giles when he thought he had waited long enough, "how do you know so much about Bishop Robert?"

"Simple, the priest that rescued me from Tewkesbury is Doctor John Morton, Master of the Rolls. He supported Lancaster then but threw himself on Edward's mercy when Queen Margaret was captured. Anyway, Bishop Robert and he are competitors for the King's favour and anything and everything Bishop Robert does is noted by the Doctor."

"I don't understand?"

"Until recently, Bishop Robert was the King's most valued advisor but his continued support of the Duke of Clarence has angered King Edward and now Doctor Morton is constantly at His Majesty's side in the Bishop's place."

"I see. Do you know *why* Clarence has been imprisoned these past six months?"

Luke considered for a moment. " I suppose Edward eventually lost patience with him. He has continued to claim that the crown is rightfully his, based on some obscure rumour that King Edward is not the son of the Duke of York. Some say his brain is addled and it's only a matter of time before George Clarence becomes a raving madman. The strange thing is, your Bishop Robert has continued to befriend him."

"But Bishop Robert has never supported Clarence's claim to the crown, has he?"

"No, he never strayed from his allegiance to King Edward."

"So why does he befriend him and why has he never told me of this friendship?"

"God knows. It doesn't make sense."

"Oh I think it does," seethed Giles, after a moment's thought, "don't you see? Clarence married my mother Eleanor on a whim and when he realised his folly, forced his unwanted wife into a convent and off loaded her son into the care of his good friend the Bishop."

"Or, your grandfather did make the arrangements for your mother to enter the convent as you have been led to believe and Clarence does not know he has a son, which would explain why you must never meet him," suggested Luke.

Giles sighed "When I was a boy I thought the Bishop might be my father and that he had to pretend otherwise because he was a man of the cloth. I challenged him once."

"Goodness, what did he say?"

"That it was not so and that not even my mother really knew the identity of my father."

The recollection of what he now knew to be a lie and the implications it had for Eleanor's virtue, cut deep into Giles' heart releasing uncontrollable anger. Without taking his leave of Luke, he stuffed the notes into his script and made straight for the door, somehow expecting the cold to freeze his emotions and hold back his growing hatred of Bishop Robert.

Chapter 3

The Palace of Westminster 15th January 1478

Luke paid the landlord and made his way back to the Palace of Westminster to resume his duties in the service of Doctor Morton. His earlier assignation with Margery had been ruined by his seizure and he was worried that she may not have returned to her post before she was missed.

The wedding banquet was already in progress in the King's great chamber and the sound of music and cheerful voices rang throughout the palace in celebration of the happy event. As Luke made his way along the lower corridors, servants passed him carrying greasy platters, trays of meat bones and half eaten food, empty jugs, messy bowls of unfinished sauces and basket upon basket of unneeded bread. When he reached the top of the main gallery he could see page boys stationed at every doorway leading into the banqueting hall, fidgeting and yawning as they waiting to be hailed by their masters. But as Luke made his way along the back corridors, to where Doctor Morton's chamber's were located, he detected a strange atmosphere. Clerks with earnest faces and hurried strides were bearing armfuls of scrolls and writing materials from storerooms to offices with an intensity associated more with a crisis than with a wedding celebration.

"There you are," sighed Doctor Morton as Luke entered the chamber, "where have you been man? I could do with your assistance here."

"Is something amiss? Why are you not at the banquet?"

John Morton, Doctor of civil and cannon law was certainly dressed for a royal occasion. His large girth was swathed in a fine woollen cassock, deep green in colour and decorated with gold and silver embroidery at the neck and cuffs. A matching skullcap covered the crown of his head, below which, a circle of iron grey hair framed his florid face and on the ledge of flesh that rose above his waist whenever he was seated, there swayed a large silver and gold cross, suspended on an elaborate silver chain. He pushed the documents he was studying to one side and spread his chubby bejewelled fingers on the table before him.

"His Majesty has seen fit to convene Parliament tomorrow in order that George, Duke of Clarence undergo trial by his peers, on an attainder of high treason," he announced, in a tone that implied the decision to be imprudent.

"A public trial ... of the King's brother ... *tomorrow?* The man has been locked in the Tower for the past six months. What can he have done to provoke such haste?"

"I don't know. All I have been told is that the trial will take place tomorrow because most of the nobles are in the capital for the wedding and available for parliamentary duty. I doubt they would have attended otherwise."

Luke dropped heavily onto the bench under the window.

"I am to collate any relevant documents that will support King Edward's accusations should they be challenged," continued Morton, mopping his cherub like face with one of his kid gloves. "It's too much to prepare for tomorrow: even if I knew the specific nature of the accusations."

"I wouldn't worry. Who would dare challenge the King?" asked a bemused Luke.

Morton raised his eyebrows by way of reply.

"Oh no, not even Bishop Robert would dare to call the King's accusations into question in so public an arena," protested Luke.

"Probably not. But who is preparing the indictment? It should be my task. How can I collate the documents if I am not privy to the indictment?"

"Perhaps His Majesty will send for you after the banquet," suggested Luke helpfully.

The door swung open wide and William, Lord Hastings blustered in unannounced. He too should have been at the banquet but had excused himself when the whisper of the impending trial reached his section of the table. His tunic was damp with drink and stained with dropped food, his flushed face betraying the large quantity of wine he had consumed. A seasoned solider of some fifty years and King Edward's oldest friend, Hastings mistrusted Doctor Morton and privately questioned Edward's wisdom in employing the ex-Lancastrian. So the inebriated Lord was easily convinced that Doctor John was behind this quickly arranged, reckless trial.

"Did *you* persuade Edward to try George Clarence for high treason?" he bellowed, "what in God's name do you think you're about man?" The old warrior moved so close to Morton, that the cleric recoiled from the sight of his rotten teeth and the smell of his disgusting breath.

"It had nothing to do with me, my Lord Chamberlain," said Morton, with as much dignity as he could muster. He covered his nose and mouth momentarily with one hand whilst indicating a chair for his visitor with the other. Hastings ignored the offer.

"Somebody put pressure on him, they must have done," persisted Hastings, "no way would he have taken such a step without consultation."

"Richard Gloucester perhaps?" ventured Morton, "Clarence treated him disgracefully over the matter of Anne Neville."

Clarence had opposed the marriage of his brother, Richard Duke of Gloucester to Anne Neville, because he was married to Anne's sister and coveted the Neville inheritance.

"Don't be a fool man that was settled long ago," roared Hastings, "if it's not you, then I'd wager our beautiful lady Queen has been whispering 'sweet pressures' in the King's ear." He tapped his nose knowingly and leaning forward, whispered loudly into Morton's face, "bedroom pressures, know what I mean?"

Morton assured him that he did not know what he meant, he being a man of the cloth but Hastings just sneered and left as abruptly as he came. Luke winced, for Clarence's diabolical treatment of Gloucester's wife was just one of several unpleasant stories Giles would learn about the Duke soon enough.

Lord Hastings was not the only one to assume that Doctor Morton was the King's confident in respect of the pending trial. Lady Stanley also believed that he was involved and appeared at his office door only minutes after the Lord Chamberlain had left. She too entered without being announced and instantly dismissed Luke, ordering him to 'close the door' behind him. Luke was happy to escape, he was nervous of this inscrutable lady with her hooded eyes and thin lips and besides it was probable that Margery had been ordered to wait close by for her mistress. He was not disappointed, Margery was standing by the window of the back-room used by those lesser mortals who wished to see the Doctor but had to wait for his convenience. He closed the door quietly and playfully tried to steel up on her without her noticing but she sensed his presence and squealed coquettishly when she realised who had startled her. Luke gently took her in his arms and placed a light kiss on her mouth.

"I'm so sorry about this morning my love, can you forgive me?"

He expected her to protest that there was nothing to forgive and to show concern for his well being but instead she gently pushed him away and preened herself for a speech she had been preparing in her head since she had left the King's table only moments ago.

"Yes," she said slowly, "of course I can forgive you. Your affliction is to be pitied but I'm not sure I can constantly watch your suffering without it affecting my own humours." She turned away from him and stared out of the window, feigning to hide her pain from his view.

"What are you saying? You know I recover with the help of my medicine."

"It's more than I can endure. The attacks have become so frequent. Two weeks ago at the tavern and now again this morning."

Resting his forefinger gentle under Margery's chin, Luke turned her face to his.

"True but it has been two months since I had an attack before that. What has changed my love?"

"Nothing sweetheart, I just need to be sure of my future."

"But your future is mine … we are betrothed … we are to be wed … aren't we?"

"Of course but perhaps it would be better to leave our final vows until you are completely well and your memory has returned."

"It may never return."

"It will," she insisted, "and who knows, you may be an Italian nobleman of great wealth with castles in Florence and Venice."

They heard the door of Morton's office banged shut and Margery's name shouted with irritation from along the passage.

"I must go," she sighed, "we can still be friends and I shall see you every time Lady Stanley visits Doctor Morton." Smiling broadly she placed a swift peck on Luke's cheek and hurried after the tapping heels of her mistress.

The panic Luke had fought in her presence now crashed through his barriers, causing bile to rise in his gut and sweat to cover his body like the plague fever. What had happened to Margery to make her reconsider their relationship? Only this morning she had taken a considerable risk to meet him outside the Palace of Westminster and showed no indication of this change of heart. Dear God how was he to cope without her? Would it truly help if he regained his memory? Sadly he thought it might, that is, if he proved to be a rich nobleman from Venice. He returned to Morton's office with his pain clearly etched on his face. The Doctor brought him a stool and bid him sit.

"I'm sorry," said Morton sincerely, " but really Luke, Margery is a shameless whore."

"How dare you. You have no idea how sweet and gentle she can be."

"In truth, I have not," agreed Morton, "but I fear your judgement and understanding of the way some women operate verges on the naïve."

"Does it indeed? Well perhaps your own judgement is jaded by a lifetime of church doctrine. Anyway, how did you know? Of course, Lady Stanley. What had she to do with Margery's sudden change of heart?" snapped Luke.

"Nothing at all. Like Lord Hastings, Lady Stanley assumed I was responsible for persuading the King to put Clarence on trial tomorrow but she was at the banquet and saw …" Words failed the Doctor and he rotated the loose ring on his little finger whilst he considered his choice of words: a mannerism Luke knew to mean he was experiencing embarrassment.

"Apparently the King saw Margery this morning after the marriage ceremony and well, you know how Edward is used to every woman he lusts after, falling into his bed and …"

"We are betrothed, she should have told him …"

"Oh Luke, you know King Edward takes any woman he wants, whether she be, betrothed, handfast or barely reached womanhood. It's his greatest weakness and one day he will answer in heaven for his insatiable appetite."

"But she didn't have to succumb to his lust. The King constantly boasts that he has never taken a woman by force."

"Oh Luke, grow up! Edward is not only a handsome virile man, he is the King of England. What young woman could resist the attention of such Majesty?"

Luke was devastated. Morton had spoken the truth but what really hurt was that deep in his heart he had always known that someday Margery would betray him.

"Does Bishop Robert know about the trial?" he asked flatly, forcing himself to focus on something other than his loss.

"Yes, he left for the Tower immediately after the ceremony. But why has the King not consulted me? Why have I not been summonsed to the royal presence?"

"What did Lady Stanley have to say about the trial?"

"She is as much in the dark as I am, which means that if Hastings is correct and the Queen is the instigator of this mischief, Her Majesty is keeping it to herself."

"She is the most likely protagonist," reasoned Luke, "Clarence executed her father on his own warrant and it would be the end of the House of Woodville should Clarence ever manage to dislodge Edward from his throne."

"He will never do that Luke, there is no support for the man but you are correct in one respect, Queen Elizabeth is obsessed with taking revenge for the death of her father."

By the time Giles returned to Clipberry his anger had abated and as always, after one of his uncontrollable outbursts, he felt guilty and exhausted. Cold and miserable he climbed the stone steps that led into the great hall, to find the place virtually deserted. Mary and the other servants were returning tomorrow and those that had not been seconded to the Palace had duties enough without forming a welcoming party for their young master. Only Woof raised his head to see who it was that might shift him from his position before the dying fire and so without disturbing the hound, Giles heaved a couple of logs on to the remaining embers and then removed his wet boots and outer clothing. The light was just beginning to fade and full of fear that the certainties in his world were failing, Giles slumped into the Bishop's chair, pushed his cold feet under Woof's warm body and fell into a fitful sleep, only to be woken moments later with Mark's stern voice assaulting his ears and the cold draft from the open door freezing his body.

"You might have let me know you were returning home," complained Mark, " I have spent the last two hour searching for you."

"Where else would I go?" replied Giles sulkily.

"To the Palace of Westminster? To find the Bishop and challenge him with those damned notes?" countered Mark, "don't tell me you didn't try to find him?" He didn't wait for an answer but rang the hand bell in the grate. Within seconds a child of no more than eight years responded by popping his head around the door and grinning at his betters.

"Find me something to eat," snapped Mark, "and some ale."

The head disappeared and immediately Mark was chastened by the expression on Giles' face. "Alright, so I shouldn't vent my anger on Peterkin. You are safe and that is all that really matters. Did the Bishop tell you what you wanted to know?"

"I told you, I have not seen Bishop Robert. But the man we pulled from the crowd this morning told me things about our Bishop that will surprise you."

"How does he know him?"

"Luke is retained by Doctor John Morton, Master of the Rolls and it is Morton who has replaced Bishop Robert in the King's favour."

"I didn't know the Bishop had lost favour with the King. He is still on his council and he officiated at the royal wedding today. In what way has he lost favour?"

"Edward is displeased with Bishop Robert because he is George Clarence's legal advisor. Apparently he visits the Duke every day in the Bowyer Tower."

"Rubbish," cried Mark, "we would know if the Bishop had anything to do with George Duke of Clarence.

"No, it is not rubbish Mark. In fact it makes a sort of sense if I am Clarence's son and he doesn't know I exist. Consider, why am I not yet settled in a career? With the Bishop's influence I could have been a King's herald by now or in Sir Matthew Pawson's service. Even a Chancery post is not beyond his power but no, any one of those or a thousand other opportunities would mean I would be free to mix and communicate with those in high places."

"You do mix and communicate with those in high places. Only yesterday you were at the Palace of Westminster and you know the Tower better than I know this place."

"But I am always escorted by his Grace," persisted Giles. "He dare not leave me alone for fear of what I might learn and 'heaven forbid' I could meet the Duke of Clarence."

"Giles you are becoming obsessive. There has been no chance of you stumbling across George Clarence in the past six months. He has been imprisoned in the Tower."

"Exactly. He caused King Edward so much embarrassment His Majesty silenced him with imprisonment. What if Clarence's indiscretions also prompted the Bishop to arrange for me to enter that Monastic House in Yorkshire. Remember? He suggested I should consider 'a life of devotion' when I return from Oxford. Well I have worked it back and it is precisely six months since he wrote to the Abbot."

"You are making something out of nothing," said Mark sternly.

"No I am not. The Bishop's secret visits to George Clarence in the Tower, my mother's note instructing the Bishop to keep me from the Duke and the Bishop escorting me everyplace I might learn something about the man, all suggest a secret is being kept from me. You may think it irrelevant but the Duke's imprisonment in the Tower and the arrangement for me to visit the Benedictine Abbey in Yorkshire were concluded at the same time. My guess is that I *am* George Duke of Clarence's first born, legitimate son and therefore in line for the throne. A fact King Edward wishes to hide."

"For God's sake Giles, that is treason for sure." Mark sprang from his stool and hurried to the side door where the young boy had returned struggling with a large tray on which was precariously balanced a trencher of cold meat, cheese and two quart pots of ale. More kindly than before, Mark took the tray in one hand and held the door open whilst the bemused child retreated. Returning to the fire and placing the tray on the stool, Mark pulled up another on which to sit, whilst Giles reached for one of the pots and pulled a piece of chicken from the trencher which he fed to Woof. Mark continued to feed his supper to the hound whilst the two men drank their ale in an awkward silence. Eventually Giles could stand it no longer.

"I intend to prove my theory by speaking to George Clarence," he said resolutely.

Mark stared at his young master in horror and then covered his face with his hands.

"Oh Giles I'm so sorry," he began from behind his hands, "you haven't heard. You left the tavern before the news broke."

"Heard what?"

"The King has convened parliament tomorrow. George, Duke of Clarence is to be tried by his peers on a charge of High Treason."

It was Giles' turn to be horrified but it lasted only moments before a sardonic smile played on his lips and he clapped his hands in mock appreciation.

"So let it be," he spat through clenched teeth, "all the indiscretions will be aired in public and if the Bishop defends the Duke of Clarence, as I believe be will, then perhaps the King will execute them both."

Chapter 4

The House of Lords – Westminster 16th January 1478

Luke accompanied Morton to the House of Lords well before dawn on the day of the Duke of Clarence's trial. The Doctor wished to be available should His Majesty remember that he had not briefed his most able legal advisor and wished to scan the notes Morton had sat up most of the night preparing. Servants were already at work lighting candles in the sconces around the chamber walls and chandeliers bearing many more lighted candles, were being hauled up by pulleys into the roof and suspended securely at a height that would provide maximum light in the chamber below. The King's throne was set on a dais at one end of the hall, with a second high backed chair, for the Duke of Clarence, facing the throne but off set to the King's right. Also at the front were two tables, situated either side of the House, one for Bishop Robert and his clerks and the other for Doctor Morton and his party.

With Luke in attendance, the Doctor sat in his appointed place and closing his eyes, he tried to relax his mind, mentally marking off the points of accusations he had prepared in anticipation of the indictment.

It was not long before the troubled nobles of England began to file into the chamber, none were certain what to expect and most would have made some excuse for their absence, had they not attended the wedding on the previous day. The exception to this sombre assembly was the group of Woodville lords, who chattered excitedly in anticipation of the sweet revenge to be wrought on the Duke of Clarence: the man they believed threatened the survival of the House of Woodville.

The Lords rose when King Edward appeared from the anteroom with his stepson, Dorset, close on his heels and carrying a scroll across his folded arms like a precious sceptre.

"Is Dorset to read the indictment?" hissed a horrified Morton in Luke's ear, "has the King become a slave to the Woodville's petty vendettas?"

Luke was thinking only of Margery as he glowered at the six foot imposing figure of the King from his front bench advantage but Edward was too preoccupied to notice the anger on Luke's face. Begrudgingly, Luke had to admit that although the King's person looked magnificent in his robes and crown, his face was drawn and harrowed with the weight of what was to come and despite his own pain, he felt some sympathy for the great man alone on the dais.

King Edward signalled to the guards at the far end of the House and the ancient oak doors swung open, revealing the well guarded Duke of Clarence framed in the doorway at the opposite end of the hall to his brother, the King. One of the guards nudged him forward and smiling broadly and acknowledging the nobles as he passed, George Clarence slowly made his way to the front of the House. Without meeting the King's sorrowful eyes he bowed deeply towards his brother and then sat in the chair provided, with all the ostentation of a monarch approaching his throne. Bishop Robert Stillington followed the Duke at a respectable distance and sat at the table opposite Luke and the Doctor.

With renewed interest in Morton's rival, Luke observed the Bishop as he deliberately shuffled and sorted the documents before him. Like his own master, John Morton, Bishop Robert was a doctor of civil and cannon law and like Morton he was a 'career churchman,' having a suffragan deputising for him in his See of Bath and Wells. Today though, he wore full regalia, an elaborately embroidered cope covering his vestments and he even carried his crosier, which was such an unusual sight that Luke wondered whether the display was to remind the King that he was answerable, firstly to the church or whether he was playing mind games with Doctor Morton, who was his clerical junior. Luke concluded it was the latter, as the thin, grey faced Bishop stared defiantly across the floor of the House and all but snarled at Morton, sitting restlessly on Luke's left.

"He blames me for this trial," hissed Morton, in Luke's ear, "he thinks I persuaded the King to accuse his brother Clarence of treason."

"Cannot the King act for himself?" whispered Luke, "does he have to be acting on the advice of a councillor?"

Doctor Morton shook his head impatiently. "He would not embark on such a dangerous course of action without taking advice, unless Lord Hastings is correct and the Queen has driven him to denounce brother George."

"But surely the King would resist her pleas. Clarence is his brother?"

"If she refused him her bed, as Hastings implied she might; well then I'm not so sure," sighed Morton and put his finger to his lips to hush Luke as the proceedings were about to commence.

King Edward had waited patiently for Clarence to settle and now that he had his brother's attention, he took the scroll from the Marquis of Dorset and much to the amazement of the hushed parliament, began to read the lengthy indictment himself.

He began by explaining that this trial was *not* about past treason: no reference would be made to '69 when George Duke of Clarence had conspired with the late Earl of Warwick to dethrone him and install George as England's king. This trial was *not* about his brother's subsequent traitorous alliance with Lancaster, for George had forsaken both Warwick and Lancaster and King Edward had forgiven him. This trial concerned 'new treasons' in which George had publicly claimed that he was the Duke of York's true heir: that King Edward was a bastard and not York's son. He further accused Clarence of secretly retaining a document drawn up and signed by himself and Queen Margaret of Lancaster in which he was named Lancaster's heir should her son die without issue (the Prince had indeed died childless at Tewkesbury.) The indictment continued at length, citing the many other instances when the Duke of Clarence had assumed the authority of a King, undermining the King's justices and flouting the law.

As Edward drew to a close, Luke began to feel light headed and gripping the arm of Morton's chair, he closed his eyes and prayed that he might remain upright long enough to find his way out of the chamber. A distant voice, which appeared to be echoing in his reeling head, was calling for a witness to come forward and the general shuffle of bodies made it possible for him to leave his seat and melt into the back line of standing clerks. Luke rummaged in his script for the phial of green salts and somehow managed to withdraw the stopper. The precious salt spilt into his script but Luke scooped a few grains between his forefinger and thumb and placed them hopefully under his tongue. He was succumbing quickly to the swimming sensation which always preceded his collapse, when the fizz and sharp sting from the salts awoke his senses sufficiently to enable his escape into the anteroom, where a steward rushed to his assistance. Luke did not loose consciousness but the undiluted salt was burning his mouth, causing him to cry out with pain and permitting green foam to escape from either corner of his mouth. The spectacle struck such fear into the steward that he ran from the room calling for God to save him from the devil's works. Left alone, Luke relaxed and slowly began to recover. He rinsed his mouth out with wine from a cup on the side table, being careful not to swallow even the merest drop. He had never prevented an attack in this way before and was unsure whether he had done so now but he felt well enough to stand, so slowly he made his way back to Morton's quarters and in the safety of his own small room, he lay down on his bed and pulled a blanket over his head.

It was pitch black in Luke's tiny, windowless room when he awoke hours later to the sound of Giles Butler's voice emanating from beyond the leather curtain that divided his sleeping quarters from the Doctor's main office cum living area. Carefully, Luke swung his long legs to the floor and tested himself in the upright position and as everything seemed to be working normally he pushed aside the curtain and rubbed his aching eyes whilst adjusting to the dancing light created by the draught from the open door.

"I'm sorry to disturb you Doctor Morton," Giles was saying but when Luke stepped into view Morton abandoned his visitor in the doorway and assisted Luke to a chair by the grate.

"Have you had another seizure?" asked Giles, watching Morton fuss about his new friend with a blanket, " I am here because Bishop Robert has not returned from Westminster and has not sent a message to say he would be late, which is most unusual and....and I wondered if he were with you but obviously he is not."

Giles concluded his rehearsed speech letting his final words trail away as he realised the Doctor was not listening and anyway he had concocted the excuse to visit because he was desperate to discover the outcome of the trial. Mark, who hung back in the corridor, had only agreed to the pretence because Giles had promised they could stay overnight at Alice's tavern after their visit.

"Come in man and close the door," called Morton, as he caught sight of Mark hovering in the corridor.

Embarrassed by their deceit, Mark clumsily collided with the manservant making his way to the kitchens in search of hot water for Luke's medicine and between them they left the door off the latch.

Resuming his welcome, Doctor Morton offered his visitors mulled wine from a large sizzling jug in the grate, insisting that it would ward off the feverish colds they had most likely contracted by walking out on such a bitter evening. Giles declined but Mark was happy to partake of the cure, grasping the warmed goblet whilst the Doctor filled it to the brim with hot, spicy liquid. Without warning and with the jug barley upright, Morton let rip a short blasphemous cry of terror, spilling some of the hot wine onto Mark's boots. It was Woof: the dog had been left outside in the corridor but sensing the warmth emanating from the grate, the huge hound had nuzzled the door open, slunk unnoticed passed Giles and Mark and brushed his wet tail across the back of the Doctor's legs, before stretching himself out in front of the fire.

"We need him for protection on our return journey," apologised Giles, "even without a bark he looks pretty intimidating being so large."

"Indeed he does," agree Morton and jovially expressed a hope that he would not smell too much as the warmth from the fire dried his fur. They all laughed and at the Doctor's invitation pulled stools up to the fire whilst he patted Woof's head, mumbling something about having liked the dogs at old King Harry's court. In the comfortable silence that followed Morton considered the reason for Giles' late visit. Surely he knew this would be the last place Bishop Robert would seek solace after this dreadful day. He concluded it was Luke, Giles had come to see and so the good Doctor generously excused himself on an indeterminate pretext and departed into his own sleeping quarters. Quickly Luke leaned forward and whispered to Giles not to mention his belief that Clarence was his father and in lowered tones Giles replied by begging for information about the trial. Luke sat back and recanted the detail as if it were of casual interest to his friend, during which time, the manservant returned with hot water and Morton reappeared and took up the account of the trial from the point at which Luke had left the House due to his attack.

"Nobody accused the Duke from the floor of the House and nobody other than Duke answered the King's charges," declared Morton, refilling his goblet, "Bishop Robert never got to his feet and neither did I. A few witnesses were called to substantiate dates and times but they spoke neither for nor against the Duke. It was most strange."

"Did the Duke of Clarence ask for forgiveness?" enquired Giles.

"Certainly not. At no point in the proceedings did he show any outward sign of remorse or humility. Not even when the Duke of Buckingham announced him guilty of all the charges."

"Buckingham?" echoed Luke, "I thought Richard Gloucester was Seneschal of England, should he not have delivered the verdict?"

"He probably asked to be excused such a distasteful duty, but I doubt he will refuse any of Clarence's estates which are sure to be his now that Clarence is attainted," sneered Morton.

Giles was about to ask him to elaborate on his appraisal of Gloucester but he caught Luke's warning look and forwent his curiosity.

"After the verdict, Clarence became angry and stupidly challenged the King to a 'trial by combat', which His Majesty quite rightly ignored." Morton sighed. "In the end the Duke was forcibly removed from the House protesting that his case had not been heard out. And once the King was beyond earshot, Gloucester threw a typical Plantagenet tantrum, accusing the Queen of forcing His Majesty to condemn Clarence and swearing to avenge his brother's disgrace."

"Will he be put to death?" whispered Giles, as he imagined the Duke being dragged away into the Tower dungeons, never to see daylight again.

"I very much doubt it." said Morton, surprised at the concern he perceived on Giles' face. "That would be fratricide and besides, King Edward is not a vindictive man."

"Then why go through the humiliation of the trial?" queried Luke.

"I have no idea," replied Morton, distracted by the appearance of his young visitor, whose face had turned a deathly white.

Poor Giles, his imagination was providing images of the man he believed to be his father being hung, drawn and quartered, before he had made himself known to the Duke but the bells of Westminster Abbey interrupted his thoughts as they rang out for Vespers. Morton abandoned his concern for Giles' curious reaction to the fate of Clarence and rose to take his leave but not to the Abbey, his prayers would be said in the chapel of St Stephen within the Palace of Westminster. Luke made to go with him but Morton bid him remain in his seat.

"Entertain your guests Luke and enjoy what's left of the evening," said the Doctor, patting Luke's arm and smiling at both Giles and Mark. "You've been unwell," he soothed and then added as he closed the door, " for once, I can say prayers for us both."

"You are very fortunate to have such an understanding master," said Mark with feeling, "Bishop Robert would not be so considerate." He looked hard at Giles and then walked to the casement and pulled back the drapes which covered the glassed filled fenestralls. "We should be on our way master Giles if we are to reach the city gates before they close, it's dusk already." Mark tried to sound casual but failed. Giles laughed.

"You go on to the tavern Mark and take Woof with you. I want to talk to Luke about ... well you know. Can I bed down here tonight Luke?"

Luke spread his hands to indicate that the office was available for Giles to sleep in and so without waiting to be persuaded further, Mark called Woof to heel and left for Ned's tavern and of course Alice, with whom he wished to spend the rest of his life.

When they were alone, Luke brought brandy wine from the side cupboard and filled Giles' cup nearly to the brim. Somehow Giles didn't think Doctor Morton would mind, Mark was right, he was a very considerate master, so why did Luke not want Morton to know that he believed the Duke of Clarence was his father? He put his question to Luke.

"Ah, well, the Doctor keeps his distance from the Duke of Clarence"

"Why is that?"

Luke paused, unsure whether he should confide in the young man he had only recently met, but he liked Giles and identified with his need to find his father.

"It all began when the great Earl of Warwick quarrelled with King Edward and openly supported Clarence's claim to the crown," began Luke, "Warwick married his eldest daughter Isobel to Clarence in the hope that he would become father-in-law to King George."

Giles nodded. "I know the story. There was no support for Clarence amongst the English nobility so he and Warwick fled to France to beg help from the French king."

"Yes, but King Louis wasn't interested in replacing Edward with his brother George. Louis supported Lancaster and as Queen Margaret and her son were in exile at his court he agreed to provide Warwick with men and arms with which to oust Edward provided he forsook York in favour of Lancaster."

"Why should Warwick agreed to that?" asked Giles.

"Because Queen Margaret proposed the marriage of her son, Lancaster's Prince of Wales, to Warwick's younger daughter Anne."

"I see," said Giles, "Warwick abandoned Clarence and Isobel to become the father of a future Queen Anne. No wonder George Clarence deserted him and returned to his Yorkist family but what has all this to do with Doctor Morton?"

"Morton was at King Louis' court too, because he was also in exile in the service of Queen Margaret." Luke took a deep breath, he knew Giles would loose his temper if he phrased his next sentence insensitively. "The Duke of Clarence holds Doctor Morton responsible for Warwick accepting King Louis plan in favour of Lancaster."

"You mean it was Morton's *idea* for Warwick to abandon Clarence and York in favour of Lancaster?" said Giles curtly. Luke nodded.

"The Doctor was terrified of what might have been disclosed at Clarence's trial today because *he* masterminded the brief revival of Lancaster or so he tells me. I have no recollection of events prior to Tewkesbury but fortunately for the Doctor, King Edward restricted his indictment to the treason's Clarence committed *after* the King and George Clarence were reconciled at Tewkesbury."

"Surely King Edward knew of Morton's previous links to Lancaster?"

"Of course he did, after the battle of Tewkesbury Morton threw himself on Edward's mercy but how the Doctor described the importance of those 'links with Lancaster' is guess work. For Edward to have recognised the Doctor's exceptional administrative abilities and appoint him Master of the Rolls, suggests that the crafty Doctor may have underplayed his political acumen in favour of his administrative qualities."

Both men sat in silence for a few moments. Giles tried to piece together the sequence of his father's inconsistent loyalties and how they intertwined with Morton's change from Lancaster to York. Amongst his thoughts Giles found another loose thread.

"I've noticed that the Doctor is less than charitable about the Duke of Gloucester. Has that anything to do with the Duke of Clarence?"

"No. Three years ago Edward invaded France but withdrew his armies for a bribe of £5000, to be paid every year for the next ten years and Morton was involved in drafting the legal documentation. Somehow he managed to include a clause which committed King Louis to ransoming Queen Margaret from the Tower of London. Gloucester was unimpressed and openly accused Morton of harbouring Lancastrian sympathies."

"It seems strange that Doctor Morton is so trusted by King Edward and at the same time mistrusted by both of his brothers," mussed Giles, rubbing his forehead with the heels of his hands.

"You should try and see the Duke of Clarence Giles and ask him outright if he married your mother."

Giles sighed and nodded his agreement. " I need to speak with the Duke when Bishop Robert is not in attendance. It is not going to be an easy task."

CHAPTER 5

The Kings Chambers. Westminster 16th January 1478

King Edward sat at the open window in the anteroom of his bedchamber, wearing only silken hose and an open necked shirt. He had dismissed his knights of the wardrobe before they had completed his disrobing, needing to be alone to allow his hurt to erupt unseen. That was an hour ago and now the cold night air that had dried his tears, drifted round the room like a vengeful spirit, wafting the drapes and redirecting wisps of smoke in a chilling dance of accusation. Time and again he had told himself he had no reason to feel guilty, Clarence had tried more than once to usurp his crown and it had to stop. He watched Sir Matthew Pawson clear away the uneaten food from the small table where he had meticulously prepared supper for the King and his latest mistress, Margery but Edward was in no mood to entertain and had not sent for her. He followed Matthew with his eyes as the knight gently padded back and forth with the tray. Strangely, he had allowed Sir Matthew to witness the extent of his grief: knowing instinctively that his pain was Matthew's and to shut him out would have been unthinkable. The knight was in his mid thirties with thinning fair hair, blue eyes and a smooth pink and white complexion that made him appear somewhat younger but it was his heart shaped face and pouting mouth that endeared him to Edward's ladies so that they adopted him like a playful puppy. Thoughtfully, Sir Matthew left the jug of claret and a silver salver of dates on the little table. He knew Edward's culinary preferences as specifically as his own and the palm fruits, so sticky and sweet, might just be sufficient to tempt the royal palate, in spite of the anguish that had destroyed the royal appetite. The knight hovered by the King's chair. He wanted to close the window but was unsure how His distraught Majesty would react to such presumption. It was Sir Matthew's purpose at all times to care for the King and he knew the physicians would hold him responsible should His Majesty catch a chill from that open casement. Boldly he made his decision, pulling the window shut and closing the shutters as determinedly as if he had been commanded to do so.

"I'm sorry Your Majesty but you will certainly catch the winter ague on a cold night like this," apologised Matthew, "and with an open shirt too," he dared to scold.

"Go away," Edward sighed, "you fuss like a wet nurse, just leave everything and go."

Matthew withdrew immediately. It disturbed him to witness the huge frame he so admired, cowed and defeated and he desperately wanted to pick up the velvet dressing gown from the robe stool and place it about the King's shoulders but he dare not. He slid quietly between the double doors, closing them carefully behind him as if not to wake a sleeper. From the dejected appearance of Matthew's retreating figure, Edward could only guess at the injured expression on the knight's face but for once he was prepared to let the little effeminate man sulk: he needed to be alone, to consider what to do about brother George.

Edward's peace was short lived, within minutes the Lord Chamberlain, William Hastings, threw open the door leading from the Presence Chamber and announced the arrival of Cecily Neville, Dowager Duchess of York and Richard, Duke of Gloucester.

"My mother? God's teeth Will, keep her out of this chamber. She'll think we run a whorehouse." He waved his arm around the room indicating the single candelabra providing minimal soft light and the profusion of silk drapes and plump cushions.

Hastings grinned and helped Edward into his velvet grown.

"I can tell them you have already retired my liege but as you are so clearly *alone*, might this not be a good opportunity to dispel some of Her Grace's doubts about your nocturnal habits?"

"Don't be so pompous Will," scolded the King, but he was in no mood for banter. His relationship with his mother had been difficult since he had married Elizabeth Woodville fourteen years ago. She considered Elizabeth too lowly born to be Edward's Queen but more significantly she blamed their marriage for Warwick's defection. The great Earl of Warwick, her brother's son had been in Europe finding a suitable Queen for Edward and returned to find that he had secretly married Elizabeth Woodville. Cecily fervently believed that Warwick would never have turned traitor and dragged her son George Clarence into treason had Edward not caused him such humiliation.

The King suspected this would be her argument now. However, he knew his mother had travelled at great personal risk, the Thames was still frozen and unsafe for journeys by barge, which meant she and Richard had braved the icy roads from Baynard's Castle.

"Show them in Will, she has not called to chastise us about the decor."

Hastings grimaced, he considered the Dowager Duchess to be a formidable lady, capable of observing every detail of the perfumed antechamber and storing the images for future reference. However, when the King was suitably dressed and seated at the small table pretending to have just completed a solitary meal, he formally announced their arrival. Richard Gloucester glared at Hastings as they passed in the doorway, he was not in the habit of waiting to be formally announced before attending his brother, the King. Edward greeted them both warmly, preventing the Duchess from kneeling before him by catching her elbows as she started to bend.

"Why has Your Grace ventured out at his hour?" he inquired gentle, "Dickon, could you not have persuaded our mother to wait until the morning to make this journey?"

"No I could not," snapped Gloucester, "and well you know it."

There was an awkward pause during which the King observed his aging mother. She looked frailer than when he had last seen her some weeks ago at the Christmas Day celebrations. During the lavish entertainment, she had swallowed her pride and begged Edward to release George Clarence from the Tower, complaining bitterly that it was more than her heart could stand to see the loathsome Woodvilles enjoying the festivities whilst her son George was so cruelly confined. Edward was aware he had handled the situation badly, scolding the Duchess for her dislike of Elizabeth's kin and insisting that he had offered George every opportunity to apologise for his appalling behaviour. This time he intended to remain calm, no matter how disparaging Her Grace was about the Woodvilles, although he had no intention of releasing Clarence, now or in the future. Never-the-less he was confident that once he had explained George's conduct at his trial today, his mother would understand.

"Edward, Richard assures me that you do not intend to sentence and execute your brother George but I would like to hear the words for myself."

"Oh does he? and just when did we discuss the matter with you Dickon?" began Edward acidly but the panic in Richard's eyes chastised his anger and reminded him of the resolve he had so quickly abandoned.

"Of course we have no intention of executing George, Madam. Although he does deserve to be put to death?"

"Then why have you dishonoured York so publicly with this charade of a trial, or was it pressure from your Woodville Queen?" snapped the Duchess.

"Any pressure we succumbed to, was from you madam," retaliated the King. " For the last few weeks we have been taunted by your anguish, so eloquently expressed at the Christmas festivities. George has had every opportunity to repent his treason and seek our forgiveness but he has been obdurate. We thought if we brought him before his peers, there to face his own death by *their verdict of guilty*, he would beg for our mercy and then we could release him with only cautions and financial penalties." Edward had not taken his eyes from his mother's face throughout his explanation and she could not help but be moved by the sincerity and pain she witnessed in his. "But when George realised his treason was official, he challenged us to trial by combat," concluded Edward.

The Duchess caught her breath and put out her hand for Richard to take and steady her. Edward pressed home his advantage.

"Trial by combat," he repeated, "George actually announced publicly that he was prepared to fight and kill us in order to take the crown or loose his own live in the attempt, when all we were doing was trying to find an honourable way to release him back into our court. Some brother!"

All three sat in silence whilst the implications of George's, 'challenge to the death' crept unwillingly into their hearts.

"George has clearly taken leave of his senses," ventured Richard, "his wits are addled and he his not responsible for his actions at this time, although he must certainly remain imprisoned for the foreseeable future. Would you not agree Madam?"

Cecily did not answer her youngest son but rose stiffly from her chair and crossed to where Edward sat with his head in his hands. Gently she wrapped her arms round his shoulders and pressed his huge frame against her frail body, kissing the top of his head by way of apology and reconciliation. Peering from beneath her embrace the King watched Richard move to the table to refill his cup and for a brief moment he saw his father. Richard was so like him both in appearance and in his mannerisms. Smaller than average with dark hair and fine features, there was no mistaking he was York's son. For just a second Edward considered the possibility that George was correct, that he, King Edward, was not his father's son, for he bore no resemblance to him. He closed his eyes, allowing his mother's perfume to fill his senses as his mind drifted back to his childhood years at Fotheringhay. Long, long ago before his father the Duke of York had even thought of claiming the throne of England. How would his father have managed the deluded George Duke of Clarence?

Chapter 6

The Tower of London 16th February 1478

Bishop Robert spent the days following the trial in attendance on the Duke of Clarence who had summonsed him to the Bowyer Tower within hours of his re-incarceration there. The Duke had been furious, screaming at servants and supporters alike, demanding a retrial, at which he would show conclusively that he was the rightful King of England. The Bishop had been obliged to write down Clarence's account of how his mother, Duchess of York had taken a soldier to her bed whilst accompanying the Duke of York on one of his missions in France. The result of their union being her first born son Edward, now bastard King and half brother to her second surviving son George, Duke of Clarence, who was England's rightful King. The poor Bishop had been mortified, such treason in his own hand was insufferable and he had begged the Lord Chamberlain to grant him an audience with King Edward so that he might explain how his position of trust had been compromised. Unfortunately, Lord Hastings considered it a kindness to His Majesty to intervene in those petitions which concerned Clarence and denied Bishop Robert his request.

So each evening after Vespers, Robert had returned to his manor in Clipberry Street, retiring immediately to his own chamber with only a jug of Claret. The following day, after celebrating mass and breaking his fast with little more than bread and cheese, he had again set out for the Tower of London and the treacherous George. The cold early mornings and freezing late evenings had destroyed the Bishop's health and by Sunday, 16th February, Bishop Robert was unable to rise from his bed. His head throbbed. The winter ague had crept into his aging bones so severely that even lifting his head from the pillow was painful. He informed Mark that he would spend the day in bed and that when Sir Matthew Pawson arrived he was to be shown up to his bedchamber.

Giles resolved not to visit the Bishop in his sickbed until later that evening. Bishop Robert had been so involved in the frenzied activity surrounding the aftermath of George Clarence's trial, that he had forgotten about the box Giles had received on his birthday and so far, Giles had avoided telling his guardian about its contents. With the Bishop confined to his bed, Giles decided he must take the opportunity to visit Clarence and if he was successful in gaining entry to the Bowyer Tower then by this evening he would be able to confront his guardian with the truth about his father and admit to withholding the note his mother had intended for His Grace.

The clatter of hooves on the cobbled yard heralded Sir Matthew Pawson's arrival and Mark opened the door to the great hall to welcome him as usual. He was concerned to hear that Robert had taken to his bed and enquired of Mark what the Bishop had eaten these last few days.

"Some of the royal venison has been very strong this week," fussed Matthew as he accepted the cup of watered wine Mark had just poured from the jug on the sideboard, "I told the head cook only yesterday that he was not to serve it to the King this week, in *any* guise," he pursed his lips and nodded to Giles who had just wandered in from the buttery. "You'd be amazed at some of the dishes that find their way to the royal table under the veil of being 'fashionable' at the court of the French King Louis."

"It isn't anything he's eaten," assured Mark, "His Grace has been out in all weathers, trailing back and forth from the Tower." Matthew and Giles exchanged knowing looks as Giles picked up the second cup Mark had filled and drank in silence. Neither wished to comment on the precarious politics surrounding the King's brother.

"He still wishes to beat you at chess though," volunteered Giles as he put down his empty cup, "I'll take you up if you like?"

Giles didn't wait for Sir Matthew to reply, or for Mark to finish refilling Matthew's cup. He started to climb the wooden stairs leading to the Bishop's private chambers. Giles was in a hurry, he wanted to be about his own business at the Tower.

"Just knock and go in," he said, indicating the bedchamber door, "Bishop Robert asked for you to be shown up here."

As Giles started to descend the stairs he heard Sir Matthew knock on the door and then call out in a strangely intimate voice.

"Knight to King's Bishop, may I come in?"

Mark had Dexter and Old Sal saddled and waiting and was passing the time of day with Arthur when Giles joined him in the stables. He had insisted on accompanying his young master on what he considered to be a dangerous mission to the Tower.

"I don't suppose you told Matthew where we are going?" whispered Mark, as they mounted.

Giles shook his head, spurred his horse and made a dash for the gate, determined to be gone by the time the noise of the horses hooves on the cobbles brought anyone to a window. Mark encourage Old Sal in the same fashion, following Giles into Clipberry Street and maintaining speed until they reached Clerkenwell, where Giles reined in Dexter and allowed Mark to catch up with him.

There had been no frost now for two nights and the snow had turned into dirty slush, leaving small puddles of icy water in ever crevice and pothole and the two men were splattered with mud from the short dash they had made from the Bishop's manor. The capital's citizens were mostly indoors trying to keep the seeping wet out of their clothes, despite the persistent tolling of bells across the dank Sunday morning air, demanding their attendance at the myriad of churches.

Travelling at a gentler pace, Giles and Mark followed the city walls passed Moregate, Bishopsgate and Aldgate to the first gatehouse of the Tower of London. As they approached, Giles reminded Mark to appear, 'relaxed' and to keep their story as near to the truth as possible, because this evening they would have to account for their adventure to Bishop Robert; a fearful task that Giles pushed to the back of his mind for now.

The Tower gatekeeper, Tom Stokes, was a tiny sinewy man with eyes of steel blue that scrutinised every soul who asked for entry to his ancient stone charge. From his vantage point in the gatehouse he had seen the two conspirators approach long before they were prepared to confront him and his unexpected hail caused Giles to falter and momentarily loose his nerve. Was gaining entrance to the Tower on false pretences a punishable offence? Giles was certain it must be.

"Master Giles its good to see you sir. Is the Bishop not with you today then?"

"Good morrow Master Stokes," replied Giles as heartily as his recovered nerve would allow, "No, Bishop Robert has the winter ague and cannot leave his bed. I am come to let the Duke of Clarence know of his condition."

"Come in and warm yourselves young sirs, its cold enough to freeze your tits off," chortled Stokes as he help Giles dismount. Mark secured the horses and followed the gatekeeper and Giles under the raised portcullis and into the first checkpoint of the great fortress, where a fire roared in the grate and the smell of drying leather pervaded the room. Stokes called for additional cups and immediately a servant brought both cups and more strong ale to the rough table set by the fire.

"It's a bad business this trial of Clarence," said Stokes sipping his ale like a little bird, "Bishop Robert should take care not to get too close to Duke George. I've tried to hint as much to him but he's too high and mighty to take any notice of the likes of me."

"I think the King would expect his brother to engage a lawyer under the circumstances," said Giles, " and the bishop has acted for him before."

"Um, but the Duke is up to something even now. There's much comings and goings of his retainers. I'm surprised the King doesn't put a stop to all his visitors."

Giles didn't want to gossip with Tom but neither did he want to raise his suspicions as to their purpose, so he chattered aimlessly until he thought they had lingered long enough.

"I'll have Duncan here take the message across to Bowyer if you like. It's a long trail round to the north side," offered Stokes, when Giles said they should be on their way.

"Oh no, no," said Giles getting to his feet, "the Bishop insisted I deliver it myself but if Duncan could show us the way, I would be most grateful? "

Mark and Giles took their leave of Stokes and followed Duncan, a lad of about twelve summers with thick matted hair and a running nose, who was evidently used to escorting riders into the massive edifice for he trotted in front of the horses at a nimble pace. He guided them through the array of towers surrounding the gatehouse that spanned the causeway across the moat and signalled to the keeper that his companions were to be admitted. Silently Giles prayed that they would not be challenged at the third and final gate which was set in the grey soaring walls surrounding the mighty Tower complex itself. The drawbridge was down and the portcullis raised but one of the two guards on duty was new and walked forward to meet them as they approached so that Giles was obliged to reiterate the details of his errand.

"Where's your authority?" demanded the surly guard."

"I don't need authority," replied Giles indignantly, "I am Bishop Robert Stillington's ward. I've told you my business today and Duncan here has been assigned by Master Stokes to escort me to the Bowyer Tower. Now either let me through or send a messenger to the Duke of Clarence and ask for *his* permission."

The second guard hawked and spat and then ambled over to join his associate. "It's right enough what the lad says. Let 'em pass, unless you fancy a hike round to Bowyer to check?"

The new man nodded his acceptance of his more experienced colleague's assessment and stood aside, allowing the three to enter the Tower, that ancient symbol of London's impregnability. It was an unpleasant ride along the west side of the fortress, hemmed in by the high wall of the inner bailey and the wall that retained the odorous moat but none of the duty soldiers question their presence and the guard in charge of Bowyer Tower itself, seemed unconcerned when Giles said he needed to deliver his message from the Bishop to the Duke in person. Mark tossed Duncan a penny to take care of the horses and said that another would be his when they left.

"The Duke's rooms are at the top of them steps behind that door," said the guard, nodding towards a small but solid door in the corner of the guardroom. "It 'as to stay locked at all times, them's my orders. If you go up there I'll be obliged to lock it behind you and you'll 'ave to knock when you want out again and you'll 'av to leave your dagger 'ere with me."

This was so much easier than Giles had dared to hope and he readily agreed to being locked in. Mark cast him an anxious look as he removed his dagger and handed it to the guard who then unlocked the door and pulled a bell rope hanging on the wall.

"That's to let 'em know your coming up," said the guard as he closed the door behind Giles. The key turned smoothly in the lock and the noise it made echoed round the spiral stairway. It was dark and cold in the confined space that preceded the steps and Giles paused to reassert his determination as well as gain his night sight before climbing carefully up to the first landing. A second guard sat outside the only doorway leading off and from behind which, Giles could hear several people talking in earnest, although he could not make out their words. The soldier informed him that the Duke occupied the top floor and as he climbed still higher Giles wondered how many retainers and servants were with the Duke in his tower prison? Panic was beginning to undermine his resolve as he realised there would be little use in calling for assistance from the top of the Tower. The Bishop had said Clarence had lost his wits and that was Morton's opinion also. Was he being foolhardy in facing this man? He was soon to find out, for as he turned the final bend in the spiral and reached the top landing the door opposite was already open with the figure of a large man blocking the way beyond. Knowing that he may be denied entry if he haggled with those guarding the Duke's person, Giles had prepared a short speech designed to take the guard by surprise and raise the Duke's curiosity. Without waiting to be challenged by the man blocking the doorway, Giles shouted his prepared speech into the void behind him.

"My name is Giles Butler, I am Robert Stillington's ward and my mother was Eleanor Butler. I have reason to believe that the Duke of Clarence is my father."

Giles would have continued with references to their marriage but a harsh voice from behind the guard ordered that Giles be brought before him. He was pushed roughly into a very comfortable room with tapestries covering the walls and several rugs and soft cushions littering the floor. The room was brightly lit by candles, not only in wall sconces but also in standing holders and table sticks. Clearly the Duke had moved many home comforts into his prison. When Giles' eyes had readjusted to the light he realised he was standing less than three feet away from the man he thought to be his father and momentarily he was lost for words as his heartbeat increased and the palms of his hands became hot with sweat. George Clarence had risen from his chair and crossed to the door. He was younger looking than Giles had expected and taller than he had imagined but incredibly he could see his own likeness in the Duke's face and he struggled to contain his excitement. Clarence also registered shock as he recognised his own youth in Giles' face but it was the name, *Eleanor Butler* that had alerted him.

"You are Eleanor Butler's son?" cried the Duke, the delight in his face initially helping Giles to relax but within seconds the Duke's demeanour had changed and he appeared menacing and wild eyed.

"Bishop Robert has kept your existence from me," he snarled, so close to Giles that he could smell the wine on his breath, "now why do you think that is?"

"I truly have no idea Your Grace," whispered Giles, "I hoped you would know the answer to that question."

"When did your mother die boy?" asked the Duke harshly.

"On 30th day of June, in the year of our Lord 1468," stammered Giles. He rummaged in his script and found the notes which he handed to Clarence, explaining that they were in the box his mother had left him for his last birthday and adding shamefacedly that he had not as yet, shown them to the Bishop. As Clarence read the two notes his mood changed again. Raising his hands and thanking God for hearing his prayer he hugged and kissed Giles, calling him his saviour and a gift from the Almighty. He turned to his startled squire and ordered him to take a message to his brother the King, at Westminster.

"Tell him I have some wonderful news that concerns a certain Lady Eleanor Butler and that I await his pleasure."

As he prepared to leave, the nervous squire repeated the message under his breath for fear he might forget the exact wording.

"Stupid boy," railed Clarence, "just make sure he understands the lady's name, Eleanor Butler. Now go."

"Your Grace. How might I gain an audience with King Edward?" whimpered the squire, backing away from the Duke for fear he would lash out at him for daring to speak.

"You wear my livery, *that* should be sufficient," growled the Duke, simultaneously removing his signet-ring and throwing it across the room for the squire to retrieve from behind a chest by the door.

He summonsed a second servant and ordered a flagon of his best Malmsey with which to celebrate this most joyous of occasions. Tears filled Giles' eyes, he could not have anticipated the Duke would react so heartily to his news.

"Come, come," chided Clarence, wrapping his arm about Giles' shoulders, "this is time to celebrate not wallow in tears." He took a silk cloth from his sleeve and handed it to Giles. As he did so, Giles noticed the ring on the Duke's forefinger; it was exactly like the one his mother had given him. He fumbled inside his tunic and pulled out the leather thong on which was threaded his mother's ring and showed it to his father.

"You have one just like it My Lord. Did you have them made as wedding bands?"

The Duke appeared stunned by the question but quickly regained his composure, looking closely at the ring hanging from Giles' neck.

"Er, yes," he stammered, "the initials on mine are er, GP for George Plantagenet and on yours er …?"

"EB. Eleanor Butler," said Giles proudly.

"Quite. Well Giles Butler, drink your Malmsey," said Clarence, walking Giles to the brazier, one arm still firmly around his shoulder, "you'll have to get use to Malmsey wine sir, if you are to be my son." The Duke grinned and leaving Giles standing by the brazier he returned to sit in his chair by the window where he fell into deep thought for several minutes. Giles manfully drank the rich wine from the silver goblet.

"Now, what am I to do about our less than honest Bishop?" mussed Clarence, rousing himself from his reverie. Giles was shocked at the vicious tone of his father's voice and begged him not to deal harshly with Bishop Robert, because, as Giles explained, it was his mother who had forbidden the Bishop to inform the Duke of his existence. Clarence smiled patronisingly and Giles felt uncomfortable.

"For now we will keep this little secret between ourselves. Robert need be none the wiser," purred Clarence, meeting Giles' gaze with narrowed eyes and again Giles felt uncomfortable, "but be assured boy, when I am King I will grant you the Earldom of March. Call it, 'a gift from your father'." He laughed as if he had cracked an amusing joke.

Giles wonder how Clarence thought he would ever be King but mindful that delusion was probably part of the madness, he thanked the Duke graciously. Clarence continued to laugh uncontrollably so that Giles imagined it must have been a private joke, for he saw nothing amusing in what had been said.

A watery sun appeared low in the sky as Mark and Giles left the Bowyer Tower and made their way back to where Duncan waited with the horses.

"Well?" enquired Mark impatiently, "what did the Duke of Clarence have to say about your claim?"

"Not here Mark, lets ride out to Westminster and hire a room for the rest of today. I need to think through what Clarence has said to me and discuss it with you in private before I face the Bishop."

Mark was happy to agree, the rest of the day at the Westminster ale house meant he would see Alice and that suited him very nicely.

"In fact, we will hire a room for the night," said Giles resolutely, and he spurred Dexter into a trot, glad not to be making for Clipberry.

CHAPTER 7

Westminster Ale House 16th February 1478

As they approached the ale house, Ned's stable man, Joel, recognised Mark and hailed him from the top of the stack of hay he was forking into the stalls. Mark took the horses across to Joel while Giles went into the ale house to find Ned and hire a room for the night.

"Come into the back Master Giles," cried Ned, shaking Giles' hand vigorously, "I have a favour to ask of you. I suppose Mark Taylor is with you?"

"Aye he's taking care of the horses."

In the back kitchen a mouth watering aroma rose from the piglet roasting on the spit. Giles had not eaten since he left Clipberry Street that morning and as his nervous excitement receded, his appetite was returning. Ned brought Giles a black jack filled with his best ale and pulled up a stool alongside him.

"My Alice has set her heart on your man Mark and I wondered if you might put in a good word for her?"

"I'm sure Mark is just as smitten with Alice as she with him … ," began Giles.

"Not a good word with Mark, master Giles, I mean with Bishop Robert Stillington. You see, I want Mark to come and work here in the tavern. Alice is my only child and one day all this will be hers and her wedded husband's. Do you think the Bishop will release Master Taylor?"

Giles was sure Bishop Robert would resist such a proposal. He would welcome Alice into his own household to work alongside Mark's mother but he would not release Mark from his service completely.

"Mark has said nothing to me about wanting to leave the Bishops houschold," protested Giles, "but should he do so in the future, he can count on my support."

Ned realised that in his haste to settle his daughter's future he may have spoken too soon so he thanked Giles and then offered him more ale and some hot meat from the spit. Before Giles could reply, Mark and Alice appeared though the buttery door carrying rugs and bolster cases for filling with straw.

"Master Giles and Mark are staying the night father and they need a private room in which to conduct their business." Alice hesitated and then taking a deep breath added. "I'm going to put them in the rooms across the yard, it's high time we opened them up again."

She did not wait to hear what Ned had to say but walked straight back through the buttery and out into the backyard closely followed by the taverner who had abandoned his task of carving the roast. The rooms to which Alice referred were situated on the upper floor of a stone building which ran at right angles to the tavern, the far wall of which formed a passage way between Ned's property and the next block of buildings. An external flight of stone steps led up to a small wooden door giving access to the upper rooms, the area below being a derelict forge. Giles and Mark hurried after Alice as she mounted the stone stairs but Ned remained in the yard below. The small doorway opened into the first room from which a second door gave access to a large comfortable chamber with a proper bed, a chest, wash stand and candle sconces fixed to the walls.

"My this is grand. Can we afford such luxury?" teased Mark and Alice giggled as she spread the rugs around the floor.

"This room is for master Giles, you can sleep next door," she said coyly, "but you will need to fill the bolsters with straw first." Alice bobbed and curtsied towards Giles and was about to leave when she suddenly remembered.

"Just watch yourselves on the steps," she warned, "they are awful slippery when wet."

Left alone, Mark was eager to hear about Giles' encounter with the Duke of Clarence and prompted him to tell. Giles closed the door and looked out of the widow to make sure there was no one in the yard below to overhear.

"Clarence *is* my father," said Giles confidently, "he had no idea of my existence but I resemble him closely and he admitted to marrying Eleanor and giving her this ring as a wedding gift." Giles pulled his mother's ring from beneath his shirt. "Clarence had one made for each of them, bearing their own initials and guess what? he still wears his on his right forefinger."

"So what happens now?" asked an amazed Mark.

"Difficult to say. The Duke is furious with Bishop Robert for keeping him in the dark but I hope I persuaded him that he was only carrying out my mother's wishes."

Mark detected a note of concern in his friend's voice.

"What's bothering you Giles or should I address you now as, My Lord."

Giles ignored Mark's quip and began to pace the floor, shaking his head slightly as if straining to find a connection between the facts as he had just reported them and an uncomfortable niggle in the back of his mind.

"There is a lot more to this," he eventually said, resigned to not having enough information to make the connection. "The remaining questions are: *why* was my birth kept from the Duke and *why* was my father's identity kept from me?"

"Well the rabbit is out of the bag now and it would appear that Bishop Robert is the key. You must confront him now you know the truth," reasoned Mark.

"The Duke made me promise not to challenge the Bishop until he had spoken with him, which is why we are staying here tonight Mark. My father has sent for the Bishop and by tomorrow everything will be out in the open."

Alice brought them food, blankets, extra candles and logs for the fire, which entailed three journeys across the yard and up the stone staircase. Each time Mark went to her aid, making sure she negotiated the steps safely.

"For heavens sake Mark, stop bobbing up and down whenever Alice appears. If the stairs are as treacherous as you seem to imagine, Ned would have them repaired."

"It was on those stairs that Alice's mother fell to her death," said Mark, "Ned is not altogether happy about Alice reopening these rooms."

"Oh I see."

"No you don't, not completely," replied Mark, pulling a stool closer to the fire. "Your father hid his sister-in-law, Anne Neville in these rooms, so that she could not marry his brother Richard, Duke of Gloucester."

"But she *is* married to Gloucester"

"She is now. But after she was widowed at Tewkesbury she went to live with her sister Isobel, your father's second wife. Clarence wanted to place Anne in a nunnery so that her share of Warwick's estates would pass to his wife. He hid her from Gloucester in these very rooms, whilst making the arrangements for her to take the veil."

"And Richard Gloucester found her here?"

"Not until he had searched the length and breadth of the Capital but eventually somebody tipped him off and someone else reported the tip off to Clarence. He immediately dispatched his men to remove Anne but they were too late, Gloucester had already rescued her. Unfortunately Clarence's retainers made a frenzied search of these upper rooms and somehow poor Janet was pushed to her death down that stairway."

"And now Ned blames the Duke of Clarence for his loss," sighed Giles. It was becoming a familiar story.

"Yes he does," replied Mark hotly, "and considering Clarence also murdered midwife Twynho, Ned's aunt, perhaps he has good reason and perhaps it might be better if you didn't boast that he is your father."

Giles noted the anger in Mark's voice and was surprised at his defence of Ned, who presumably had charged the Duke of Clarence handsomely for imprisoning Lady Anne Neville on his premises. Giles felt the vein on his temple begin to pulsate but he had no energy with which to express his anger.

"Look Mark, I'm the same person I was before my birthday when I had no idea George Clarence was my father. I have only spoken to him once in my entire life and I do not feel responsible for those he has wronged. Furthermore, I have no intention of hiding my relationship to him, for fear that the hatred he has earned is somehow transferred to me. Is that clear?"

Mark swallowed hard to prevent himself from arguing with Giles. He could see the enlarged vein on his temple, which was a sure sign to those who knew him that he was about to erupt. Nodding briefly to his young master Mark took his leave, descended the stairs carefully and strode purposefully across the yard in search of Alice. She and Ned hated the Duke of Clarence and openly made crude and spiteful remarks about him. Mark feared he would find himself in the middle and unable to support either faction, unless he could gain a quick release from Bishop Robert's service.

"Fat chance," he said to himself under his breath as he entered the main building in search of consolatory ale and the reassuring smiles of Alice Twynho.

The following morning Giles woke with a throbbing head which he attributed to a restless night dreaming of the frightened Lady Anne Neville laying alongside him in his bed. She had begged him not to hurt her, threatening him with Gloucester's wrath should the Duke discover how he had misused her. In the crazy logic of dreamland he desperately tried to explain that he was not the Duke of Clarence, only his son but the ravished lady had taken no heed of him and screamed and screamed until he had woken in a hot sweat. He called out for Mark, expecting him to be asleep in the adjoining room so when he failed to respond Giles went to find him, only to discover his bed had not been slept in. Angry with Mark for abandoning his duty, Giles descended the stairway without the recommended care and slipping on the slimy green moss that covered the bottom two steps, he tripped and fell headlong into the muddy yard. Fortunately, only his pride was injured but as he relieved himself in the cess pit at the bottom of the yard he reflected on Mark's obvious concern over Ned's reaction to Clarence being his father. He had no wish to spoil Mark's relationship with Alice; he clearly loved the girl. Giles recalled the way the two had looked at each other on the wedding day of the royal children and inevitably his thoughts turned to Margery. His imagination explored the memory of her kissing him goodbye, until embarrassed by the affect of the images, he quickly tied his points and tried to eliminate the improper manifestation by concentrating on cleaning the mud from his hose with freezing water from the trough by the back door. Given his confusion, it was not surprising that his face flushed crimson when he entered the taproom to find Margery and Luke breaking their fast at the table directly opposite him.

"Giles, what in God's name are you doing here at this time in the morning?" hailed Luke as he recognised his new friend.

"I … er … I. er … stayed here last night. I needed time to consider what I should tell the Bishop and …"

Luke banged this blackjack on the table.

"My God … you've seen the Duke of Clarence! What did he say … did he acknowledge you as his son?"

Margery spluttered her mouthful of drink all over the table as she registered Luke's question and her unladylike attack was prolonged by a fit of coughing when Giles nodded his assent. The two men embraced and Luke congratulated Giles with genuine joy, empathising with his friends happiness.

"He even looks like me," enthused Giles as he accepted Luke's offer of a seat next to the recovering Margery. "Honestly Luke it could not have been more conclusive."

"You are the Duke of Clarence's by-blow?" interrupted Margery.

"Indeed *no* my lady, the Duke married my mother before my conception." announced Giles, with pride, "but before you misunderstand, my mother was dead before His Grace married Lady Isobel Neville."

"You must tell the Bishop as soon as possible," urged Luke, " gossip circulates round Westminster at an alarming rate and it would be unfortunate if he heard the news from someone other than yourself."

Giles sobered immediately.

"My father is furious with Bishop Robert for keeping my existence from him and has asked me not to tell him of my discovery before he speaks with him. If I return to Clipberry, I will be forced to lie to the Bishop or break my promise to my father."

"You can't stay here indefinitely. What will you do?"

Giles thought for a moment before making a decision.

"I must warn the Bishop of the Duke's displeasure. I know he has deceived me for years but he was only carrying out my mother's wishes and it would be vindictive to allow him to face Clarence unprepared."

Ned brought a bowl of hot oats for Giles with a side bowl of honey and whilst the landlord busied himself clearing the mess Margery had spluttered over the table, Giles became aware of the coolness between Luke and his lady.

"What brings you and Margery here at this hour?" asked Giles trying to dispel the tension.

"Perhaps you would care to answer that?" said Luke to Margery icily.

"Of course," replied Margery smiling coquettishly at Giles. "The Queen returned to Windsor some days ago and naturally Lady Stanley accompanied her. I remained at Westminster at the *King's* request, but now I must return to Windsor to join Lady Stanley. For the time being you understand?"

Giles did not understand but the disconcerted grunt from Luke warned him not to pursue further explanation and the sound of horses being reined in quickly and men jumping to the ground in obvious haste averted their attention. Two of Doctor Morton's men burst into the tavern calling for Luke as they entered.

"Whatever is the matter?" cried Luke getting to his feet.

"You are to return to Westminster at once, Master Lazarus, there is some serious crisis," explained the senior of the two retainers, "just what it is, I have no idea but Doctor Morton has need of you immediately. He say's the lady must wait until tomorrow to return to Windsor."

"I can take Margery to Windsor, if that will help?" offered Giles.

Margery pouted at her abandonment but only until Luke had

thank Giles and left with Morton's men.

"I must find my squire before we leave," said Giles, unsure of the motive for his gallantry, "Mark is probably out in the stables with the horses."

Rising quickly he escaped through the main door, hoping to find Luke still in the yard, so proving he was not instantly wooing the deserted lady but Mark was not to be found in the stables.

He was hiding himself in the loft used by Alice as her bedchamber, his knees drawn up to his chest, bound by his long arms and laced fingers. He felt deeply guilty. How could he possibly have predicted that he would feel differently about Alice once he had made love to her? Not that he *loved* her any the less now he had lain with her, he had not found himself to be so shallow as to have mistaken lust for love. However, satisfying his hunger for her body had calmed him and given him pause to consider other aspects of his proposed marriage contract, in particular, those aspects that Ned was earnestly seeking. The taverner wanted an apprentice to learn the trade and take over from him in his old age. A most generous arrangement but on reflection Mark thought he recognised other motives behind his prospective father-in-laws open handedness. He recalled that on each occasion he had visited Alice in the last six months, Ned had instantly found him a job to do and as soon as Mark was harnessed to the task, Ned had left the tavern on the pretext of urgent business. Not that Mark shunned hard work, the Bishop could be a hard task master himself but he had always treated Mark particularly well, teaching him to read and write, to play chess and to ride. He had even given him Old Sal for his twentieth birthday but it was the freedom to accompany Giles wherever he went that Mark was nervous about relinquishing. His life was varied and interesting, with a great deal of personal freedom, never any hardship and only a small amount of physical drudgery. Why should he forego his way of life to ease Ned's? He could still marry Alice and take her to Clipberry Street where she would be made welcome and where her own life would be so much improved. If only he had considered all this *before* he had lain with her. To offer an alterative to Ned's proposal now would seem like a lame excuse for not wanting to wed.

"There you are Mark," scolded Alice, standing on the fourth rung of the ladder and poking her head up through the hole in the loft floor. "Master Giles is looking for you to ride to Windsor with him but father says to excuse yourself, as he needs you here so that he can settle some business down by Paul's Wharfe. Will you speak to master Giles?"

"No Alice I will not," said Mark gently. "I can't ignore my duties just to please Ned."

"But master Giles is so kind and he knows it would mean we could spend the day together," she pleaded, " I'm sure…."

"No," interrupted Mark, "Giles may well agree but Bishop Robert would not. He has only recently allowed Giles to leave Clipberry with just me in attendance and I am sure he would be angry should I permit my master to ride to Windsor alone. Please tell *Master* Giles I will be with him immediately."

"Very well but you *must* explain to him today that you will not be at his beck and call once we are man and wife."

Mark swallowed hard, last night's romp in the loft had also affected Alice. Did she consider that they were now effectively handfast?

Chapter 8

Windsor Castle – 17th February 1478

Throughout the journey to Windsor, Mark rode two or three lengths behind Margery and Giles. He reckoned they were less likely to include him in their conversation if he kept his distance, leaving him free to ponder his own problem. So preoccupied was he with his cooling ardour that he barely noticed their behaviour, whispering, laughing and dawdling for most of the journey. However, Mark did notice how they separated and waited for him to join them before making themselves known to the gatekeeper at the entrance to the great bailey of Windsor Castle.

"See to the horses Mark, I shall escort Margery to Lady Stanley's quarters. I'll meet you in the kitchen and take refreshment with you before we return," said Giles stiffly.

He did not wait for a reply but after dismounting and helping Margery to do likewise, he took her formally by the arm and whisked her across the bailey and up the external stairway into the central keep. Neither spoke as they hurried along the passageways but each was aware of the other's expectations. They had flirted shamelessly throughout the journey and now, if they were to find themselves alone, as Margery expected and Giles desperately hoped, then the parry and thrust of innuendo which had prolonged their gentle ride but heightened their desire, might find relief. Margery finally halted outside a door at the far end of a long gallery and knocked impatiently. A small round creature eventually opened the door.

"Is Lady Stanley within, Dilly?" enquired Margery, knowing full well that she was unlikely to be anywhere other than with the Queen at this time of day. The round bundle named Dilly bobbed and curtsied and without raising her head, moved aside to allow Margery and Giles to enter the chamber. She coughed to indicate she had instructions to convey and then spoke into her chest as if her chin were pinned to it.

"She's with the Queen, mistress. She said to tell you to go straight to Her Majesty's apartments as soon as you arrived."

"Thank you Dilly, you can leave the key as you go."

The strange round bundle rummaged in her apron pocket and produced a large iron key, which she handed to Giles. A funny little smile played on her lips and Giles forgot himself and winked at her as she shuffled out. As Dilly trundled down the long gallery she heard the key turn and the iron lock clunk smoothly into its housing. She chuckled to herself. If the castle gossips were only half right about mistress Margery, then that young man was in for a fine old tumble.

"And good luck to 'em both," she chortled aloud into her chest.

The kitchens at Windsor Castle were large rambling buildings situated many paces away from the main living quarters, their multiple ovens being a constant fire hazard. They generated intense heat throughout the day, much of which escaped through the double doors of the main entrance leading into the court yard and the stable buildings beyond. Even in the depth of winter these doors remained open to provide respite for the army of cooks and scullions who laboured within and a comfortable focal point for journeymen, visitor's servants and apprentices, who made time to rest and socialise in the warm air. A couple of old wine casks and an upturned log used to keep the doors open, doubled as stools and makeshift tables at which the enterprising cooks supplied refreshment to those drawn to the warmth and enticing aromas.

Mark had long since eaten his fill and was beginning to wonder what had delayed Giles when his attention was drawn to an impressive group of visitors entering the main gate. Although they rode close by him, he failed to recognise the insignia displayed on the cloaks of the retainers but the two lords were clearly distinguishable by their exquisite attire and high antics. Mark reckoned both men to be in their early twenties and from their similar appearance probably brothers. Both had auburn hair, pale complexions with green hazel eyes and fine features, but the shorter of the brothers had a cruel mouth which in spite of his good mood twisted into a sneer, whilst the taller man laughed and joked honestly. An under-cook returning from the stores and carrying a sack of apples, set his load down at Mark's feet and watched the lords as they climbed the steps of the keep two at a time, laughing and punching the air.

"Who are they?" enquired Mark.

"Our King's step-sons. Little'n is Marquise o' Dorset an' big'n Lord Richard Grey. Seem to be in fine fettle, don't they?" grumbled the cook and then without waiting for Mark to comment, he lifted the sack of apples and disappeared into the haze of heat.

Several apprentices hurried from the stables to relieve the retainers of their horses but two of the younger squires followed them into the stalls emulating their lord's cheerful glee with boisterous back slapping and hugging. Mark was curious about their high spirits and bored with waiting for Giles, he followed the squires into the stables pretending to check on Old Sal and found his chestnut in a stall next to where the squires were stood shouting orders at the stable hands. He had managed to remove two apples from the cook's sack whilst it resided at his feet and now he fed them to his delighted cob whilst eves dropping on the squires.

"Lets find some ale and toast George Clarence's journey into hell," proclaimed the smaller of the two.

"Good idea," agreed his companion, "all of London will know by now that King Edward has passed sentence of death on his tiresome brother."

"How do you reckon the Queen finally persuaded His Majesty to execute George?"

"Who knows. Perhaps she refused him her bed."

"The King wouldn't execute his brother for *her* fading favours.

He can have any young filly he fancies. Lucky sod."

"It's called patricide."

"What is?"

"When you kill your brother ... or is it fratricide? Who cares? Our Marquise is delighted and his temper has improved beyond belief, which bodes well for the like us."

They both laughed and with arms around each other set off in the direction of the kitchens. Mark could hear Giles calling his name, so he untied their horses and walked them out into the yard to discover an animated Giles flushed and excited with news he was bursting to divulge.

"Mark, Mark, you will never believe what has happened. This is the most wonderful day of my entire life. Today I have fallen in love with the most beautiful creature in all of God's creation and guess what Mark, she has agreed to become my wife."

Giles paused and waited for Mark to enthuse and congratulate him but Mark stood motionless, first stunned and then angry with his young master.

"How can that be?" said Mark through clenched teeth as if he feared to be overheard. " I presume you are referring to Margery?"

Confused and aghast at Mark's indignation Giles nodded.

"Well, you might just have overlooked the fact that Margery is virtually handfast to your new friend Luke."

Giles threw his head back and laughed heartily. "No, no Mark, Luke has broken their agreement. Margery told me during our journey here this morning. Poor Luke feels unable to commit himself to marriage until his memory returns and as there seems to be no likelihood of that happening in the near future, he considered it a kindness to release Margery from her contract."

Mark stared back at Giles in astonishment. Had it not occurred to the young pup that Margery had made a remarkable and instant recovery from her break up with Luke and did he really expect Luke to understand her rapid transfer of affection to Giles? Mark kept his thoughts to himself but instead tried to persuade Giles to keep his news a secret for the time being, at least until he had heard Luke's version of his split with Margery.

"Damn you both," said Giles light-heartedly. "That's what

Margery made me promise."

"To keep it from Luke?"

"No, to keep our love a secret for fear the Queen should hear of it. The Queen, like Doctor Morton, Ned and Alice and God knows who else, hates my father."

Mark thought it unlikely that the Queen would be interested in the love life of a servant of one of her ladies-in-waiting but he still enquired about the nature of Queen Elizabeth Woodville's hatred of George Clarence. Giles explained that when Clarence and the Earl of Warwick took up arms against the King ten years ago Edward had not believed them capable of insurrection and had dispatched the Queen's father to investigate the source of the rumours. Unfortunately, the aging Lord was captured by Clarence and executed without trial. Ever since the queen had demanded retribution.

"Lets get out of here," said Mark, handing Dexter's reins to a perplexed Giles. "I have something to tell you but not here where we might be over heard," and without waiting for Giles to respond, Mark mounted Old Sal and rode towards the main gate. Once free of the small village that sprawled before the Castle, Mark spurred his cob into a trot and Giles was obliged to similarly encourage Dexter.

"So what have you to tell that is so private?" asked Giles crossly, when he was eventually trotting alongside Mark. He was annoyed that Mark had taken his news badly and hurt that he failed to congratulate him. Mark took a deep breath and very deliberately and concisely repeated what Dorset's squires had said about King Edward condemning the Duke of Clarence to death. Giles reined-in Dexter and Mark turned in his saddled to witness the explosion.

"That's ridiculous," screamed Giles angrily but his indignation was curtailed by Dexter, who, startled by the sudden outcry directly above his ears, reared on his hind legs, forcing Giles to redirect his efforts into consoling the confused beast.

"Doctor Morton assured me that the King was only trying to frighten my father into more prudent behaviour when he tried him for treason," continued Giles more evenly when Dexter seemed sufficiently reassured. Mark remained silent and Giles walked Dexter forward to join him. "I warrant that Clarence appeared so unperturbed by being found guilty of treason that Edward is calling his bluff still further."

"Yes, yes probably."

"Yes *definitely*," snapped back Giles so fiercely that Mark resolved to say no more.

"Bishop Robert will know what's behind this nonsense," continued Giles, "I need to speak with him anyway and this time I will not be denied the truth." So saying, Giles dug his spurs into Dexter and galloped off down the London road. Mark sighed and nudged Old Sal to follow but at a more reasonable pace.

Margery straightened her wimple for the tenth time and conceded to herself that she could no longer delay her attendance on Lady Stanley. She would be able to leave the old crow's service once she had established herself as the King's long-term mistress and then if His Majesty eventually tired of her, well, she would remain at court amongst wealthy noblemen, who would appreciate her feminine skills and reward her with practical gifts of such value that would ensure her independence. So why had she lain with Giles? And why had she agreed to marry him? Margery closed the heavy door behind her and turned the key. She made her way along the passageway and took the shortcut via an outer walkway which led back through a small anteroom into a wider gallery with polished wood flooring and high windows and which led directly to the Queen's chambers. She continued the conversation with herself in an audible whisper.

"Well, one night in the King's bed hardly constitutes a long-term relationship but it's a start and if all else fails, well Giles is the Duke of Clarence's son and surely King Edward will make him an Earl or something?"

At the sound of footsteps climbing the stairway further along the gallery, Margery stopped talking to herself and hurried forward to discover who else was making their way to the Queen's chambers. The heads appearing above the stairwell were those of the

Marquise, Thomas of Dorset and Lord Richard Grey, the Queen's sons by her first marriage. Without looking either man in the face, Margery curtsied and stood back to allow the two lords to proceed her. Both men had encountered her in these corridors on numerous occasions, although neither had chosen to acknowledge her. Unfortunately, Margery was about to discover that her means to independence had turned her world into a precarious place. Before she realized what was happening Dorset put his hand around her throat, lifted her up and forced her back against the wall.

"Now what is this little whore doing in the Queen's gallery Dick?" snarled Dorset, pushing his face so close to Margery's that she could smell his foul breath.

"Leave her be Tom, we've important news to impart to our mother," slurred Grey.

Still holding Margery by the throat the Marquise pushed his other hand down her bodice and squeezed her left breast. She tried to prevent his mauling by twisting her body towards the wall but he thrust his knee hard into her groin to hold her fast whilst he twisted her left breast so viciously that she all but fainted with the pain. He let her drop to the floor, wiping the blood from his fingers across her cheek and then spitting at her over his shoulder as he followed Grey down the gallery.

Margery remained on the floor for several minutes in a state of shock and pain. It had never occurred to her that her ambition to become the King's mistress would offend anyone. How dare Dorset treat her so roughly? The King would hear how his step-son had behaved and then he would be sorry. She got to her feet and straightened her gown, her groin was sore and blood was seeping through her bodice but if she could reach the room used by the Queen's ladies unseen, she might be able to repair the damage before having to face Lady Stanley. She hurried passed the main entrance to the Queen's chambers with her shoulders hunched forward so that the man-at-arms could not see the stain on her bodice. Normally she would have bid him good day but now she looked straight ahead to the end of the gallery where she turned the corner quickly and pushed open the small door of the room allotted to the Queen's ladies. Thankfully she was alone and able to breathe more freely but her groin was throbbing and the pain in her breast was acute. Never mind, by tomorrow there would be evidence of her mistreatment, a colourful bruise which together with the gouge marks on her breast would be more than enough to convince King Edward of what she had endured. She soaked the inside of her underskirt in some red wine from the jug on the side table and cleaned the blood from her face and breast. The stain on her bodice was not so easily removed but she wetted the surrounding area with the red wine so that the dark patch was uniform and therefore less noticeable. Satisfied with her efforts she poured herself a full cup of wine and slumped onto a bench to await Lady Stanley's return.

Beyond the silence of the ladies room she could hear the sound of muffled voices in the adjoining chamber. The Queen was laughing and cups were being banged together in salute. The other voices were male and probably those of Dorset and Grey but she could not hear what they were saying. Margery began to doze with the effect of the wine and her mind wandering back to the one night she had spent in King Edward's bed. She smiled to herself as she remembered his compliments and expressions of pleasure so, why had he insisted that she leave Westminster so soon? Her wonderings were sharply interrupted by the icy shards of Lady Stanley's voice demanding she wake up.

"Be alert girl, Her Majesty is asking for you."

"*Me*? She doesn't know of my existence, how can she be asking for *me*?"

"Oh she knows of your existence my lass, believe me. Now *get in* there."

Lady Stanley's hooded eyes were inches from Margery's face and her thin dry lips barley allowed the words to pass between them as she suppressed the anger heaving in her chest. Margery's fear of Lady Stanley released her from the bench like an arrow and before she had time to consider the Queen's request further she had entered the royal chamber for the very first time. Of course she had peeped in through the ladies room door but the high screens across the entrance virtually block the view completely.

Now she absorbed its beauty and heady fragrance as if she had been invited to step into heaven. Folds of purple velvet hanging on golden rods covered every wall, their hems richly embroidered with gold lozenge motifs. Black and white floor tiles offset to form a clever chequered pattern, had the same golden lozenges sparkling in alternate black tiles like wrongly placed chess pieces. The vaulted ceiling was painted a pale green with each curve and arch delicately gilded. Persian rugs with gold fringes were placed beneath every chair, stool and side table and matching both in richness of colour and design, embroidered cushions were strewn around the floor and benches. A chandelier bearing twenty or so candles hung from the centre of the ceiling and all around the perimeter of the room upright sconces with golden back guards, held branches of five candles. Even though the afternoon light had not yet faded the uprights were lit, encouraging the gold throughout the room to twinkle and dance in its magnificence. Sweet smelling herbs released their perfume into the warm air, provided by a log fire set into the exterior wall, with the new and fashionable back vent which drew the smoke away from the room and up through the hole in the roof. For a very brief moment Margery was seduced by the richness that surrounded her.

"Your Majesty, my servant, Margery Goodman," announced Lady Stanley, with such distaste that Margery looked around for the object of her mistress' displeasure.

"You may leave us," replied the Queen, who was standing so close to Margery that she could have reached out and touched her. Blinking, Margery refocused her gaze on the beautiful woman who now smiled graciously and indicated a chair where she should sit. Margery had observed the Queen on numerous occasions but never so up close. She knew Elizabeth Woodville to be in her early forties but she looked at least ten years younger. Her hair was rich auburn with no telltale signs of grey and she had white silken skin without a single wrinkle, except when she smiled and to Margery's surprise she continued to do so. Her mouth was full and generous and her teeth, even and sparkling white and her huge grey green eyes laughed and danced with delight at the girl's obvious amazement. She did not appear to Margery, to be the hard, cruel,

Woodville bitch, that the gossips reported. A young page boy served them wine in gold goblets and them left them alone as Her Majesty instructed.

"My sons tells me you are the King's new favourite," said the Queen softly, studying the wine in her goblet to avoid witnessing Margery's embarrassment. She did not wait for a reply. "It is quite usual for a man to take more than one woman to his bed, especially when he is as rich and as hansom as Edward Plantagenet." She paused briefly to allow Margery to absorb her words. "And as he is King, it would be unrealistic to try and restrict his natural appetite." Again she paused, if Margery was to be of use to her she must understand her acceptance of Edward's lust. "No mistress lasts for ever," she sighed, as if genuinely sorry for those he discarded, "his appetite is quickly jaded with plain and simple morsels. But let us speak no more of the King's weakness."

The Queen turned to face Margery and as the pale sunlight streamed through the open shutters it caught the girl's face, revealing how very young and unblemished her beauty was. Elizabeth Woodville drew in breath to control her rising envy, it was some time now since her mirror had recorded such flawless beauty without assistance from her 'miracle pots'. She continued but with less sympathy for girl than before.

"From what Lady Stanley has told me, you are a strong, single minded young woman, unlikely to be swayed from your *ambition* by the inconvenience of tugs at your heart."

Margery noted a sourer, much harder edge to her voice and looked up to meet the Queen's intense and glittering eyes.

"This is a man's world Your Majesty, but if God has been gracious with gifts of beauty, then a woman has options and can, if she so chooses, achieve independence for herself."

The Queen held Margery's gaze: surely the girl was not mocking her? Society gossips still whispered how Elizabeth had bewitched the King with her beauty when she had 'accidentally on purpose,' met him in the forest whilst he was hunting on her father's estate. Elizabeth mentally reprimanded herself, the girl would not dare to mock her. She was simply defending herself against Lady Stanley's pious judgement and anyway, Elizabeth agreed with

Margery, it *was* a man's world. Here was a kindred spirit who would serve her well for nothing more complicated than financial remuneration. Excellent!

"I need you to be my eyes and ears at court," said the Queen more kindly. "Most men are arrogant enough to believe that women have little understanding or interest in politics, especially frivolous, pretty women."

Margery suppressed a giggle, she knew this to be true. Her presence had often been ignored by Lord Stanley and Doctor Morton whilst they discussed courtly matters.

"You will report everything you hear to Lady Stanley, who will relay your information to me only," continued the Queen, "however insignificant. Do you understand?"

Margery nodded.

"Information is the source of all power Margery. Beauty fades with time and we have to find an alternate commodity with which to barter. Even the smallest indiscretion can be very important when matched with other factors. Now, can I depend on you?"

Again Margery nodded.

"In return I will provide you with lodgings at both Westminster and here at Windsor and when the King tires of you, I will promote your services to other noblemen, that is, if His Majesty does not recommend you to someone himself."

Margery winced visibly.

"If you think Edward will remain interested in you for more than a month or so child, you are deluding yourself," said the Queen harshly, "it's the way men are. Come now, you don't need me to tell you that, do you?"

"No," replied Margery, brightening at the thought of conspiratorial involvement with the Queen of England. Margery Goodman and Elizabeth Woodville, sisters armed only with their beauty and unacknowledged intellect, determined to infiltrate the world of lustful, arrogant noblemen in order to relieve them of their power and in Margery's case, their riches. What a fantastic prospect!

"You and I will not speak again," said the Queen, satisfied that Margery was aware of the opportunity she presented, "It is important that others believe you are still Lady Stanley's maid: a servant who is just pretty enough to engage the attention of the King and his cronies. Now go," the Queen raised her goblet, "and may we both prosper from your endeavours."

Margery curtsied low before the Queen and in so doing revealed the seeping wound and multi-coloured bruise developing on her left breast.

"He'll not touch you again," said the Queen stiffly as she caught sight of the wound. "I can promise you that."

Chapter 9

London 17th February 1478

Giles reined in Dexter as he entered the small courtyard in front of Clipberry Manor, just as the Priory bells were tolling for Nones. Even though the light was failing and men would soon be finishing work for the day, the yard was strangely inactive. A small light flickered from the stables and Giles walked Dexter towards it, calling for Arthur to take his horse. A scruffy stable lad appeared carrying a lantern and hugging some sack cloth to his frail body in an attempt to fend off the chill. The meagre light shone on the child's face and Giles was struck by the fear in the huge round eyes that searched beyond him to the gate and the superficial defences of the bailey walls.

"Lord preserve us, whatever has frightened you and where is Arthur and the other stable hands?" asked Giles as he dismounted and handed his reins to the boy.

"In the 'ouse sir, somat awful's 'appened," croaked the child.

Without waiting for further explanation, Giles climbed the flight of stone steps and burst into the unlit great hall, to find all the servants huddled together in front of the hearth. His sudden entrance caused them to stiffen with fright, whilst the draught from the opened door wafted the idling fire into life, throwing long fingers of dancing shadows into the far reaches of the hall. Giles froze, a bizarre sense of fear rendering him immobile and before he could recover his nerve, Mary pushed her way to the front of the frightened huddle and with intermittent wails and sniffs, proceeded to inform him of the dreadful happening that had taken place that afternoon.

"King's men master Giles ... proper dressed sir ... bearing the arms of England they did, all did ... all five of 'em, burst into here, just as you did now master Giles. Swords all drawn and flashing, pushing us around like we were ... dangerous felons. It was terrible ... terrible."

"God Almighty Mary, what did they want?"

"The Bishop master Giles, they arrested Bishop Robert."

"I don't understand, why should they arrest the Bishop?"

Mary wiped her eyes on the heels of her hands and sniffed long and hard, then turning to find Elias, the bottler, she grabbed him by the arm and whimpered, "show him Elias, you show him."

Elias shuffled forward, a willowy man in his late fifties with wisps of thinning grey hair, bony features and black beady eyes, which in total gave him the appearance of a man of learning. He could neither read nor write but amidst a flock of panicking servants he would be the natural choice for someone in authority to trust with a message. Obediently Elias fumbled in the pocket of his leather apron and produced a scroll of vellum which he handed Giles. At the same moment the huge oak door was flung open again, causing a second draft to draw the flames high up the fire back.

"Why are the lamps unlit?" said Mark as he carefully closed the door, fearful of creating another draft. "What on earth is everyone doing in the dark?"

Hearing Mark's voice, Woof left the corner he had retreated into when the King's men had arrived and padded over to push a wet nose into his master's hand. Mark crouched down to pat Woof but continued to hassle the servants.

"Come on you lot, move it before grumpy Giles gets here and wants his supper."

The disconcerted servants were grateful for the order to disperse and moved readily to their tasks, leaving Giles, Mark and Woof alone in the great hall.

"Oops," cried Mark in a silly voice, hiding his face in the thick fur of Woof's neck and feigning fear of reprisal for bad mouthing his young master.

"Stop arsing about," snapped Giles, "the King has arrested Bishop Robert, and if these bloody lamps were lit I could read the warrant and determine *why* he's been arrested."

Mark was speechless, why should the King arrest Bishop Robert, there must be some mistake? A lamp flickered along the screened passage and Mary nervously re-entered the hall. The two young men waited in silence whilst she lit the cresset lamps and the three branch candelabra either end of the trestle table.

Giles broke the seal on the scroll and gasped in disbelief as he read the few lines of the warrant. Mark waited until his mother retreated to the kitchen and then peered over Giles' shoulder and read aloud.

"This warrant authorises the arrest and imprisonment in the Tower, of one, Robert Stillington, Bishop of Bath and Wells, on the charge of making utterances which are not in the best interest of His Majesty King Edward."

"It doesn't make sense," said Giles, "this hasn't been drawn up by a lawyer. Apart from the lack of legal pomposity, no man trained in the law would use such phrases as, 'making utterances' and 'not in the best interest of.' A lawyer would refer to, slander, lies or even treason. These words suggest a minor indiscretion. It's ridiculous."

"Are you sure it's the King's signature and seal?" asked Mark.

"How can it not be? But I know how we can be certain."

Without further hesitation Giles made his way up the wooden stairs and along the gallery to the small room next to the Bishop's bed chamber and Mark followed, pausing only to collect a cresset lamp from the side table. The room served as a Chancery now but it had been the school room when the boys were younger and both knew the lock had been broken years ago. Tentatively they entered the office, conscious that they were about to search the Bishop's private records. Five summers since, Bishop Robert had been Edward's Chancellor and Giles reasoned that there would be letters bearing the King's seal still filed away in some of the dusty wooden boxes and so Mark lit another cresset and set it on the high writing desk where it provided further illumination of the musty room. It was still as the young men remembered, with boxes of scrolls stacked precariously against two of the walls, some even resting on the ceiling crossbeam and balanced on a stool next to the desk was a small open chest containing an assortment of unsharpened quills, pieces of pumice, and several tiny bottles of ink. Amongst the quills Mark found a bone handled knife which he and Giles had given the Bishop for his saint's day many years ago but he put it to one side, Giles was already pulling at a wooden box, marked with the dates he thought referred to a period when the Bishop was high in the King's favour. He was correct, two of the documents it contained were from the King, bearing his signature and the great seal. Giles spread one of them out on the desk and placed the warrant alongside.

"There, you see, it is the King's seal and look, the whole of the warrant is written in the King's own hand."

Mark examined the two seals and then the hand writing.

"Why would the King compose and write the warrant himself? he asked.

"Perhaps he wished to keep the real reason for the Bishop's arrest a secret."

"Why?"

"I have absolutely no idea," said Giles, turning away from the light so that Mark could not see the horror on his face but try as he might, he could not keep his rising panic to himself. "Oh Lord help me Mark, I'm beginning to think this is all my fault. If I hadn't made myself known to my father and he hadn't informed the King …" His words trailed away as he allowed his body to sink down the wall coming to rest on the floor with his knees under his chin.

Mark frowned but remained silent.

"Yesterday morning I made myself known to my father, whose first response was to get word to the King. Now this morning King Edward passes sentence of death on Clarence and by noon has Bishop Robert confined to the Tower."

"So what? There is no evidence to link the sentencing of Clarence with the arrest of the Bishop, or with your meeting the Duke," said Mark.

Giles rummaged in his scrip for the note Eleanor had intended for the Bishop.

"Read it again," he demanded.

Mark read the short note aloud. *"My Dearest Robert, I beg you, ensure my son Giles, never encounters George, Duke of Clarence. Tell the King. God bless and keep you, Eleanor Butler."* Again Mark waited for Giles to explain further.

"Don't you see, my mother implores my guardian never to let me contact my father; *never* to contact him. But in my usual headstrong way, I *did* contact him and now it seems more than a coincidence that both Clarence and the Bishop are in trouble the very next day. There *is* something more to all this Mark, I'm sure of it. Somehow I have betrayed the King by ignoring Eleanor's warning."

"You've betrayed *the King*?" howled Mark in disbelief.

Tears welled in Giles' eyes. "I've been less than honest about yesterday's meeting with my father," he sniffed, "hear me out Mark before you judge me to be a complete ass."

"Go on then," said Mark more soberly, "tell me what really happened."

"Oh it happened just as I said," defended Giles, "it was how my father reacted to the news, which I misrepresented."

Giles got to his feet and started to pace up and down, trying to make sense of the jumbled thoughts which had troubled him since yesterday morning.

"He was unbelievably excited to learn that I was his son, which is an odd reaction. It isn't as if he had not sired other sons. Why was I so special?"

"How do you think he should have reacted?"

"Well, he could have been shocked, embarrassed or even angry if he thought I was seeking recognition or financial support. Or he could have been welcoming, reassuring and shown some interest in how I had faired until now but the only emotion he displayed was sheer excitement. I have tried to interpret his reaction differently but I always return to the same conclusion. He was ecstatic, over come with joy and yet he never mentioned my mother other than to ask the date of her death. He could have spoken of his love for her or even tried to explain why he had abandoned her."

"But he told you about the matching rings. He said he had had one made for Eleanor and one for himself."

"No, not really," said Giles sadly, touching his mother's ring inside his shirt. "When I saw his ring, *I* suggested that he had had them made as a pair, he even hesitated before agreeing with me."

"What are you saying Giles, that the Duke of Clarence isn't your father after all?"

"Oh he's my father alright," replied Giles bitterly, "being so close to him was like looking at my own face in polished silver but he doesn't give a damn about me or my mother."

"Then what *are* you saying?"

"That my birth has remained a secret because it poses some kind of threat to the King. Clarence has made Edward aware that the secret is out and the King has wrongly assumed that Bishop Robert betrayed him. Eleanor also knew of the danger and in her note, warned the Bishop, both to tell King Edward that Clarence was a threat and to ensure that I never encountered the Duke."

"But what danger, what threat?" persisted Mark, "it doesn't really make sense Giles."

Both young men sat silently considering the logic of Giles' argument.

"Dear God," exploded Giles, "this is the second time recently that Edward has acted without a lawyer when both Clarence and the Bishop were involved."

"What?"

"My father's trial. King Edward conducted the prosecution himself. Why did he not trust Doctor Morton?"

Mark shrugged. "Why didn't he?"

"Because it would be natural for the prosecution to delve into Clarence's earlier treason and if Morton had done so *Bishop Robert*, might have been forced to defend Clarence by revealing some secret hidden in events before 1471."

"No Giles. If the Bishop knew something that would help Clarence's defence, even if it damage the King, then all he needed to do was inform the Duke, who would be more than capable of presenting the damming evidence himself."

"You're missing the point. The King trusted the Bishop not to *deliberately* divulge the 'secret' but he could not risk an in-depth discussion between the lawyers which might raise difficult questions about those early years of his reign. My father gained some important knowledge from our meeting yesterday and armed with that information he challenged the King.

Well it was not Bishop Robert's fault. Tomorrow I will go to Westminster and seek out Doctor Morton. He has access to King Edward and surely he will be able to help me secure the Bishop's release?"

Baynard's Castle was not Richard Gloucester's favourite place but it was his mother's London home and it would have been ungracious not to have accepted her invitation to stay there for Christmas and the wedding celebrations that had followed in January, or at least, that was how his wife Anne had argued when they were making arrangements to travel from their Yorkshire home. They had intended returning after the customary few days of nuptial feasting but King Edward's clever timing of George Clarence's trial had made it impossible for them to return as planned. Richard's mother Cecily, was fearful for the fate of her son George and had turned to her youngest for comfort and reassurance and so he had felt obliged to extend their stay.

This was the additional fourth week and Richard was becoming impatient to return to Middleham Castle. Both Anne and their small son Ned, quickly succumbed to winter fever and Baynard's was always damp and cold at this time of year, situated as it was on the banks of the River Thames. Even now, Cecily's physician was attending her three year old grandson in his bedchamber across the gallery. The child's coughing and wheezing had been so severe that even at this late hour, Richard had insisted the doctor be called and now the anxious father sat in his own chamber with his door ajar so that he might be certain Ned had finally settled. However, the boy's mother was unaware that the doctor had been summonsed as she had also retired early with a sore throat.

At their home in Yorkshire, Richard shared a bedchamber with his wife but his mother's household was more formally run, here each had their own bedchamber. Of course he could go to her at any time and before retiring, he had enquired about her condition only to be informed by her ladies that she had taken a sleeping draft in honey and lemon and was sound asleep. So he had retired to his own room, dismissed his squires and was now keeping a vigil on the closed door of Ned's room.

Sat alone in the stillness, Richard's recurrent nightmare of childhood terror manifested itself in wakeful panic. It was from that chamber across the gallery that without warning, the eight year old Richard and his eleven year old brother George, had been roused from their sleep and hurriedly escorted to a waiting boat on the Thames. Only three weeks earlier the notorious Queen Margaret of Lancaster had put to death their father, elder brother Edmund and their uncle Salisbury and rumours that she was fast approaching the Capital had prompted Cecily to hastily rouse her small sons and ship them to the Low Countries, into the care of Philip of Burgundy, a sworn ally of the House of York.

Richard shivered as the memory of childhood terror swept over him again and again. He poured himself some more wine in an attempt to ward off the unattractive panic and continuing to distract himself in this way he eventually fell asleep, only to be woken some hours later by Ned tugging at his sleeve.

"Wake up papa, wake up. Come ... see. The King and Grandam in the hall ..."

"No Ned, you must have been dreaming," yawned Richard, stretching his cramped limbs and reaching for some more wine to clear the rough taste from his mouth. "What are you doing out of bed? Where is nurse Collins?"

"The King is here," insisted Ned, jumping up and down and tugging at his father's sleeve with two small white hands.

Richard reach for a coverlet from his bed and wrapped it around the infant's shoulders, then telling him to hold it tightly across his chest he took the child's other hand and pointed to the door, indicating he was willing to be led to the hall. When they reached the top of the staircase all was dark and quiet below. Ned looked over the banister in disbelief.

"Gone," he howled.

Richard knelt beside him and brushed the tears of frustration from his small face. In the weak flickering light, shed by the single torch at the top of the stairs, the child looked like a ghostly spectre of some previous life. His dark sunken eyes were too large for the rest of his features and the grey circles beneath them told of his ill health. Richard lifted the child into his arms, the sensation of bone protruding through meagre flesh tugged at his heart and he silently prayed for the health of his son. Still trying to sooth Ned's protests he carried him back along the gallery to his bedchamber but when they reached the door, Ned tightened his grip on his father's neck.

"Sleep in your bed papa?" he whispered tentatively, fearing the refusal.

Without answering, Richard cross the gallery to his bedchamber and laid the child in his own bed. Content, Ned seemed to fall asleep almost immediately so Richard closed the door and still in his day attire lay on top of the bed next to his son. The child snuggled into the crux of his father's arm and slept soundly.

Richard could not sleep. His brother George filled his thoughts and he prayed fervently that Edward might find a way to reconcile himself with their wayward sibling. He glanced at the hour candle which showed less than an hour past midnight and realised that his mother may well have been in the hall as Ned had insisted. She always rose at this time for Matins but surely Edward was not here too: no the lad was mistaken.

Before he finally fell asleep Richard resolved to go to Westminster tomorrow and ask Edward's permission to leave the Capital and if granted, by noon his little family would take leave of the Dowager Duchess and embark on their journey north to Yorkshire and their home at Middleham Castle, or so he planned.

Chapter 10

Palace of Westminster 18th February 1478

Winter was by no means over but a few frost-free nights and warmer days had quickly released the mighty Thames from the grip of ice, allowing river traffic to reclaim its watery highway. Surviving islands of dirty ice still hugged the banks and tributaries, heavily burdened with filth and sewage defrosting rapidly in the early warmth. Lord Francis Lovell pinched his nose and held his breath as he disembarked from the royal barge which had carried him and his Lord, Richard Duke of Gloucester, from Baynard's Castle to the King's Steps at Westminster. He dreaded travelling on water, even the short distance from Baynard's had made him feel queasy, so hearing the Abbey bells calling the faithful to early mass, Francis paused, ostensibly to admire the Abbey building which rose majestically into the misty sky. His pale, freckled face was tinged with a green hue and his long red hair whipped round his cheeks and clung to the sweat released by his sickness. Francis wiped his forehead on his sleeve and tucked what he could of his hair under his velvet cap. With his feet now on solid ground he was recovering quickly but was forced to hurry to maintain pace with the Duke. Francis slithered along the greasy path that led into the palace yard and stumbling on an icy patch shaded from the watery sun, his feet rushed from under him. Instinctively he grabbed Gloucester's sleeve and both men laughed as they grappled to maintain their balance. Like the Dukes of Gloucester and Clarence, Lord Francis Lovell had spent his youth as a ward of the Earl of Warwick. The Earl's daughters and the King's brothers had been his constant childhood companions and he loved both the Duke and his Duchess as his own kin.

"We will cut through the great hall Francis and you can find me that lawyer who is handling the sale of Crosby Place for the grocer's widow."

"William Catesby my lord. Have you decided to buy the manor then?"

Gloucester nodded and grinned as Francis slipped once more, this time stumbling into the backs of two red capped judges, deep in conversation. They too were making their way to the great hall and both turned angrily to see who had dared to collide with their lordships but recognising the King's youngest brother they graciously broke ranks to allow him to pass into the hall before them. Even at this early hour, preparation for the daily duty of administering the King's Justice was under way. Lawyers, sheriffs, sergeants-at-law and their myriad of clerks filled the great arena dressed in their official garb like dozens of penned exotic birds, strutting and calling to one another in sounds known only to others of their kind. Richard Gloucester paused to determine his route through the crush.

"Much as I love my mother, Francis, I hate Baynard's. It invokes too many childhood demons, which I am unable to exorcise. Besides I need a London home of my own, if only to sleep in the same bed as my wife without announcing my intentions to the entire household."

Francis grinned and was about to take his leave of the Duke in search of the lawyer, Catesby, when a commotion broke out across the hall. A sergeant-at-law in his white hooded tunic and scarlet hose was denying a young man access to the chambers beyond.

"You cannot see Doctor Morton today sir. I have had strict instructions from the Doctor himself not to allow anyone into his chambers".

"I'm not *anyone*" complained Giles, beginning to loose his temper, "I am the Duke of Clarence's first born son and I'll thank you to convey my request for an audience, to Doctor Morton immediately."

Those near enough to hear the outburst laughed and two burly bailiffs moved forward threatening to remove the 'witless youth' from the hall but Richard Gloucester had heard Giles' claim to be Clarence's son and noted the likeness of the lad to his brother.

"Bring that young man to me," snapped Gloucester to Francis Lovell, "I'll be ...," he turned, looking for somewhere private to interrogate Giles, "there," and he pointed to a door he hoped would lead to an office.

Francis vanished into the crowd whilst Gloucester walked straight into the room behind his chosen door, much to the consternation of an ancient short sighted clerk. The startled fellow was warming his half gloved hands over a brazier prior to starting work, his vellum, scrolls and writing materials were all laid out on the large desk that filled most of the tiny office. Screwing up his eyes and peering in the general direction of the opened door he demanded to know if fire had broken out somewhere close by.

"There is no fire. I am commandeering your office for a few minutes, on the King's business," shouted Richard Gloucester, wrongly assuming the ancient to be hard of hearing as well as short sighted.

"All business in the great hall is the King's young sir," squeak the clerk defensively, as he shuffled his bent body towards the intruder, "and there's no need to shout, I'm not deaf." He was now within inches of Gloucester and simultaneously bending his knees and jerking his torso backwards, his head came up sufficiently for him to identify the insignia hanging round the Duke's neck. "Good God, please forgive me your Grace, my eyes are weak and ... and ..."

The petrified clerk hurriedly tried to collect the scrolls from his desk, dropping and retrieving them in alarming succession. Gloucester helped him to secure his load and eventually calmed, he bowed himself out of his own domain and in so doing, backed into Francis returning with two sergeants escorting a protesting Giles. Francis instructed the men to release their charge but to wait outside the door. Free from the rough hold of his escort Giles brushed himself down and faced Gloucester defiantly. He was immediately struck by how different his father and uncle appeared to be. No bejewelled velvet and rich ermine adorned Gloucester's body. He wore a fine woollen hooplander beneath his black cloak but there was nothing in his dress to suggest he was the King's brother. Giles had heard that Gloucester was a small man but he was amazed to find him no taller than himself but with dark hair and smaller features. His face had the pinched look of someone who had suffered a long period of ill health, with thin lips that struggled to smile and Giles marvelled that his father and his man could be brothers. In the poor light, the eyes that stared intensively at him appeared to be deep blue, harsh and unforgiving so the unexpected gentleness of his uncle's voice took Giles by surprise.

"I heard you claim to be the Duke of Clarence's son. A by-blow of his misspent youth? Well lad you certainly look like him."

"No My Lord, the Duke married my mother before I was born."

Francis hissed in disbelief but Gloucester raised his hand to silence him.

"Explain yourself boy. You'd better have proof of your claim."

Giles told his story from the beginning. How his mother, Eleanor and his father, George Duke of Clarence had been married and how he had been born as a result of their union. How Eleanor had been confined to a Nunnery and he had been raised by the Bishop. He explained about the casket, opened four weeks ago and the notes it contained. Fumbling in his script, Giles produced the two small scrolls which he handed to the Duke.

"After I had read the one with my name on it, I was so angry with the Bishop for lying to me that I broke the seal and read the second note," admitted Giles.

Even as he spoke Gloucester was reading the notes and then, without comment, he passed them to Francis. When Francis had finished he looked up confounded.

"Neither of these *say* that George Clarence is your father," he said.

"No my lord, that is why I went to see the Duke myself."

"You've spoken to Clarence?" asked Gloucester.

"Yes Your Grace. He acknowledge me as his son and confirmed he wed my mother."

Gloucester just gaped in amazement. Giles reminded him so much of George at fourteen that he was involuntarily warming to the lad. Giles decided to confide in his uncle. If he could convince Richard Gloucester that he had inadvertently been responsible for Bishop Robert's arrest, then perhaps he would help secure his release.

"The Duke of Clarence was furious with the Bishop for keeping my birth a secret... but....well, there must have been a reason for not telling him." Giles hesitated, he needed to be honest about the concern he had for Clarence's reaction to his news.

"My Lord, when I identified myself to the Duke he reacted very strangely, as though ..." Giles paused again trying to recapture the inappropriateness of Clarence's response, "... as though my very existence was the solution to his own problems."

"How could that be?" sneered Francis.

"I know how unlikely it sounds my Lord but it is the only way I can describe my father's strange excitement. He immediately despatched a messenger to tell the King of my revelation and he was determined to punish Bishop Robert for keeping my existence from him. If Clarence led King Edward to believe that Bishop Robert was the source of his discovery then perhaps that is why the Bishop was arrested for 'making utterances that were not in His Majesty's best interest.' "

"I do not understand," Gloucester said shaking his head.

"In truth, neither do I Your Grace but that was the day before yesterday and since ..."

"Since then," cut in Francis Lovell, "the Duke of Clarence has been sentenced to death and the Bishop of Bath and Wells, arrested and held in the Tower."

"And Bishop Robert doesn't know that I opened the note address to him or that I visited my father," added Giles.

"There can be no connection," snapped Gloucester but he knew brother George was capable of the most outrageous acts.

"I am determined that King Edward should know that Bishop Robert has not revealed my identity to the Duke: that if anyone is to blame, it is me," wailed Giles, "that is why I wanted to find Doctor Morton. I need his help to convey my guilt to the King but by God's truth Lords, I know not of what I am guilty."

"Except breaking the seal on your guardian's note and keeping its content from him," said Gloucester with a wry smile and then slapping Giles heartily on the back continued, "whatever the truth of the matter, you obviously need to express your concerns to the King. I shall be delighted to witness his reaction when you claim to be Clarence's legitimate first born and I am sure the Bishop will forgive you."

Giles still looked worried. Gloucester took his arm and ushered him towards the door.

"And don't worry about Clarence," he added kindly," Edward will not execute his own brother however difficult he his. I promise you, Edward is calling his bluff; trying to frighten him into apologising for his bad tempered behaviour."

Although Giles had been in Westminster Palace many times, he had never before entered the King's private chambers. As he followed his uncle Richard and Francis Lovell along the corridors and galleries he wondered at the sheer luxury unfolding before him. Polished wooden floors and wainscoting gleamed in the light that streamed though coloured glass filled windows, conjuring rainbows in their path. Tapestry clad walls and floors strewn with enormous Persian rugs, depicting ancient battles, ferocious beast, and exotic vegetation, hushed the noise of human movement throughout the wonderland. From the ceilings hung banners displaying the arms of knights who had defended the realm over the centuries and from pots acquired from the far reaches of Christendom, rose the fragrance of fresh herbs and expensive spices. Men-at-arms guarded every doorway along their route, each wearing a costly tabard, bearing the arms of England and York. So many turns and twists did their short journey take that Giles began to feel dizzy, loosing his sense of direction until a curious feeling of unease crept over him as he drew nearer the Presence Chamber and the centre of Royal power.

Gloucester halted outside double oak doors adorned with golden embossed 'suns in splendour', King Edward's personal insignia, while men-at-arms wearing embroidered tabards displaying the same insignia guarded either side of the entrance. A squire seemed to appear from nowhere as they approached and bowing low before the Duke, opened the doors with a theatrical flourish. Giles felt the panic manifest itself in his gut, expecting to come face to face with the King of England, regaled in magnificent robes and enthrone amidst a room filled with fantastic jewel-encrusted artefacts.

They walked into a small dark antechamber in which the shutters were closed and the only light glowed falteringly from a brazier at the opposite end of the room. As Giles' eyes became accustomed to the darkness he could make out the figures of Doctor Morton and a large rough looking man huddled together deep in conversation. Both men rose when they recognised Gloucester but it was the carelessly dressed man that advanced to greet them. As he drew near, Giles could smell his foul breath and sweating body.

"Dickon! What can I say at a time like this? I am truly sorry."

He grasped Gloucester about the shoulders and pulled him forward into a bear hug, but the Duke pushed him away and stared back at him with questioning amazement.

"Jesu, you haven't heard," stammered Lord William Hastings, taking a step backwards.

"Heard what, Will?" retorted Gloucester.

Hastings gathered himself and wiped a huge flabby hand across his brow.

"Dickon, George Clarence was executed at first light this morning."

"What?" screamed Gloucester advancing on Hastings and unsheathing his dagger as he moved. Hastings stood his ground.

"He knew he was to die Dickon. Bishop Robert Stillington heard his confession and gave him absolution and then … ," Hastings drew a deep breath and without taking his eyes from the blade that twitched in Gloucester's hand he released the final words in a rush, "and then he was clubbed unconscious and … and drowned in a vat of Edward's best Malmsey."

Gloucester, Francis and Giles stood speechless. It was difficult enough to absorb the fact that Clarence had been executed but the method by which he had died beggared belief. Francis was forced to choke back a laugh of incredulity, whilst Giles' confused brain struggled with the significance of 'being drown in best Malmsey'. Gloucester was the first to come to his senses. He turned sharply and with his dagger still unsheathed, kicked open the door leading into the Presence Chamber. Hastings moved to prevent him but he was gone, the door slamming behind him.

"God's bollocks," cursed Hastings who had received specific orders from the King that he should not be disturbed.

The chamber was empty but Gloucester could see candles burning on the alter in the King's private chapel beyond. Even as he strode down the small aisle the huge frame, that was his brother King Edward, rose wearily from the prie-dieu and turn to face the inevitable verbal onslaught. He stared in alarm at his brother's unsheathed weapon but Gloucester threw it at the wall in disgust at the King's panic.

"Before God Edward, what have you done?" began Gloucester. But those were the only words Edward heard, for whilst his young brother raged, he seriously considered telling him the truth. It was very temping. Richard was devoted to him, totally loyal and utterly trustworthy but his mother had made him promise not to confide in Richard.

The King dragged his thoughts back to the present. His brother's rage was spent but still he demanded to know why Clarence had had to die.

"For pity's sake Dickon, he was a bloody traitor. He took up arms against us in '69, he supported the readaption of Henry VI in '70, his support for us at Barnet and Tewkesbury was simply expediency and ever since he has been publicly denouncing us as a bastard and promoting himself as York's true heir. Do you need more? I can go on if you have an hour or two to listen."

"But you promised our mother."

Edward looked into Richard's tear stained face and his own pain resurfaced. He drew his younger brother into his arms and both wept for their errant brother George.

"Why?" Richard was still asking minutes later, choking on his tears.

Edward shook his head. "I cannot tell you. I will not endanger your soul with the knowledge of my own sin. It is better and safer for you not to know my reasons."

"But Edward if I could only understand …"

"No Dickon. That must be an end to it. No!"

King Edward summonsed Sir Matthew who brought wine, bread and fruit with which to break their fast but neither had any inclination to eat. Richard sat by an open casement trying to clear is head with the chill air. He could not accept Edward's reason for refusing to explain and moodily he dredged his own mind for a more satisfactory explanation. Edward had promised their mother that George would not die; that he was only calling his bluff. So what had changed his mind so suddenly? Surely it had nothing to do with Giles being Clarence's son? How could it be? No, it had to be Queen Elizabeth Woodville and her parasitical kin. That evil mother of hers, Jacquetta was a known practitioner of the black arts. Had they not connived and trapped Edward into marriage? Had they laid another trap for Edward? Perhaps even used witchcraft to force him to do their bidding? Richard warmed to his own reasoning. The Queen blamed George for the death of her father and Richard recalled her well earned reputation for relentless pursuit of revenge. He didn't actually believe in witchcraft but he readily convinced himself that she possessed the guile to persuade Edward that it was necessary for George to die. Richard swallowed hard and gritted his teeth, convinced he had reasoned correctly and that the Woodville bitch was responsible for George's death: that Edward had concocted the story of protecting Richard from 'a soul destroying truth' to hide his own weakness. He grimaced and wiped the tears from his eyes. The only protection he needed was from Her Majesty's disfavour, lest he too should warrant an early grave. Annoyed and hurt by Edward's apparent deception, Richard wanted to strike out at his brother; at hand he had Giles' news.

"Apparently you were not the only one to marry beneath yourself in secret," announced Richard spitefully, "it seems George was wed to some country wench prior to his marriage to Isobel Neville. Their *legitimate* son is waiting outside to make himself known to you."

"Giles Butler is here?"

"Indeed sire, doubtless he will ask why his father had to die. Will you tell him or shall I, that his soul is safer if he remains in ignorance?"

"Matthew, show Giles Butler in at once," ordered the King, ignoring his brother's sarcasm.

Doctor Morton had been concerned and surprised to find Giles in the company of Richard Gloucester but with Francis Lovell remaining in the anteroom he was unable to express his disapproval. Instead he offered both men wine and after some time had elapsed asked Giles casually what had brought him to Westminster so early.

"I was trying to find you, Doctor. To ask for your help in securing the release of Bishop Robert from the Tower," said Giles guardedly, remembering Luke's advice, not to tell Morton that Clarence was his father.

"Bishop Robert Stillington – in the Tower?"

"Yes he was arrested yesterday evening. I hoped you could speak to the King for me."

Morton looked towards Hastings anticipating an explanation but the Lord Chamberlain shrugged his heavy shoulders and shook his head.

"I know he heard Clarence's confession but I have no knowledge of his arrest."

Before Morton could question Giles further, the door opened and Matthew announced that the King wished to speak to Giles immediately.

"Master Giles for God's sake plead for Robert while you have the King's ear. I'm sure he has done nothing wrong," begged Matthew wringing his hands.

"That is precisely why I am here Matthew," replied Giles as he straightened his tunic.

"Oh God bless God bless," simpered Matthew, brushing invisible specks of dust from Giles' shoulders.

Giles followed Sir Matthew into the Presence Chamber and was instantly chilled by the cold air entering from the open casements. Both the King and his brother were trying to refresh their humours and dry their tears by letting the sharp air strike their faces. The King turned as Matthew announced, 'Giles Butler Your Majesty' and Giles knelt on one knee as Matthew had instructed him. The King came forward and taking Giles hands in his, lifted him gently to his feet. Giles looked into King Edward's face and was relieved to see the likeness of his father. His earlier encounter with his uncle Gloucester had shaken him but there was no doubting his relationship to Edward. He was bigger and broader than Clarence but both man had lantern jaws and moved with a grace often lacking in over large individuals. Edward's skin was as fair but less lined than his father's even though he was much older and his hair was thicker too but falling about his face, framing and enhancing his features just as Clarence's had done. His eyes were the same sparkling blue and although both had a full and generous mouth, Edward's lacked the cruel twist that had so startled Giles when Clarence smiled.

Edward kissed Giles on both cheeks and whilst doing so asked for the evidence he had shown Clarence two days earlier in the Bowyer Tower. Giles felt uneasy, the King had wasted not time in coming to the point and he was sure that he had deliberately whispered so that Gloucester could not hear. He stiffened his shoulders in resistance to the King's urgency but Edward sensed his reaction and reinforced his demand with a harsh stare whilst tightening his grip on Giles' arms.

"Now would be *very* sensible," he said and Giles knew he had no option but to comply.

"Robert Stillington knew nothing about the notes Sire," said Giles as he took his time rummaging in his script.

The King was visibly shocked and Giles was convinced that Edward believed that the Bishop had told Clarence about the contents of his birthday box.

"The notes and the ring were in my casket which I opened *after* the Bishop had left for Westminster." He handed the documents to the King and waited whilst he read them.

"The casket was a gift from your mother, for which birthday?" asked the King casually.

"My eighteenth, Your Majesty."

"Indeed. You do not look your age Giles," said Edward quietly, "you could be taken for no more than, say, sixteen or even fifteen summers." The King glanced over to where Gloucester stood gazing out of the window, "and the ring?" He held out his hand in anticipation. Reluctantly Giles removed his mother's ring from the thong around his neck and kissed it before handing it to Edward. The gesture touched the great man but he could not allow sentiment to influence him now.

"Does Bishop Robert know of this?" he asked holding the ring between his forefinger and thumb.

"He may do," Giles answered honestly, "my father had one made for himself at the same time as this was made for my mother. They were probably their wedding rings but Bishop Robert does not know my mother left it for me in the casket."

Edward's eyes opened wide in amazement.

"George told you he had a pair of rings specially fashioned, of which this is one and he wore the other?" Edward asked, choosing his words carefully and speaking so deliberately that Giles wondered about their significance.

"Yes your majesty."

"And he acknowledge you as the son of Eleanor Butler, his first wife, their marriage having been solemnised?" he continued, in the same exaggerated tones.

"Yes Sire, but Sire, Bishop Robert Stillington had no idea that I had visited my father in the Tower. The Duke was furious with the Bishop for having kept my birth a secret and insisted I should not tell him of our meeting so that he could punish him for… Could it be Sire, that my father deliberately led you into believing that the *Bishop* was the source of his information, knowing full well that you would … ?" words failed Giles as he realised he was implicating the King himself in some kind of conspiracy.

"Nonsense," scoffed Edward, "I have no interest in how Clarence discovered he had a son by his supposed first marriage. My dispute with Bishop Robert is about another matter entirely."

But Giles knew it was a lie and even Gloucester sauntered over, curious to discover what had forced the King into such a defensive outburst. Edward recovered quickly, acknowledging Giles as his nephew and suggesting he should attend Clarence's funeral here at Westminster and then accompany his father's remains to Tewkesbury Abbey where they were to be interned in the family vault. However, he also warned Giles against referring to his father's death as anything other than, lawful execution and suggested he should remain at Clipberry until the interest in his demise had receded.

"In time I may see fit to grant you a knighthood and possibly a manor house to sustain you. I will send for you when I am ready to discuss your future."

There was an awkward silence. Giles was not aware of just how difficult it was for King Edward to converse with him.

"George Clarence may well be your father but you only met him the once and then for just a few minutes," said the King falteringly, "your grief can not be compared with those who had known and loved him all their lives."

To Giles' amazement tears welled in King Edward's eyes and he turned away. For a brief moment Giles felt sympathy for the man who had ordered his father's death.

"Will Bishop Robert be released now you know the truth?," Giles asked tentatively, but Edward did not hear or chose not to hear. He had already moved away to the open window where he gazed up at the watery sun and allowing his tears to flow freely he prayed for forgiveness. At a brief nod from the distressed King, Gloucester summonsed Sir Matthew and Giles was escorted out of the Presence Chamber.

"Well?" whispered Matthew as soon as the door had closed behind them, "will Bishop Robert be released?"

"I expect so," replied Giles, "I certainly made it clear to His Majesty that the Bishop had not spoken carelessly."

Doctor Morton poured a cup of wine and trying to appear casual, ambled over to offer the cup to Giles. He was curious to discover why the King had granted him an audience at such a difficult time. Morton considered himself Edward's closes advisor but he had not been consulted about the trial or the execution of Clarence and Robert had been arrested and Giles summonsed to attend the King all without his knowledge. He felt excluded from the 'inner circle' and he needed to interrogate Giles whilst he had the chance. To Giles' surprise, Sir Matthew drew himself up to his to his full height as Morton approached with the wine and looking faintly ridiculous he held up his hand in a forbidding gesture against the Doctor's advance.

"Master Giles is too distressed by this father's death to engage in chit-chat," declared Matthew, placing his arm around Giles' shoulder in a gesture of protection and comfort.

In the moments of confusion that followed, Matthew ushered Giles out of the antechamber, across the corridor and into a small but elaborately furnished bedchamber, which Giles assumed must be Sir Matthew's, as he unlocked the door with a key hung round his neck on a silver chain.

"How did you know Clarence was my father?" asked Giles disengaging himself from Matthew's consoling arm. Sir Matthew tapped his ear and made a moue.

"I eavesdrop," he said coyly. "You seem to be taking his death very stoically."

"I only met him once and he couldn't wait to be rid of me so that he could torment the King with whatever secret I inadvertently revealed." Giles sipped the heavy brandy wine Matthew had poured for him. " Matthew, you don't happen to know what that was, do you? I mean, has your eaves dropping made you party to some fantastic secret involving myself, the Bishop, Clarence and possibly the King?"

Matthews eyes took on the appearance of an alert owl.

"Gracious no," he protested, but then reconsidered, "however, there is something very strange going on. For two days now His Majesty has declined to see any of his councillors, not even that ale swilling sot Hastings has been allowed into the royal presence *and* he has temporarily dismissed virtually all of his personal household, leaving me to fetch and carry day and night without a break."

"Won't you be missed now?"

"Probably, but even the indispensable have to take a piss occasionally." Matthew warmed to his gossiping. "Do you know, even his latest amour, pretty little Margery Goodman has been sent packing back to Westminster, although I understand she will be back tonight." Sir Matthew grinned and winking knowingly, added, "there are some things our King cannot go without for long."

Poor Giles, the name of the King's new mistress rang in his ears like a thousand tocsins.

"But she's betrothed," he stammered.

"Not any more. She gave Luke Lazereth his marching orders on the day the young Duke of York was wed. My informant in Morton's office, you understand I can't name names, assures me he pleaded with her to reconsider but the lady was quite merciless …"

Giles had heard enough, he put down his cup and made for the door leaving the amazed Matthew opening and closing his mouth like a landed cod.

For an hour or so, Giles wondered the galleries of the King's Chambers like a sleepwalker, eventually being guided back to the great hall and out into the yard by two guards who remembered his arrival with the Duke. He recalled nothing of his return journey, his thoughts were on Margery, sweet, gentle, beloved Margery. Only yesterday they had lain together between the perfumed coverlets of her bed where she had so decorously agreed to become his wife. Damnation, she had lied to him, told him Luke had deserted *her*, when she had left Luke to become the King's plaything. He felt so ill he believed that he would soon die from a broken heart and in his delirium gazed across the river and considered the comfort of a watery grave.

The early sun had surrendered to the more seasonable fog that now rolled in from the Thames and Giles began to shiver as shock and damp effected both his body and spirits. Fortunately, Mark had spotted him being escorted through the great hall where he had been waiting and had fought his way through the crowds to find Giles huddled against a wall shivering uncontrollably.

"What's happened?" he cried, removing his own cloak and wrapping it round his master. Are you ill? Have you spoken to the

Doctor? Giles look at me. Will Bishop Robert be released?"

Giles shrugged his shoulders and stumbled down the path towards the King's Steps. He neither knew nor cared; the Bishop, his father and now Margery had all deceived him and the extent of their disloyalty made him nauseous.

Moored at the bottom of the steps, was Gloucester's barge, the pennant displaying his White Boar and personal motto blowing in the breeze. Giles threw back his head and laughed in disgust as he read: *Loyaulte me lie*. Loyalty binds me.

Chapter 11

Clipberry Manor 31st May 1478

Bishop Robert Stillington was not released as Giles and Matthew had hoped. In the days and weeks that followed, Giles discovered that it was possible to more-or-less recover from a broken heart and with Mark's help, he set about managing the Bishop's affairs at Clipberry Manor. Robert sent for his books, fresh clothes and even wine from his cellar but neither Giles nor Mark were allowed to visit him. The King had strictly forbidden all visitors, possibly mindful of the problems caused by his liberal approach to Clarence's imprisonment, or so Giles surmised. Sir Matthew Pawson continued to visit them each Sunday, eager for news of his friend but Giles had nothing to report and as there had been no mention of the Bishop in the corridors of the King's household either, Sundays were gloomy and depressing days.

By the last Sunday in May the weather had at last improved and in the late afternoon Giles, Mark and Matthew took wine out into the herb garden and sat on the turf seat surrounded by clumps of lavender and rosemary to enjoy the welcome warmth and the promise of summer. No-one spoke as the fragrant smell of rosemary reminded them of how in previous summers the Bishop would commandeer the seat and recount the many uses for the herb, which was his favourite plant. All three had been forced to listen to the Bishop's remedies many times in the past and all three would have gladly listen now if only Bishop Robert were free to be with them.

"The Bishop's internment has provided me with a much needed break from Alice and her father," sighed Mark, "Ned is keen to set a date for the wedding but I cannot agree without first speaking to the Bishop."

He was about to voice his misgivings about his proposed marriage when Arthur trundled down the gravel path calling for Master Giles. He had a visitor.

Giles returned through the buttery and was startled to see Luke standing with his back to him looking out of a window in the great hall. He had not spoken to Luke since that day in February when he had accompanied Margery to Windsor. Mark had convinced him that there was nothing to be gained by admitting to Luke he had seduce her and Giles had salved his conscience by promising himself that he would confess all to his new friend when both Luke and he had completely recovered from Margery's deceit.

"Its good to see you Luke," lied Giles, summonsing a hearty welcome, "some wine for Master Lazarus Arthur."

"No, no, just some watered ale. I've been unwell and I am still taking my medicine."

Luke did not look well. His swarthy skin had a yellow tinge and the whites of his eyes were creamy and watery and he dabbed at them repeatedly with a piece of cloth.

"I also suffer from the summer ague," moaned Luke, but I have not come to advise you of my ill health. I need to speak to you privately."

Giles' heart sank. Had Luke discovered his dalliance with Margery?

Arthur returned with the watered ale and Giles filled cups for them both whilst suggesting they should retire to the Bishop's chancery where they would not be disturbed. If he was to be scolded by Luke for seducing the despicable Margery, he would rather it was done in private. As they climbed the stairs Giles notice how Luke used the hand rail to aid his ascent and how the few steps caused him to breathe heavily; he should not have left his sick bed. Giles ushered Luke into the one time school room and indicated that he should sit on the comfortable backed stool whilst he climbed on the high stool by the desk. Luke dabbed his eyes and cleared his throat.

"As I said earlier, I have been ill for several weeks now and I have spent days on my sick bed considering the notes your mother left you and the subsequent fate of George Clarence."

Giles breathed out audibly. He had not come about Margery.

Luke cleared his throat again. "Most of the gossips believe that Elizabeth Woodville persuaded King Edward to have Clarence executed, as indeed does the Duke of Gloucester. He has returned to Yorkshire by-the-way, apparently hurt and confused by what he judges to be Edward's capitulation to the Queen's demands."

"But you think otherwise?" pressed Giles.

Luke grimaced. "Yes but I don't believe that his death had anything to do with you visiting him either. Clarence has hounded King Edward for the last ten years with the story that he is not the son of the Duke of York and that he, George Clarence, is the rightful king of England. Suppose Clarence was correct and King Edward is *not* the Duke of York's son. Suppose Bishop Robert provided George Clarence with irrefutable prove that *he* was York's legal heir but not until after his trial."

"It's possible I suppose. The Bishop's health suffered dreadfully after the trial. Clarence insisted that Robert attend him all day, everyday, demanding that he should find evidence for his claim to Edward's crown. The pressure might well have broken him and induced him to provide Clarence with what he needed. That is, if he actually had the proof you speak of."

"That supports my assertion still further," said Luke, "but see how everything else fits my theory. Once aware that Clarence had proof of his illegitimacy, Edward had little option but to silence him and arrest the Bishop. The Bishop has been spared death because he would claim the 'right of Clergy' and besides Edward needed him to hear Clarence's confession. He could not risk another priest speaking to brother George lest he divulge his secret. George Clarence knew he was to die and after absolution expected to be taken to the execution block …"

"… where he would proclaim his proof from the scaffold," interrupted Giles, "but Edward had some thug club him senseless and stuff his unconscious body into a barrel of Malmsey wine to drown, ensuring the truth would never be aired. God help the Bishop, if you are correct Luke, he will remain a prisoner for the rest of his life."

"The Bishop is not the only one in need of divine intervention," warned Luke, "if Edward was forced into executing his own step-brother because he was England's rightful King, surely the life of his step-brother's son and heir is a mere trifle?"

Giles, jumped from his stool and paced the room. "I actually told King Edward that it was I and not the Bishop who betrayed his secret to Clarence."

"You did what? But how did you know there was a secret?"

"I worked it out. I had no idea of the nature of the secret only that there was one." Giles shook his head. "You may have determined the reason for Clarence's bizarre execution Luke but I am convinced that it was something *I* said to Clarence that caused him to challenge Edward. Besides there was nothing in our conversation that remotely touched on Edward's legitimacy. I don't think you have solved Edward's secret Luke."

"You can't be certain and anyway, the nature of the secret is not really relevant," persisted Luke, " Clarence died because of it and you are his legitimate son. Surely your life is in danger as well?"

"No. The King said he would send for me when he was ready. He is waiting to see if I pursue my notion of a secret and *become* a threat to him. All I need do is abandon my interest in the reason Bishop Robert was imprisonment and wait until King Edward feels safe enough to call me nephew."

CHAPTER 12

Westminster 20th June 1478

Ned Twynho, landlord of the Westminster tavern, perched on the edge of the log wedging open the buttery door. He was wearing his best jerkin, a crisp clean white shirt and the new blue hose Alice had bought him for his Saint's Day and so he shifted cautiously on his rough make-do seat, fearful that he might soil his fine attire. The ale in his cup was icy cold and much appreciated on this hot June morning. It had been a clever idea of young Mark's to lower flagons of ale into the well to keep them chilled in hot weather, thought Ned but where was the young pup now, he had not been near the place in weeks? Oh Ned had heard all the scandal about the Bishop being held in the Tower and the doubtful story about Master Giles being the son of the Duke of Clarence and of course, the numerous versions of the Duke's bizarre death but none of these events warranted Mark's long absence. Ned had been forced to employ Peter Linton to help in the tavern whenever he had business at St Paul's Wharf and it was an expense he could do without. True, Mark had got word to Alice apologising for his absence and explaining his preoccupation with the Bishop's business at the Manor and he had promised to visit the first time Master Giles journeyed to Westminster but that was of little use to Ned, who was travelling to St. Paul's Wharf more than once a week now.

"The pair should have wed this Springtime," grumbled Ned to himself, as he strode back into the tavern, where Peter was taking orders from two foppish gentlemen wriggling about in an alcove seat which was so small that it necessitated their sitting extremely close together.

"I'll be on my way now Peter," he called over to the stocky youth who wore a shock of gold red hair, beneath which, glinted almond shaped green eyes. His high cheek bones supported fat rounded cheeks between which nestled a small snub nose and tiny mouth; the total effect being the appearance of a huge tom cat. The lad was oblivious to his feline resemblance and he stood mesmerised whilst the two fops teased him with meows and pathetic jokes about cream and mice.

"Get the wine lad before you take root," snapped Ned, "Alice is working in the new lodge if you need anything but don't leave the tavern. If you shout from the buttery door she will hear you."

"Here pussy, pussy, pussy," jibed the taller of the two fops and both fell about laughing.

Peter grinned inanely and disappeared to fetch the wine whilst Ned, shaking his head in mock despair, left for his rendezvous at St. Paul's Wharf. Had he been aware that at that very moment Mark was relinquishing Old Sal into the care of Joel, Ned's stable lad, he may well have delayed his departure.

Mark was surprised to find Peter Linton apparently in charge of the tavern. He knew the lad vaguely but could not place him.

"Mistress Alice is in the new lodgings over the outbuilding and Master Twynho has just left for The Wharf," replied Peter to Mark's enquiry as to where the landlord and his daughter might be.

Mark nodded with some relief, for it would be easier to talk to Alice without Ned's oversight. He ordered ale and invited Peter to join him. A couple of blackjacks of Ned's fine cool ale would bolster his courage and help him explain to Alice how his situation had changed. He kept telling himself he still loved and wanted to marry her but he was not prepared to leave the service of the Bishop to work in the tavern. If Alice still wanted to marry him, then she must make a new life with him at Clipberry Manor in the service of Bishop Robert.

Peter returned with a jug of ale and two blackjacks and pulled up a stool alone side Mark's chosen table.

"Are you Master Twynho's new apprentice?" asked Mark hopefully.

"I wish," replied Peter sadly, "I am the third son in my family and need to learn a trade but Master Twynho only employs me when he's going out and he'll not need me at all when Mistress Alice is wed this summer."

Mark eyed Peter over his raised blackjack but the lad had no idea who he was talking to.

"So the more business Master Twynho has at St. Paul's Wharf, the more work there is for you?" prompted Mark

"Yes sir, Master Twynho visits widow Rosy Burrows most weeks now. Them should be wed by Michaelmas if Mistress Alice weds this summer."

Peter excused himself as a dusty traveller opened the door and called impatiently for the landlord and Mark smiled to himself as he reviewed Peter's information. So, Ned's business was with Rosy Burrows, widow of taverner Burrows who owned The Wharf Tavern on St. Paul's Wharf. But why must they delay their nuptials until after Alice was wed? When Peter returned Mark found him happy to gossip further, so he ordered another jug of ale and when Peter brought it over, he refilled the lad's blackjack as well as his own.

"Master Twynho has proposed marriage to widow Burrows," whispered Peter, conscious that he was gossiping but enjoying the experience just the same. "She is very wealthy. Taverner Burrows invested in shipping," he tapped the side of his nose knowingly, "the abbey clerics say it's the devil's business, there being no work involved in investment but I hear that even the King dabbles in shipping, so why shouldn't the taverner? Anyway, Burrows died two winters since, leaving Rosy over *three hundred pounds*."

"Hell's teeth, but I still don't understand."

"Well, according to her cook, who is a good friend of my father, she is willing to sell up and move in here as the new Mistress Twynho, especially as the master has converted the old outbuildings into such a fine lodge for them to spoon in. But it seems she wants to be a lady now. Expects someone else to do the work. Expects Alice and her man to take over the daily grind of the tavern so she and the Master can lord it over them from their new love nest." Peter leaned forward and whispered in Mark's ear. "According to her cook, she is so determined to have this placed fully staffed *before* she moves in, that she has postponed her own marriage until Mistress Alice is wed." Peter brought his fist down sharply on the table to confirm the accuracy of what he had divulged.

"Mark, oh Mark, I knew you would come," cried Alice from the buttery doorway.

Mark jumped to his feet and crossed the tavern floor as if sprung from a trap. He pushed Alice gently into the buttery before him and close the door from behind his back. His heart raced: oh how their separation had refreshed her appeal. She looked wonderful to his unfamiliar eye. Her beautiful hair seemed more luxurious than he remembered, falling about her uncovered white shoulders and delicate neck. Her eyes sparkled with delight and her lips, no longer chapped with winter chill, quivered within inches of his face. He could smell the sweet scent of lavender which clung to her clothing as she had just gathered the first crop for drying and he tried to remove two tiny blue buds which had become attached to trim of her bodice but his courage failed him. She laughed and taking his hand in hers she cupped it firmly around her breast and at the same time brushed her lips against his.

"Come," she whispered indicating the ladder to her bed in the eaves, "father will not be back till nightfall."

In a mist of fresh yearning Mark was helpless to resist and turned to follow her fragrance in the direction of the loft ladder but at that instant Peter opened the door with such force it sent the couple stumbling across the floor.

"I'm sorry, I didn't realise you were just behind the door," gabbled Peter, "I need a fresh flagon." He edged himself towards the outer door and then fled across the gravel towards the well. Alice and Mark laughed enjoying his embarrassment.

"Come," sighed Alice, "let me show you what father has done for us."

She took Mark's hand and led him across the newly gravelled yard towards the renovated outbuilding. He could only stare in amazement at its transformation. The entire front had been faced with new stone as far as the first floor and the upper storey had been freshly plastered. Even the wooden timbers had been newly stained. Glass replaced the horn windows and the old dangerous outside steps that led to the first floor had been replaced by a sturdy oak staircase with a handrail and enclosed in a stone and wood shelter complete with locking door and enormous iron door handle.

"How do you mean, 'for us'?" questioned Mark, recalling what Peter had said about the converted outbuilding.

"Well, father hasn't exactly *said* it is to be our marital home but why else would he spend so much on doing it up?" She smiled up into his face and then stood back confused by the expression of concern that clouded it. "What is it Mark? Aren't you pleased with our new home?"

Mark led Alice back to the log by the buttery door and insisted she sat down.

"Alice sweetheart, I love you with all my heart," he lied, "and I will be happy to marry you tomorrow," he added more truthfully being resigned to wed for honours sake, "but I cannot leave the Bishop and my duties at Clipberry. If we are to wed you must leave the tavern and your father and join the Bishop's household at the Manor. Your chores will be lighter and life far easier, I promise."

The colour drained from Alice's cheeks.

"No, no," she stammered, "it has always been agreed: you are to learn the trade so that you can take over when father is old and unable to cope."

"Maybe, but it has never been my wish to take on the ale house. Your father has never *asked* if I wished to do so."

"He shouldn't need to," snapped Alice angrily, "it is the most generous settlement ever. Better than most daughters would dream of."

"But when your father remarries things will be different. His new wife will take over from you as mistress of the tavern," countered Mark and then added cautiously, "she may have other plans for you and I."

"Don't be ridiculous," cried Alice, "father will never remarry; he still frets over my mother. If that's the best excuse you can think of to avoid marrying me, you had better leave and never return."

Poor Alice, the fears she had pushed to the back of her mind during Mark's long absence now rose like demons to confirm her worst imaginings. Tears burst forth and shaking with fear she screamed at Mark to go. He had little option. Customers, as well as Peter, startled by her hysteria, rallied to ensure he left the premises immediately, hustling him through the back yard and into the street. Several cowardly kicks and punches landed on his legs and torso and someone pulled a knife and sliced into his upper arm. Mark thought it was Peter Linton but in the struggle of flailing arms and legs he could not be certain. If Joel had not ventured from the stable to see what the uproar was about he may even have left without Old Sal but unimpressed by the odds of six or seven to one, Joel slapped the animal sharply on her rump to urge her into the tumble and threw Mark the reins. The pack broke apart for fear of being trampled and so with blood seeping from his arm Mark scrambled onto the back of Old Sal and clutching the reins in his right hand, kicked hard and made for the Abbey, there to wait for Giles who was visiting Luke in Doctor Morton's quarters.

He had slowed Old Sal to walking pace as he entered the Abbey Gate. The sun was burning his face and his mare was sweating from the short gallop. To his surprise Giles was walking Dexter across the yard towards him.

"What are you doing here," shouted Giles, "had a lover's tiff already?"

"Not exactly," replied Mark stiffly, "why are you not with Luke?"

"The man is seriously ill and unable to cope with visitors. I've just lit a candle in the Abbey for him and then I was coming to find you at the ale house. Lord but it's hot."

Giles was preparing to mount Dexter when he noticed the blood still seeping from Mark's arm.

"Christ man your arm is bleeding. Have you been in a fight?"

Without saying a word Mark turned Old Sal and retraced his steps though the Abbey Gate and started along the London road. Giles mounted and urged Dexter on until he was walking alongside the despondent Mark.

"What is it Mark, for God's sake what is it?"

Reluctantly Mark related the morning's events. When he had finished Giles let out a long slow sigh.

"Do you still want to wed Alice?"

Mark shrugged. If Giles had asked him that question yesterday he would have said that his feelings were irrelevant, that he owed her marriage because he had lain with her. However, if Giles had asked the same question prior to Alice's hysterical outburst, the resurgence of his desire would have prompted a 'yes', but now he just felt numb. They travelled for some time in silence whilst Giles considered Mark's plight.

"We will continue as far as Newgate together and then you must return to Clipberry Manor and get that arm seen to. I shall take my refreshment at The Wharf," said Giles. Mark was about to protest but Giles held up his hand to silence him.

"You are Bishop Robert's manservant and I am responsible for you in his absence. I have no intention of releasing you from your duties at Clipberry, regardless of whether or not you are prepared to take on the tavern and that is what I shall tell Ned *and* Rosy."

When they reached Newgate, Mark tried once again to prevent Giles from interfering in his dilemma but it was a half hearted protest. All he wanted at that moment was a long cool drink and somewhere to rest his throbbing arm so, shrugging submissively, Mark pulled Old Sal's reins left, towards West Smithfields and on to Clerkenwell, whilst Giles turn right towards Ludgate and the sound of the cathedral bells heralding the midday Angelus.

The narrow streets leading to the river at St Paul's Wharf were crammed with traders having purchased goods, recently unloaded from the daily barges moored there. Hand carts and pack horses jostled for position with individuals shouldering heavy sacks of grain and wool destined for the warehouses of local traders. Giles guided Dexter through the throng and on to the quayside where the shouts and cries of price fixing and deal sealing vied with those of hucksters and booth owners selling refreshment to the river men and their customers. The heat and clamour of the quayside was stifling and flies buzzing over a nearby heap of filth were turning their attention to the sweat glistening on Dexter's hide.

Giles turned his mare in order to view the dwellings that lurched towards the river. The Wharf Tavern was a three-storeyed building with black timbers, bright yellow washed plaster and open, glazed windows which drew quayside workers towards the delicious aromas of freshly baked bread and meats cooked with spices. Above the door hung a skilfully painted sign depicting the view of the wharf as seen from that side of the sign. Giles wondered if the artist had painted the opposite view on the reverse side but the hustle of loading and unloading was too dense for him to bother to look. Instead he walked Dexter into the tavern's integral stable and after handing a dirty groom a coin to ensure his horse was watered and rubbed down he pushed his way through the traders to the tavern entrance. Some customers had abandoned the stuffy taproom and were propped against the outside walls whilst others were trying to escape the heat by leaning out of the windows.

The dimly lit, large taproom was packed with thirsty hot bodies taking a midday break and two sweat covered barmaids struggled to satisfy the demand for wine and ale, whilst several pot boys carried precariously stacked platters from kitchen to consumer via circuitous routes around tables and standing customers. There was no fire in the taproom today but a smoke blackened staircase to one side of the hearth led to the upper storeys and also down to a cellar below.

At the back of the taproom an open door provided Giles with a glimpse of a garden beyond and much to his surprise, in the adjacent window seat, with his back towards him, sat Doctor Morton, deep in conversation with a gnarled faced man Giles believed to be a seaman. Between these two unlikely companions, sat a clerk, scribbling on a piece of parchment and on the table next to him, his satchel of writing materials and several scrolls bound with red ribbons. Giles was curious and was about to push his way to the Doctor's table when a buxom barmaid with black broken teeth and breath that even Woof would recoil from, tugged at his sleeve and demanded to know, 'what he wanted'. Before he could answer, a pot boy threaded his way between himself and the barmaid carrying a stack of dirty wooden platters, followed closely by an elderly man demanding to be allowed through to the yard for he was in need of an urgent piss, so Giles was obliged to shout his order over their heads.

"Don't move, else I'll not find you in this mob," the slattern shouted back.

Giles clung to the handrail of the stairs to await her return. She was some time but the ale was worth the wait, the nectar cooling his mouth and throat as he drank long and deeply and the freshly baked bread and creamy white cheese, thrust into his free hand by the returning pot boy, was far better than he could have hoped for at such a busy time.

"My Lord of Clarence," hailed Morton, as he turned to find a barmaid but spotted Giles instead, "come and join me Giles. Andrew and the captain are just leaving."

As he made his way past the stairs to the Doctor's table he was aware of two people joining the throng from the staircase and turned to find Ned Twynho and a lady, he presumed to be Rosy Burrows, virtually treading on his heels in the crush.

"Master Giles," cried the startled Ned Twynho as he registered the significance of Morton's salutation, "what are you doing here?"

"I need a word with you Ned," replied Giles severely, taking advantage of the man's surprise at Morton's recognition of his new status. "Please excuse me Doctor Morton but my business with Master Twynho cannot wait."

Giles left his food and drink on Morton's table and opened the door to the garden, indicating to Ned and Rosy that they should both pass through before him. Once outside Rosy turned and faced Giles angrily.

"This had better be important young man. I don't take kindly to being ordered about in my own hostelry."

Giles did not flinch. The woman before him was about thirty summers, tall and thin, with a long nose and tight lips that betrayed a mean disposition. Her black, beady eyes stared unblinking into Giles'.

"My business is with Master Twynho mistress," restated Giles flatly, "but you may wish to stay and hear what I have to say."

He waited for her to depart but curiosity over came her dignity and she led them though beds of thyme and lemon balm to a lychgate set in a thick yew hedge which marked the end of the herb garden. Beyond the hedge and to the left, was a large stew pond and to the right an orchard of apple, pear and plum trees.

"Get on with it," she snapped, satisfied that they were alone and far enough away from the tavern not to be overheard.

A nervous Ned introduced Giles to Rosy Burrows as, 'the widow of his good friend taverner Burrow' and then waited for Giles to declare his business.

"Mark visited Alice this morning Ned, for the first time in weeks."

Ned nodded but said nothing.

"He went specifically to tell her that he was not prepared to work in the ale house after their marriage."

"What?," snarled Rosy.

"But it was agreed that he should move in and learn the trade," whimpered Ned.

"No Ned. *You* agreed that with Mistress Burrows. Alice assumed, as did you, that Mark would be grateful for the opportunity."

"And why isn't he?" shrieked Rosy.

"Because he prefers to remain in the Bishop's service and after this morning's fiasco I have no intention of trying to persuade him otherwise."

"What fiasco?" asked Ned tentatively.

"Mark suggested to Alice that she might be more comfortable at Clipberry Manor once Mistress Burrows becomes the new Mistress Twynho and moves into the renovated lodgings behind the tavern," continued Giles, watching Ned cringe as he imagined his daughter's reaction to the news of his forth coming marriage. "It appears she knew nothing about her new step-mother and refused to believe her father had so soon forgotten her beloved mother." Giles was enjoying himself now. "It seems Alice flew into a rage, demanded Mark be forcibly removed from the tavern."

Ned gasped and sat down heavily on the grass. His schemes were unravelling and he felt helpless in the face of Rosy's indignation.

"What ridiculous rubbish," sneered Rosy, "where is this Mark? Hasn't he the guts to come and face us himself?"

"He would have done madam," said Giles, "had he not been

viciously stabbed by Ned's new manager and forced to take to his bed with a serious loss of blood."

"God save us Master Giles, how did that happen?" cried Ned.

"I'm not sure. Mark believes Peter pulled a knife in the scuffle that followed his expulsion into the road. He only escaped because Joel came to his aid."

Ned scrambled to his feet and took Giles by the shoulders.

"Please take me to Mark I must apologise for Peter's over zealous protection of my Alice. I will engage the very best physicians to ensure he recovers."

Giles panicked slightly, realising he had overstated Mark's injuries. It took him some considerable time to convince Ned that Mark's stab wounds were not life threatening and that he needed rest more urgently than an apology and that the best course of action would be for Ned to return home and sort things out with Alice. Without taking his leave of either Giles or Rosy, Ned hurried from the garden intent on returning to Westminster. Rosy pursued him as far as the garden door, threatening to cancel their, 'understanding' if he could not abide by their agreement. To the amusement of all those in earshot her protests went unheeded and she was obliged to returned to the garden and vent her anger on an unfortunate potboy gathering sage for the cook.

When Giles returned to the taproom, Doctor Morton was still sat in the window seat with a jug of claret. Another potboy brought a second cup for Giles and Morton filled it with the quality red wine from his jug.

"I visited Luke earlier this morning," said Giles, "he seems seriously unwell."

Doctor Morton nodded and wiping his cherub like face with both hands leaned forward and coughed nervously.

"I have sent to Italy to employ the services of a very successful physician, Antonio Benivieni" whispered Morton. "His methods are considered to be against the teachings of the church in England but he practices with the consent of Rome in his own country. I first consulted him when we realised Luke would probably never regain his memory and it is he who supplies the green crystals." Morton sighed and fidgeted with the gold rings he wore on most of his fingers. "I cannot imagine life without Luke. He has been like a son to me and I will do anything, *anything* I can, to prolong his life."

"When does Doctor Benivieni arrive?" asked Giles, respectful of Morton's deep concern.

To bring a doctor from Italy would incur enormous expense and if the English Church deemed this man's methods heretical, Morton was taking a considerable risk.

"He should arrive in the next week or so." Morton smiled sadly and added. "God willing he will come in time."

"If there is anything I can do to help, now or when Doctor Benivieni arrives, you must send for me at once," said Giles. "I have not known Luke long but we have become good friends and I would dearly like to be of assistance. Maybe I could help nurse him if the Italian doctor prescribes regular treatment or intensive care of some kind?"

Morton smiled and patted Giles' hand.

"Thank you," he said with genuine warmth, "I will remember your kind offer. I promise you."

CHAPTER 13

The Tower of London 22nd June 1478

Perhaps it had nothing to do with meeting Doctor Morton in The Wharf and offering to help nurse Luke back to health. Perhaps the good Doctor did not speak to his close friend, King Edward, on behalf of the Bishop. Maybe it was just coincidence that a herald from the royal household, arrived at Clipberry Manor only two days later with a summons for Giles to attend His Majesty in the royal chambers at the Tower of London. Either way, Giles was excited and nervous, his entire future and perhaps his liberty, depended on King Edward's deliberations since the death of the Duke of Clarence. And what was to become of Bishop Robert? Was his fate also to be revealed today?

The King's herald could tell him nothing. The young man, wearing the arms of England on his tabard was an arrogant young buck, annoyed that he had been forced to walk the hot dusty roads form St Paul's Wharf to Clipberry Manor in Clerkenwell and back to the Wharf, where he had a barge waiting to take Giles to the Tower.

"Had I known you owned a nag," he said, waving a dismissive hand at Dexter, who was being walked across the yard by Arthur to graze in the paddock, "I would have ridden out to this Godforsaken manor and you could have made your own way to the Tower."

He wiped his hand across his mouth to prevent the spittle from running down his chin. He appeared to have more teeth than his mouth could comfortably accommodate and his angry outburst had caused him to dribble unattractively. Giles had not replied to this or other taunts with which the impertinent youth had tried to goad him, as they walked back to the barge. He was preoccupied with his own thoughts and so intent on giving a good account of himself that he was virtually unaware of the journey up stream until they were approaching London Bridge. Then, without warning, the leading oarsman counted loudly to three and in one movement the men raised their oars from the river, allowing the barge to be swept naturally by gushing water through the narrow arches of the bridge. The dipping and rising of the craft caused Giles' already nervous stomach to retch but the pleasure of witnessing the green face of the herald somehow enabled Giles to retain its threatening contents.

The Tower beckoned as the barge manoeuvred towards the quayside, the great Norman keep surrounded by a dozen or more attendant towers linked by high crenulated walled walkways. The soaring double swathe of curtain wall and the stinking moat reminded Giles of his last visit when, under false pretences, he had gained entrance to the Bowyer Tower and now as a result of the events that had followed that visit, he was returning under hostile escort. They entered through the Lion Gate, the narrow paths and high walls sucking them into the heart of the structure but when they reached the centre they walked out onto a huge expanse of green. Here the soldiers of the garrison lived with their families, creating a small village within the Tower fortress. The herald hurried on, filtering his way through women drying washing and preparing food, children playing, infants crying and off duty soldiers enjoying a drink and a game of dice. Two guards, lazing against a catapult in the warm sun, recognised Giles and hailed him as he scurried after the herald. At the foot of the central keep known as the White Tower, they were greeted by Sir Matthew Pawson who was insufferably excited. Amidst his twittering and the wiping of his brow with dramatic flounces, Matthew managed to convey the news that had reduced him to this dithering state. Bishop Robert had been released. He was with the King and Doctor Morton even now awaiting Giles' arrival. He would take Master

Butler up stairs at once.

"Stop blathering you stupid faggot," scoffed the herald, "I have my orders. I will announce Master Butler."

Sir Matthew, rarely visited the Tower and was relatively unknown to the heralds who worked and lodged in the fortress, otherwise, this arrogant youngster would not have dared show such disrespect. Matthew recovered his composure instantly and drawing his dagger with one hand he grasped the surprised herald with the other and thrust him roughly against the wall. The herald fumbled for his own weapon but Matthew raised his knee and struck him in the groin with such force that the boy doubled up in pain. With the flat surface of his blade under his victim's chin, Matthew raised the herald's face to within inches of his own and smiling sweetly said that *he* would show Master Giles into the great hall. Matthew and Giles climbed the stairs to the fading curses of the humiliated herald and when they reached the entrance, Matthew nodded briefly to the guard and with his usual aplomb, swept open the double doors and announced the arrival of 'Master Giles Butler.'

A long oak table stretched the full length of the room, at the far end of which sat King Edward. On his left was Doctor John Morton and on his right, facing the Doctor across the table, sat Bishop Robert Stillington. Morton rose and smiling a welcome, he hurried to the opposite end of the table to greet Giles. King Edward welcomed Giles cautiously and then touching the Bishop lightly on his arm but still focusing on Giles, explained that his good friend, Bishop Stillington, would be returning to his manor at Clerkenwell. The Bishop did not even look at Giles but nodding slightly to His Majesty got to his feet and with bowed head walked straight passed his ward and out of the hall. Somehow Giles maintained his composure, his reunion with the Bishop could wait a few hours more.

Gently Morton ushered Giles to the seat vacated by his guardian and resumed his own. The King relaxed and rang the silver bell to summons Sir Matthew and order refreshment but the knight had anticipated the King's request, returning instantly bearing a jug of claret and followed by two page boys carrying silver trays.

On one tray were four silver goblets, embossed with gold vine leaves and encrusted with emeralds, and on the other, two silver dishes of dates which were temporarily set to one side for fear of ruining the taste of the wine. Sir Matthew filled the three goblets and placed the jug on the tray. At an almost indiscernible nod from the King, he bowed low and swept the boys out of the hall before him.

After his journey from Clipberry Giles was in need of refreshment and drank deeply from the beautiful cup before him but even the urgency of his thirst could not distract him from the supreme quality of the wine. King Edward laughed at the pleasure registering on Giles' face.

"I'm glad to see you appreciate fine wine nephew," he said reaching for the jug and refilled Giles' cup. "Now, listen to what I have planned for you." He looked towards Doctor Morton who cleared his throat and prepared to speak.

"His majesty has considered this most unusual situation Giles. That is to say, you being the legitimate son of his beloved brother, George Duke of Clarence." Morton paused and glanced towards the King for approval but Edward waved an impatient hand and he continued quickly. "Ultimately you are to join the Royal Household, responsible to me, Master of the Rolls. But first you will go to Oxford next term and study Civil Law."

Giles did not want to go to Oxford but he knew he must, as all the administrative posts in the Royal Household were filled only by educated men.

"Thank you Your Majesty. I am most grateful," ventured Giles.

"You will reside in my quarters at Westminster," continued Morton, "you will move there immediately and until you go to Oxford, nurse your friend, as you yourself suggested."

"Yes of course, I will be pleased to do so," stammered Giles somewhat taken aback by the thought of moving out of Clipberry Manor, "I will speak to Bishop Robert about moving as soon as he is settled back in the Manor."

The King leaned forward and to Giles' surprise took his hand in his as he spoke.

"The arrangements have already been agreed with Bishop

Robert. You are to attend your friend Luke as soon as you leave here today."

"Robert will arrange for your belongings to be transferred to Westminster," added Morton. "Now is there anything else?"

Giles felt as though he was tottering on the edge of a precipice: one false move and the King, who still held his hand, would ensure a fall to his death, so asking for the return of his mother's ring was either extremely foolhardy or the request of a total innocent. The King perceived it to be the later and felt sorry for Giles whilst refusing.

"I had your mother's ring buried with your father's body in Tewkesbury Abbey," Edward said softly tightening his grip, "I know she left it as a keepsake but believe me the past is best forgotten." He smiled at Giles but could read the anger in the boy's face.

"If you are to take your rightful place in my household Giles," warned Edward, "you must let go of the past. And understand this too, it is imperative that you have no further dealings with the Bishop."

The King's steely blue eyes focused unblinkingly on Giles, who was beginning to piece together what must have taken place before his arrival. Fortunately he had the good sense to fain ignorance.

"Why can I not see the Bishop, Your Majesty? I don't understand."

"It is as well you do not," replied Edward sincerely, "there is no more to be said. You will do as I say." He dropped Giles' hand, picked up his goblet and drained it in a gesture of finality. "See to it John. It is your responsibility now."

The King put down his cup and reaching for one dish of dates, he offered the other dish to Morton. The fruits on the King's dish were whole, still containing the stones but the others had been stoned and stuffed with marchpane. John Morton squeezed the two largest into his mouth and licked the sticky oozing juice from his fat fingers before pushing the dish across the table towards Giles. Giles shook his head.

"No, thank you," he said, moving the dish aside and turning his head as if it gave off a foul odour. "I can be sick even with the smell of marchpane. It's the almond oil I think."

"God's breath," swore Edward in amazement, "it must be a family trait boy, for I too cannot bear the taste of marchpane." Edward coughed and quickly rang the tiny silver bell that summoned Sir Matthew, ordering him to 'show out' Giles Butler, when a small side door creaked open and a pretty female head peered into the hall.

"Oh Beth sweetheart, I forgot," cried Edward rising from his seat and extending both his arms to his most cherished daughter. " Giles wait! I promised Beth that she could meet her new found cousin."

The girl pushed the door wide and ran into the arms of her father.

"I knew you'd forget papa, I knew you'd forget," she cried pummelling his chest in mock anger.

Giles turned to see 'the most beautiful creature on earth,' which was how he later described her to Luke. She was taller than most girls of thirteen or fourteen summers with corn coloured hair that hung to her waist and held in place by a simple gold circlet around her head. High cheek bones, large wide dark eyes and the fullest mouth Giles had ever wished to kiss, all caused his senses to tingle with delight. Her youthful body, encased in close fitting cream silk, moved with such natural grace and sensuality that he was obliged to avert his gaze for fear of appearing lustful. To his surprise and embarrassment the King laughed with pride at his obvious attraction.

"I'm pleased to meet you cousin Giles," Beth said soberly and then she moved close to him and whispered in his ear. "I thought my uncle George was great fun. He was always upsetting the grown ups. I hope we can be friends?" she giggled and planted a huge wet kiss on his cheek.

"That will do madam," scolded the King at the same time signalling to Sir Matthew to show Giles and Morton out of his presence.

A temporary bed had been made up for Giles in Luke's chamber, with the promise of his own room when he returned from Oxford.

The good Doctor had servants enough to nurse Luke but he wanted Giles to sit with him and keep his spirits high. As he explained on their return journey to Westminster, Luke had become morose confined so long to his sick bed with so few visitors. He had spoken frequently of his new friend and so when Giles had offered to nurse Luke, Morton was prepared to manoeuvre events to that end.

"So the King released the Bishop on the understanding that I would be living here from now on," prompted Giles as they entered Morton's chambers at Westminster.

"Indeed. His Majesty and I were drinking together only last evening, when he let slip that he had no reason to keep poor Robert in the Tower any longer but was unable to release him whilst *you* resided at Clipberry." He paused. "Why is that Giles?"

"I have no idea," lied Giles, "but the Bishop must have agreed to the conditions otherwise I would not be here now. Can I see Luke?"

Luke was feeling better and able to sit up with the aid of several pillows to support his back but Giles thought he still appeared unnaturally yellow and that the loss of flesh from around his face and neck had aged his friend considerably. Fortunately for Giles, Luke was not one of those individuals who are obsessed with their own ill health and so he brushed aside Giles' attempts to sooth his condition with kind words, demanding to know what events had led to Giles moving in and sharing his chamber. Carefully Giles recounted every detail, concluding with the appearance of Edward's eldest child, Beth.

"Tell me again about Princess Elizabeth," said Luke when Giles was done, "I will close my eyes and imagine every detail. Her beauty will prove the tonic that no amount of Italian wonder potions can provide."

A faint smile played on his lips as Giles retold every delicious detail, finding new words, sometimes appropriate, often not, to describe both her appearance and the effect she had on his senses. Suddenly Luke opened his eyes and turned on his pillows.

"Giles stop it. She is your cousin, you must not lust after this beauty. Now, *I* am no relation at all," he teased.

"Rubbish, both my father and my uncle Gloucester married their cousins, although I believe they needed dispensation from the Holy Father."

"Which *you* would not be granted."

"It hardly matters. King Edward will not allow me to court her affection, especially if he is illegitimate as you believe. He will use the marriage of every one of his offspring to entrench his family in the Royal Houses of Europe."

Voices in discourse brought the Doctor hurrying to Luke's chamber. Apart from good food and wine there was nothing John Morton preferred to an argument based on sound reasoning with intellectual companions. Unfortunately for the Doctor the discussion halted as soon as he entered the bedchamber but he was well pleased with the instant improvement in Luke's mood. It was a brilliant idea of his to take young Giles under his wing, even if he was the son of the despicable George Clarence.

That first night at Westminster Giles was unable to sleep. Even when Luke eventually drifted into shallow slumber, his mind wondered endlessly over the implications of his sudden departure from Clipberry Manor. Without Giles to help manage the Manor, the Bishop would not release Mark to take up duties at Ned's Tavern but with Giles gone, would Mark prefer to work for Ned Twynho? Would the Bishop allow Giles to keep Dexter and did he blame Giles for his arrest and imprisonment in the Tower? Would he ever see Woof again and Arthur and Mary?

It was too ridiculous, he was bound to encounter the Bishop sometime in the future: the King could not expect to keep them apart for ever. Restless and unable to lay comfortably on his unfamiliar bed, Giles got up and crossed to sit at the table where the hour candle burned steadily behind its guard. A calf hide box containing writing materials had been left open and underneath, virtually hidden from view was a piece of cleaned parchment or palimpset. An idea occurred to him so he rummaged in the box until he found a piece of charcoal which he used to write down the messages contained in the two notes his mother had left and King Edward had confiscated. He could recall them easily now but he might not find it so simple in the future. Then he tried to sketch his mother's ring, making several attempts before managing to draw the tiny ivy leaves correctly. They weaved round the band and through the initials, branching left and then right in perfect symmetry. Eventually he propped the sketch against the writing box and leaned back to judge its accuracy when his movement caused the hour candle to flicker and for a brief moment cast a shadow across the sketch. Giles gasped at the distortion that manifested itself and then vanished. By God's grace had that brief moment shown him the truth, the King's secret and the danger both he and Bishop Robert faced?

For some time Giles stared at his sketch, uncertain what to do with the evidence. Common sense told him to destroy it but he may not be able to recreate another accurate drawing in the future. And what if he should need this proof?

An old tapestry hung on the wall against which Giles was sat and moving the stool quietly to its far edge, he climbed up and began searching the seam between the tapestry and the backing material to find a loose thread or place where the backing was coming away. The hanging was very old and there were several places in need of repair so, he selected a spot near a fleur-de-lis on the border, which he would be able to find easily at a later date and tucked the parchment into the seam. Then making the sign of the Cross, Giles vowed to tell no one what he thought he had discovered, not even Luke.

PART 2

"She, for an Edward weeps and so do I."
(Richard III - Wm. Shakespeare)

CHAPTER 14

London 10th March 1483

Giles Butler graduated from Oxford as a Doctor of Civil Law in the Summer of 1481, entering the royal household as a Chancery clerk where he relieved Doctor Morton of his responsibility for King Edward's investments in merchant shipping. His shrewd dealing provided Morton and himself with personal fortunes, at the same time filling the King's coffers beyond His Majesty's expectations. An unsurprising royal favourite, Giles was knighted in '82 when the King also rewarded the faithful Doctor with the See of Ely. So Morton resigned his post as Master of the Rolls and moved to the Bishop's Palace in Holborn, vacating two of his rooms at Westminster for Giles' use.

The health of Morton's surrogate son Luke, improved after the Italian doctor performed surgery to relieve the pressure on his brain but unfortunately he lost the use of his left arm whilst under the knife and although his seizures had been eradicated his memory appeared lost for ever.

Alice Twynho and Mark Taylor were not married and somehow, Mark persuaded Bishop Robert to allow him to join Giles at Westminster as his squire. Robert regained some favour with the King but apart from the occasional visit from Sir Matthew Pawson, he saw no-one, becoming his own gaoler in his Manor at Clipberry.

By the spring of 1483 George Clarence had been dead for five years yet King Edward had not explained, even to the closes members of his family, why he had put his brother to death in such a bizarre manner. His Majesty had become less approachable and less tolerant of the mistakes of his subjects, indulging heavily in drink, food and lewd company. He had long since dispensed with the services of Margery Goodman but her arrangement with the Queen ensured she had plenty of noble suitors who paid well for her favours and she had also renewed her acquaintance with Giles and surprisingly, they developed a relationship which worked to their mutual advantage.

Jane Shore had become the King's permanent mistress and according to rumour had replaced the Queen, not only as the focus of his desire but also of his affection. Whilst Edward grew slothful and unfit for battle, his youngest brother, Richard Gloucester, was busy fighting the Scots on his behalf and at the Christmas celebrations he was received with great acclaim throughout the capital for his success and bravery in the battlefields north of the boarder.

By 1483 the Exchequer, which was housed in the Tower of London, no longer dealt with the royal revenue. Years earlier Doctor Morton had persuaded King Edward that income from land, taxation and customs could be more beneficially controlled if it were paid directly into the King's coffers but his treasure, the crown jewels, other precious objects and gifts of great value were still housed in the mighty fortress of the Tower of London.

It was in the Tower room above the Treasure House on the tenth day of March 1483 that Giles had spent most of the day overseeing the calculation of Edward's share of the profits from one of his shipping ventures. The merchant ship Rising Sun, was even now on the Thames awaiting permission from Sir Giles to up anchor and continue her journey north to Norwich. Recently returned from Venice, she had brought home the King's agents and the substantial profits acquired from selling baled wool to Venetian merchants. It was part of Giles' brief to inspect the leather money bags and certify that the merchant's seals had not been tampered with, to count and record the profit and pay off the agents and sea captains. Earlier Giles had been aboard the galley to inspect her cargo and assess the customs revenue due on the Venetian goods being brought back into England. It had been a long day and he was glad to see the back of the hard nosed agents.

The vessel moored by the steps of St. Thomas' gate and guarded by six men-at-arms from the King's household was the royal barge which had brought him to the Tower for the days business. Giles watched as his escort loaded the money bags ready for their return journey to Westminster and the replenishment of King Edward's coffers. He was about to take his leave of the chief clerk of the exchequer when the Treasurer, Sir Douglas Hatton, appeared and asked if he might have a private word, for it was a delicate matter and one that Sir Douglas was in two minds whether to discuss. He was a fussy little man with unfashionably short, grey hair and an even more unfashionable pointed white beard. His hands appeared to shake involuntarily when he refrained from tapping his thighs, which he seemed to do most of the time. Sir Douglas started by referring to the many times he had assisted with the King's 'little financial adventures' as he called the accounting sessions that regularly took place in the chamber above the Treasury.

"I'm sure I should not be concerning myself with this," he said, slapping his thighs quite viciously, "but I really do not understand the reason for it."

"For *what* Douglas?" asked Giles, irritated by the Treasurer's vagueness and eager to be on his way.

"The Marquis of Dorset and Richard Grey have been in the Treasury these last three days packing the King's treasures into ... well, manageable size bags."

"Have they been removing the treasure from the Tower?" asked Giles in amazement.

"No, just re-packing it. That's what I don't understand," wailed Sir Douglas, "and they haven't shown me any authorisation."

"Then ask for it man. You have every right."

"I have, I have asked, both yesterday and today but the Marquise told me to 'bugger off.' He said he hadn't time to fart about with bits of notes and anyway as *he* was Deputy Constable of the Tower he didn't need permission from me to do the King's bidding."

"He said that ? He actually said he was doing the King's bidding?"

"Yes."

"Then leave it Douglas. As long as nothing is removed then no harm is being done. You know what Dorset is like; that arrogant pup is just winding you up. The King must have his reasons for bagging the treasure," Giles patted Sir Douglas on his arm. "If they remove the bags without showing you their authorisation get word to me and I will ask the King for an explanation myself."

"Oh thank you Sir Giles, thank you," simpered Douglas, "I'll do that. Yes sir, if they remove *even one bag* I'll contact you at once."

Having delivered the investment profits personally into the King's hands, Giles considered informing His Majesty of the activities of Dorset and Grey in the Treasury but courage failed him. If the Woodville brother's were about the King's business, as Giles expected and the Marquise of Dorset learned of his interference, then the vindictive, bullying Marquise would certainly make Giles' life a living hell. So he decided instead to discuss the matter with Sir Matthew Pawson but when he crossed to knock on the knight's chamber door, he could hear Matthew in earnest conversation with a guest, whose voice he knew but failed to identify.

Tired and weary, Giles returned to his own chambers in search of warmth and sleep. He cherished the privacy and comfort afforded by the two adjoining rooms which he had acquired courtesy of John Morton. Although the second chamber, which had been Luke's bedroom and was now Giles' office, had to double as Mark's sleeping quarters. Since Woof slept at Mark's feet, it was inclined to smell more like a kennel than an office and so Giles worked in the lager room at the big table and only stored his scrolls and writing materials in the smaller one.

He opened his door to find Mark and Margery Goodman sprawled around the table, consuming quantities of his best wine and gossiping about Robby Morton, Doctor Morton's nephew and successor in the Rolls office. Giles slumped into the vacant chair and groaned at the inebriated state of his squire and lady friend.

"You see Sir Giles," stressed Margery, as she undertook to bring him up to speed with their discussion, "Robby had arranged to meet me for an afternoon of relaxation." She giggled and sighed dramatically. "And God knows I need a break from the fumes released by the Lord Chamberlain."

"I understood Lord Hastings to be the gentlest and leased demanding of men in the bedchamber," said Giles sarcastically as he reached for the jug of wine.

"Only because he is constantly in his cups and virtually legless when he gets to bed."

"Exactly."

"Well anyway, Robby failed to keep our rendezvous so I went to his office where I found him feverishly searching through enormous boxes of scrolls and parchment. The Queen's brother Earl Rivers, had sent urgently for some document that Robby could not find. There was a dreadful scene. The Earl's man was stamping about in rage, saying it was more than his life was worth to return without the document Lord Rivers had requested."

"What could possible be so important?" asked Mark.

Margery shook her head by way of reply and pushed her empty cup towards Giles, who still held the wine jug.

"And that was the *second* disturbance I've witnessed today. Earlier the young Prince of Wales was screaming and cursing like an old soldier in the Queen's chambers."

"Enough Margery, I'm tired," said Giles and relinquishing the jug he left the table, kicked off his shoes and dropped face down onto the huge bed, for which he had paid a local merchant handsomely some weeks previously.

"Don't you want to know why the young Prince was so cross?" demanded Margery.

"*I* do sweetheart," slurred Mark, who was well in his cups, inducing a state of boldness that would otherwise have been unthinkable.

She kissed her forefinger and placed the moist digit on Mark's lips. He lurched towards her across the table, his legs and arms falling carelessly in all directions like a dropped marionette.

"You must promise not to tell anyone? If Lady Stanley hears of it she will know that I have been gossiping."

Margery placed the side of her face close to the surface of the table so that she could look into Mark's face.

"I promise. Go on, tell."

"Well, apparently the Prince had made some disparaging remarks about his uncle Gloucester in the King's presence. Something to do with the wars Gloucester and his northern armies are fighting in Scotland. The precocious young Prince congratulated his father on deploying savages to engage savages, thereby ensuring only savages died in the process."

"Oops."

"Quite. The King expressed such displeasure at the boy's observations that the Prince reluctantly conceded that his uncle may not be a savage but his men from the North and the Scots of course, most certainly were. When pressed for the source of his uncompromising opinions he admitted they were learned from his tutor and uterine uncle, Lord Rivers."

"Whose agent dare not return without Robby's lost documents?"

"The same. Well, the King gave immediate instruction for his son and heir to travel to Yorkshire after Easter and spend some time at Middleham Castle under the tutorage of the hither-too 'savage' uncle Gloucester so that he might learn at first hand the error of his assessment of both his uncle and the men of the North."

"How do you know all this?" asked Giles from beneath his pillow.

"Because," replied Margery in a superior tone, satisfied to have gained Giles' attention at last, "the Prince sort an audience with his mother this morning whilst *I* was in attendance. He is determined not to go to Middleham after Easter. You should have heard him curse, quite the seasoned soldier but beneath his bravado he was really frightened, finally begging his mama to intercede for him."

"Lord Rivers must have filled his head with dreadful stories about northerners," said Giles, rolling over and propping himself up on one elbow, "how did the Queen react?"

"Oh she tried to sooth him; promising to have a word with the King but there's little hope of her persuading him to change his mind."

"Yes she will," leered Mark, "she will seduce him with her con..jugal arts."

"I don't think so," said Margery, shaking her pretty head and making a moue, "Her Majesty has not allowed the King into her bedchamber for sometime now. She is taking his affection for Jane Shore *very* seriously."

Mark pushed back his stool and got to his feet cautiously. The wine had gone to his head, chiefly because he had not eaten since dawn and his stomach rumbled loudly causing Margery to giggle.

"I am in serious need of sustenance," slurred Mark by way of an apology and gripping his stomach he started to move towards the door.

Woof appeared from under the table and padded after him.

"You must be hungry too old friend," added Mark reaching down to pat Woof's upturned head but stumbling onto the foot of the bed as he missed his target.

"For God's sake Margery, take this idiot down to the kitchens and feed him. He obviously won't make it alone."

Margery pouted but Giles had pulled the pillow over his head again and was clearly not in the mood for the tumble she had hoped for.

Left alone, Giles undressed and climbed into his bed, he would not eat tonight, he was so tired slumber would sustain him until dawn but just as sleep began to claim his consciousness, the gentle face of Earl Rivers impressed itself upon his mind's-eye. Lord Rivers was rarely at court. He spent his time at Ludlow Castle where he tutored the Prince of Wales but according to Margery the Prince was at Westminster today, so was Lord Rivers here too? Why should Rivers in-still such fear of Gloucester in the young Prince and what were his nephews, Dorset and Grey, really doing in the King's Treasure House. And what was his agent looking for in the Office of the Rolls? There was something else, something Sir Douglas had said but sleep overwhelmed his tired brain and he failed to recall the Treasurer's words.

Giles woke the next morning with a sense of unease and he lay for some time trying to untangle the threads of disquiet. He decided to visit Doctor Morton at his manor in Holborn and seek his advice regarding Sir Douglas' concerns at the Treasury. He was also intrigued by the thought of Earl Rivers deliberately poisoning the mind of the young Prince against his uncle Gloucester. What possible reason could he have for creating such fear?

Giles dressed quickly and kicked Mark's still booted foot protruding from beneath Woof's shaggy coat. Mark had not even made it to his bed last night and both he and the dog jumped at the impact but only Woof got to his feet. The animal stretched, padded to the door and pawed at it.

"Come on Mark, the dog needs a piss and I'm to the kitchens, I could eat a horse."

Mark sat up and rubbed the sleep from his eyes.

"No chance of meat, it's still Lent," he yawned.

He was a sorry sight but Giles had no time even to poke fun at his squire. He had not eaten since noon yesterday and the watered wine he had just consumed served only to intensify the pangs in his belly. He left Mark and Woof and descended the spiral stairs next to the garderobe tower, stopping only at the least offensive latrine to relieve himself. A small door at the bottom of the stairs open out into the kitchen yard but unfortunately, as Giles started to cross the cobbles the smell of Lenten fish filled his nostrils. He turned on his heels and telling himself he would not die of starvation within the hour, resolved to buy bread on his way to Holborn. He wandered into the Palace yard and sat on a mounting block to wait for Mark, when a man he vaguely knew, hurried up the pathway from the King's steps where the barges were moored. He was tall and gaunt with pursed lips and eyes that narrowed in order to focus on his surroundings. As he walked towards him, Giles recognised the golden leopards embroidered on his tunic. He was one of Earl Rivers' retainers.

"Sir Giles Butler, is it not?" enquired the tall fellow in a haughty affected voice.

"Indeed sir, you have the better of me," replied Giles.

"I never forget a face and can always fix it with a name,"

continued the man with such triumph that Giles had to restrain the urge to offer his congratulations.

"Andrew Dymmock, we met briefly at the Feast of the Nativity if you remember? the Prince of Wales spent last Christmas at Westminster."

Giles did remember and asked Sir Andrew if his presence at Westminster now, meant that Earl Rivers was also here?

"Oh no. He escorted the Prince to the King's court last week but returned immediately. *I* am to accompany the Prince back to Ludlow for Easter but right now I am on a terrible mission to inform the King of the most dreadful accident."

"How so?"

Sir Andrew drew in breath and shook his head.

"Lord only knows how he managed it but the Tower Treasurer, Sir Douglas Hatton, fell to his death from the parapets of the White Tower last night."

"Douglas Hatton is dead? echoed Giles, "he fell from the parapets? To do that he would have to climb into the crenulations."

"Indeed he would," Sir Andrew agreed, "presumably he was drunk, unless of course, he jumped deliberately. Either way, I must convey the sad news to the King."

He took his leave of Giles and pushed his way through the lawyers and clerks making for the great hall where the day's business was about to get underway. Mark and Woof arrived, reasonably tidy but smelling of fish, so that Giles turned his head away.

"What's the matter? " asked Mark, innocently stuffing the remains of a fish pie into his mouth. Woof cleared the crumbs almost before they reached the cobbles. "What's the matter?" he repeated.

"The fish in that pie is none too fresh," replied Giles, "*and* the Treasurer, Sir Douglas Hatton is dead."

Giles, Mark and Woof arrived at Morton's manor in Holborn to find the bailey looking like a stone mason's yard. Everywhere building work was underway. The old gatehouse had been demolished and an almost completed, enormous new structure, towered in its place. An extension to the east wing was being roofed and the wall of the west wing bore scaffolding in readiness for yet another extension.

An aging servant showed them into the great hall where all the furnishings had been stack in the centre of the room and glaziers were fitting coloured glass into fenestralls for the magnificent new windows. The old manservant called for the bottler and ordered wine to be brought to the hall whilst he struggled up the stairs to inform His Grace of Sir Giles' arrival.

"Can you smell what I can smell?" whispered Giles, salivating visibly, as the aroma of roast chicken drifted into the hall from the door left ajar by the departing bottler.

"It can't be, it's still Lent," protested Mark, as if the mere mention of meat during Lent constituted sacrilege.

Woof knew nothing about Lent, only that it had been awhile since he had encountered the smell of cooking meat. He scampered over to the half open door and pushing his snout into the gap, widened it sufficiently to enable him to bolt into the dark passage beyond. Before Mark could follow and haul him back, the old servant reappeared at the gallery rail and begging their pardon for not descending the stairs to escort them back up again, he announced that Bishop Morton would receive them in his solar.

Mark followed Giles into the solar and gasped in wonder at the luxury with which Bishop Morton had surrounded himself. The walls were hung with new, brightly coloured arrases, non of which depicted biblical stories as far as Mark could tell. Fur wraps and rugs were strewn about the floor like straw in a barnyard and plump cushions disguised the hard surfaces of wooden stools and benches. Three braziers filled the room with excessive heat and the sweet scent of fresh herbs rose in the warm air from the several dishes placed strategically around the room. Morton welcomed them both enthusiastically.

"Where's your hound?" he asked Mark, "surely you've not come without him?"

Morton had a soft spot for the dumb animal and had secretly hoped that when Mark moved from Clipberry Manor they would find the dog over crowded their two roomed apartment.

"You know I would be glad to have him here, if you find him too much to manage at Westminster," he added wistfully.

"Thank you, Your Grace but we are doing fine," laughed Giles, who considered the Bishop's weakness for the dog, heart warming.

"He's here somewhere, Your Grace," said Mark, "he made his first call at your kitchen. He could smell …"

Giles coughed and interrupted Mark's flow for fear he might mention 'roast chicken' and embarrass the Bishop.

"Go find him Mark and Luke too. I need a private word with His Grace."

"Luke is in the orchard tending the plum trees," Morton called to Mark as he left, "they seem to have developed a mould this year. Now, you want a private word?"

Giles described what had taken place at the Treasury on the previous day and the subsequently reported death of Sir Douglas Hatton.

"It's an odd coincidence don't you think?" concluded Giles.

Morton remained in deep thought whilst he struggled to find a rational explanation for Giles' story but eventually he conceded defeat.

"It might be best if you confront the King with your concern," he said slowly, "a man has died in unexplainable circumstances and the repackaging of the King's treasure by Dorset and Grey is most odd as you say."

"I would if the Marquise of Dorset was not such a vindictive man. If there is a simple explanation for his involvement and I go wailing my concern to the King, Dorset will make me pay dearly for my meddling."

"Very true," agreed Morton, "both the Marquise and his mother have a reputation for extracting vengeance in the most artful manner." He puffed up his cheeks and blew out audibly in acknowledgement of Giles' dilemma.

"It is virtually impossible for a man to fall accidentally from the parapets," said Giles, "he would have to climb into the crenulations first and in the White Tower the walls supporting the crenulations are at least shoulder high."

"Indeed? Well, if we rule out accidental death, that leaves suicide or murder," said Morton, " and if Sir Douglas was murdered, Dorset and Grey must be responsible."

"Because he threatened to report them for not showing their pass; surely not?"

"Well, for someone else to have murdered him, for some reason unconnected to the packing of the King's treasure, would be stretching coincidence, don't you think?"

"If Dorset and Grey *murdered* the Treasurer because he threatened to report them for their lack of authorisation, what were they *really* doing in the Treasury?"

Both men retreated into deep thought.

"Preparing to steal the King's Treasure," proclaimed Morton with great triumph.

"No, that's preposterous," cried Giles, "much as I dislike the arrogant Marquise I do not believe he would steal from King Edward. They are good friends and.."

"… whoring partners?" prompted Morton.

"Yes, whoring partners. Besides Dorset and Grey are totally reliant upon King Edward's patronage. It is inconceivable that they would steal from the King when he is so sympathetic to their needs."

"Suicide then?"

"Well," said Giles slowly, "perhaps Douglas Hatton was fearful of what Dorset and Grey might *discover* whilst they where rummaging in the treasure bags and took his own life rather than face the consequences."

"A discrepancy that might come to light. Of course, well done Giles."

"Perhaps Douglas feared that the King already suspected him of theft," suggested Giles encouraged by Morton's praise.

"Aye and perhaps Dorset and Grey were only *pretending* to repackage the treasure whilst they were searching for evidence of his dishonesty."

"Of course: the bastards did have authority from the King. They taunted poor Douglas by pretending not to have," growled Giles. He disliked Dorset intensely, despite Douglas' possible guilt.

"But we have only formed an hypothesis," warned Morton, "which is nothing if we cannot proof it to be correct. I will speak to the Coroner, I partly know the man. If Sir Douglas' body shows signs of being assaulted I will learn of it." Morton rose from his chair and paced the floor. "I still find it difficult to believe that Douglas Hatton allowed them into the Treasury, let alone the Treasure House without somebody's signet, especially if he had some irregularity to hide."

"That's it, that's what I forgot," cried Giles, "Dorset told Sir Douglas that because he was Deputy Constable of the Tower he did not need authority to enter the Treasury."

Morton stopped pacing and turned to face Giles his mouth open, displaying broken and blackening teeth.

"Dorset is not Deputy Constable of the Tower. One of the last tasks I performed as Master of the Rolls was to transfer the authority vested in Constable Dudley, to his deputy, Earl Rivers."

"Well he told Sir Douglas that he was."

"Then he lied! I tell you, the Deputy Constable is Lord Rivers. Constable Dudley had become infirm but the King insisted he should retain his title and income, so for all practical purposes his deputy, Lord Anthony Rivers took on his duties."

"Maybe Dorset has been made deputy in place of Rivers," suggested Giles.

"I doubt it. The King would have consulted his council if a change was to be made, especially as whoever is deputy is in fact *acting Constable*, with access to the garrison and the armoury as well as the Treasury. You can check it out with my nephew Robby. He keeps those records as my successor at the Rolls."

A knock at the door preceded the reappearance of Mark, accompanied by Woof and Luke and whilst Morton fussed over the dog, Luke and Giles exchanged greetings. Luke was wearing a long leather apron, hidden in which was his lifeless left arm. The sleeve of his right arm was rolled to the elbow and his face and hand were covered in dirt. Somewhere on track to the solar he had removed his mud-caked boots and filthy hat which hitherto had controlled his unkempt hair, now straggling hopelessly about his beaming face. Giles was happy but surprised to find his friend so absorbed in the cultivation of soft fruit. He needed some interest to divert his attention from his ill health and crippled arm but Giles could not help remembering the stunning young man he had once been. A handsome gallant of Mediterranean appearance who had accompanied the beautiful Margery to watch the wedding procession of the young Duke of York and Lady Anne Mowbray. Giles sighed, that winter's day felt like a life time ago.

CHAPTER 15

London 25th March 1483

Giles did not wait for Morton to contact the coroner but instead, attended the inquest being held in a small courtroom located on the ground floor of the White Tower. The coroner sat on a low dais behind an enormous table that almost filled the raised platform. He was dressed in black as befitted the occasion and was assisted by a snivelling clerk, who shuffled and fidgeted with his writing materials at the far end of the board. The jury comprised of off-duty men from the Tower garrison, peeved to have had their free time commandeered by the coroner but Giles was confident that these soldiers would be aware of how difficult it was to 'fall accidentally' from the parapet and would not be fooled by an attempt to explain the Treasurer's death in this way. They stood almost to attention behind the coffined body which was placed on trestles and covered by a dark red cloth that fell to the floor on all sides.

Apart from a clean shaven man of about thirty summers who vaguely resembled Sir Douglas, Giles was surprised to find that he was the only other non-officer in the courthouse. Such hearings were usually well attended by ordinary folk in search of a snatch of scandal with which to brighten their dreary lives but being Holy Week, perhaps the Tower folk had more urgent duties to attend.

The coroner opened with a few words of condolence for the benefit of those who had known and cared for the old Treasurer in life and around the courtroom heads nodded in agreement with this sentiment, before the guard who had found Douglas' body was called to present his evidence. In a rehearsed fashion he described how he had discovered the dead man on the ground about ten paces from the door of 'this very courtroom, face down, arms and legs stretched out in a star shape'. The guard claimed to have smelled drink on the dead man's clothing and as he still clutched the broken remains of a Claret jug, he believed the Treasurer was drunk when he fell.

There was a long pause whilst the sound of the clerk's quill scratching out the evidence for the records seemed to fill the courtroom. Neither the guard nor the coroner himself had made reference to the difficulty a drunken man would encounter climbing a five foot wall into the crenulations and Giles considered voicing his unease when the coroner broke the silence by asking the jury to examine the body. A man-at-arms walked forward and pulled back the sheet. Without leaving their places in line, the soldier-jury glanced into the coffin. There was no disquiet amongst their number, no mumblings or whispers of 'foul play', just the nodding of heads in unison. One or two crossed themselves as a mark of respect as the coroner announced his verdict of 'accidental death'.

Giles was stunned. It was a mummery, a staged performance with everyone having learned their part. Even the public had been warned off. What about Douglas' relative, surely he was entitled to the truth? But what was the truth? Had Sir Douglas been murdered or had he committed suicide? Either way Giles was convinced that someone with great influence had corrupted the court and for the rest of the day he agonised over having remained silent during the proceedings. He must consult with Bishop Morton immediately.

Two days later Giles had still not spoken with Morton. On the Thursday before Good Friday, he was obliged to accompany King Edward on his journey around the Capital where the King performed the unpleasant but traditional ceremony of washing the feet of the city's poor. A humiliating experience designed by the Church to remind all mighty monarchs that Christ washed the feet of his disciples on the eve of his Crucifixion. Giles had struggled not to laugh as grubby individuals were brought one by one before the King, who kneeling on a blood red velvet cushion with a bowl of scented water before him, solemnly perform the task of washing their awful feet. Amusement lay in His Majesty's apparent unawareness that men-at-arms from the royal household had some hours earlier, rounded up six or seven paupers from church porches, fed and paid them and then instructed them to clean their filthy feet in the nearest duck pond, prior to the 'royal washing'.

Giles was also one of the King's household men required to attend his Majesty on Good Friday *and* Easter Saturday. The former was an endless series of services in the Abbey interspersed with traditionally meagre quantities of bread and watered wine. The latter was a dreadful day spent fishing. It had rained incessantly and Giles was drenched to the skin by the time they returned to Westminster, whilst the King, having been sheltered from the worst of the deluge by Giles and other knights, had thoroughly enjoyed the experience and was planning a second trip early in the following week. He had enthused to Giles personally throughout the Easter Sunday celebrations, joking that if they went fishing regularly during Lent they might even save his household the expense of Lenten fish. However, for this year Lent was over and meat of every description was on the menu for Easter Sunday dinner, which was a fine affair held in the great hall when over a hundred guests and members of the royal household sat down together. Dorset and Grey escorted their mother, the Queen to her seat at the top table to the left of King Edward and then Dorset took his coveted seat at Edward's right hand, the place usually reserved for the King's favourite. The young Duke of York sat to the left of the Queen, for once allowed to eat with the adults but the Prince of Wales had returned to his own court at Ludlow with Sir Andrew Dymmock to join his uncle, Lord Rivers for the Easter festivities. Bishop Morton was personally honoured by the King's request that he should bless the meal and all those about to partake in it. Bishop Robert was not in attendance.

After dinner Giles and Morton retired to Giles' chambers and following several cups of brandy wine Giles broached the subject of Sir Douglas' death, expressing his disquiet about the verdict and adding that now he considered suicide unlikely.

"Why? Surely it is still the most plausible explanation? Douglas was fiddling the accounts and committed suicide when he thought he was about to be found out," said Morton, " we should be grateful that the court did not consider it. At least with a verdict of 'accidental death' his body will be buried in God's acre."

Bodies of suicides were usually tossed into the city ditch as the church forbade their burial in consecrated ground. Giles shook his head.

"I have rarely left King Edward's side since the inquest. If there had been any reports of missing treasure from the Tower or rumours that Sir Douglas had committed suicide because of irregularities I would have heard. What did your friend the coroner have to say about the state of Hatton's body?"

"Nothing much. There was a large lump on his forehead but that was easily explained by his hitting his head on the ground when he fell."

"Or by a heavy object being used to render him unconscious, before being pushed over the parapet."

"Well yes, I suppose so," agreed Morton wearily.

"There is no motive for suicide. And another thing; I am convinced everyone at the inquest had been instructed as to what to say. We should be considering the possibility of murder."

"Oh I don't think so," said Morton draining his cup and setting it down a little too deliberately for a sober man. "Perhaps the King has decided to keep the matter a secret. He might well be embarrassed by the activities of a dishonest treasurer and *instructed* the coroner to bring in a verdict of accidental death."

Giles refilled Morton's cup and then shuffled back in his seat.

He was about to protest when he heard the gentlest of snores emanate from Morton's ample bulk. He got to his feet and pulling a coverlet from his bed, Giles draped it over the Bishop and tucked it round his legs. Infected by the cleric's slumber, Giles yawned and stretched out on his bed but before the surfeit of food and drink dragged him into sleep, an annoying thought flitted across his mind. If Morton slept until supper time, he would sup at Westminster and expect Giles to put him up for the night and that meant relinquishing his precious bed.

They both slept until supper time but it was Morton who roused first, his legs were stiff and he was cold. The evenings were still chilly at the end of March and the fire was all but burnt out.

"Sir Giles, what hour is it?" mumbled Morton, rubbing his portly legs and wriggling his toes in an attempt to force some life back into them. He quickly downed the abandoned cup of brandy wine and got to his feet. He needed to relieve himself but the light was fading and even though he had resided in these quarters himself he still needed a lamp to find his way to the garderobe.

"Lord, it's dark, what hour is it?" yawned Giles climbing off his bed and searching for a taper to light the covered lamp.

"You didn't light the hour candle but my belly says its well passed supper time."

Morton took the lamp Giles had managed to light and made his way to the latrines, leaving Giles to light candles and stoke up the fire with wood from the leather pannier. When first waking he was never in a good mood and he stumbled about the chamber spilling the remains of the brandy wine and stubbing his toe on a log that had rolled from the pannier and come to rest in the middle of the room.

"Where the hell is Mark?" he grumbled aloud, irritated by the realisation that Bishop Morton would be staying the night. "He should be here attending to my needs not sleeping off his dinner in the kitchens with some slattern wrapped round his thighs."

As if on cue, the door flew open and a very agitated Mark burst into the chamber.

"Giles, where is Bishop Morton? He is needed in the royal bedchamber immediately. The King is dying and he is asking for the Bishop."

"*Dying*? He can't be. Mark, are you drunk?"

Morton's large frame appeared in the doorway and Mark abandoned trying to make Giles comprehend and turned to appeal to the Bishop directly. The lamp Morton was holding clearly revealed the horror and panic in Mark's face and once he had heard the message, Morton wheeled-about and surprisingly quickly for a man of his girth, set off down the corridor with his robes bellowing in the draught he caused behind him. Giles followed in his wake.

When they reached the royal chambers, men-at-arms were everywhere and Giles sensed the fear in these otherwise hardened bodyguards who had been warned of the imminent death of their King. Sir Matthew Pawson received them as they entered the side chamber; he was pale and shaking uncontrollably. Morton pushed him to one side and made straight for the royal bedchamber but Giles remained in the adjacent room where the King had been sharing supper with his mistress, Jane Shore. She was still there, distraught and weeping. She pulled on Matthew's arm begging him to allow her to see the King but Matthew shook his head and whined at her reproachfully.

"You know women are not allowed in the Death Chamber." He tore his arm away from her grasp, "for the love of God leave me alone."

Giles interceded, taking Jane gently by the arm he led her to a chair and bidding her sit, he found himself a stool and sat beside her. She was very scantily dressed with as much of her heaving bosom displayed above her gown as hidden beneath. Her round, unpainted face was stained with hot tears and even though her dark eyes were ringed red, Giles could appreciate her appeal, for she had a natural beauty more usually associated with very young girls.

"Why is everyone so sure His Majesty is dying?" asked Giles softly, "has he had some kind of heart seizure?"

Jane sobbed and nodding her pretty head, she covered her face with both hands and cried unashamedly. For the first time since he had entered the chamber Giles looked around him. The table had been cleared but a spilt cup of wine lay on the floor and an upturned stool and a torn drape suggested some kind of struggle. Pulling gentled on the hands masking Jane's face, Giles asked calmly what had taken place.

"We only had a light super," she sobbed, "Edward wanted to be able to satisfy me tonight, having abstained during Holy Week."

Under different circumstances Giles would have laughed. Pious men forwent pleasures of the flesh for the forty days and forty nights of Lent but for Edward, Holy Week was quite long enough.

"We had finished our meal when Sir Matthew brought a plate of sweetmeats to the table. I dislike palm fruits but poor Edward cannot resist them." She started to cry again, "I removed the marchpane from one or two and ate it to be polite but when Edward had consumed two, maybe three dates he turned white and gripping his belly he fell to the floor writhing in agony."

Giles tried to calm her but she was sobbing uncontrollably, so he turned to the still shaking Matthew, who took up the story.

"Mistress Shore summonsed me right away and I immediately sent for His Majesty's physicians. Oh Sir Giles, surely he will not die, he is a strong man?"

"I have no idea Matthew," said Giles honestly, "from what Mistress Shore has said, it would appear the King has been poisoned by the sweetmeats. Perhaps the dates were rotten or fermenting as a result of the distance they must travel to reach our shores."

"But she ate them too," screeched Matthew, "you said you did, I heard you." He was shaking Jane by her shoulders and Giles had to pull him away.

"Stop it Matthew. Nobody is blaming you for the condition of the fruit and anyway, if there was some mould, it could not have been much. You would have noticed if a significant number of pieces were decaying."

Matthew slumped down onto the floor and began to cry.

Throughout the next hour, physicians and senior noblemen filed into the bedchamber leaving their squires and servants in the adjacent room with Jane and Giles to wait and pray for their King. The door to the bedchamber was much too thick to hear what was happening beyond but with its every opening the waiting room fell quiet as they all strained to catch some sound or sight of the happenings within. Giles ordered Matthew to organise refreshment for those waiting, as it was going to be a long night and many were already claiming the most comfortable benches and chairs on which to snatch a few hours sleep.

Crowded together they soon began to feel warmer and satisfied with the wine Matthew had reluctantly provided, one by one the servants fell asleep in the darkening chamber.

All had been quiet for some time when the door opened and Thomas, Marquis of Dorset left the royal bedchamber, stumbling over two dozing servants in his eagerness to escape. Viciously he kicked out at the prone bodies that hindered his exit and their shrieks of pain woke others, until the entire huddle of servants was awake and listening to the sound of retching and heaving coming from the King's bedroom. Sensibly, someone kicked the door shut and the waiting room darkened once again and sleep crept over the watchers.

Giles woke some hours later with cramp in his right leg. Slowly he became aware of rhythmic movement not far from his painful limb and as he gathered his senses and remembered why he was not in his own comfortable bed, his night sight revealed that the movement beside him was in fact two persons coupling. At first he smiled and endeavoured not to disturb the pair whilst at the same time rubbing his cramped leg but then he realised that Jane Shore was the only female in the room. It was inconceivable that she had so quickly recovered from her distress and concern for the King's approaching death and succumbed to the amorous overtures of some magnet's servant. So who were the couple so close to his right leg that he could feel the heat from their panting on his thigh? Giles gently pulled himself round so that he could rest on his right side and look down at the top of the heads of the pair beside him. He had to shut his eyes quickly and fain sleep as the man rolled away from his partner and without standing, fumbled to pull up his hose. However, Giles still had a clear picture in his head of the moment before the man moved and with his eyes tightly shut he examined every detail. The woman was indeed Jane Shore; she had her left hand flat on the floor by her side, fingers splayed and pressing against the ground. Her head was turned towards Giles' thigh and he could clearly make out the pain on her upturned face. Her mate was none other than the Marquise of Dorset and although Giles knew that his personal loathing for the man could have affected his judgement, he was still convinced that Dorset had forced himself on Jane but how had he prevented her from crying out for help? Giles remained still and sightless until drawn broke and men began to yawn and stretch in their crowded billet. Only then did he open his eyes and to his surprise everything seemed normal, there was no evidence of the despicable violation he knew had taken place.

The air was stale and fouled by the concentration of so many bodies but some inspired soul flung back the shutters and opened wide the glass filled window just as the bedchamber door opened and Bishop Morton appeared. He looked ghastly; a night without sleep had left him sallow and red eyed and his usually immaculate attire was hideously stained with damp vomit which still retained much of its original odour.

"It's over," he said dramatically, dropping onto a stool vacated for his use by a man close to the doorway.

"The King is Dead. God Save King Edward V," trumpeted Dorset, " I will inform my mother, Her Majesty the Queen."

"The King is *not dead* my Lord Marquise, I refer to his fever, his sudden illness. *That* is over, not his life, man."

The room erupted with good cheer. The King was much loved and his death would have been sincerely mourned. Jane Shore shrieked with joy and fled into the sickroom without waiting to be granted permission. Giles turned to observe the stunned Marquise of Dorset whose expression of amazement gave way to one of fear and Giles relished the moment. If Jane Shore complained to the King about his amorous advances, Dorset would be in serious trouble, thought Giles – good.

"I shall make my way to the Abbey and beg a clean habit," sighed Morton examining the wreckage of his fine tunic.

"And some hot water and strong smelling herbs as well," teased Giles, "come, I will walk with you."

As Morton and Giles made their way along the corridors and galleries of Westminster, joyful servants, aware that their beloved King was no longer expected to die, bowed and curtsied with alacrity. Such was his own relief, Bishop Morton acknowledged their delight with nods and 'good days', usually reserved for those of higher status and even exhausted as he was, he moved with such a spring in his step that Giles was obliged to scurry after him in order to keep up.

"What ailed His Majesty?" asked Giles when they were alone.

Morton shook his head and looked about him to ensure there were no eaves droppers.

"You know how the physicians arrive at their diagnoses; silly men, drawing stupid star charts and rambling on about the body's humours in relation to the planets," he sneered, "I think their 'star charts revealed' that Edward was having a seizure brought about by over eating, after fasting for Lent."

"Not everyone has the courage to trust in the likes of your Italian Doctor friend."

"I don't need Antonio Benivieni to tell me that King Edward suffered some kind of food poisoning," snapped Morton, "he was much recovered as soon as he had been violently sick and had emptied his gut."

"It was the palm fruits I think, if Mistress Shore has told me correctly," said Giles and then he repeated Jane's story, including her explanation for Edward's light supper.

"So the physicians were wrong, Edward had not overeaten. Well that's no surprise," concluded Morton, convinced that his own theory had been proven. They were approaching the Abbey gatehouse.

"I'll take my leave of you Giles. My Chaplin has been staying at the Abbey during Easter, he will escort me back to Holborn once I'm scrubbed clean of royal vomit."

Giles ambled back to the palace deep in thought. He felt uneasy about the way Edward's illness had been portrayed as fatal. Who had started that rumour? Was it Dorset? He certainly misunderstood Doctor Morton when he announced Edward's illness was over and the Marquise might well be involved in the death of Sir Douglas Hatton but Giles failed to find anything that linked the two events. However, he had not yet spoken to Robby Morton, Master of the Rolls and he decided that after a wash and change of clothes he would pay Morton's nephew a visit. Discovering who really was the Deputy Constable of the Tower was not going to settle his unease but if Dorset had been lying about that too, well, at least it would be worth making a few more discrete enquiries.

Chapter 16

Westminster 31st March 1483

Robby Morton had been in his office for several hours when Giles called. He was a smaller, rounder version of Bishop Morton of Ely but unlike his uncle, Robby was prone to sweat under pressure, making it difficult for him to lie with conviction and therefore rendering him unsuitable for promotion. He had already heard the news about the King's ill health and was genuinely relieved that Edward was recovering from his 'seizure'. He had also heard that Sir Giles had been present throughout the night and he pumped him relentlessly for information with which he planned to gossip later.

"Robby, I need to contact the Constable of the Tower, Lord Dudley," lied Giles, who considered it about time *he* asked some of the questions.

"What about?"

"The King's business," lied Giles again, tapping the side of his nose to indicate that the said business was private, "where can I find the man? He hasn't been in the Tower for the past week."

"He is ailing and has returned to his estates in Wales," said Robby, "If you're business has anything to do with his being the Constable, then I suggest you speak to his Deputy, the Marquise of Dorset."

"Since when was Dorset, Dudley's deputy?" asked Giles innocently, "I thought Lord Rivers held the post."

"He did but Andrew Dymmock notified me earlier this month that Lord Rivers wished to transfer his office of deputy to his nephew, Dorset."

Roses are White

"Is that legal? Can such a transfer be made without the King's authorisation?"

"Not officially," agreed an agitated Robby. It was his responsibility to record all royal appointments, but as Dymmock had pointed out at the time, His Majesty would not object to the transfer.

"I think you should notify the King of the new arrangement," said Giles.

"I will, I will Sir Giles but it is so difficult in my position." Robby brushed the sweat from his brow with the back of his hand and then leaning forward across his desk, appealed to Giles. "You see, Earl Rivers is in the habit of instructing Dymmock to undertake tasks that are really Chancery business."

"Is he now?"

"I'm afraid so Sir Giles." Robby pulled a cloth from his sleeve and mopped his face vigorously. "On the day that Dymmock notified me of Dorset's new post, I discovered that he had been in the Chancery earlier and actually paid a clerk to make copies of at least two documents held there. Of course I dismissed the clerk at once."

"What a liberty," sympathised Giles, "which document did he have copied?"

It was Robby's turn to tap the side of his nose to indicate that such information was none of Giles' business but he was clearly nervous about the activities of Sir Andrew Dymmock and Giles made a mental note to inform Morton of his irregular behaviour.

In the days that followed Easter Sunday, King Edward's health slowly improved, although he kept to his bed as the physicians were fearful that his sanguinary humour might flounder in the chills of early April. Much to Giles' irritation he remain in the King's favour and found himself entertaining the royal invalid to the detriment of his duties in merchant shipping as well as his social life. To make matters worse, by the 7th April His Majesty had become morose about his recent brush with death and the more he considered how close he had come to leaving his realm to a twelve year old boy and a council of fractious nobles, the more he sort Giles' council. The rift between the Queen's kin and the established nobility had festered and widened over the past fifteen years so that only the King's own forceful personality prevented outright hostilities. By the time he retired that night, Edward had concluded that his illness was a personal 'wake up' call from Almighty God; that it was his holy duty to heed the warning, but a method by which he might reconcile the fractious magnets eluded him and try as he might, Giles was unable to suggest a solution either.

On the morning of April 8th King Edward dispatched Sir Matthew to summons Giles before he had even broken his fast. The knight felt misused and undervalued in the menial role of messenger but as Giles had been woken by Matthew's persistent knocking, he was in no mood to tolerate the man's hurt pride.

"Matthew, I did not ask you to call: you were sent by the King. So complain to him, not me, about the inappropriate use of your valuable time."

Sir Matthew pouted. "Well you're in for a grim day as far as I can tell. The King is up and shouting orders to all and sundry. If you'll take my advice you will persuade him back to bed and forget all this ... reconciliation nonsense."

Giles said nothing but hurried to the King's chamber to discover for himself the implications of Matthew's ramblings.

The King sat at a small table swathed in a purple velvet dressing gown with a fine woollen scarf wound round his neck. He wore fingerless gloves and a velvet cap trimmed with ermine. His barber had already shaved him and the remains of his breakfast were being cleared away even as Sir Matthew announced Sir Giles' arrival.

"Good day Sir Giles," called King Edward, "come and listen to the brilliant scheme by which we intend to unite our 'bitching' nobles." Edward held out his hand and Giles knelt and kissed his ring. "Have you broken your fast Giles? Matthew, bring food and wine. Go man, hurry." Edward nodded to a stool and bade Giles be seated at the opposite side of the table. "Now, let us see how you react to our plan," said the King full of intrigue which Giles failed to comprehend.

"In a little while our fractious friends and family will all join us here in this chamber. We will instruct them, one-by-one, to swear allegiance to our son, the Prince of Wales and then they must declare, each to the other, how their previous enmity will, from this day forth be forgotten and replaced by love, courtesy and care for the well being of each other." Edward beamed at Giles across the table. "Well?" he said dramatically, "have we your approval? Is it not time that distrust and hatred be banished from our court?"

"Er, yes er... of course Your Majesty, I'm sure the ploy will work well," stammered Giles, confounded by Edward's apparent naivety and then to his amazement the King burst out laughing.

"Don't be ridiculous Giles," cried King Edward with glee, "the plan is pathetic, childish in the extreme. We cannot *command* old adversaries to kiss and make good their differences, at least not with sincerity."

Giles stared back at the King. Had His Majesty's illness affected his mind?

"But our point is well made," continued Edward more soberly, "like you, our high and mighty nobles will humour their King and make all the right noises of reconciliation in the belief that our recent vision of death has addled the royal wits."

Still Giles dare not comment.

"They will pledge themselves to each other unreservedly," persevered Edward, "confident that the exercise be some mummery to appease our fevered brain."

"But in future disputes you will hold them to the promises they make," declared Giles, picking up the threads of the plot, "so forcing cooperation when previously they would have been openly hostile to each other."

Secretly Giles was amazed at the King's ingenuity and proud to be taken into his confidence. Edward laughed.

"Good plan, eh. Once they have openly agreed to co-operate

with each other, there can be no going back without confessing they thought us deranged."

Matthew returned with wine, bread, cheese and a selection of cold meats but Giles was too engrossed in the conspiracy to break for food.

"May I make a suggestion Sire?" asked Giles, emboldened by the trust Edward had placed in him. The King nodded his assent.

"Perhaps Your Majesty should consider making your brother Gloucester, Lord Protector? God forbid he should need to assume the role but…"

"It's a brilliant idea Giles," cried Edward, slapping his hand down hard on the table and making the bread bounce on its platter, "however, we will also take care not to need our good brother's services by eating and drinking more frugally in future." Edward smiled benevolently at Giles. "Still, if death had claim us last week and Gloucester had been nominated Lord Protector…" Edward rubbed his chin, "well, let us say it would have redressed the balance of power."

The King laughed nervously and raised his goblet to toast Giles. No further explanation was required, clearly the only power that needed redressing was that wheeled by the Queen and her Woodville relatives. Giles drank the wine Matthew had poured for him and in the comfortable silence that ensued he decided that there would never be a more suitable opportunity to ask Edward about the activities of Dorset and Grey in the Tower Treasury. Unfortunately, before he could formulate his question Sir Matthew appeared and announced that the Her Majesty the Queen and her son the Marquis of Dorset were in the antechamber in response to the summons.

"Quick Giles help us to our bed. If the plan is to work they must not think we have recovered our health completely. And Matthew, clear the table, remember we have not left our sickbed."

Giles helped the King climb back into his great bed and arranged the pillows and coverlets about him.

"Now leave us Sir Giles," said Edward winking conspiratorially, "oh and Giles, send John Morton to me, he can see to the legality of making Gloucester Lord Protector."

Giles bowed out of the King's presence unaware that he would never speak to King Edward IV again.

Margery hurriedly made her way to Giles' apartment in search of comfort and reassurance. The Queen had been in an awful mood ever since King Edward's sudden illness a week ago. Nervy and jumpy, she had even shouted at Margery, calling her 'a silly whore', much to the delight of Lady Stanley but *that* Margery could handle. It was the Marquise of Dorset's visit to his mother's chambers this morning that had truly frightened her. The summons from the King to attend his reconciliation gathering had annoyed Her Majesty and at first she had been determined to ignore it but when Dorset arrived with his own summons and accused his mother of alienating the entire Woodville family by her obduracy, the Queen had actually begged her son not to insist she attend. Bewildered, Margery had watched and listened from behind the screened entrance. Normally the roles were reversed and it would be the Marquise who begged for concessions, but when he had grabbed his mother by the wrist and physically pulled her towards him, the memory of his violent attack on her own person flooded back. The pair had edged their way out of Margery's sight and an exchange in angry low tones was all she could make out but the Queen must have eventually agreed to attend the King's summons because Dorset had left, warning her not to change her mind and to meet him before noon in the antechamber.

Panicked by the apparent domination of the Queen by Dorset and the dangers that forecast for her own safety, Margery had escaped the Queen's chambers to find her friend Giles. Now she knocked on his door but there was no reply, so gently she turned the handle and pushed it open but the room was empty. Margery crossed to the office curtain and called Mark's name but there was no reply, so reasoning that they had not gone far, the door being unlocked, she smoothed the top cover of the unmade bed and stretched out to await their return. Resting her head in the hollowed pillows where Giles had been sleeping, she could smell his scent and to her surprise she found it strangely arousing. Why was he not here when she needed him?

Margery pulled the top pillow into her arms and hugged it tightly. Without realising, she drew much of her own strength from the Queen's self assurance but since this had faltered, Margery's confidence was also crumbling. Until this morning, she assumed the Queen would be Regent if King Edward died but now she feared that the Marquise might assume that role. Stroking the top of the hugged pillow, Margery confided her fears to an imaginary Giles.

"If only we could find love, perhaps even marry. Is it too much to ask?" she whispered, tenderly kissing the pillow.

"Is what too much to ask?" echoed Giles as he entered the room.

"Giles! Hello," called back Margery in a loud cheery voice, as if it would drown her earlier words. She sat bolt upright and threw the pillow onto the floor.

He removed his sword belt and throwing it carelessly over the discarded pillow he climbed onto the bed beside her. He had returned from the King's chambers full of self confidence and self importance. Had not the great King survived assured death and commanded Giles be at his bedside throughout his recovery? Had His Majesty not taken Giles into his confidence, laughing with him about how he proposed to dupe some of the mightiest Lords of England? And had Edward not received, with enthusiasm, Giles' suggestion that Gloucester should be named Lord Protector, should His Majesty's mystery illness return and claim his life? He had even joked about the imbalance of power the appointment of Gloucester would redress. Never had Giles felt so self assured and now on his return to his quarters, he finds the beautiful, sensual Margery in his bed: it was heady stuff.

The new macho Giles would take, not too roughly, for that was not in his nature, the gratification and pleasure that were his manly rights. Margery read the signs accurately: the arrogance in his eyes, the smile that was so nearly a sneer and the body language that so many of her over mighty clients displayed whilst flaunting their sexual prowess in the pathetic belief that they alone, could satisfy any women beyond her wildest imaginings. She disguised her disappointment behind a professional smile and nimbly untying the points on her gown and kirtle she pulled off her clothes and slipped naked beneath the coverlets. Giles took his time undressing, not wanting to appear too eager. After all Margery was only a whore, a very high class whore who knew exactly how to please him but certainly not the love of his life. He climbed into his bed and pulled her towards him, feeling the soft contours of her body in order to enhance the excitement of which he was so assured. Momentarily he hesitated, normally she took charge of their lovemaking, eager to please, knowing what to do to excite him but now she held back. No, that was not what was happening, for she snuggled up to him responding to his caresses but.... so what was it? Was she actually *waiting for him to please her?*

In the brief moment that followed Giles thought he heard Margery sob; something was terribly wrong.

"What is it dearest?" he asked tenderly, instantly loosing touch with his new bullish image.

"I'm sorry Giles," sobbed Margery, her head still pressed into his chest, "I'm so afraid."

For a second, Giles believed that she was afraid of him. Terrified, he held her at arms length so that he could read the truth in her eyes.

"What have you to fear? – Margery look at me. Surely you are not afraid of *me*?"

"Of you? oh no Giles. Why should I fear you? It's *Dorset* I fear. The Queen has somehow lost control of him and I'm petrified that if Edward dies then he will take charge of.... of well, everything."

Once unleashed, Margery's terror was uncontrollable. She clung to Giles and shook as she explained the depth of her fear.

"Truly I think he will stop at nothing. He's a mad man where women are concerned, stalking them as if he were hunting wild animals."

"Shush, be still, be still."

"Besides he hates me, because all those years ago, his mother scolded him for attacking me," sobbed Margery, touching the scar on her left breast which she would have as a life long reminder of his savagery, "It's only his deference to the Queen that stops him from coming after me now and now – now that he no longer fears her – he'll come for me and, and he'll kill me. I know he will."

"Stop it Margery. It won't happen I promise you. Dorset will never touch you again."

She wiped her eyes on the back of her hand and looked earnestly into his, searching for conformation of his words.

"And Edward is recovering," continued Giles, "whatever made you think otherwise?"

Margery sniffed and chewed her bottom lip.

"Only this morning Dorset told the Queen he was seriously ill. Why should he lie?"

"I have know idea dearest," said Giles honestly, "but I do know something, which if you have a mind to repeat to Her Majesty, will put the Marquis of Dorset back in his cage for the foreseeable future."

Margery brightened. "Oh Giles what is it? Please tell."

"Well, on the night Edward was taken ill, I witnessed the Marquis coupling with the King's mistress, Jane Shore."

Margery shrugged and sniffed hard. "Edward may have given her to Dorset."

"You can't be serious? Besides I believe he forced himself upon her."

"What? Edward would not tolerate such savagery," cried Margery brightening again, "but if Dorset forced himself on Jane, she may well tell His Majesty herself," she added, thinking the information may be worthless after all.

"I don't believe she will, otherwise why did she not call for help at the time? The room was full of sleeping servants. No, Dorset would not have dared touch her if he thought she would cry out. He was taking a terrible risk of discovery as it was."

"That would be part of his pleasure," said Margery with disgust, "and so would blackmailing his victim." She smiled at Giles and cupping his face in her hands she kissed him tenderly.

"Thank you my love for that juicy poison and I am sure the Queen will thank you too when I tell her," and then breathing seductively into his ear, "now let me show you just how grateful I am."

CHAPTER 17

Westminster Palace 9th April 1483

By 9th April King Edward was well pleased with his own recovery, boasting that his constitution was second to no man's. He still felt weak but that was to be expected after such violent bouts of vomiting. Edward was also congratulating himself on yesterday's well staged charade, which had successfully culminated in the sworn enemies of his court, promising to 'love one another' as the holy book demanded. The King began to chuckle to himself as he recalled the old warhorse, William, Lord Hastings, gritting his teeth and swearing to set aside his hatred for the Marquis of Dorset and then there was that pompous ass Harry Buckingham, promising to adore his Woodville in-laws with such eloquence that Lord Grey actually believed him and burst into tears of repentance for previously bad-mouthing the Duke. Edward began to laugh aloud. He remembered his mother's angry glare when he ordered her to embrace his Queen, who from that moment on would be her dutiful daughter. Tears of laughter began to roll down the King's face as he recalled the look of disgust on his Queen's face when he bade her kiss his mistress Jane and swear to comfort her should he be taken unexpectedly.

"Really that was unforgivable of me," choked Edward, trying unsuccessfully to control his mirth.

He pulled himself together and taking a gold ring from the velvet pouch around his waist, he placed it inside one of the drinking cups on the small table. He had arranged to have supper with Jane, and had dispatched Sir Matthew to escort her from her house off Bishopgate. Edward played with the ring inside the cup. She would accept his trinket as a token of his love but tonight he intended to persuade her to also accept his offer of quarters in the Palace of Westminster. She had promised to 'live in,' when the annulment of her marriage to William Shore was granted by the Holy Father but it was taking for ever and Edward wanted her close, especially now he had been forced to face his own mortality. To hell with what Elizabeth had to say about it, Jane was witty, excellent company and his friends adored her, which was more than could be said for his Queen. Jane may not be as beautiful as Elizabeth but she faired as well in bed and anyway Elizabeth was showing signs of aging after forty or so summers.

Edward broke wind painfully and rang the tiny silver bell that usually summonsed Sir Matthew. A young knight appeared, apprehensive as to his stand-in duties but the King only required something to eat. His belly had been rumbling unattractively and he thought it best not to wait until supper before responding to its complaint. He ordered the man to bring him some sweetmeats and then stretched out comfortably on the cushioned bench to await the return of Sir Matthew and Mistress Shore.

On a table set in the serving lobby the young knight discovered several cold dishes prepared for inclusion in the royal supper. Amongst the fruit and cheese was a selection of sweetmeats arranged on a silver plate which the knight brought to the King as instructed. With his head resting on a velvet cushion and the plate of sweetmeats at his fingertips, King Edward allowed his senses to drool over the promised pleasures of a much needed night with his lovely mistress, Jane Shore.

It was growing dark when Mark took Woof for his last walk before they retired for the night. As usual, Woof made straight for the waters edge, where Mark assumed the most interesting doggy smells must lurk, when a barge drew alongside the King's Steps and Sir Matthew Pawson and Mistress Jane Shore joined them on the quay. Woof bounded about Sir Matthew, recognising him from the time when they had lived at Clipberry Manor but Matthew ignored the dog and tersely bade Jane, make haste. She smiled at Mark and ruffled Woof's shaggy coat by way of apology, then lifting her gown ankle high she hurried after her impatient escort but before they reached the opposite side of the palace yard the sleepy buildings surrounding them burst into life. Lamps, candles and torches were all being lit and carried from chamber to chamber. Men started to shout orders and the scream's of women signalled alarm, whilst down in the courtyard horses and dogs caught the sense of human urgency, whinnying and barking in sympathy. Mark thought a fire must have broken out in the kitchen block where frequent minor fires occurred but no smoke appeared from that quarter. Then a herald shouting for Sir Matthew to come at once, bellowed the sad news into the night air. The King had had another seizure and was fighting for his life. All knights of the body must attend His Majesty immediately. Mistress Shore let out a shriek of terror and fled in the direction of the King's bedchamber but Sir Matthew could not move, gasping for breath he gripped his throat and fell to the ground in a swoon. Mark rushed to his aid but the herald reached him first, so calling to Woof to follow him, Mark made for Giles' chambers to inform his master of the King's relapse.

At the end of the first gallery he met Giles and Luke hurrying towards him.

"Go to the Abbey Mark and alert Bishop Morton, he should be with the Abbot," cried Giles over the heads of two screaming maid servants pushing by in the opposite direction.

When Giles and Luke reached the King's apartments they learned that Bishop Morton was already at the King's bedside, as was the Marquis of Dorset, William Lord Hastings and Mistress Shore. The bedchamber door was firmly shut and guarded by two knights of the body but they recognised Giles and allowed him and Luke to enter the adjacent room where Matthew was being given watered wine by the deputising knight.

Giles surveyed the scene. The supper table, set for two, was undisturbed but cushions from the couch were strewn on the floor.

Giles asked the terrified young man what had happened.

"Go on Peter," urged Matthew, "tell Sir Giles what you know."

Sir Peter tossed his long golden locks out of his face with a shake of his head and looked into Giles's face with beautiful deep blue eyes.

"After Bishop Morton left earlier, His Majesty sent Mathew to fetch Mistress Shore whilst he prepared to receive her in the bedchamber. Sir John and Sir Henry attended him," whispered Peter and then coughed nervously, "His Majesty was suffering from bouts of wind and his belly was rumbling most offensively. Of course it was only to be expected when he had eaten so little since his illness."

"But embarrassing when entertaining a lady," encouraged Luke.

"Quite so Sir. His Majesty asked for something to eat and I found those sweetmeats already prepared, in the serving lobby." Peter pointed to the dish of marchpane on a stool beside the couch. "After I had served them I retired to the lobby and some minutes later I heard the King screaming in agony. When I returned to see what was amiss, I found him rolling on the floor gripping his belly and retching to no avail. Naturally I called for Sir John and Sir Henry and … well with the help of the men-at-arms we carried his Majesty to his bed and sent for his doctors."

Giles took a closer look at the dish of marchpane and his heart sank. He crossed to the window and opened the shutters, revealing the absence of the glass-filled fenestralls behind them. Giles leaned out but it was far too dark to see.

"For heavens sake Sir Giles close the shutters," whined Matthew, "before we all die of the ague."

Closing the shutters slowly Giles struggled to control his rising concern when the sound of footsteps in the corridor preceded the arrival of Bishop Robert Stillington. He was ushered in by a dishevelled squire who had ridden out to Clipberry in all haste to bring him to the royal presence. Bishop Robert appeared apprehensive at the prospect of facing the King and needed to be convinced that the squire had correctly summoned him. Sir Peter tried to reassure him, saying that he had heard the order issued himself and that as soon as the King drew breath between retching and vomiting, Bishop Robert's name was the first he breathed.

Robert sighed, nodded briefly to Matthew and allowed the squire to lead him into the King's bedchamber.

"Perhaps Edward needs to make his peace with your guardian," ventured Luke, "according to Bishop Morton, Bishop Robert has hardly been at court since George Clarence was executed."

"I don't think he has been anywhere since then," replied Giles sadly.

The great oak doors of King Edward's bedchamber swung open and the Marquis of Dorset with Jane Shore on his arm entered the antechamber. Jane was ashen, her wimple all askew and her manner that of a broken doll. She allowed Dorset to seat her on the couch and lift her feet so that she might lie there.

"Women are not allowed in the death chamber," he said softly," dragging his hand around the contours of her breast, "it will not be long before he meets his maker."

Jane was oblivious to his mauling, so he squeezed her flesh until she winced and then satisfied he had her attention, he kissed her brow and returned to Edward's chamber.

Within the hour summonsed priests arrived ominously bearing the Eucharist and shortly after Bishop Morton appeared in the doorway.

"He's gone," he said simply.

Whilst those in the waiting room knelt in prayer, a single bell tolled from the Abbey, awakening Westminster to the sorrowful news. One by one church bells across the capital reiterated the message in every hamlet and village for miles around.

Dorset joined them once again and seeing Jane sobbing helplessly, he appeared to comfort her by holding her close and whispering in her ear but she was inconsolable and clearly offended by his words, she struggled to release herself from his grip.

"My Lord, you should inform Her Majesty at once," said Bishop Morton sternly, hoping his tone implied more than just a reminder of his duty.

Incensed at the reprimand but nervous of challenging the Bishop, Dorset turned on Sir Matthew who was sobbing dramatically in Sir Peter's arms.

"Stop whimpering, you insufferable sodomite and get this place cleared. It looks like a whore's boudoir," he screamed.

He kicked Matthew's thigh as the miserable knight scrambled to his feet, sending him sprawling across the room. Luke and Giles instinctively sprang to his aid. Dorset hawked, spat and then left.

"Dear God," sighed Bishop Morton, "whatever will become of us now?"

He sank onto the couch and covering his cherub like face with two chubby bejewelled hands the weary Bishop sobbed uncontrollably. His was a personal loss, for John Morton mourned the passing of yet another much loved and cherished friend.

This was not the moment for Giles to confide his suspicions regarding Edward's second seizure. He too mourned King Edward, in the last five years he had grown close to him and since the week before Easter, Edward had sort Giles' companionship to the exclusion of those such as William Hastings and Thomas Dorset whom he normally favoured. He shivered as he remembered his assurances to Margery regarding her safety from Dorset. The poor girl's worst nightmare was about to unfold, so taking Mark to one side he instructed him to find Margery and to escort her to Clipberry Manor where she would be out of the reach of the Marquis of Dorset, at least for the time being.

"Matthew, you should go too. Mark's mother will see to your accommodation and when Bishop Robert returns you must convince him of your need for his protection."

Matthew stopped tending his bruised thigh and hustled Peter into collecting a few items from his chamber whilst Mark went in search of Margery.

"We can't hide at Clipberry for ever," whined Sir Matthew, "I still have duties to perform here and Dorset will discover where we are soon enough."

"Dorset will be curtailed immediately the council confirms the appointment of Richard Gloucester as Lord Protector. Is that correct?" asked Giles turning to Morton.

The Bishop wiped his eyes on his sleeve and nodded.

"I have spent most of today with His Majesty drawing up the codicil to his will. Richard Gloucester is named Lord Protector but how did you know Giles?"

"We should also leave now," said Giles to Luke, ignoring Morton's query, "the Mayor and Aldermen of London will soon arrive to view the body as will any lords spiritual and temporal who happen to be in the capital. I trust someone has sent for Archbishop Rotherham, he should be here by now?"

Wearily Bishop Morton got to his feet. If there was one thing his long life had taught him, it was that there was little point in dallying over what could not be changed but still the prospect of a boy king filled him with foreboding. Whatever the new order was to be, he must find a niche for himself in which he could prosper. Dammed pity he was unable to dissuade the King against appointing Gloucester as Lord Protector.

"Get some sleep Giles whilst you can, there are busy days ahead," said Morton with more optimism than he intended.

Sleep was the last thing on Giles' mind, so when he and Luke were clear of the guards and men-at-arms that surrounded the King's chambers, he suggested they should take a walk in the night air. The full moon and clear skies provided ample illumination and the comings and goings of noblemen and city dignitaries, together with the bustle of stablemen tending their horses, made midnight seem more akin to an overcast midday.

"Why are we going this way?" complained Luke, as he followed Giles along the narrow path that ran close to the soaring walls of the palace.

"I'm looking for something that was thrown from the window where Edward and Jane were to eat their supper," replied Giles, staring up at the casements.

"If you tell me what we are looking for … ," began Luke but Giles had already spotted what he was seeking and leaped forward.

"There, on the gravel, look Luke, just there."

"It's a mouse or a vole," cried Luke, "whatever makes you think it was thrown from the chamber above?"

"Not the rodent Luke, the *palm fruit* that it was gnawing before it scurried away. Don't touch it," Giles pulled Luke's hand away from the remains of a sticky, half eaten fruit, "it may be poisonous." Several more lay in the vicinity.

"Poisonous?" repeated Luke, "I doubt it. The creature that

disappeared into the undergrowth hadn't been poisoned."

"If there is nothing wrong with the fruit then why was it thrown from the window?"

"I have no idea Giles. What makes you think it was smothered in poison?"

"Edward was murdered, I'm sure of it," said Giles emphatically."

Luke sank to the ground, slowly sliding his back against the wall as he assimilated words he could not credit.

"You're not making sense Giles."

Giles crouched beside him.

"When Edward was taken ill for the first time last week, his physicians said he had suffered a seizure but both Morton and I believed he had contracted food poisoning, primarily because he was so sick and then, because his bowels were water for days afterwards. Jane Shore had eaten the same meal as the King, except for the palm fruits which she loathes. So I suspected they were the cause of the King's sickness."

"But you did not suspect he had been deliberately poisoned?"

"No, not at the time. There was no telltale discolouration of Edward's lips, otherwise even the physicians would have noticed and anyway he recovered."

"Exactly Giles, he recovered."

"So when he was taken ill tonight for the second time," persisted Giles, ignoring Luke's objection, "I naturally inspected the dish of sweetmeats Sir Peter had served but discovered it contained only marchpane. Now, I know Edward dislikes marchpane. I was present when he refused it most forcefully at the Tower years ago."

"So it wasn't the marchpane that caused his illness."

"Ah, but when I looked more closely at the dish I detected a trail of a sticky substance from the centre of the plate to its edge. As if something had been swept from it."

"Which is why you opened the shutters to see if anything had been thrown out."

"Yes but it was too dark to see. However, the fenestralls behind the shutters had not been replaced, suggesting that after someone had hurriedly cleared the dates from the dish, there had been insufficient time to replace the glass, before closing the shutters."

"Perhaps Sir Peter or Matthew cleared the dates from the dish for fear you might accuse them of serving the King with rotten fruit," suggested Luke, " you did suggest the fruit might have been mouldy when Edward was sick last week."

"That explanation is fine, except that King Edward died this evening."

"But not from eating palm fruit," insisted Luke, "Edward died of successive seizures as his doctors will undoubtedly conclude."

Giles removed his cap and using it as a glove, scooped up the offending fruits. He stared up at the window and then at the sticky mess in his cap. The dates had been scraped from the plate and disposed of through the window, he was certain of that but if he was correct and the fruit had been smeared with poison, why had the mouse survived after gnawing at them? Was he missing something or was Luke correct and the fruit thrown out of the window, not because it was contaminated with poison but because Matthew feared it was the source of Edward's stomach upset for a second time and as he had prepared the dish he disposed of the evidence?

"But Edward died, " he said aloud. "Come on, let us get back before you catch the ague and Bishop Morton holds me responsible."

"That's a waste of a good cap Giles, you can't wear it again," scolded Luke as he clambered to his feet.

Giles grimaced and linking his free arm in Luke's, marched him back to his apartment. Embers were still smouldering in the grate and Luke used his good hand to add wood to encourage the fire to burn, whilst Giles unsheathed his dagger and slit open one of the dates in his ruined hat.

"Look at that," said Giles, triumphantly holding out the cap for Luke to examine the cut fruit.

"What am I supposed to be looking at?"

"The cavity left by the stone is filled with more mashed up date. See!" Giles used the point of his dagger to extract a gooey substance from the centre of the fruit. "I'd wager that has been soaked in poison. Don't you see Luke? the mouse hadn't reached the centre of the date when we disturbed it."

"Or the fruits have been stuffed with morsels of date soaked in some fancy brandy," said Luke, irritation showing in his tone.

"Well we can soon see which one of us is correct," countered Giles angrily and sheathing his dagger he made for the door and the back staircase at the side of the garderobe tower. Luke followed his friend to the bottom of the stairs where a small door led into the tower itself. To Luke's consternation Giles kicked open the door and instinctively both men covered their nose and mouth with their hands. The smell was overpowering and Luke pitied the poor soul whose job it was to keep the sewage tower unblocked and functioning. Meanwhile Giles dropped his cap just inside the opened door and then pulled it shut.

"An underground stream runs along the base of that tower before it joins the river," choked Giles, "that's why the chambers at this side of the Palace are troubled with rats. If I am correct and the dates contain poison then by tomorrow there will be one or two less of the foul creatures."

They returned to Giles' chamber in silence but as Luke poured watered ale from a jug on the sideboard into two cups, he wondered if his impulsive friend had considered how he intended checking that disgusting hole for dead rats tomorrow but he kept his thoughts to himself. Giles set about cleaning his dagger with an old cloth when he suddenly dropped it onto the table as if he had cut himself.

"The murderer is not an accomplished poisoner," he said, staring wide eyed at Luke.

"What?"

"When Mark and I were small, we used to watch old Arthur set rattraps at Clipberry. He used scraps of food smeared with arsenic to lure the creatures into the traps but if he was over generous with the arsenic, when we checked the traps the following day, we found the rats alive, gasping for breath and swamped in vomit. "

"And the point of this unpleasant tale?"

"That the murderer made two attempts to poison the King. The first attempt failed because *he used too much poison* and Edward recovered."

"Giles, what are you saying?"

"Too much poison causes the victim to vomit naturally. Edward vomited violently when he was first taken ill last week. He was strong and healthy and having just eaten, his stomach was full of supper which helped to clear the poison when he was sick."

"If I was intent on poisoning the King of England, I would learn all about the properties of the substance first," said Luke.

"Perhaps the murderer expected just one date to be sufficient to kill Edward but he is greedy for the fruit and could have stuffed two or three into his mouth at once. If he swallowed large chunks rather than chewing carefully, multiple amounts of the fatal dose would enter his stomach, causing him to vomit immediately."

"Perhaps."

"And his doctors would automatically prescribe a physic to flush any bile from his system. Any remaining poison would be ejected, leaving him weak but able to recover. However, this evening, the much weakened King was given a second dose of poison on an empty stomach and death came quickly."

"It takes a very composed individual to attempt the same murder a second time," said Luke with a shiver.

"Not necessarily, officially the King suffered a huge seizure after the first attempt, a second, similar seizure was to be expected sooner or later. The method of poisoning had to be the same to ensure that only Edward died and the murder went undetected."

Giles joined Luke at the sideboard where he was re-filling their cups. Both men were sombre, neither wished to consider the names of suspects. Giles was the first to break the silence.

"Who would do such a thing? Who would benefit? Edward's heir is barley twelve and the prospect of a boy King is historically catastrophic."

"Quite," agreed Luke, "but *if* you are correct and we find a dead rat on your cap tomorrow, we will be forced to report the matter."

"But to whom Luke? The murderer has to be someone close to the King. Someone who knows his culinary likes and dislikes and those of his mistress, Jane Shore and that means someone close enough to share his table."

"Dear God, it doesn't bear thinking about."

"Anyone could access the palm fruits before they were served.

There is an entrance from the rear of the serving lobby and although Sir Matthew keeps the key, I suspect it is left open most of the time but we can check," said Giles, "however, I think we can rule out kitchen staff and the like. No one would dare hire a servant to poison the King for fear that they would tell His Majesty."

"You're right. Any servant would anticipate a reward in excess of the hirer's price for exposing such a plot. If you want the King murdered, the only safe way is to perform the task yourself."

With an unsteady hand, Luke downed his ale.

"Giles, *if Edward was murdered,* the one thing we do know is that the murderer was present prior to our arrival at the King's chambers tonight. He had to be, for who else would need to dispose of the remaining palm fruits in such a hurry?"

"You're right Luke."

Giles disappeared into his office, returning with parchment and writing materials.

"We must make a list whilst it's still fresh in our minds. Now who was in the King's chambers when we arrived tonight?"

"Sir Matthew, Sir Peter, Sir Henry, Sir John," reeled off Luke.

"Mistress Shore, Bishop Morton, Lord Hastings, the Marquis of Dorset," added Giles slowly, as he had the task of writing the names.

He moved the lamp so that he could see more clearly and underscored Dorset's name. How convenient it would be to discover that the Marquis had murdered King Edward, thought Giles vindictively, but it didn't make sense. With Edward gone Dorset and his Woodville kin were powerless. Giles even considered a personal motive for Dorset's guilt, such as his lascivious greed for Jane Shore but the more he tried to implicate the Marquis the more it became apparent that without the King's sponsorship, Dorset, like the Queen and Earl Rivers, was exceedingly vulnerable. Even the young King, Edward V, would be removed from their influence as soon as Gloucester arrived in a day or so. Mentally, Giles struck Thomas, Marquis of Dorset from his list of suspects and snapped out of his ruminations to find Luke staring into space with a look of horror transfixed on his ghostly face.

"Are you ill Luke? What is it?"

With difficulty Luke swallowed and coughed by way of communication. Giles poured him some more ale and held the cup to his dry and quivering lips.

"Come and sit by the fire and warm yourself," soothed Giles, "You've not slept tonight and all this talk of murder has been a shock to your humours. You shall sleep in my bed tonight and I warrant you will feel much recovered by first light."

Luke pushed away the cup Giles was holding to his mouth.

"I'm well enough," he said, coughing again to clear his dry throat. "There is something I must tell you: something that may have a serious bearing on events *if King Edward was murdered.*"

Instantly Giles was still, waiting for Luke to explain further.

"You know that Bishop Morton rescued me from certain death after the battle of Tewkesbury in 1471?" began Luke.

Giles nodded impatiently whilst Luke rummaged in his script and found the jewelled brooch depicting the Prince of Wales' Feathers. He handed to his friend.

"It is beautiful Luke," said an amazed Giles, "and worth a fortune."

"When Morton found me he was mourning for the Prince of Lancaster."

"Margaret's son, the Lancastrian Prince of Wales?"

"Yes. Morton had been stationed at the Abbey to provide the boy with an escape route should he need to flee the field and because I had this jewel in my closed fist he believed that I had been dispatched by the Prince to find help. Morton took me back to the Abbey in the hope that warmth and good wine would revive my memory."

"But it didn't."

Luke shook his head.

"And all this has some bearing on tonight's events?" asked an incredulous Giles.

"I fear it has. After the battle we left Tewkesbury Abbey disguised as monks and made our way to Chepstow to rendezvous with Jasper Tudor in the hope that he would arrange our passage to France. But when Morton came face to face with Jasper's weasel of a nephew Henry, he dropped to his knees and addressed him as,

My Sovereign Lord."

"He did what?"

"I was struggling with total memory loss at the time and stood my ground but Morton's spontaneity obviously pleased the Tudor lad, because he promised Morton that he would make him Archbishop of Canterbury once he was England's king."

"That was twelve years ago Luke. At the time Morton supported Queen Margaret and the Prince of Lancaster. His death and the defeat of Margaret's armies left Morton leaderless and with an urgent need to escape the Yorkist rout. Encouraging Tudor's aspirations was nothing more than expediency."

"Well it didn't win us a passage to France. Henry Tudor may look like a sickly weasel but his brain is razor sharp and a fine match for John Morton. He sent his newly 'loyal subjects' to Brecknock Castle in Wales with letters for his mother, the Countess of Richmond."

"This is all very interesting but I don't see what bearing it has on Edward's murder."

"We spent several days at Brecknock Castle as the guest of young Henry Stafford and his aunt the Countess of Richmond. You know Stafford as the Duke of Buckingham. Brecknock is his family home and where he spent most of his time after the death of his father."

"Oh come on Luke get to the point of all this."

"The night before we left, the four of us met in the Stafford's solar but it was Morton who took charge of the meeting. I was there in body but in no fit mental state to partake, other than to agree to support Morton in his endeavour. He addressed the three of us very formally, saying that if we intended to secure the throne for Henry Tudor then we must undertake long term strategies, as the Yorkists were well entrenched for the foreseeable future."

Giles sat bolt upright in his chair. Now he could see where Luke was leading.

"Morton told Buckingham that he must stop sulking about his enforced marriage to Catherine Woodville and make himself useful at court. He was to get close to the King and seek out his weaknesses for future exploitation. He suggested that the Countess should marry a Yorkist Lord as soon as possible for fear that King Edward might confiscate her lands and fortune. She was to come to an arrangement with her new husband, insomuch as he would receive all her estates, provided she was permitted to retain her own considerable fortune, as this would be needed later to fund her son's bid for the crown."

"Holy Mary, Mother of God. Who did she wed?"

Luke swallowed hard and bit his lip. "Within two weeks of our leaving Brecknock the Countess of Richmond married Lord Thomas Stanley."

Giles sprang from his chair, knocking the table and shaking ale out of the cups.

"Lady Stanley is *Henry Tudor's mother?*" cried Giles, "did King Edward know?"

"Yes, of course he did, as he knew of Morton's devotion to Queen Margaret and Buckingham's objection to being married to Catherine Woodville. What he didn't know was that all three were party to a long term plan to dethrone him."

"And what did Morton promise to contribute to this long term plan?"

"He undertook to throw himself on Edward's mercy and use this considerable administrative skills to gain knowledge of the King's Chancery," said Luke flatly, "and if you are correct and Edward has been murdered then I think they may have made their first move towards installing Henry Tudor as King of England."

"I don't believe it." said Giles quietly, "I mean, I don't believe Morton poisoned the King. He love him like a brother, I know he did." Giles wiped a tear from his eye, he found it inconceivable that his mentor and friend, Bishop Morton, could have murdered King Edward. "I can accept that twelve years ago a desperately unhappy and desolate Morton plotted his revenge on the Yorkist King, the man who had destroyed his beloved Margaret and killed her son," conceded Giles, "I can even believe that twelve years ago he infiltrated the abhorrent regime that was the source of his despair with the *intention* of destroying it. But I refuse to accept that he has managed to hide his hate behind a show of devotion and service all these years."

"Put like that Giles, I am inclined to agree," said Luke. "Once Morton sensed a successful career in Edward's service he would have no further use for revenge and truthfully, he has never mentioned the conspirators in connection with their plotting, from that day to this, which is why I had forgotten about it."

They sat in silence for awhile staring at the spilt ale that was spreading slowly across the table.

"Surely Buckingham will have come to terms with his enforced marriage to Catherine Woodville now they have children," ventured Giles.

"Maybe but Lady Stanley won't have 'come to terms' with her role, will she? She gave up her independence and her estates to buy a position at the Yorkist court. My God Giles, Lady Stanley could easily have found an opportunity to smear the fruits with poison."

"But she wasn't there to throw the residue out of the window."

"No, but Morton was. You sent Mark to the Abbey to find him last night but he was already there when we arrived. Think about it Giles, Morton would see the palm fruits on the plate, recall his conversation with you about their being the source of Edward's food poisoning last week, consider the coincidence of a second batch of rotten fruit and then, consider the possibility that Lady Stanley had deliberately contaminated them. Realising the danger she was placing him in, he cleared the offending fruit out of the window."

"No Luke no, Morton did not dispose of the dates because he suspected Lady Stanley of contaminating them. If he saw the dates he may well have considered the coincidence of a second batch of rotten fruit but that would be the limit of his wondering because King Edward was still alive when he arrived and as far as Morton knew, suffering from nothing more than another bout of food upset. If the dates had been on the plate when I arrived, I would not have considered poison, so why should Morton?"

"Well who else is there? Lord Hastings is, I mean was, Edward's oldest friend. What possible motive could he have for killing his King and Jane certainly didn't. As for the knights, well one or the other may have harboured some grievance I suppose. We will have to look into the possibility but I doubt we'll find a motive for murder. Which leaves the Marquis of Dorset."

"But Dorset is a Woodville and who are they without Edward's patronage?" sighed Giles, "but my uncle Gloucester is above suspicion and when he arrives from Yorkshire in the next day or so I will confide in him."

"Until then we can observe those who were in the supper room and note any unusual behaviour," suggested Luke.

"Unusual behaviour," repeated Giles, "what about the activities of Dorset and Grey in the Treasury last week. And Hatton's death. The inquest was rigged for certain. Could Edward's murder be linked to those events?"

"Maybe," said Luke thoughtfully, "they have one thing in common, both Douglas Hatton and King Edward have died without anyone suspecting foul play."

"Other than me," corrected Giles, "*and* the Marquis of Dorset was at both scenes. But there is no reason for Dorset to murder the King," wailed Giles.

Luke got to his feet and opened the shuttered windows. Dawn was breaking and below in the court yard churchmen were preparing a bier on which to move the King's body to St. Stephen's Chapel.

"Giles, if Morton is involved I shall stand by him."

"You can't mean it?"

"I'm sorry Giles. I owe him my life. Not just for my rescue at Tewkesbury but also for the twelve years he has supported me since. Morton believes that I am at least a Lancastrian knight, perhaps a Lord of Lancaster. He alone has faith in my identity and sustains my hope. If he needs me now or later, I will be there for him, no matter what the implications."

Chapter 18

St Stephen's Chapel Westminster 10th April 1483

Eventually, Luke fell asleep on Mark's bed but Giles was unable even to doze, for the thought that John Morton might be involved in the death of King Edward confused his loyalties beyond toleration. Morton's mentoring and support had sustained Giles after Bishop Robert had abandoned him but if he were implicated in Edward's murder, then Giles would be forced to denounce him and as that would affect his friendship with Luke, he fervently prayed that his friend's suspicions were unfounded.

Unable to contain his anxiety any longer, he rose from his chair and grabbing his cleaned dagger, rushed down the backstairs to the service door of the garderobe tower and kicked it open. He drew his dagger from its sheath and with one hand over his nose, used the weapon to fumble inside the stinking tunnel for his cap. It had only been a few hours since he had so confidently left it there but now he prayed that the morsels of dates were gone and that there would be no sign of a dead rat. Now, he was desperate to be proved wrong, for Edward not to have been murdered, Morton to be guiltless and his friendship with Luke unthreatened. Almost immediately his blade stabbed into something soft that twisted forcefully on its entry, causing Giles to drop the dagger in fright but not before withdrawing his arm fractionally. There in the doorway, was his cap covered in vomit, with an enormous black rat, feet in the air, impaled on his blade. Retching at the sight, Giles pulled his dagger free and kicked the cap and its gruesome load deep into the sewage chamber. Hurriedly he closed the door and with his heart bursting with panic, raced out into the courtyard and into the fresh morning air. Self pity filled his heart as he stamped about the yard in angry despair. Why must he be alone? What had he done to loose his mother and father, Bishop Robert, George Clarence, King Edward and now in all probability, John Morton *and* Luke?

Through tear filled eyes he could make out the flickering candles that lit the windows of St. Stephen's Chapel and determined to confront his maker with the unfairness of his solitude, he crossed the courtyard to the west door, which slightly ajar, enabled him to slide through without disturbing the peace within. Before the alter, monks from the Abbey were preparing the King's body for public viewing; tradition dictating that the royal corpse should be laid bare for men to view and be assured that death had been natural. Unnatural death does not necessarily involve a visible wound, thought Giles ruefully as he watched the monks remove Edward's shift and eager to see if the poison had left any discolouration around the King's mouth he drew nearer the corpse, genuflecting towards the alter as he reached the head of the bier. Several incense burners puffed their sweet odour into the surrounding air and Giles retched, more at the thought of the putrescence they were preparing to disguise, than at the excess of cloying sweetness that filled his nostrils. King Edward had been in excess of six feet tall and although in his later years he had gained some weight, his corpse was still an awesome sight. The solid white mass looked more like an oversized marble effigy than a corpse, the artist having generously defined the arms and legs with huge muscles and the neck with strength to support the burden of Atlas. Attendant monks laboured like worker ants, cleaning and dressing the sculptured block but they moved silently aside as Giles leaned over the head to examine the mouth. It had been cleaned and prepared for display like every other chiselled feature and although Giles bent so close to the lips he could have kissed them, he could detect nothing that might confirm his diagnosis.

Something rustled in the darkness beyond the pool of candle light containing the body and Giles stepped outside its halo to see what had moved in the shadows. Knelt on the cold stones with his head in his hands and with the trace of tears still running between his fingers was William, Lord Hastings. To his right, kneeling more comfortably on a prie-dieu, was Bishop Morton who was still shuffling to ease the cramp in his legs when Giles touched his shoulder. Morton turned his tear reddened eyes and sore face towards Giles.

"What hour is it?" he sighed, "we accompanied the body from the death chamber and have been here since."

"Not yet noon," replied Giles softly.

The sorry sight of the rotund Bishop struggling to his feet and toppling as he tried to stand on a lifeless leg, convinced Giles that Morton truly mourned Edward's passing. Hastings sat back on his heels and wiped his wet nose across the back of his sleeve.

"I can't believe he has gone," he wailed in broken tones, "we fought so many battles together, often against the odds and he just ups and dies of nothing."

The chapel door swung open and a cold draught of air heralded the entrance of the Marquis of Dorset. He genuflected briefly towards the alter and then stode purposefully towards the three men in the shadows.

"My Lords, there will be a full meeting of the Council tomorrow at noon in the Queen's council chamber," he announced, "the wheels of government must not be allowed to grind to a halt whilst we bury one King and crown the next."

"We should wait till Gloucester gets here," snapped back Hastings but Dorset ignored the remark, turned on his heels and retraced his steps, oblivious of the rude gesture Hasting was making at his retreating figure.

"I doubt that Edward's reconciliation plans will hold. What do you think Giles?" said Morton, offering Hastings a hand up from his kneeling position.

"They had better," snarled Hastings, "if the rest of us support Gloucester's Protectorship that popinjay and his Woodville family will have no choice but to follow suit. God I need a drink. Well Sir Giles, did I hear you offer this old soldier a glass of your best Claret with which to drown his sorrows?"

"Of course Lord William, I should be honoured. Your Grace, will you join us?"

Morton declined and waited until they had left the chapel before summonsing a lay brother to convey a message for him to Lady Stanley.

"Make sure she is alone before delivering my message," insisted Morton, "invite her ladyship to join me at Holborn for supper tonight and if she appears undecided as to whether to accept, tell her that Bishop Morton says, the time has come."

When Luke awoke some hours later he discovered Giles and Hastings deep in their cups. Unable to join them, as too much wine invariably induced one of his attacks, Luke bid them farewell and made his way back to Holborn, arriving just in time for supper. He rode his mare into the bailey and hailing the gatekeeper as he entered, they briefly exchanged wagers on the prospect of a down pour before morning but when he reached the stables Luke's heart missed a beat, for there was Lady Stanley's carriage, pulled under cover in case of rain. A groom hurried to help his one-armed master dismount and relieve him of his mare when a second rider galloped into the bailey.

"What the hell is going on Luke?" roared Henry, Duke of Buckingham as he reined in his magnificent black stallion and swung from the saddle with the style and flourish of a man confident of his authority. He didn't wait for an answer but summonsed the groom, still busy with Luke's horse to, 'move his fat arse and attend to his stallion.' He didn't even pause to see that the lad came as ordered but mounted the steps to the great hall two at a time and then rapped impatiently on the oak door with the hilt on his dagger. Luke picked up the dropped reins of his own horse and led her into a stall, followed closely by the groom struggling to calm the nervous sweating beast abandoned by the Duke. The groom grinned at Luke, expecting him to comment on the arrogance of Morton's supper guest but the arrival of Buckingham had thrown Luke into a state of panic and uncharacteristically he snapped at the surprised groom.

"That lad, was the Duke of Buckingham, so you had best ensure his stallion is well tended whilst in your care, otherwise you will answer to me, after his lordship has kicked your arse."

A second groom, who had wandered off to the kitchens in search of food, appeared in the doorway to see what all the noise was about and surprised by the activity he dropped the chicken leg he was gnawing and bolted across to the stable block to resume his duties. He took the brush from Luke's good hand and red faced, begged to take over the task he was hired to perform.

Luke climbed the steps to the great hall deep in thought. There could be only one reason Morton had invited Buckingham and Lady Stanley to supper so soon after Edward's death but praying that by some miracle he would be proved wrong, Luke entered the hall and joined the Bishop's guests.

The meal was a formal affair at which neither guests nor host discussed the reason for the hurried summons but when they later retired to Morton's solar and the servants had been dismissed the excitement was almost tangible. Lady Stanley was accompanied by her husband Lord Thomas, who was some years her junior and who she called to heel by rapping her knuckles on the edge of her stool whenever he moved a yard or two from her side. He was an unkempt individual with a few wisps of thin white hair that formed a collar around a head as smooth and pointed as the sharp end of a hen's egg. Stanley's eyes were two black spots that crowded his beak of a nose and his mouth was as tight and cruel as his wife's. His agitation manifested itself in his constant rubbing and rolling of his hands as if he were washing them; a mannerism Luke associated with miserly avarice. The pair were attended by a knight called Reginald Bray, who fussed constantly over his mistress, finding a pillow to support her back and placing her feet on a low stool to avoid any possible draughts. Bray was short in stature and of indeterminate age and he obviously irritated Lord Thomas, who frequently swatted at him with the back of his hand in an attempt to rid him from his personal space. Buckingham flounced about the solar flicking imaginary specks of dust from his expensive doublet and referring to Lady Stanley as, ' my lady aunt Margot' which seemed to annoy the lady as she tightened her lips and narrowed her eyes each time he addressed her by the title. For all his confidence, Buckingham was not a handsome man. Luke thought he had the face of a 'court fool,' round with popping eyes and a crooked mouth that he opened so wide when he started to speak, that it was possible to see the tonsils at the back of his throat. Luke thought he had perhaps developed his flamboyant antics to disguise his ridiculous appearance, for he was certainly the most arrogant individual he had ever encountered.

Morton began by addressing the meeting formally and specifically welcoming Lord Stanley and Sir Reginald Bray. He explained that Lady Stanley had already taken the two into her confidence regarding the purpose of the group but never-the-less, he retold the story of his escape from the field at Tewkesbury, the subsequent meeting with the Tudors at Chepstow and the conspiracy spawned at Brecknock. Lord Stanley gasped with outrage when Morton told how he had advised his lady to find a husband who would gain her entrance to the Yorkist court but she grabbed his wrist and bade him be silent as if he were an errant child.

"The question is, are we all still of the same mind?" said Morton deliberately, "I have to admit, that over the last twelve years I grew to love King Edward and I have served him faithfully to the best of my ability."

"Hardly the loyalty Lancaster expected of you Bishop," snapped Lady Stanley.

Morton ignored the reprimand and continued patiently.

"But with his untimely death, I find myself once again attracted to the prospect of a Lancastrian sovereign." He turned to Buckingham. "My Lord, are your wounds salved now or do you still seek retribution for past wrongs?"

"Oh believe me Bishop, the pleasure I experience from inflicting pain on a Woodville will never be surpassed and my desire for that delightful sensation never sated."

"My Lord Stanley?"

Stanley wrested his arm from his wife's grip. This was serious business and he would speak for himself. He rubbed his nose hard with his freed hand as if to engage his brain in independent mode, at the same time moving out of his Lady's reach.

"I care nothing for the honour of York nor for that matter for the honour of Lancaster," he trumpeted, glaring at his wife defiantly, "my interests lie in the prosperity of the Stanleys, more specifically, the Thomas Stanleys. And in that context, if my stepson can be crowned without fuss and too much bloodshed, then he has my blessing."

Lady Stanley sniffed as if a foul odour had drifted under her nostrils and Bray coughed discreetly. It was to be expected that a monarch's stepfather would receive certain privileges but Lord Thomas was embarrassingly blunt.

"Well John, perhaps you would care to explain your own reasons for resurrecting our twelve year old pledge," ask Lady Stanley coldly, "apart from my son's promise of Canterbury of course."

Reginald Bray smiled knowingly and Luke and Morton exchanged glances. Bray must be carrying messages between Tudor and his mother, even now. Morton chose his words carefully.

"The King's death will inevitably result in a struggle to control the young Prince of Wales. The Woodvilles on one side and the established nobility, led by Richard Gloucester on the other. There is no place for me in either camp. Gloucester is so narrow minded he will consider my past alliance with Lancaster reason enough to exclude me and...."

"Ah, a man of perception then?" quipped Buckingham.

"No my lord, a man without imagination. And as for supporting the Woodvilles, well that is a pointless exercise as I am sure my Lord Stanley will confirm."

"Very true," agreed Lord Thomas, "they will keep everything in the family. Only Woodvilles will prosper under a Woodville regime."

"Not least because there are so many of them. They breed like vermin," spat Buckingham, apparently unconcerned that his own wife was the Queen's sister.

"So for me, Henry Tudor is a natural choice," persisted Morton, smiling graciously at Lady Stanley, "and the See of Canterbury, just the incentive I need to ensure the success of our venture."

"And what have you to say Sir Luke, Lord Luke or whoever you claim to be? Are you ready to support our Welsh cousin?" asked Buckingham, flashing his tonsils in Luke's direction.

Luke turned in his chair so that he might observe the reactions of Lady Stanley and Bishop Morton to the words he had been preparing since the beginning of the meeting.

"I will protect the Bishop's plans with my life, providing no-one here has murdered King Edward to further the cause of Henry Tudor."

"You think the King was murdered?" gasped Lady Stanley.

"No," lied Luke, "but you must agree that his death at this time is most fortuitous."

"Meaning?"

"Well, Edward's heir has not yet reached his majority and his mother the Queen, could reasonably expect to be Regent. Yet Edward has willed Gloucester the Protectorship, in order to curb her power." Luke scanned the stunned faces of his audience. "I have no reason to think him murdered, but for him to die at this precise time, suggests a powerful motive."

"How do you mean?" snapped Lord Thomas

"Because with carefully managed encouragement, the Woodvilles and those supporting the Lord Protector could be goaded into tearing each other apart, leaving the way clear for Henry Tudor to pick up the pieces."

"Now that is creative," mocked Buckingham, "how about it my lady aunt Margot, did you slip something nasty into King Edward's loving cup?"

"No I did not but I would like to express my gratitude to anyone who did." She cast her hooded eyes around the meeting trying to identify a possible murderer. "As Luke has so eloquently pointed out, there could not be a better time for our plans to be activated."

"Well I do not echo your gratitude my Lady," said Morton, still reeling from Luke's proviso, "is it possible that one of us murdered Edward?"

"Don't be ridiculous Bishop," sneered the Duke, "neither you nor I would warrant it worth the risk and my lady aunt Margot had not perceived the timely advantage until now. Luke on the other hand clearly recognised the coincidence but that is all it is, a very convenient coincidence. Seriously now, is there anything else to suggest foul play?" Buckingham's challenge was met with blank looks. "You have a nasty suspicious mind Luke, I salute you," concluded Buckingham with a supercilious bow.

Luke felt uncomfortable but he was as convinced as he could be without conclusive proof, that those present in Morton's solar were not responsible for Edward's death but were only taking advantage of it.

"Very well, then let us proceed," said Morton, casting a scathing glance at his protégé. "As Luke so aptly pointed out, our task is to encourage as much conflict between the Woodvilles and Gloucester as possible. We must spilt up and take sides. By gaining their trust we should be able to incite sufficient hatred to goad them into destroying each other politically and with luck, physically as well. Then, when they are at their lowest ebb we will invite Henry Tudor to resolve the conflict, blaming the situation on the inherent weaknesses of a realm headed by a boy King."

A thin smile played on Lady Stanley's lips and Lord Thomas shuffled in his seat. Buckingham nodded approvingly, whilst Bray actually clapped his hands. Only Luke felt unhappy, he knew his friendship with Giles must end but worst than that, he found himself disapproving of Morton's plan.

The Bishop had an assignment prepared for each of his guests. Lady Stanley was to continue in the Queen's service, supporting any adverse comments she should voice about Gloucester and his followers and if she had not already done so, to send financial aid to her son in France. Lord Stanley was to develop further his association with Will Hastings, making it clear that he supported Gloucester as this would cover Lady Stanley's activities because it would be assumed that Stanley and his wife were of one mind. Morton himself, would try and befriend the Marquis of Dorset and guide the council whilst the Duke of Buckingham was assigned to the Duke of Gloucester and Reginald Bray was the go between Henry Tudor and his mother. Luke was to keep Giles Butler's nose out of their affairs.

"Although our task is to encourage hatred and conflict, the

difficulty will be ensuring that neither protagonist is actually successful," warned Morton, " remember, victory is reserved for Lancaster alone and therefore we must all stay in touch and keep each other informed, discreetly of course."

Luke promised himself one more visit to Westminster to speak to Giles honestly but thereafter he would be Bishop Morton's spy.

CHAPTER 19

Westminster 15th April 1483

It was five days before Luke summonsed enough courage to face Giles. He knew that by exonerating Lady Stanley and Bishop Morton from involvement in Edward's murder, Giles would assume that his fear of a revival of the Brecknock conspiracy was also unfounded. Resigned to being deceitful but taking some comfort from having already explained to Giles that he would support Morton because he owed him his life, Luke accompanied the Bishop to Westminster on the morning of April 15th. Morton had hired a barge to take them to the Palace and they were amazed at the many wherries, barges and other small craft all making for the same destination. King Edward's death had attracted large crowds to the chapel of St. Stephen and as Morton remarked, those who could afford to do so seemed to have travelled on the river. Not only did they have to queue to disembark at the King's Steps, they were also jostled by loyal citizens who thought they were queue jumping as they made their way along the pathway leading to the Palace yard. Men-at-arms were desperately trying to control the crowd streaming up the path from the quay as it merged with the crowd pouring in through the main gate but to no avail as a bottleneck was being created at the chapel door by churchmen insisting on single file through the Chapel. As many stopped to light a candle and say a prayer for King Edward's soul, the courtyard was fast becoming jammed with impatient mourners. A couple of hawkers, a relic seller and a pie man were taking advantage of the crowds to making a few pence and moving slowly, Morton caught sight of a cut purse plying his trade. The Bishop extended his foot and the slippery thief tripped, sprawling full length on the ground whilst his victim, realising his script was no longer hanging on his belt, and spotting his purse lying in the mud alongside the man on the ground, shouted 'thief, cut purse'. Luke and Morton did not stop to witness what happened next but they could hear the screams of the grounded wretch, as several bored mourners set about kicking him mercilessly.

When they eventually entered the great hall, Morton told Luke he would join him later in Giles' apartments, he had an emergency meeting with some of the councillors.

"Dorset, Grey, Hastings and Stanley, I think," said the Bishop, "something to do with French pirates in the channel." He shook his head in exasperation. "Why it takes five of us to authorise Edward Woodville to set sail after them, I fail to understand."

Giles' door was open and Luke detected an unpleasant smell emanating from within. He stood for a moment in the doorway watching Giles, who with his back towards him, was angrily throwing items of clothing into a pair of panniers on the bed and grumbling furiously to himself.

"Giles?"

At the sound of his name he spun round and glared at Luke.

"What do you want?" he said rudely and returned to his packing.

The pulsating vein on Giles' forehead should have warned Luke of his raging temper but he was curious to know why he was preparing to leave.

"What's all this?" he asked, pointing to the panniers, "and why are you so angry?"

Giles slapped the leather flap over one of the bags and pursed his lips in a vain attempted to control the abuse bursting to be released.

"It has been nearly a week now since Edward died and not one of those bastard Woodvilles has had the grace to inform the Duke of Gloucester," spat out Giles with such venom that Luke took a step back.

"Are you certain?"

"Mother of God Luke, of course I'm certain. Lord Hastings has been drowning his sorrow in my claret for the last four days and nights but this morning he cleared off to enquire about the arrival of the Lord Protector, only to return within the hour to say that, as yet, no message has been sent to Yorkshire."

"That's appalling Giles. Where is Lord Hastings now?"

"God only knows. He is supposed to be writing a letter for me to take to Middleham, informing Gloucester of Edward's death and explaining that the Duke is now Lord Protector but whether he will manage it before I set off at midday isn't worth a wager. The man's a toper Luke. Twice in the past three days, he has spilt his guts in my hearth and he breaks wind like an elephant. For pity's sake, remove the fenestralls from the window and let some air in. It's as stale as a taproom in here."

It was much worse but Luke held his tongue and removed the glazed panels from two of the windows.

"I'll come with you if you want," offered Luke.

Giles sighed and sat down heavily on the bed. His friend's generosity chastised his temper. He knew how difficult a journey it would be for Luke and he had just been inexcusably rude to him. Damn his temper.

"Thank you Luke but no. I must ride hard, possibly through the night. Mark will come with me and Hastings is arranging an armed escort and letters so that we can have fresh horses at Northampton and York should we need them. Please excuse my poor manners, I'm truly sorry."

Woof stuck his head out from under the table where he had taken refuge. The tone of Giles' voice had reverted to normal and he thought it might be safe now to welcome Luke. The rest of his shaggy body soon followed his head and he pushed his wet nose under Luke's good hand. Luke grinned and patted the dog's head.

"Sir Giles has certainly inherited the Plantagenet temper Woof but he will soon be on the receiving end when he informs his uncle Gloucester of the king's death and the small matter of their forgetting to let him know about it."

"That will be nothing, compared to telling his grace that Edward was murdered," groaned Giles.

"You will tell him that?" asked a startled Luke, "there were dead rats in the garderobe then?"

"I'm afraid there were. There can be no doubt that Edward was poisoned but don't worry, I'll not suggest that you think Morton may have a motive for the murder."

"I-I don't any more," stammered Luke, "in fact I am certain that neither Bishop Morton nor Lady Stanley had anything to do with his death."

Woof padded over to Giles and sat squarely in front of him with his head on one side.

"He wants to know if it's safe to approach you," said Luke, trying to divert the conversation from Morton. He hated deliberately misleading his friend.

"Sorry old thing," apologised Giles, rubbing Woof's shaggy coat, "could you take Woof to Holborn whilst Mark and I are in Yorkshire? Mind, Bishop Morton must understand that he's only on loan"

Both men laughed and Woof made the most of their better mood, running from one to the other, bounding round their feet in genuine pleasure.

"Whilst I'm away, could you ask Bishop Morton to look into something for me?"

"What is it?"

"Some time ago I had business with his nephew, Robby Morton. In passing, he informed me that Lord River's agent Andrew Dymmock, had illegally secured copies of a couple of documents in his keeping. I enquired about the nature of the documents at the time but Robby was not forthcoming. I need Morton to acquire that information on my behalf."

"Very well, but he should be here before you leave. He and other councillors are in the chancery authorising Edward Woodville to take ships into the channel in pursuit of French pirates.

Has the information you need some bearing on Edward's death?"

"French pirates?" mused Giles before answering his friend, "er no. Well it may have."

Luke and Woof watched patiently whilst Giles finished his packing. Giles felt sorry for Luke and guilty about refusing his company to Yorkshire but his lifeless arm hampered his riding and his general ill health would slow them down.

"Whilst I'm away, you could make some enquiries about our remaining suspects," said Giles by way of compensation. "Somebody murdered King Edward. You have just eliminated Bishop Morton and Lady Stanley and we eliminated Dorset and Jane Shore earlier because they both will struggle without Edward's support. So, we need to examine who else was in the King's supper room between the palm fruits being served and our arrival?"

"The knights of the body!"

"Exactly and if one of them is responsible for applying the poison to the palm fruits, he is unlikely to be acting on his own initiative, which means manipulation by a third party. So be very careful what you say."

Mark arrived looking sheepish but excited. He had been to Clipberry Manor, ostensively to tell Mary that he would be in Yorkshire for the next few days. Unknown to Giles, Mark had been visiting Clipberry on some pretext or other every day since he had delivered Margery into his mother's care and had become smitten by the lady's indubitable charm.

"You'll never believe it Giles, Bishop Robert is visiting his See of Bath and Wells. He left Clipberry two days ago," announced Mark.

"Your right, I don't believe it. He has never once visited the cathedral since his investiture. Why should he go there now?"

"His pupil, John Alcock doesn't believe it either. He was furious when mother told him Bishop Robert had left and apparently he turned the manor upside down looking for evidence of where he might have gone."

Giles pondered Robert Stillington's absence from Clipberry, whilst Luke fussed over Woof and Mark considered what he might need for his first trip beyond Westminster.

"How is Lady Margery faring away from the luxury of the court?" asked Luke innocently, "I may reacquaint myself with the hussy while you are gone. To think I once contemplated marrying the whore."

"Oh she is fine," sang Mark, beaming inanely into space.

Both Luke and Giles gaped at the love struck man before them. Even though Mark was more of a brother than a squire to Giles, it had never occurred to him that Mark would aspire to a courtesan such as Margery.

"In your dreams," laughed Luke, as he regained his composure "you could never afford her."

"Who said anything about paying her?" crowed Mark.

He made the longbow man's sign of contempt and Luke responded with an equally rude gesture but then slapped Mark on the back and congratulated him on his achievement. After all she must have fancied him not to charge for her services. There followed an exchange of chauvinistic claims and wagers during which Mark's sexual prowess underwent a transformation. Giles watched in horror as they horsed around: it had never occurred to him that Margery favoured others by not charging. He had always assumed he was in someway special to her and that she had favoured Mark in the same way hurt him deeply. With the vein on his temple beginning to pulsate once again he bawled at Mark to take the panniers down to the stables whilst he found Hastings and the letter he was to deliver to his uncle and Lord Protector of England.

It was dusk when Giles and Mark reined in their horses before Micklegate Bar, the impressive gateway to the city of York that welcomed travellers from the south.

"The Duke of York and his son Edmund had their heads displayed on those spikes after the battle of Wakefield," said Mark, pointing to the rods of iron protruding from the crenulated towers set either side of the central gatehouse.

A ghastly shrivelled head of some poor wretch more recently impaled, stared ghoulishly into the distance from its elevated post and Giles shivered.

"Wakefield? Your father died at the battle of Wakefield, didn't he?" he asked.

Mark nodded. Both he and Giles had grown up with Mary's gruesome stories about the cruelty of the Lancastrian Queen Margaret and her henchman Lord Clifford. Mark's father had died that winter's day fighting for York and the day after the battle, Mary had discovered his body hacked to pieces in a ditch. Along with other battle-widows she had journeying to London, walking most of the way and carrying her three year old son Mark, eventually finding employment in Bishop Robert's household, although he was only a common priest at the time.

"I suppose Prince Edmund was your uncle too," mused Mark, "he was seventeen when Lord Clifford cut of his head after the battle."

They walked their horses through the gateway and down the hill towards the bridge that straddled the River Ouse. The working day was over and the narrow streets and alleyways were full of filth and rubbish in which beggars and urchins rummaged for scraps of food and discarded clothing. By the time they reached Ouse bridge the dirt carts were out in force, pushed by harden men in long leather aprons and bands of dirty cloth wound round their brows. Relentlessly they rammed their wooden boards under the heaps of rubbish, releasing not only the stench of rotting filth but also rats that had ventured from under the bridge in search of tasty morsels. Most retreated back into the murky water but others nipped into the open doorways of shops and dwellings that clustered along the river's bank, lurching precariously towards the fast flowing Ouse. Giles haled a Beagle making his way towards the castle and asked directions to the Benedictine Abbey of St. Mary's. The Beagle raised his staff and pointed towards the towering edifice of the Minster that reached high above the crooked roofs and spires.

"You need the northern gate at Bootham, sir. St. Mary's is just west of the Minster but beyond the city walls."

Giles thanked him and using the tower of the cathedral church as a guide, they crossed the city and found the Benedictine Abbey on the far side of Bootham Bar as the Beagle had said. It was an ideal resting place for the night, for the Abbey was virtually on the road north to Middleham and they could start out early in the morning, leaving before the city gates were opened if necessary. As they waited for the brother hosteller to allocate them beds in the guesthouse, Giles warned Mark not to mention the nature of their business for fear that someone might ride out to Middleham before them and break the news to the Duke prematurely.

"We need food and a good night's sleep," explained Giles, "Gloucester will doubtless saddle up immediately he learns of his brother's death and we will be returning to London without a break."

"I have never ridden so many miles. My legs are unsteady and my arse is so sore I shall have to sleep on my belly tonight," groaned Mark.

Giles was in much the same state and would have made do with a light supper in favour of retiring early but Abbot Booth had invited him to supper in his lodge and it seemed churlish to refuse.

There was a chill in the air when Giles made his way from the Abbey guesthouse to the Abbot's lodgings and he wished he had not removed his riding cloak before making the short journey. He had heard that winter clung to the northern parts of the Kingdom well into Spring but it was mid April and he was surprised to feel such bitter cold striking his face and neck but once inside the lodge, Giles forgot his discomfort. A huge log fire roared in the grate and several charcoal braziers ensured that even the alcoves and furthest parts of the room were heated. The chamber was sumptuous and the supper table laden with fare fit for a King.

Abbot Booth had invited his nephew, Oswald Garvey, to join them and all three men chatted amicably as they ate their way through five courses of the best food the Abbey could provide. A member of the prestigious Corpus Christi Guild, Oswald, had recently travelled to York from King's Lynn. He was a younger version of his uncle, tall and willowy with just a hint of the stoup that the cleric had already developed. The Abbot's tonsure had long been a natural feature and the merchant's hair was thinning in the same monkish style but it was their similar mannerisms that made Giles wonder if the title of 'nephew' was one of expediency.

At first Giles did not recognise Oswald but as soon as the merchant reminded him that he had done business with him at the Tower just before Easter, Giles recalled the agent who had secured such a good price for King Edward's wool in the Venetian markets.

"Are you here to inform the Duke of Gloucester of the King's death?" asked Oswald casually, when the three had retired to the Abbot's parlour to continue drinking the amazing brandy wine the cellarer had procured for their delight.

"What? When did you hear the news?" asked Giles, confounded by the question.

"Actually I heard of his demise on the Tuesday after Easter Sunday," replied the merchant, "I was staying with my father-in-law Master Thorsby, Mayor of Lynn, having sailed into port at King's Lynn on Easter Day."

Giles could only gape at Oswald and watch dumbfounded as he poured more brandy wine into all three of the silver cups.

"I arrived in York on the 9th and immediately conveyed the sad news to my Guild Master," continued the merchant, "he arranged for a mass to be said in the Minster that evening. No expense was spared. King Edward supported us merchants and we mourned his passing."

"Edward had two seizures," explained Giles, "the first on Easter Sunday and the second on April 9th. He didn't die until the day you arrived here in York."

"So the mass was not wasted after all," declared Oswald, unconcerned about the discrepancy, "the Guild Master will be pleased and so am I, for I was to bear the cost, as my story appeared unconfirmed, until now of course."

"Who brought the news to Mayor Thorsby on Easter Tuesday?" demanded Giles.

"I couldn't say but Mayor Thorsby seemed certain of his source, because I questioned him myself, thinking it strange that I hadn't heard even a whisper at the Guild Hall in King's Lynn."

"Whoever he was he either had second sight or the message was corrupted by being repeated several times," said Abbot Booth helpfully, "I've known that to have occurred before now."

"I must beg to be excused my Lord Abbot. I have an early start tomorrow," said Giles, who wanted to be alone to consider Oswald's revelation without constant interruption. He got to his feet before uncle and nephew could launch a joint protest, thanked the Abbot warmly for his generosity and prepared to leave.

"I have letters to write before I retire," he lied.

Despite his exhaustion Giles slept fitfully. His brain repeatedly created different scenarios to account for the release of the news of King Edward's death before he had actually died but none were satisfactory. He eventually gave up trying to sleep and followed the Benedictine monks into the Abbey church for the office of Matins. Mark was also awake well before daybreak so they skipped breakfast and slipped out into the cold morning air to collected their horses from an almost awake lay brother and set out on the road leading north.

By mid morning they had climbed out of the clinging mist and were riding along the high ridge, sheep trader's roads of lower Wensleydale. Mark was thrilled, he had never before seen hillsides that forced their peaks above woodland cover.

"Look Giles, the other side of the dale, is that snow still lying on the tops?"

"Most certainly, winter hangs around up here. Look there! that must be Jervaulx Abbey, one of several Cistercian Houses in this area. I bet they didn't enjoy roast venison with truffle sauce for supper last night."

"Neither did I," declared Mark, "but the claret was the finest I have ever tasted and the most plentiful." He licked his lips and kicked his mount into a trot. "Come on Giles its freezing and we must be nearly there now."

Sure enough within moments they could see the great castle at Middleham dominating the rise before them. Giles was nervous. Time and again, during the last two and a half days, he had rehearsed the words he would use to explain the death of King Edward to his brother Richard Gloucester but even as he entered the castle's outer courtyard from the eastern gatehouse, he was still preparing his speech.

As they rode towards the wooden bridge that spanned the moat and gave access to the inner courtyard, four riders appeared and rode out towards them. The first was a young boy astride a docile pony which he desperately tried to spur into action, at the same time shouting words of encouragement and abuse, much to the amusement of the other three riders. The second was an older youth in his early teens who, leaning forward, slapped the pony's haunches with his gathered reins. The startled animal shot forward and the small crowd of onlookers cheered as the boy raised himself in his stirrups and treated his audience to a display of horsemanship. As pony and rider flew past Giles for the second time, he thought he heard a snap of leather and watched in horror as the saddle slipped, flinging the child to the one side of his pony, leaving him gripping desperately to the beast's main. Giles turned his own mount and was alongside the unsaddled boy within seconds, pulling on the reins and calling to the frightened animal to slow down. It stop as abruptly as it had set off, causing Giles to loose his own balance so that both he and the child dropped to the ground and rolled together on the wet track.

"Gi-les," screamed the delighted boy struggling to clear the dirt and straw from his mouth, "Papa it is Sir Giles!"

"Are you hurt, my Lord," ask Giles, rubbing his own bruised back.

"I'm fine thank you Giles," replied Ned, grinning mischievously and getting to his feet. "Its Giles papa, Giles has come to Middleham."

The others soon reached the accident scene and dismounted. Gloucester could see and hear, that his son Ned was none the worse for his fall but Giles was still sat in the mud, strangely distracted and clearly anxious.

"Are you injured Sir Giles?" asked the Duke, offering his hand by way of assisting the knight to his feet.

"N-no Your Grace, I'm fine, truly." Giles scrambled up and brushed the dirt from his tunic. The anxiety was not so easily removed from his face.

"Then what news do you bring from the Capital that concerns you so?"

What else could Giles do? He reached into his script and

produced the letter that Hastings had prepared and whilst Gloucester broke the seal and read the detailed account of his brother's death, the onlookers were briskly dispersed by the fourth rider. He was a falconer, his charge sat hooded and jessed on his left wrist, waiting patiently with the rest of the group, whilst Gloucester digested the contents of Lord Williams letter. The silence was difficult and uncomfortably long but eventually the Duke folded the parchment and pushing it into the back of his gloved hand, turned away from the group and stared into the distance, wrestling with his emotions and trying to summons enough control to give instruction to those waiting for him to speak. Only Ned was brave enough to question his silence.

"What is wrong papa? Does the letter Sir Giles has brought mean we cannot fly the new falcon today?"

"That is right," said his father flatly and he gripped the boy's shoulder so tightly that Ned knew he must make no further protest.

"John, take our guests to the hall and see to their comfort. Then take Ned to his tutor and inform my Lady that I shall be back before dark." Gloucester turned to Giles, blinking hard to force back the tears which would not be restrained for much longer. "Forgive me nephew, I must be alone for now," he croaked, then mounting his horse and without looking back, galloped out of the courtyard, turning west behind the castle towards the moor beyond.

Ned watched him go and followed his progress up the hillside until the only visible sign of a rider was a moving speck along the top of the ridge but then it too disappeared as one fold of moorscape lapped the next. With no further sight of his father, Ned's thoughts returned to the guests and he tried to remember his training.

"Sir Giles, allow me to introduce you to my half-brother, John of Gloucester. John, this is my cousin Sir Giles …" he paused for moment but before Giles could say 'Butler', Ned remembered and introduced him as Sir Giles of Clarence. "Is that correct?" he asked.

"It's near enough. I'm delighted to meet you John. Ned told me all about you when he came to Westminster for the feast of the Nativity. Actually, if I remember rightly he described you as a larger version of his father but without the wrinkles."

John clipped Ned's ear and both laughed until John remembered that their morning's sport had just been cancelled.

"What news did you bring that so disturbed our father?" he asked, at the same time signalling to a groom to take the horses.

"King Edward has died," said Giles softly, "and the Duke is appointed Lord Protector of the young King."

The elder boy reached for his young brother and drew him close. Ned looked into John's face with large brown eyes and read the fear.

"Protector of the young King? What does that mean John? Will papa have to live in London?"

"You can all go and live in London, at Crosby Hall and I can come and visit you there," said Giles, realising for the first time that Gloucester's appointment might be best for England but that it would have a devastating effect on family life at Middleham Castle.

Ned disengaged himself from John's protective arm and without warning, fled across the wooden bridge, through the inner gatehouse and out of sight. John shook his head.

"Poor lad, when he returned from London after Christmas he was ill for weeks. The physicians say he must not travel such distances in future."

"Oh no, I had no idea he was so unwell," cried Giles.

"He does everything possible to build up his strength but he seems to be fighting a loosing battle. Cannot the Lord Protector be based at Middleham?"

"I doubt it. Perhaps after everything is sorted out. I really don't know."

John took Mark and Giles into the great hall, ordered food and wine and gave instructions for their stay. Then he excused himself, saying he must inform the Duchess of their arrival and then find Ned, who he expected had gone to ground in a secret place John wasn't supposed to know about.

"Who is this John of Gloucester?" asked Mark when they were alone in Giles' extremely comfortable quarters.

"I only have Ned's version of the story which he volunteered last Christmas at Westminster, when I found him sobbing under the dinner table. I felt something brush against my knee and lifted the cloth. There he was huddled in a ball, so as I was bored and perhaps a little merry, I slipped under the table, replaced the cloth and tried to comfort the boy."

"He was missing his brother John?"

"Yes. Apparently Gloucester was 'friendly' (Ned's word) with John's mother during the period when Anne Neville was 'nearly a queen of Lancaster' (Ned's words again). John's mother has since married and as John's stepfather was an 'unkind brute' (again Ned's description) so Gloucester arranged for him to live at Middleham."

The knock at the door was John returning from his unsuccessful search for Ned.

"My Lady begs your attendance in her solar Sir Giles. If you come at once I can take you to her but then I must find Ned before papa returns or I shall be in big trouble."

Mark made a mock bow to Giles and stretched out on the comfortable bed. Giles shut the door behind him with a bang and hurried after John who was fast disappearing down the gallery of the west wing.

CHAPTER 20

Middleham Castle 17th April 1483

Lady Anne Neville, Duchess of Gloucester, fixed her needle into her canvas and moved the frame to one side as 'Sir Giles Butler' was announced and shown into her solar. He bowed, kissed the lady's hand and looked once more into the face which reminded him so much of his dead mother. It was macabre, he could only recall his mother as she had lain in her coffin fifteen years ago but her translucent skin, her huge hollow closed eyes and the strands of chestnut hair that had escaped her wimple had left a permanent impression on the young Giles. So when he first met Anne, at a Christmas court, he had been terrified by the similarity in her appearance. Her eyes were open of course, huge brown doe like eyes, too large for her small face and colourless lips. Her chestnut coloured hair caught up in a net of gold was just as he imagined his mothers to have been. He even anticipated her skin to be cold and solid to the touch and was embarrassed to recall how he had jumped when she had held out her hand to him and it had, indeed, felt cold and clammy. Later he had learned that Lady Anne did not enjoy good health but Giles could not banish from his mind's eye her likeness to his coffined mother. Now she smiled weakly and asked after his health. Mortality was never far from the Lady's thoughts for her son Ned suffered from the same inflammation of the lungs that had haunted her since childhood.

"John tells me that you bring news of King Edward's death. He was not ill when we left his court in January. Did he die of natural causes?"

"His doctors concluded he had a seizure," replied Giles, startled by her directness.

"Come Sir Giles, a healthy man such as Edward can expect to reach his sixtieth year and he was barley forty summers." Anne paused but Giles offered no further comment. "Oh well, doubtless I shall learn the truth all in good time."

By way of compensation Giles offered his condolences on the loss of her brother-in-law and was surprised to notice the scorn which played momentarily on Anne's lips.

"You forget Sir Giles, I am the daughter of the Earl of Warwick. I do not share my Lord's worship of the mighty Edward but I am sorry to hear of his passing."

Giles said nothing but wondered how Anne and Richard would manage their differing regard for the dead King in the weeks that lay ahead and was embarrassed to find she was already considering her situation.

"John gives me to understand that Edward willed Richard the appointment of Lord Protector of England. Is Elizabeth not challenging the legality of this appointment?"

"Madam?"

She smiled at the confusion her question appeared to cause him.

"I have no brothers Sir Giles. My sister Isobel and I were my father's sole heirs and accordingly he allowed us to study with the boys of our household."

She sighed and smiled wistfully, remembering the happy days when the were all children together at Middleham, in Warwick's care. Warwick, the father she still loved and still mourned.

"I have enough knowledge of the law to know that only the King's Council and Parliament can appoint a Lord Protector," she shrugged and added, "but then whenever did the law stand in Edward's way?"

The revelation stunned Giles. No one else had challenged the legality of the King's will in this regard. Not even Bishop Morton and he would certainly have commented on its illegality, had he sensed that Gloucester might be prevented from assuming the Protectorship. Surely, Lady Anne must be mistaken?

It had been dark for some hours when Giles heard the sound of a horse clatter over the drawbridge of the northern gate. His room was directly above the gatehouse and as he had not retired to bed, Giles opened the casement immediately and peered out just in time to see the rump of a white horse disappear through the gate. Was it the Duke returning from his vigil on the moor? Giles thought it most likely. He had remained dressed and waiting since supper, determined to speak to his uncle tonight if at all possible. As yet, his grace was unaware that his brother had been poisoned and as Lady Anne had asked Giles outright if the King's death had been natural, he wanted to alert his uncle to the true nature of Edward's demise before his Lady made her own thoughts known on the subject.

Giles made his way to the great hall and perched on a stool close to where Mark was snoring gently, wrapped in an enormous woollen blanket. The hall was full of sleeping servants and visitor's servants similarly cocooned, their bodies rising and falling as they snuffled and snored in their sleep. Giles waited in the dark, certain that the Duke would walk through the hall on route to his private quarters but he had not appeared, so Giles wandered over to the screened entrance to check the stairway and the courtyard below for any sign of his uncle.

On his arrival at Middleham, Giles had not noticed, that at the top of the stairs and to the left was a chapel and now, the sight of candles flickering in the nave tempted him to open the door and look in. Knelt at the alter and with his head bowed, Giles recognised the figure of his uncle but not wishing to disturb him, he began to retreat but Gloucester jumped to his feet and with his dagger drawn demanded that who ever was there should stand in the light. Giles did so instantly and Gloucester sheathed his weapon.

"Gracious Giles, you should know better than to creep around in the dark. What are you doing here anyway?"

"Waiting for you my Lord. I need to speak with you."

"Surely it can wait until the morning?" but Gloucester read the agitation in his nephew's face. "Very well, I doubt I shall be sleeping much anyway. What is it?"

There was no way of telling the truth gently and Giles was torn with pity as he looked into his uncle's dirty tear stained face. The candlelight may have exaggerated the paleness of his complexion but there was no hiding the thick red trickle from his mouth where he had bitten his lower lip so hard that it had bled. Nor was there any way to disguise the rawness around his eyes or the sweat that had soaked his hair and run in rivulets down his neck, drenching the collar of his open shirt.

So as simply as possible Giles told the story of the two attacks on Edward's life. How he had recovered from the first and succumbed to the second. How on both occasions the King had eaten the palm fruits and how on the second occasion the residue had been thrown from the window and later consumed by an unfortunate rat. How the disposal of the remaining dates placed the murderer in the room when Giles and Luke arrived which in turn provided them with a list of suspects.

Gloucester's reaction was predictable, the vein on his temple enlarged and began to pulsate. At the same time he started to shake and Giles feared he might throw a fit but most of his energy had already been expended with hours of riding on the freezing moor and his fury was only momentary. With a cry of anguish that must have been audible for miles around he fell in a heap on the alter steps, exhausted and deflated like a child's bladder ball. Giles hesitated, unsure whether to stay or retreat discretely. He took a couple of paces back towards the doorway but Gloucester heard him move and without lifting his head he bid him stay.

"You have done well Giles and deserve my thanks."

The Duke pulled himself up and sat on the alter steps, legs crossed, like a scruffy urchin. Giles took the piece of parchment from his script on which he had penned the suspects names and handed it to him.

"Come here boy, and sit by me. Let us consider which of these whoresons could possibly benefit from Edward's death."

Roses are White

He patted the stone step beside him and so taking a candle from its sconce on the wall and holding it so that they might consider the list, Giles joined his uncle on the alter steps. The flame flickered causing the names on the parchment to dance in the intermittent light and Giles felt guilty about those who were innocent but whom he had presented as possible suspects to the most powerful man in the realm.

"I'd stake my life against Will Hastings harming his King," sighed Gloucester, wiping a tear from his face, "and as for John Morton, well, you know him better than I nephew but he has everything to loose and nothing to gain by Edward's death, wouldn't you say?"

Giles nodded but said nothing.

"Which leaves the arrogant Marquis, Jane Shore and three knights of the body. It *has* to be Dorset."

Gloucester got to his feet and for some time expressed his rage by thumping a nearby pillar with both fists, turning and likewise thumping the air. Eventually he had control of his tears and was able to express his anger in words, cursing the Marquis in such vile terms that if only half his curses were unleashed on the man he would be already bound in hell suffering unthinkable torture. Giles dare not speak, let alone disagree with the Duke but an altogether different solution was forming in his own mind, a solution that drew in several of the other odd happenings in the past weeks. However the problem was how to prove his theory, although one thing was certain, he had best keep this thoughts to himself for now.

The following morning Giles woke to the sound of Mark's impatient knocking on his chamber door. Unusually he had over slept and angered by his own sloth, jumped out of bed and carelessly pulled on his clothes and boots before answering the knocking. Mark was not amused by the delay, he had been to the kitchen and brought a selection of cold chicken, ham, goat's cheese and fresh white bread together with watered ale for Giles' breakfast and he thought the least his master could have done was to acknowledge his rapping. So, instead of bidding Giles 'good morning' he set the tray down on the small sideboard with a firmness that denoted his displeasure, crossed the room and flung open the shutters. Daylight streamed in, clearing the stale night air and flooding the chamber with the warmth and promise of Spring.

"Thank you Mark but it is not your place to sulk. I'm the one with the bad temper around here. Remember?"

"Oh no Sir Giles, you come a poor second to your uncle Richard," said Mark, his annoyance fading, "according to the lady with whom I had supper last night, when the vein on *his* left temple signals an impending outburst the servants go to ground like foxes at dawn."

Giles grinned, he could well imagine the havoc a full blown Plantagenet fury would reap on any household. He reached for the watered ale and noticed the beautifully prepared tray of food and his grin broke into a laugh.

"You rouge Mark. This tray was prepared by your supper companion, wasn't it? You slept in her bed last night and rose late yourself. You feared I might have been looking for you this morning and this tray of food was to calm my anger."

Mark grinned and the colour in his face confirmed Giles' suspicions.

"It's as well I've found my lady friend, for it was she who lent me this black doublet and hose with which to pay proper respect to our dead King." mocked Mark, crossing himself and then wiping an imaginary tear from his eye.

"You idiot, stop arsing about. We should both hurry, Gloucester will be eager to reach London as soon as possible. I'm surprised I have not been roused by one of the servants before now."

"I doubt we are returning today Giles, from the activity in the courtyard and stables it would seem uncle Richard intends taking half the garrison with him to London."

Giles stretched his still aching body in front of the open window which provided a panoramic view across the dale and happily contemplated a leisurely day in the fresh air. He was in no hurry to returned to London. Mark helped himself to a chicken leg from the tray.

"I'll be on my way then," he said hopefully, through a mouthful of chicken "you can find me in the buttery or there-about if you need me," and without waiting for an answer Mark disappeared, only to return briefly again and poke his head around the door. "Oh and by-the-way it appears we missed a ' midnight requiem' in the chapel."

"Shit!"

"And you had better wear your black tunic, this place is in serious mourning."

Giles cursed under his breath again. The last thing he wanted was to offend his uncle and he feared he may have done so by not attending the mass. He broke his fast, washed and changed into his black tunic and hose and went down to the great hall in search of forgiveness. It was as Mark had hinted. Black drapes were being hung on narrow rods around the walls, covering the bright red and gold paint work and fine tapestries. In the centre of the hall stood Lady Anne, organising the removal and storage of all the colourful cushions, silks and even some hanging banners that threatened the sombre mood she was at pains to create. Servants were either wearing black tunics or black tabards to cover their own garb. Middleham was in deep mourning. There would be no sport, no music, no dancing and certainly no entertainers for some time to come.

The Duchess spotted Giles on the staircase and beckoned him to join her by the fire. She too was wearing black, a heavy velvet that coffined her frail body and mocked her alabaster skin so cruelly that Giles believed she would scare her own ladies should they encounter Her Grace in some poorly lit gallery.

"I thought we would be travelling south today," said Giles after they had exchanged greetings, "why does my uncle delay his departure?"

"You are not married Sir Giles? You have no children?"

"I have not my lady but you answer my question. I apologise for my impertinence."

"You have no reason to know how things are," she said sadly, "Ned cannot travel and I cannot leave him alone. The young King will need a Lord Protector for the next two years at least and I doubt that my Lord Richard will deem it prudent to leave the Prince in Woodville hands and travel north during that time. Do you?"

Guilt swelled in Giles' breast. When he had suggested to Edward that his uncle should be Lord Protector he was thinking only of the influence he might wield with King Edward and of course, the curbing of Dorset's power. Anne caught his embarrassment and touched his hand gently.

"But there are other reasons for his delay. We – he did not sleep last night. He spent every hour until dawn writing letters to our friends in the area, informing them of Edward's demise and asking them to rendezvous in York. They need time to prepare for their journey south but he is moving as fast as he reasonably can, messengers and harbingers were dispatched at first light this morning."

Giles tried to hide his embarrassment. How could he have been so stupid as to imagine Gloucester would simply call for a horse and set off at full gallop to London?

"I fear I slept too well my Lady and missed the requiem. I need to speak with my uncle and offer my apologies."

"He is in his chancery, writing to those who should have made it their business to inform him officially of Edward's death: condolences to Edward's widow and his sworn allegiance to the young King. But before you go to him will you walk with me? My Lord has told me of the manner in which King Edward died and I would like to enquire about certain details."

Without waiting for his reply, she slipped her arm into his and led the startled Giles across the hall and into the chapel where their conversation would not be over heard.

Lady Anne ushered Giles into the chair reserved for Gloucester and sat in her own chair beside him.

"I note with interest that John Morton's name is on your list of suspects and I would like to hear what evidence there may be against the slippery doctor."

"None what-so-ever," said Giles, shocked at the Lady's keenness to implicate Morton, "he is on the list simply because he was in the King's chamber's when the palm fruits were thrown from the casement. He had no motive to commit murder and besides he loved King Edward like a brother."

"No one on your list has a motive that we know of as yet," said Lady Anne reasonably and then added, "you say Morton loved Edward like a brother. George Clarence was Edward's brother but expediency overcame his brotherly affection."

"If the love of Edward is no defence against being his killer," countered Giles, "then equally suspect is Lord Hastings, Jane Shore, Sir Matthew, Sir Peter, Sir Henry, Sir John."

"Sir Giles?"

"Madam I protest. I was reared a Yorkist and all my adult life I have served King Edward faithfully."

"Exactly," she cried triumphantly, "and so has every other soul on your list, except John Morton. Believe me Giles I know what foul intrigue that toad is capable of inciting."

Of course! Giles recalled what Luke had told him. It was Morton who conceived the plan to permanently bind Warwick to the House of Lancaster by marrying his daughter Anne to queen Margaret's son.

"If Morton had poisoned the King he would not have criticised the physicians for failing to diagnose food poisoning," explained Giles, "he would have been grateful for their incompetence as it provided cover for the crime. Instead he called them pathetic fools for consulting their star charts rather than observing Edward's symptoms."

"Then why did he not come to the same conclusion that you did when Edward was taken ill the second time?"

Giles hesitated, this was exactly how he and Luke had reasoned and he was suddenly conscious of having only Luke's word for Morton's innocence.

"Because he went straight to the King's bedside and failed to spot the dish of sweetmeats," said Giles, hoping his explanation was near enough the truth.

"Did you not tell Morton about your suspicions after you and your friend found the discarded fruits?"

"No. We did not know who to trust so we told no-one."

They sat quietly for some minutes until Giles decided to try out his new theory on the Lady but before he spoke she surprised him with a second scenario of her own.

"Might it be that the Woodvilles were loosing their influence over King Edward?"

"I have no reason to believe so madam. Have you?"

"Not specifically but the Prince of Wales was destined to spend some time here at Middleham away from the influence of his uterine uncle Rivers and my Lord Richard has been named Lord Protector. You infer that Edward still favoured his mistress, Jane Shore who was causing his Queen serious concern as long ago as Christmas."

"What are you suggesting Madam?"

"I'm not sure really," she admitted, "but if a rift between the Woodvilles and Edward were sufficiently threatening, then they might considered the young Woodville reared Prince more malleable than his kingly father."

"Possibly," said Giles doubtfully, "but the loss of King Edward puts them in great jeopardy and the council would not allow … …"

"Suppose they planned, not only to poison Edward but also to keep my Lord Richard in the dark long enough to crown their protégée" interrupted Anne, " is that not motive enough?"

"I don't think … "

"Go to my Lord at once and explain what we have reasoned."

As Giles hurried along the west gallery in search of the Duke's chancery it occurred to him that the reporting of Anne's 'Woodville plot' was unnecessary as Gloucester had already decided that Dorset was the murderer. Somehow Giles could not see the Marquise carefully slitting open the dates and filling them with morsels of pulp soaked in poison. It was a delicate process, filling the cavity with just sufficient contaminated date so that it could be closed again without any sign of interference. The work of a woman perhaps? Giles shuddered, if Dorset was the murderer, had he enlisted the help of Jane Shore? Giles had witnessed her sufferance of his sexual advances on the night Edward had first been taken ill? So why should she help him? Wasn't Jane Edward's permanent mistress and besides she wasn't even at Westminster when he was taken ill for the second time? Although, God forbid, she could have prepared the fruit earlier and Dorset could have placed it on the serving dish. Matthew would not have noticed if the Marquise had removed one or two of the original fruits.

Deep in thought Giles almost stumbled into the squire who sat nodding outside the chancery door, presumably he had been there all night but he roused at Giles' clumsy approach. Giles asked the squire to show him in.

The chancery was dimly lit by a single, three branch candelabra placed on the desk at which Gloucester was working. The shutters were closed and it appeared to Giles that his uncle had not realised it was light, so intent was he on his letter writing. He put down his quill as his squire announced 'Sir Giles Butler' and ordered the weary man to pour wine for them both. Gloucester looked tired and exhausted, the red rings around his eyes betraying both tears and lack of sleep. Giles' instinct was to suggest the Duke should leave the correspondence and get some rest but he dared not.

"Giles, I want you to consider joining my household, said Gloucester, when his squire had opened the shutters and poured wine into two cups, "my brother has sponsored you these past five years and I am prepared to retain your services if you so wish."

Giles was ecstatic, he had not considered his future since Edward had died but the opportunity to serve in Gloucester's household was an honour he was delighted to accept, although he knew John Morton would be disappointed.

Hurrying footsteps in the corridor signalled the arrival of another journey worn messenger and both uncle and nephew were surprised to see the man shown into the chancery was wearing the livery of Lord William Hastings. The exhausted man apologised for his appearance but his master had insisted he reach Middleham in all haste. Whilst handing the letter to Gloucester he offered to return immediately with any reply that might be necessary. Gloucester ordered his squire to attend to the man's need for rest and refreshment and promised to send for him if an urgent reply was appropriate. Giles made to leave with the squire and messenger but his uncle insisted he stay and hear what Hastings had to say. With a preparatory deep intake of breath, Gloucester broke the seal and read the contents in silence. Giles watched as the remaining colour drained from his uncle's face and the vein on his temple began to pulsate as he read the words Hastings had penned. Then without speaking, he handed the parchment to Giles, who instantly recognised the uneven hand and the wine stains that had smudged the ink in several places. Will Hastings may have been in his cups when he put quill to parchment but the message was clearly stated. The Woodvilles were ignoring Gloucester's Protectorship and had deliberately failed to inform the Duke of his brother's demise in order to buy time. The Queen, acting as Regent, had sent to Ludlow for the young King and since the council was dominated by her kinsmen, her proposed date of 4th May had been accepted for the coronation, after which, the Protectorship would of course lapse.

Initially she had ordered an army of six thousand men to escort the boy to London but Hastings had insisted that such a large number was virtually a declaration of war against those who might challenge her authority and as he supported Gloucester's Protectorship he had threatened to retire to Calais, where he was governor and presumably safer than amid the Woodville clan. The number escorting the young King had reluctantly been reduced to two thousand but it was Hastings' considered opinion that in order to secure his Protectorship, Gloucester must first have the boy King in his charge. He therefore urged him to make haste and enter the Capital with sufficient armed men to defend his rights.

When Giles looked up from reading the lengthy letter his uncle had moved to the window where he was watching two sparrows on the parapet wall disputing ownership of a scrap of food.

"Will you do as Lord Hastings suggests my Lord and take charge of the young King before his entourage present him to the Capital?"

"I must," replied Gloucester still staring at the sparrows, " but I must also take charge of him without bloodshed." He turned to face Giles. "I admit nephew, that I find it increasingly difficult to suppress my anger, my natural instinct is to confront the whoresons head on and with swords drawn."

Gloucester returned to his desk and sat with his hands covering his face. Unsure what to do, Giles refilled his uncle's cup from the jug on the side table and offered it to him in a weak gesture of support. The Duke accepted it with a smile, recognising the spirit in which it had been offered.

"Clearly, the Queen and Dorset planned to exclude me from the council and ignore my Protectorship and if I permit them to take control of the young King they will certainly guide him into dismantling my estates and authority here in the north. On the other hand, if I challenge them and I am obliged to seize the boy by force, then he will perceive me to be the villain and ruin me the moment my Protectorship is ended. Whichever way I come at this problem Giles, I face ruin simply because my brother's son, King Edward V has been reared a Woodville."

"My Lord, I know the young Prince of Wales loved his father dearly," said Giles tentatively, "if we could *prove beyond doubt,* that his stepbrother Dorset poisoned his father, then surely he would be less eager to take instruction from his Woodville kinsmen and more inclined to accept your council."

Suddenly Gloucester was alert. Was it possible to prove it beyond doubt? The Duke was so certain that Dorset was behind the traitorous deed that the need for proof had not crossed his mind. He warmed to the idea. If Dorset could be proven guilty of murdering King Edward, then Parliament would insist on his lawful execution. George's death, as well as Edward's, would be avenged and without the boy perceiving Richard to be his enemy. In time, he would teach his Kingly nephew the honour of his Plantagenet origins and then, he would be free to retreat to his beloved Yorkshire and leave the realm in capable Yorkist hands, hopefully for generation to come. At last Richard Gloucester could see a way out of his dilemma but Giles was still not convinced that they had identified the murderer let alone the motive.

Chapter 21

Middleham 20th April 1483

Before dawn on the morning of 20th April, Richard, Duke of Gloucester and his retainers all regaled in black, made ready to leave Middleham Castle to rendezvous with the Duke's friends and supporters in York before riding south to the Capital. Giles was still forcing his dirty shirts into a pannier and cursing Mark for not attending to his duties, when the errant servant knocked on the door. He did not wait for Giles to respond but pushed the door open and demanded that Giles should stop packing and pay attention. Giles was so taken aback by his tone that he obediently dropped the pannier.

"You must come at once and see for yourself," said Mark, "it will not take long. If they leave before we return we can easily catch up."

"No Mark, I will not," cried Giles indignantly, recovering quickly.

"Giles this is about your father; you'll not believe it unless you see for yourself," and so saying Mark disappeared along the corridor and down the north gate staircase. He could hear Giles' footsteps behind him so he continued to hurry, out of the gate, across the drawbridge, threading his way between men and horses preparing to leave and up the track west of the castle, towards the moors.

"Mark, for God's sake, wait for me."

Mark stopped and rested until Giles caught up. Dawn was breaking and outcrops, hedgerows and barns were all emerging from the blackness to soften the harsh mass of moorland and breath life back into the vast expanse before them. He pointed to an isolated, ancient tree leaning precariously westwards.

"You see that tree? Just before dark yesterday, I met Lucy there." He held up his hand to stall Giles' inevitable protest. "Just listen to me Giles whilst we make our way there."

Mark forced his way through a small gap in the hedge and started the slow climb towards the oak. Giles followed obediently.

"Lucy is not a lowly kitchen wench, as I'm sure you assumed her to be. She is Lady Anne's maid."

"Indeed?"

"Yes Sir Giles, Lucy's mother was Lady Anne's wet nurse. They were born hours apart and have been friends since both could crawl."

"I don't see ... "

"Lucy told me yesterday, that the King's brothers, your uncle Richard and your father, George Clarence were sent to Middleham at an early age as wards of the great Earl of Warwick but that was long before he fell out with King Edward. Warwick's two daughters, Edward's brothers and other children from the castle, including Lucy, were constant playmates and that tree was one of their secret meeting places. You know what children are like Giles, they met there, they left messages tucked under its exposed roots and carved their initials into its great trunk."

"What have I come to see Mark?" asked the exasperated Giles as they finally reached the tree and walked round it's huge girth. " Surely you haven't dragged me up here to show me where my father played when he was a child?"

Mark pointed to a series of carved hearts in the tree's bark. A carved arrow through each heart bore the initials of each pair of young lovers. There were six such declarations of enduring love.

LD, Mark's Lucy, linked with someone whose initials were FL, AN and RG denoted Anne Neville and Richard Gloucester and of course IN and GC denoting Isobel Neville, Anne's elder sister and George Clarence.

"What do the numbers mean?" asked Giles touching the carved digits beneath his father's initials.

"That's exactly what I asked Lucy last evening," replied Mark quietly.

"Well?"

"Each child carved their age beneath their initials. You can see that Lady Anne and Lucy were very young, they could barley cut the bark evenly."

When the hearts had been carved Ann and Lucy were six, Richard and Isobel were nine and George was twelve. As Giles remained unimpressed Mark pointed to the date carved above the hearts.

"Lucy swears that the date 1461 was carved on the same day."

"That can't be right," said Giles in disgust, "I was born in 1460, my father cannot have been twelve, er.. ten, when he married my mother."

Giles' anger flared instantly, and turning on his heels he ran back down the hillside, whilst Mark followed at a slower pace but when he returned to Giles' chamber he found his master ashen faced and sat on his bed staring into space. Mark hurriedly completed the packing and then poured Giles some watered wine.

"Come on they're assembling outside the northern gate. Gloucester will be expecting you. Please, hurry."

"Close the door Mark and sit down. There is something you should know."

"But I want to say my good-byes and Gloucester will expect you to ride with him."

"Lucy must wait Mark. You were the one that said we could catch up if they left without us. Now sit."

An agitated Mark perched on the chest at the side of the bed. He had already left Lucy to show Giles the oak tree and he had promised he would not leave without saying good-bye.

"Mark, I believe that King Edward was my father."

"Mother of God Giles," swore Mark.

"If the dates on that tree are correct, Clarence cannot have sired me."

"I agree but what makes you think that King Edward was your father?"

"A combination of things. To begin with, I resemble Edward

just as surely as I resembled Clarence. Edward was eighteen in 1460 and certainly old enough to have married Eleanor but most significantly he *knew* that Clarence was not old enough to have been my father and still allowed me to claim that he was."

"Are you sure?"

"Definitely. When I showed King Edward my mother's notes he asked my age and when I told him, he said I looked much younger."

"So why didn't he refute your claim there and then?"

"Because it masked the fact that *he* was my father. Edward realised that I had the appearance of a fourteen year old and that had I actually been fourteen, then George would have been fifteen when he married Eleanor. It was the perfect cover for his secret. I looked like George and with my youthful appearance I could *just* be his son."

"Even so. Your mother must have been in her twenties. Could he expect folk to really believable that a young widow would fall hopelessly in love with a fifteen year old?"

"It is not so ridiculous but he took no chances. He confined me to Clipberry until the fuss over Clarence's death abated and then packed me off to Oxford. By the time I returned the difference between our ages became less apparent, I aged and Clarence was forgotten."

"How about your uncle Gloucester, he certainly knew the age of his brother George?"

"Yes but he didn't asked my age. It probably never crossed his mind at the time, which is not unreasonable since one of his brothers had just executed the other and remember, he returned to Yorkshire almost immediately. I wasn't in his company long enough for him to consider my age seriously and now, well, I'm established as George's son and I am old enough to be any age between eighteen and twenty five."

"Poor Bishop Robert," sighed Mark, " it must have been a terrible burden all these years. No wonder the King confined him to the Tower when he thought he had betrayed him"

"And kept him there, when I intimated the Bishop had a secret to betray."

"Even so, you can't be certain that Edward was your father. He may well have had another reason for passing you off as Clarence's boy," said Mark. "Surely King Edward would not be so foolish as to marry Eleanor. The marriage of Kings is a matter for securing treaties with foreign Royal Houses."

"It should be," agreed Giles, "but Edward ultimately married Elizabeth Woodville in secret because she would not grace his bed without a wedding band. The two situations are remarkably similar."

Both men sat in silence, oblivious to the sounds of gathering horsemen emanating from the courtyard below.

"Holy shit, Mark," cried Giles leaping to his feet. "Can you remember all the fuss when Edward announced he had married Elizabeth Woodville?"

"No."

"Well neither can I. But I can remember my mother's funeral. Can you?"

"Just about. I must have been eight at the time. Why?"

"If neither of us can remember Edward's marriage to Queen Elizabeth but both can recall my mother's funeral then the chances are that Edward married Elizabeth before my mother died, when we were to young to be aware of events."

"Don't even think about it Giles. If Edward did marry Eleanor and then married Elizabeth before your mother's death then his second marriage was bigamous. To even consider the possibility is probably an act of treason."

"Even if it's the truth?" screamed Giles, " Don't you see? Edward's secret was his bigamous marriage to Elizabeth Woodville. Somehow, George Clarence recognised the truth when I claimed to be his son. *He actually asked me the date of my mother's death*." Giles paced the floor whilst Mark tried to make sense of his outburst. "God help me, Mark. Whilst I filled in the details, Clarence planned to disgrace the King, claim the throne for himself and take revenge on the Bishop by letting Edward believe it was he who had betrayed His Majesty."

"Stop it Giles. You don't know for certain that Edward married Elizabeth Woodville whilst Eleanor was still alive or that he married Eleanor in the first place."

Again Giles ignored Mark's plea for caution.

"Edward reacted quickly to George's challenge. He cleared his household of virtually all his staff so that few were privy to the action he was about to take. He had the Bishop arrested on a private warrant and announced that George Clarence was to be executed."

"I remember the warrant written in the King's hand," gasped Mark, "but why was Clarence convinced he was safe from execution once he confronted Edward with his bigamy?"

"Because he believed Edward would not risk being denounced from the scaffold but he underestimated King Edward. In his arrogance, George Clarence never considered *a completely private execution.*"

"Clubbed unconscious, stuffed into a barrel of wine and left to drown," whispered Mark, "but what about the wedding rings Clarence claimed he had made for himself and your mother?"

Giles stopped pacing and turned angrily on Mark.

"Well clearly that was a lie," he bellowed, and then remembered the sketch of his mother's ring that he had hidden in the tapestry five years ago. "Sweet Jesus, I did see the truth that day."

Horns were calling men to make ready to move out and Giles and Mark hurried down to the courtyard to take up their positions in the troop. Couples were everywhere saying their last good-byes and Mark spotted Lucy at the top of the steps so he bounded back up them, only to find himself pushing against the flow of woman and children struggling for a vantage point from which to wave to their men folk. Giles had to elbow his way to the stables and find his horse. Fortunately, John had taken it upon himself to act as Giles' squire otherwise the beast would not have been saddled and waiting.

"Don't be angry with Mark," said John with a grin, "I know he and Lucy wanted to spend time together so I offered to deputise for him."

"That was very generous of you John but don't you want to say good-bye to your father?"

"Oh there is still plenty of time to see them leave Sir Giles and anyway the family said our farewells in private earlier this morning."

Giles threw his panniers over his horse and with John's aid strapped them securely. He mounted and was about to take his leave of John when a messenger, wearing the arms of the Bishop of Ely rode into the stable yard and yelled for Sir Giles Butler at the top of his voice. Giles made himself known to the man and was surprised to learn that he had been dispatched by Luke Lazereth and that the letter he carried was for Giles' eyes alone. He broke the seal immediately and quickly read its contents before joining the cavalcade streaming out of the castle gates.

Dearest Giles
Before leaving for Middleham, you asked me to persuade Bishop Morton to discover the nature of the documents that Lord Rivers' agent had had copies made without permission. They were two letters patent, one granting Earl Rivers the governorship of the Prince of Wales and the other granting him the right to raise troops in Wales. Bishop Morton was curious to know why Rivers should need written evidence of these powers, which he was granted nine years ago and also why it should be of interest to you? Of course I told him I had no idea!
It is also my sad duty to inform you that Sir Matthew Pawson has hanged himself from a rafter in the barn at Clipberry Manor. It is being said that he was so overcome with grief at the death of King Edward, that he lost his mind and with it his will to live. Be very careful who you tell about the nature of Edward's death. The above developments would suggest the identity of the man we were searching for, don't you think?
Your devoted friend
Luke L.

As they journeyed to York, Giles considered the contents of Luke's letter. Poor Matthew, he was certainly highly strung and very emotional. The devoted knight was devastated by King Edward's death and if Dorset was in charge now, well, Giles could imagine how he would bully Sir Matthew.

"He probably tormented poor Matthew into suicide," spat Giles, under this breath.

The letters patent that Lord Rivers had had copied, further confirmed Giles' own suspicions and he was impressed that Luke was thinking along the same lines without the advantage of having spoken to the York merchant Oswald Garvey. Giles grinned as he thought of Bishop Morton desperately trying to work out the significance of Giles' request for the information. Would the Bishop realise that Earl Rivers secured documentary evidence of his right to control the Prince *and* to muster men in Wales *before* the King was even taken ill and that the need for this evidence only became relevant *after* Edward's death. Giles thought he might.

He tried hard to assimilate Luke's information with what he already knew of Edward's murder but the fact that George Clarence was not this father took precedence in his confused brain. He could recover the drawing from the tapestry but there was no way he could confirm his belief that King Edward was his sire because Edward had had the actual ring buried with George Clarence in Tewkesbury Abbey.

Gloucester signalled to Giles to ride alongside him and as he made his way to the front of the troop he wisely decided not to claim to be the King Edward's first born. In truth Giles wished he had not even mentioned his suspicions to Mark. It had been accepted that George Clarence was his father so why complicate matters by suggesting a more sinister truth that he could not prove?

Lost in his own thoughts, Mark rode a respectful distance behind Giles and the Duke. At first he considered Giles' claim to be Edward's son but it was not long before his thoughts turned towards Lady Anne's maid, Lucy. She was delightful but was it love or just lust that kept her desirable image in his minds eye? Either way he considered her affect on his heightened senses most enjoyable and recalled similar feelings years ago for Alice Twynho but that had been a trap he was fortunate to have escaped. Did he still value his freedom or was it time to take a wife? He had all but decided on the later when an involuntary vision of Margery Goodman confused his sensibilities.

The sombre cavalcade rode into York to be greeted by the city's dignitaries, offering Gloucester condolences for the loss of his brother and assurances of loyalty to his young nephew Edward V.

The citizens had turn out in large numbers to watch the procession but their voices were muted as it was not proper to shout and cheer at men so clearly in mourning. Harbingers made their way through the crowds and directed men to their billets across the city, whilst Gloucester enquired of the Lord Mayor as to the arrangements for the Requiem Mass to be held in the great Cathedral of St Peter.

"Mark, take my things to the friary off Old Coney Street and stable the horses," ordered Giles, "then meet me at the top of Stonegate south of the Minster."

He slipped from his horse and whilst Gloucester was preoccupied with the Lord Mayor, handed his reins to Mark and nudged him in the ribs to make a move.

"Why? Are you not attending the mass?" asked a bemused Mark.

"Just do as I ask," hissed Giles under his breath and was gone.

He had spotted Oswald Garvey amongst the dignitaries surrounding the Duke and reasoned that he would be able to speak to Oswald's wife alone, provided she were at home and still make it to the Minster in time for the Requiem.

Stonegate was busy, despite the spectacle of the arrival of the Duke of Gloucester drawing folk away from their daily business. The street was wide and partially cobbled, reflecting its status as one of the most prestigious addresses in the city, where quality goods were for sale, displayed on well maintained shop fronts, nestling beneath substantial living quarters. Behind these towered larger, high status dwellings, accessible only through alley ways between the rows of shops. Giles was unsure where precisely in Stonegate Garvey lived, so he entered the nearest tavern and asked for directions.

He found the alley beyond the goldsmiths as the taverner directed, the far end of which open into a spacious court yard flanked on one side by an old manor house with a recently constructed one storey extension at right angles to the older building. Giles presumed this to be a new hall, as three huge glazed windows extended from beneath the eaves to within a couple of feet above the cobbled yard. Giles was impressed. Master Garvey must be a wealthy man to own such a house. An elderly servant waddled over to meet him as he stood admiring the costly extension. He mumbled something about his master being with the Mayor's party greeting the Duke of Gloucester but when Giles explained that it was Mistress Garvey he had come to see, the amazed servant begged his pardon and asked him to repeat his reason for visiting. It was only after Giles had assured the servant that he was Gloucester's nephew and that he had met Master Oswald when supping with Abbot Booth, that the old man reluctantly agreed to show him into the house and inform mistress Garvey that she had a visitor.

He was announced into a small but well furnished solar where a young girl of about fourteen summers sat on a huge cushion in the window seat. She had a pleasant round face, a fulsome body and the broadest grin that would endear even the sternest observer. It was not unusual for young girls to be married off to wealthy, older men and often with the lady's consent but Giles had grown up to disapprove of such arrangements since the scandal that had surrounded the marriage of a thirteen year old Woodville boy to the eighty year old Duchess of Norfolk. Mistress Garvey appeared perfectly at ease with her condition and greeted him cordially enough but her youthful curiosity could not be contained and she eagerly enquired as to the nature of his business.

"I met your husband when we both had supper with Abbot Booth," explained Giles, "and he told how he had first heard the news of King Edward's death at your father's home in King's Lynn."

"Then it is my husband you need to speak to after all," interrupted the girl peevishly.

"No mistress. You see your husband was unable to say who had delivered the news to your father's house and I thought, that as you have lived there most of your life, you might know the names of your father's associates and any local land owners who might have friends in high places and be privy to such information."

Smiling knowingly she jumped down from her cushion and crossed to the door. She opened it and after looking up and down the corridor to ascertain that no-one was listening, she closed it softly again and to Giles' surprise, turned the key in the lock.

"So Sir Giles, you think as I do, that the premature reporting of the King's death was not just a misunderstanding and that something sinister was going on?"

"No, no, of course not," protested Giles too emphatically for conviction, "but I do feel the matter needs a sensible explanation, if only to stop silly speculation."

She ignored the implication. "Well the local land owners are the Scales family but most of their estates were inherited by Anthony, Earl Rivers when he married Lady Cecily Scales. He often stays at Middleton or Castle Rising when he is in Norfolk approximately five miles from Lynn."

Giles failed to disguise his excitement and so she warmed to her theme.

"You have no idea what Oswald was doing at my father's house on 3rd April, have you Sir Giles?" she asked with an impish grin.

"Visiting his father-in-law, the Mayor of Lynn?"

Mistress Garvey giggled and shook her head very slowly. "Oswald and I were married on 4th April," she announced with pride, "I was there when the messenger arrived with the false news of the King's death."

"What! Mistress tell me carefully everything you know, *please*."

She settled herself back on the window seat and began her story as if she were telling a cautionary tale to a younger child.

"My father's oldest friend is a small landowner called Roger Townshend and on the evening before the wedding he arrived at the house with Lord Rivers. They had been in dispute over some boundary and had agreed to let the Council of the North arbitrate in the matter. They wanted Oswald to present their case to the council when he travelled north after our marriage. You can imagine what an honour it was for my husband to be so trusted and father instantly invited Lord Rivers to attend the wedding feast on the following day. That evening Roger Townshend, Lord Rivers, Oswald and my father drank well into the small hours and were seriously in their cups." Mistress Garvey made a moue and nodded knowingly. "My chamber is above father's chancery where their merriment kept me from the sleep I so urgently needed." She looked coyly at Giles from beneath her lashes. "So, when a horseman rode into the yard I jumped out of bed and tried to see what he wanted at such a late hour."

"And did you see or hear anything?"

"Not really. I watched the man enter the chancery from my hiding place at the top of the stairs. He carried a small scroll tied with a red cord and I saw him leave without it but I could hear nothing of what was said. However, I am sure that the messenger brought the false news of the King's death."

"How can you be sure if you heard nothing?"

"Not then but when I returned to my bed I could hear the five of them drinking and saluting the new young king, Edward V."

So a messenger had brought the news to the Mayor's home, thought Giles, but into whose hands was the scroll delivered? And what did this message say exactly? the king is dead…. the king is likely to die … or did it just describe the severity of his ill health and the five men assumed that death would follow? Whilst Giles tried to imagine the format of the message, Mistress Garvey rummaged in her work box, eventually recovering a small scroll of parchment rolled and tied with red ribbon and bearing a broken seal.

"I found this under the table on the following morning," she said, flourishing the scroll under Giles' nose, but it will tell you nothing."

She became animated and petulant as she recounted the state of the chancery after the five men had been drinking all night and the delicate state of health of both the bride's father and the groom on her special day, how little sleep she had had and how after all the fuss, Lord Rivers had not stayed for the wedding feast.

"May I see that?" asked Giles gently as her torrent of words diminished and her anger subsided.

She dropped the scroll in his lap and sat with her head on one side waiting for his reaction. The seal was no more than a lump of wax with no signet indent with which to identify the sender and when Giles unrolled the parchment it was blank. He held it up to the light but no message had been written and later erased. He even sniffed it to test for the use of lemon juice instead of ink, he had heard that when dry, lemon juice left no mark, but the reader would have scorched the page in order to reveal the message and it would have remained visible. How then could a blank sheet convey a message to its receiver?

The Minster bells ceased their dirge as the mass was about to commence. Panicked by the advancing hour, Giles quickly took his leave of Mistress Garvey with the promise that he would return and explain the mystery, if and when he solved it.

Mark was waiting impatiently at the top of Stonegate and together they crept guiltily into the crowded Minster from the south door. Throughout the service Giles thought of nothing but the death of Edward IV and by the time they returned to the little Augustine friary on the banks of the Ouse he was convinced he could prove to Gloucester who was responsible for the death of his beloved brother King Edward IV.

Chapter 22

Nottingham 26th April 1483

It was late afternoon on the 26th April when the rain stopped and three hundred sodden noblemen and gentlemen from Yorkshire, led by Richard Gloucester, rode into the bailey of the magnificently modernised castle at Nottingham. Since leaving York, His Grace had been constantly surrounded by his northern friends, some of whom he had not seen since they returned from war with the Scots and their reminiscing had made it impossible for Giles to speak privately with his uncle. However, last night after supper, Gloucester had announced that Lord Rivers had been gracious enough to reply to his letter. The King's party had left Ludlow and would wait for the Duke at Northampton so that they might ride into the Capital together.

It was imperative that Giles should speak with his uncle without further delay.

"His Grace is in a hot tub Sir Giles, your presence will not be welcome," insisted a sturdy squire with a sailor's gait and ruddy complexion.

He was carrying two large wooden buckets of hot water, suspended either side of a yoke, unsuitably balanced across his rolling shoulders and Giles had to dodge from side to side to avoid the slopping water, as squire and buckets progressed precariously down the gallery.

"Explain to his Grace that I would not inconvenience him so if the matter were not both urgent and personal," persisted Giles through the rising steam.

They had reached Gloucester's chamber and Giles held the door open, whilst the confused servant entered with his replenishing buckets of hot water. Within minutes the sailor like man returned, the empty buckets clanking against the walls and floor as he emerged from a curtain of steam. He simply nodded his head towards the haze as he manoeuvred himself and his yoke passed Giles, who hovered in the doorway, uncertain of how he should interpret the gesture.

"For the love of God Giles, come in and close that door," bellowed Gloucester from the depth of his hot tub.

Giles had merely wiped the dirt from his face and wrung out his hose before taking the decision to speak to his uncle and he felt embarrassed stood in his wet and dirty riding gear before the Duke, stark naked and up to his neck in steaming water.

"Now, what is so important that you must speak to me in my bath nephew?" asked Gloucester gently. He was shrewd enough not to ignore Giles' request to speak with him both 'privately and urgently'.

"Anthony, Earl Rivers is responsible for the murder of King Edward. I'm sure of it," said Giles bluntly.

Gloucester sat up in an involuntary movement that swept the water up and out of the tub, swamping the floor and surrounding rugs to a considerable radius.

"You are certain Giles? – pass me that robe – explain yourself."

The Duke abandoned his tub and wrapped himself quickly in the woollen gown Giles passed to him. Beyond the steam, the door opened again and the squire, balancing more buckets of hot water on his yoke, started to manoeuvre his second entry.

"Get out and stay out," yelled Gloucester.

Water sloshed out of the buckets as the poor man tried to turnabout and Giles, rushing to his aid, slipped on the wet tiles and almost felled his uncle as he grabbed a handful of the duke's gown in an attempt to stay upright. Gloucester struggled to control his temper but Giles had released his grip and getting to his feet, eventually managed to reverse the yoked servant back into the gallery. He closed the door and sheepishly followed his uncle into the adjoining bed chamber away from the puddles, wet rugs and slippery tiles.

"Start at the begin Giles," said Gloucester, his anger at last under control as he settled himself in a leather slung chair at one side of the brazier, at the same time indicating the stool at the other side for Giles to sit and dry himself.

"I have been making enquiries on several fronts and at last I have a clear picture of what happened but I am still at a lost to understand the motive behind the murder."

"Get on with it nephew before I catch my death," begged the Duke, his wet hair dripping onto his woollen gown whilst he attempted, with little success, to dry his feet on a silk cushion.

"When King Edward granted Lord Rivers the governorship of his son, he also granted him the right to raise troops should he need to defend the boy, presumably because he set him up in his own court at Ludlow. *That was nine years ago* but just *three weeks* before the King was taken ill, Rivers requested copies of the letters patent granting him these rights. I believe Rivers was planning Edward's death when he made this request, *anticipating the need for written proof of his authority, should it be challenged after the murder was committed.*"

"But surely Lord Rivers was at Ludlow both when Edward was taken ill at Easter and later when he died on the 9th April," exclaimed Gloucester.

"He was my Lord, more than one hundred miles away from the murder he had planned but arranged for another to commit."

"Who conspired with him Giles? Tell me, was it Dorset?"

"I believe so. When Rivers requested the letters patent, he also arranged for his office of Deputy Constable of the Tower to be transferred to Dorset, which provided his nephew with unrestrained access to both the Tower armoury and the King's treasure. The week before Easter I was at the Tower myself when the Treasurer, Sir Douglas Hatton asked for my help. The Marquis had used his authority as Deputy Constable to enter the Treasure House and go through the items there-in."

"How do you mean, go through?"

"Well, Hatton insisted that Dorset and his brother Grey were repacking the treasure into 'manageable leather bags'. He begged me speak to the King and I promised to do so if they removed any of the bags."

"And were they removed?"

"No, not at that time but before I left for Middleham, Edward Woodville was planning to take the fleet into the channel, ostensibly to deal with French pirates. He probably has the treasure aboard his own vessel even now. I should have voiced my concern when Sir Douglas was discovered dead at the foot of the White Tower but after consulting with Bishop Morton we thought it more likely that Douglas had committed suicide for fear of being found responsible for some irregularity in the accounts."

"But now you think Dorset had Hatton killed to prevent his informing Edward of his activity in the Treasury?"

"It seems likely. However, I am certain that it was Lord Rivers who provided the arsenic and the precise plan for an accomplice to murder King Edward."

"Go on."

"As soon as Edward was taken ill for the first time on Easter Sunday, the accomplice wrongly assumed that Edward was dying and so he sent a pre-arranged signal to Rivers saying the deed was done and most importantly, *that no-one was any the wiser*. This signal was a blank piece of parchment, bound and sealed with wax and delivered to Mayor Thorsby at his home in King's Lynn where Rivers had contrived to be. Thorsby probably protested at the stupidity of the meaningless note but Lord Rivers thought he had the information he was waiting for. He could return to Ludlow and wait for the official news of Edward's demise, in the knowledge that the murder had been successfully passed off as a seizure."

"And if the messenger had failed to arrive, Rivers was conveniently placed to escape via the port of Lynn and join Edward Woodville in the channel with the King's fleet and the treasure. Very clever."

"Of course, I hadn't thought of that," said Giles. "Mayor Thorsby's daughter was to be wed to Oswald Garvey on the following morning and Lord Rivers remained to enjoy Thorsby's hospitality. If he had not done so then I would never have discovered the truth. It seems that too much fine wine mixed with the euphoria accompanying the apparent successful murder, must have loosened his tongue because Rivers announced that King Edward was dead and that his young charge would succeed his father as Edward V."

"That was exceedingly careless of the Earl," said Gloucester, "considering the meticulous way in which he had arranged not to be at the scene."

"With hindsight, yes, it may appear irresponsible but if Edward *had* died that night, then the official notification of his death would only have been hours behind the assassin's messenger. Thorsby's daughter heard the celebrations from her room above the chancery and the following morning the young bride found the discarded note which she brought with her to York and showed to me before the requiem."

" So that's why you were late. Will the merchant's wife be able to testify to Rivers' premature announcement of Edward's death?"

"Certainly and when we return to Westminster I will endeavour to trace the messenger who delivered the blank parchment to Mayor Thorsby and with luck, he should be able to name Rivers' accomplice."

"Presumably Oswald Garvey also heard Rivers' announcement?"

"Yes, he informed his guild master as soon as they arrived in York and a mass was said for the King at the Minster, funded by the guild of Corpus Christi."

"Was it now? Nobody informed me."

"Well no my Lord, it was soon very clear that some dreadful mistake had been made as other travellers had not heard the news and poor Oswald was obliged to pay for the mass out of his own pocket."

"Dorset must have been panicked by Edward's recovery," observed Gloucester, " and it must have taken some nerve to repeat the murder attempt the following week."

Giles recalled Dorset's misinterpretation of Morton's announcement that, 'it was over' and thought Gloucester was probably right to assume that the Marquise was Rivers' accomplice but something still niggled in Giles' brain, something that contradicted that assumption.

"What will you do my Lord when you meet Lord Rivers the day after tomorrow?"

"Arrest him. What else?"

"But we need to discover the extent to which, Dorset, Grey and even Elizabeth Woodville, are involved. If you arrest Rivers for Edward's murder his fellow conspirators will disappear across the channel, taking Edward's treasure with them," reasoned Giles, "and then we may never know the motive for this heinous crime."

"Um ... very well. But as soon as we return to the Capital you are to set about finding the messenger who was dispatched to King's Lynn and with my warrant, arrest and interrogate Dorset. I want to know why the King's treasure was tampered with and what Edward Woodville is really doing in the channel." The Duke held up his hand to stem Giles' objection. "I mean it Sir Giles. This is high treason and I want every whoreson involved condemned to death before we crown the young boy King."

A further two soaked messengers rode into Nottingham Castle before curfew that day. The first to arrive was Sir Humphrey Percivall, a trusted knight in the service of Henry Stafford, Duke of Buckingham. Sir Humphrey was a tall man of indeterminate age with a shock of silver grey hair that contradicted his subtle frame and agile movements. His face was ghostly white without a single frown or laughter line to underscore the emotions of a natural life, emphasising the ghoulish nature of his pale blue eyes that protruded far beyond their sockets and the thinnest colourless lips that begrudged the need to part. He reminded Gloucester of a mural he had once seen as a child on the chapel wall in Jervaulx Abbey where the artist had depicted the spirits of departed souls as wisps of silver grey cloud with white, ageless faces.

Bowing low but without speaking, Sir Humphrey presented the Duke with a document pledging Buckingham's support for

Gloucester's protectorship and offered him two thousand fighting men with which to aid the enforcement of his authority. Percivall was unable to explain why his master thought that armed combat might be needed so Gloucester sent him back to the Duke of Buckingham with instructions to meet him in Northampton on the 29th but to bring no more retainers than he felt necessary for his own safety.

The Duke was about to retire, when his squire announced the arrival of the second messenger, one William Catesby with yet more news from Lord Hastings. Gloucester half hoped that Catesby's information would help them uncover the motive for Edward's murder, for it was the motive that had taxed the minds of both uncle and nephew since supper and as Giles had said repeatedly 'what possible motive had Earl Rivers for wanting Edward's death?'

Messenger Catesby was in his thirties, clean shaven and of compact build. He introduced himself as Hastings' lawyer and estate agent and offered conformation of his authority to speak for Lord William, by producing a ring bearing Hastings' seal. The faithful old warrior had deemed it prudent not to commit his message to parchment and had selected Catesby for the task because he could be relied upon to deliver an oral message verbatim. However, Catesby was a religious man with a loathing for excess and Lord Hastings' growing drink problem was causing him to doubt his master's judgement. He had been so shocked by the drunken stupor he had discovered his Lord to be in when he was summonsed, that he felt obliged to explain his concern before reiterating Hastings' dire message.

"I must deliver my message without innuendo or restraint my Lord," explained the serious faced lawyer, "anything less would be a betrayal of my master's trust. However, the nature of my message may have such bearing on the peace of the realm that I feel I must ask you to apply your own knowledge of the worthy Lord as well as the poor state of his humours, when assessing the value of what I have to say." He looked from Giles to Gloucester, expecting the Duke to dismiss his companion now that he had intimated the seriousness of his communication.

"My nephew stays," snapped Gloucester.

In truth he was impressed by Catesby's rhetoric, his loyalty to Lord Hastings and his common sense regarding the delivery of a message that may have irredeemable consequences if inaccurate. But he needed to hear it before he could judge its worth, so he simply waved his hand impatiently for Catesby to begin. Giles smiled at the agitated lawyer, conscious of his dilemma.

"Lord Hastings has uncovered a plot to assassinate Your Grace before you reach London," stated Catesby as if he were reporting the time of day.

"What?" exclaimed Giles jumping to his feet.

Gloucester managed to remain in his chair but he gripped the carved wooden falcon heads at the end of each chair arm so tightly that his knuckles turned white and the pulse on his temple throbbed as it had rarely throbbed before.

"Where did this information come from?" demanded Giles rudely.

"My Lord Hastings has recently taken to his bed, a lady from Queen Elizabeth Woodville's retinue." Catesby coughed discretely and gently touched his lips with his forefinger by way of apology for this indelicate disclosure. "It seems the lady overheard a conversation between the Queen and her son the Marquis of Dorset in which her Majesty expressed anger with her brother, Lord Rivers, for not attending the King's funeral. She was railing Dorset for not having made her intentions clear in his letter to Rivers informing him of King Edward's death."

"What were her intentions?" demanded Gloucester.

"Apparently she had deliberately withheld notification of the King's demise from yourself my Lord, so that Lord Rivers could deliver the Prince to Westminster to be crowned Edward V before you arrived to take up your duties as Lord Protector."

"So why *did* Rivers delay?"

"According to the Queen's lady, what she heard was the Marquis quoting extracts from a letter he had recently received from his uncle, in which Rivers explained that if his sister the Queen had informed *you* of the King's death immediately, as he had anticipated, then he would not have needed to delay his own departure on the pretext of celebrating St George's Day at Ludlow."

"You mean he was waiting for His Grace,?" asked Giles, "I don't understand."

"No? Well neither did the Queen," said Catesby looking directly at Gloucester as if it were he who had asked the question. "Dorset had to explained, in his own words, what he believed Rivers dared only to hint at in his letter and which the lady's maid reiterated to Lord Hastings in his bed: namely that Rivers intended to intercept your progress to the Capital and ensure that you did not live long enough to become Lord Protector. But as you delayed, so Rivers had to do likewise, excusing himself from the funeral ostensively to celebrate St Georges day."

A long silence followed whilst the Duke tried to control his anger long enough to assess Catesby's revelations.

"What cause have you to doubt the validity of this threat?" asked Giles, remembering Catesby's opening words. "Is it Hastings' constant drunken state or is his latest whore an untrustworthy gossip?"

Again Catesby coughed discretely and moved forward a pace so that he could no longer look directly into Giles' face.

"The Queen's lady, Margery, is not to be underestimated my Lord. She is a shrewd woman and by her own admission would not have repeated what she overheard were she not aware that Sir Giles Butler is accompanying you on your journey to London. Apparently she does not wish to see him perish at your side."

Catesby was aware of the sharp intake of breath from Giles but betrayed no indication that he knew the Duke's nephew was the man Margery wished to protect.

"My problem with the revelation is two fold my Lord," ventured Catesby bravely, "firstly, I cannot be completely sure that Dorset interpreted Rivers' inferences in the letter correctly, as he did not read out the precise words for Margery to repeat."

"And secondly?"

"Lord Hastings has directed me, to urge you, to pre-empt the Woodville strike and secure the Prince yourself, disposing of the Ludlow Woodvilles in the process and in the light of my first concern well … "

Gloucester broke the tension with a roar of laughter. "Excellent.

Unwittingly Lord Hastings has provided me with the excuse I needed to arrest Lord Rivers."

"I ... I fail to follow your reasoning my Lord ... "

Gloucester's face hardened and he leaned forward in his chair so that he was inches away from Catesby, who was obliged to either stare back into the Duke's icy blue eyes or step back; the latter was unthinkable.

"Believe me Catesby, I take the threat seriously and so should you."

Chapter 23

Northampton 29th April 1483

Northampton and its dignitaries had spent several days preparing for the arrival of Earl Rivers, the young King and the Dukes of Gloucester and Buckingham. There would be brisk business for the town's tradesmen and a rare opportunity for the city elders to present themselves to the princes of the realm. Harbingers had been hard at work securing accommodation and the many inns, taverns, and local religious houses were well stocked with food and drink ready to entertain the visitors due to arrive on the twenty-ninth. In the main street were three, conveniently adjacent inns and their owners, all dressed in their best attire and flush with the honour of accommodating the main parties, waited expectantly for the mighty Lords to appear. The Lord Protector was to occupy the middle hostelry with the young King and Rivers to his right and the Duke of Buckingham to his left. The keeper of the central inn had employed a local artist to over-paint his original sign with Gloucester's personal insignia, a white boar, which he intended pointing out to his auspicious guest in his welcoming speech. Unfortunately for the taverner, his carefully planned ceremony did not take place because Gloucester arrived to find confusion amongst the harbingers who complained bitterly to the Duke, that although Northampton provided ample accommodation for all parties, Lord Rivers had already left with the King for Stony Stratford. Without dismounting, Gloucester bellowed orders to one of his retainers by the name of Sir Richard

Radcliffe, to take thirty armed men and ride on to Stony Stratford but before he could instruct Radcliffe further, a small party of men led by Earl Rivers himself, trotted down the main street to where Gloucester's party was gathered and greeted the Duke like a long lost kinsman.

Although Lord Rivers was more than ten years older than Gloucester his creamy white, wrinkle-free face resembled that of a much younger man. Giles noted Rivers' likeness to his sister, the Queen, as he followed the Earl's gaze, his exquisite hazel green eyes sweeping across the group, noting who and how many attended the Duke. His full, heart shaped mouth stretched into a beguiling smile, displaying good teeth as he acknowledged Giles with the merest of nods. He purred his recognition of Gloucester's new role as Lord Protector and smoothly argued that since the King was now accommodated elsewhere, his Grace's retinue could spread, 'with deserved comfort', throughout the two inns. Giles watched bemused as his uncle smiled politely but no amount of eloquence and warm greetings could disguise Rivers' impertinent presumption. He had removed the King out of the reach of the man designated to protect his young Majesty and Gloucester had every right to be outraged but with considerable effort he remained calm. Soon enough he would wipe that ingratiating smile from Rivers' face with accusation of the Earl's involvement in King Edward's murder, at the same time thwarting the Earl's plan to assassinate his own person.

Amidst the mutual dissembling a second party of elegant and expensively attired riders burst into the gathering. The Duke of Buckingham had arrived. He swung from his saddle to greet Gloucester with all the aplomb of a French courtier and Gloucester dismounted and welcomed Buckingham warmly. Harry Bokingham, as he invariably signed himself, sniffed rudely when Gloucester presented Rivers and when he turned to introduce his nephew, Giles was nowhere to be seen. He had spotted Luke in Buckingham's entourage and had backed cautiously out of the group to go in search his friend.

Almost an hour later Giles returned to the White Boar and perched on the mounting block by the water trough. He had failed to find Luke. Why had Luke not come in search of him? He knew he would be travelling with Gloucester's party and he could not mistake where they were billeted. Mark appeared from the stable yard where he had been overseeing the care of their horses. Many young boys had been temporarily engaged as grooms to facilitate the influx of riders and Mark did not trust them to do a thorough job.

"I've taken your bags up to your room Giles. You're sharing with Radcliffe and Hastings' lawyer. The three of you will be sleeping top to tail like fish on a griddle, no snoring or farting to night Sir Giles."

Giles made no comment. His thoughts were elsewhere.

"Did you not find Luke?" asked Mark guessing correctly what was preoccupying his master.

"No and before you suggest otherwise, I *did* see him. Apart from recognising his lifeless arm, I looked him full in the face and I could have sworn he saw me too."

"If Luke had spotted you he would have sought you out immediately. What was he doing amongst Buckingham's men anyway?"

"I fear he was spying for Bishop John Morton," said Giles woefully, "he did warn me that our friendship would have to end if Morton and Gloucester became opposed over the care of the young King."

"But they haven't as yet. Have they?" Mark saw the pain in Giles' face and changed the subject. "Have you given any more thought to the possibility that our late King Edward was your father?"

"No," lied Giles, "things are complicated enough. But what *is* haunting me is Matthew Pawson's suicide."

"Do you think he was bullied by Dorset into taking his own life? The Marquise will be unassailable until the Lord Protector arrives to curb his power."

"Perhaps. Oh I don't know! Years ago I witnessed Matthew manhandle a bullying herald at the Tower. He displayed amazing physical strength and aggression for such a gentle soul but I suppose he had the backing of King Edward then."

That evening Gloucester, Buckingham and Rivers dined at the White Boar, whilst upstairs in their garret bedchamber Giles, Radcliffe and Catesby stretched out on straw stuffed mattresses and fretted over Gloucester's safety. For Radcliffe's benefit, Catesby had reiterated the warning he had brought from Lord Hastings, minimising his earlier misgivings as to its accuracy since Lord River's removal of the King to Stony Stratford appeared to underscore his master's assertion. Sir Richard Radcliffe listened intently, dropping his chin onto his chest to control his anger as the lawyer described Hastings' fear of ambush and possible assassination. Like many northern fighting men, Radcliffe admired Gloucester's leadership and courage in battle and since the Duke had found in Radcliffe's favour in a land tussle involving the mighty Earl of Northumberland, the squat, neckless Yorkshire man had devoted himself to the service of his Lord and received Catesby's perceived threat personally.

"What's His Grace doing eating supper with that fancy Woodville bugger if he knows for a fact that he plans to assassinate him?" he barked.

"I don't know," replied Catesby honestly, "perhaps he thinks if he arrests Rivers tonight, the news will reach Stony Stratford and alert the other Woodville lords."

"No news will reach Stony Stratford this night," said Radcliffe, "I've posted guards along the southern highway."

Giles rolled over on his bed and stretched to look out of the hole in the roof that served as a window. The moon was full and the sky clear and in the street below, guards were lounging by every door and alleyway as far as he could see in both directions: Radcliffe had been thorough. Giles considered telling his companions about Rivers' earlier treason but his uncle had kept to their agreement and remained silent, so Giles did likewise. To calm his apprehension he inhaled the chill night air from the gaping window and silently prayed that Gloucester would be extremely diligence. Eating and drinking with a poisoner who intended your death could have dire consequences.

"We three should take turns to keep watch in the street throughout the night," suggested Radcliffe, "none of those lads down there know what Lord Rivers intends."

"And neither do we for certain," whinged Catesby, "you can do as you please sir, but I need to sleep tonight."

Radcliffe looked hopefully at Giles. "Alright," agreed Giles, "you take the first shift. Wake me when it's my watch."

In the disturbed slumber that accompanied every first night Giles spent in a strange bed, he was just falling asleep, when someone seemed to be shaking his foot.

"Sir Giles, get yourself outside where we can talk without waking the lawyer."

Giles shook himself awake, grabbed his cloak and followed Radcliffe down the ladder that led to the first floor. At the far end of the corridor a weak light showed under the door of Gloucester's chamber and Giles nodded his understanding to Radcliffe as the soldier signalled to him to keep quiet. The guard outside the Duke's chamber was stood rigidly to attention and Giles couldn't help smiling. Radcliffe must have caught the man dozing when returning to rouse him. Once outside Radcliffe relaxed.

"About an hour ago Rivers left the two Dukes and returned to his own lodgings next door. I've locked him in, although he doesn't know it," whispered Radcliffe.

"What? How did you get the key? Wasn't there a guard?"

"The landlord saw reason soon enough," said Radcliffe, tapping the white boar sewn on his sleeve and the guard will be fine in the morning, apart from a sore head."

Pulling the cowl well over his head and wrapping his cloak tightly about his body against the chill, Giles perched once again on the mounting block by the water trough.

"Keep your eyes peeled for anything unusual Sir Giles. I shall take a quiet walk up the road towards Stony Stratford and see if there's any mischief afoot."

Before Giles could question him further, Radcliffe melted into the shadows and disappeared from view.

Moments later a column of a dozen men from Gloucester's retinue, with sacking tied round their boots to muffle the sound of marching feet, began changing the watch. The captain halted the column by the water trough and challenged Giles to reveal his identity.

"I'm sorry Sir Giles," apologised the confused captain when Giles threw back his cowl and then added cautiously, "what are you doing out here at this hour?"

"Sir Richard Radcliffe instructed me ... " but before Giles could finish his sentence the captain held up his hand, indicating that the mere mention of Radcliffe's orders was sufficient authority for him to be anywhere at anytime. Giles was impressed but as he watched the continuation of the orderly relief he became aware of someone crouching behind the mounting block.

"Don't look behind you," hissed a familiar voice.

"Luke?" gasped Giles, trying not to move his lips for fear of attracting attention from the new and alert guard posted no more than twelve feet away.

"Shut-up Giles and listen. Before dawn the King will leave Stony Stratford for London. Most of the two thousand armed men will remain behind and await the return of Rivers, Gloucester and Buckingham. *The Dukes will be arrested and executed on charges of treason.* If Gloucester's northerners resist then two thousand well armed Woodville soldiers have orders to take no prisoners."

"How do you know all this?" began Giles and then paused for a moment as the retiring column of guards past him on their return to camp. He raised his hand to their captain and watched as they disappeared behind the stables. To his horror he realised that an additional figure had join the rear of the column. Quickly he scanned the back of the mounting block but Luke had gone.

His first impulse was to follow the guards and try to find Luke but slowly, the seriousness of the message impressed itself into his brain and he fled into the White Boar in search of his uncle. Propelled by the knowledge that dawn would soon break, he bounded up the stairs and crashed unannounced into Gloucester's chamber, where he came to an abrupt halt as the warmth and calm of his surroundings startled his senses. Gloucester raised his head from a map he was studying whilst Buckingham, who had been dozing in an armed chair by the hearth, spluttered with shock and gathered his sprawling body into a more dignified posture.

"What the hell are you doing bursting in here unannounced?" raged Buckingham.

But Gloucester had become accustomed to Giles' unannounced appearances and turning his face away from Buckingham to hide his amusement, invited his nephew to take a seat and explain the reason for his sudden arrival. Without sitting down Giles blurted out everything Luke had told him and waited nervously for Gloucester to ask where the information had come from. He had no idea what he was going to say.

"You burst in here like a madman to say that Rivers intends to assassinate us? We already know that man," spat Buckingham buckling on his sword belt.

"Not quite Harry," interjected Gloucester, all signs of amusement gone from his face, "we only *guessed* that Rivers had returned simply to delay our riding on to Stony Stratford this afternoon."

"And we surmised that an ambush would be waiting for us when we eventually joined the King tomorrow," insisted Buckingham, unused to being contradicted.

"Yes Harry but we did not reckon on the King moving on *before* we reach Stony Stratford." Gloucester got to his feet and summonsed his guard. "Find Sir Richard Radcliffe and tell him we act immediately. Go man … now!"

Within minutes everyman in the White Boar was awake and ready for action. Giles rushed to the window at the sound of cartwheels on the cobbles and watched in amazement as Radcliffe and three guards, swords drawn, forced their way into Rivers hostelry and dragged the half dressed Earl out into the street. In desperation the frightened man screamed for Gloucester to protect him but Radcliffe pushed a filthy cloth into his mouth and gagged him. A guard bound his arms and ankles so roughly that he toppled and fell to his knees but on Radcliffe's order the three lifted the trussed Earl and threw him unceremoniously into the cart like a sack of rubbish.

"We should hang him now," snarled Buckingham.

"All in good time," sighed Gloucester, "now lets collect the King from Stony Stratford and arrest the remaining Woodvilles." He pulled the shutters across the window to ensure Giles' attention. "Giles I want you to ride to London immediately and explain to Lord Hastings what has happened here tonight. News of Rivers' arrest will travel swiftly to Elizabeth and she may assemble troops in the Capital. Discover what we are likely to encounter on our arrival and bring your intelligence back here in the next day or so."

Giles nodded his understanding and turned to take his leave.

"Take Hastings' lawyer, William Catesby with you ... and Giles ... God's speed."

Catesby, Mark and Giles were about to leave for London when Sir Richard Radcliffe came bustling out of the White Boar calling for Giles to wait awhile.

"I am to escort you as far as Stony Stratford and guide you round the two thousand strong army, camped in the fields beyond," said Radcliffe with a broad grin, "it would appear the Duke of Gloucester is concerned for your safety."

"He might well be," said Catesby petulantly, guiding his mare between Mark's and Giles', "it's not yet three o'clock. Folk out at this hour are usually up to no good."

The others laughed but never-the-less were please to follow Radcliffe and his half dozen men-at-arms out of Northampton and onto the London Road. Every few miles they were challenged by small groups of armed men who appeared silently from the shadows but all were Gloucester's guards, posted earlier by Radcliffe to ensure that no messenger from Lord Rivers' reached the Woodvilles at Stony Stratford. However, as they neared the town their scout reported soldiers, numbering about fifty, were stationed by the main gate but that the main army was preparing to leave.

"Can't we ride round them to the northeast?" ventured Giles, "that line of trees would provide cover."

"No way. Until the troops break camp we can't be sure how many are moving south with the King. If I was their commander I would post several hundred below the ridge, behind that tree line."

"You would, why?"

"To prevent Gloucester from retreating to Northampton after the ambush is sprung," said Radcliffe and without further consultation ordered them off the road to take cover in a small but dense copse. Whilst Giles tried to control the contents of his stomach, Radcliffe was sending a scout back to Northampton with a message for the Duke.

"We stay here, together and we stay quiet until we have further instructions from His Grace," commanded Radcliffe, "I'm taking no chances with *your* life," he added grimly, nodding at Giles, " it would be more that mine is worth."

Giles doubted that, having observed the trust his uncle placed in the northern knight but he didn't argue and they did not have long to wait. Within the hour Gloucester and Buckingham arrived in person, escorted by a dozen or so well armed men.

"We must move fast," ordered Gloucester, "the King will be ready to leave for London by now."

Buckingham dismounted and proceeded to dress Catesby in what Giles recognised to be Rivers' floppy plumed hat and velvet cloak.

"You're near enough Rivers' height," said Buckingham more to himself than to the astonished Catesby, "but mind you ride between Gloucester and myself and try to hide your face in our shadows, they will not be deceived for long."

Catesby was clearly terrified and as Giles tried to convince him that his likeness to the earl was 'amazing' the contents of his own stomach threatened again and he was obliged to turn away.

Once they had left the copse, Giles rode his mare close to the rump of Gloucester's white stallion and prayed for some of the famous Plantagenet courage, which he reasoned must surely lurk somewhere in his blood. It wasn't long before they were insight of Stony Stratford's well guarded gatehouse and the sound of guards notifying the gatekeeper of their impending arrival carried back to them on the still night air. Giles closed his eyes as they approached, it was the only way he could stop himself from digging his spurs into the sides of his mare and bolting. He heard Buckingham hail the gatekeeper and demand that the gate be opened in the name of the Lord Protector, Harry Bokingham and Anthony, Earl Rivers. As their party came to a halt, Gloucester edged his horse in front of Catesby's left flank and Buckingham did likewise on his right. Whilst the confused keeper hesitated to comply, Giles opened his eyes, grabbed the lawyer's arm and raised it above Buckingham's head indicating to the keeper that he was in agreement with the duke's demand. It worked. The heavy gates were swung open and Gloucester led his party under the archway and down the main street to a well lit tavern, where men were busy loading carts and sumpter ponies in preparation for departure. A large chestnut mare and a creamy palfrey were saddled and waiting impatiently at the main entrance and just as Gloucester's party drew up, the boy King appeared in the doorway with his household treasurer Sir Thomas Vaughan and his youngest half brother, Lord Richard Grey.

"My Lord Rivers," cried the King, who had recognised the plumes bobbing above Catesby's head, for he wore an identical cap with similar plumage.

Gloucester and Buckingham dismounted in unison and both, falling to one knee, paid homage to their young sovereign. Vaughan and Grey, peered into the gloom in search of Rivers, hesitating just long enough for Radcliffe and his henchmen to slip behind the two Woodvilles and move in so close that they could smell their perfume. Before either realised they had been deceived, daggers were pressed against the backs of their necks and Radcliff's unmistakable Yorkshire tones bid them 'hold still,' and 'call out at their peril'. Buckingham raised his voice to drown out Radcliffe's as he engaged the King with flattery and talk of the splendour of his forthcoming coronation but the boy was not distracted for long. He wanted to know where Vaughan and Grey were being taken and why his uncle Rivers was not here to greet him. It fell to Gloucester to explain the reason for the scene his young majesty had been forced to witness and although the King protested Rivers' innocence and steadfastly refused to concede that there was a plan to ambush and assassinated the two Dukes, he dutifully resigned himself to Gloucester's protection. Buckingham escorted the King back into the tavern to refresh and compose himself, whilst arrangements were made for their return to Northampton. So Giles sauntered over to where Gloucester was instructing Radcliffe to assemble the captains of the enormous Woodville army.

"Everyman will be paid off during the course of today and tomorrow, but retain the best hundred or so, we may need more men when we return to London."

"My Lord," interrupted Giles, "we should collect all their arms. A display of so many weapons when you enter the Capital will be *visual* evidence of River's aggression."

Gloucester grinned. "A good idea Giles. See to it Radcliffe." The Duke turned and put his arm around Giles' shoulder. "I saw you raise Catesby's arm at the gatehouse. Well done lad."

"How could you be so certain that it would work out like this?" asked Giles, pointing to the knights and squires leaving for Northampton under Gloucester's banners, when only an hour ago they were destined for London under Rivers' standard.

"I wasn't *certain*," laughed his uncle, " but who would dare challenge the mighty Dukes of Gloucester and Buckingham? We meant no harm to our King. Did we not pay homage to our sovereign Lord? *I am his lawful guardian,* it would be treason to question my authority as Lord Protector of the realm." With his arm still about Giles' shoulder, Gloucester guided his nephew away from the busy forecourt. "But jesting aside Giles, there is no way back now. You saw how his young Majesty reacted to the apprehension of his kinfolk. *We must proof that Rivers and Dorset murdered his father,* otherwise he will take revenge on me and mine once he is crowned and my Protectorship ends."

"We need to discover Rivers' *motive* for murdering King Edward," sighed Giles, "without it, no-one will believe he murdered the one man who maintained the entire Woodville family, however substantial the evidence."

Gloucester signalled to the groom holding the horses. "Be on your way now nephew. Bring me news of the Capital's reaction to my coup and note especially how Elizabeth and Dorset respond. Who knows, their actions may betray the motive we seek."

Out of the corner of his eye, Giles saw Catesby lean from his horse and speak to a man he thought he recognised. An involuntary shudder passed over his body and communicated his anxiety to the Duke via his encircling arm.

"It's good that you recognise the danger," he said softly, misinterpreting the reason for Giles' reaction.

Unable to explain his misgivings about the man, now laughing heartily at something Catesby had said, Giles took his reins from the groom, bowed to his uncle and mounted.

"I closed my eyes as we approached the gates earlier," admitted Giles simply.

"Well there's a coincidence, so did I," lied his uncle.

Chapter 24

London 29th/30th April 1483

As they journeyed to London, William Catesby experienced for the first time, the exaltation that follows the success of a dangerous mission. His hither-too uneventful life had been whipped into high drama by Gloucester's coup and he repeatedly rehearsed the telling of the part he had played in persuading the gatekeeper to allow them into Stony Stratford. It was difficult to communicate with the other two riders galloping at speed but at every break for refreshment he exploded with excitement. In his first version of the events, Catesby admitted to being 'shocked' when Buckingham threw Rivers' cloak over his shoulders but by noon he had 'volunteered' to play the part of the Earl and had 'hailed' the gatekeeper, mimicking Rivers' voice.

"Whatever happened to your passion for the truth?" chided Giles, as they led their horses down to a brook and prepared to take a much needed break themselves. "Is that the story your friend found so amusing this morning?"

"Friend? What friend? Oh that was John Hatton. He's a clerk-at-law at Westminster; he's more of a colleague than a friend."

"*Hatton*? A relation of Sir Douglas Hatton, the dead Treasurer?" bellowed Giles so rudely that both Mark and Catesby abandoned their wine skins to stare at him.

"I'm not certain," replied Catesby, his lawyer's instincts advising caution.

Giles said no more but rode in silence throughout the afternoon. Now he remembered why he thought he knew the man. John Hatton was the treasurer's relation who had appeared at the inquest but who, like the rest present that day had remained silent and allowed an unchallenged verdict of accidental death to prevail. So he was a lawyer *and* he had been in Lord Rivers' party at Stony Stratford. A coincidence not to be dismissed lightly. Giles' ruminations sustained him until dusk clouds began to gather and the three riders neared Westminster.

"Its after curfew," sighed Catesby, "we should stay here tonight and then we can enter the Palace of Westminster early tomorrow."

"No," exploded Mark, but then fell silent. He and Giles exchanged glances.

"What?" asked Catesby, looking from one to the other, "we can't use Gloucester's authority to break the curfew, otherwise as soon as news of the coup is brought to the Queen, we'll be sent straight to the Tower."

They were approaching the Rising Sun tavern, still known locally as Ned's ale house even after extensive renovation. Neither Mark nor Giles had been inside the improved inn since Mark had jilted Alice and Ned had married Rosy Burrows. A groom came forward as they reined in their horses, assuming they intended entering the tavern. Giles and Catesby dismounted but Mark sat still, panicked by the thought of confronting Alice and her father.

"Tend the horses yourself Mark," ordered Giles, "they've been ridden hard today and stay with them in case we need to leave in a hurry. I'll send food out to you."

Catesby stared after Mark in amazement, as without a word he took Giles' reins and led his horse into the stable yard, whilst an equally surprised groom led Catesby's mount after him. Giles offered no explanation but strode purposefully into the taproom, casting his eyes around the screened tables and dark alcoves whilst Catesby summonsed the landlord. The buttery door opened and a round faced man with a shock of red hair answered the sound of Catesby's banging fist on the bar. The lawyer explained their need to lodge for the night and ordered food and a jug of the best claret. The round faced barman nodded and yelled for Alice over his shoulder. This must be Peter Lawton, thought Giles as he noted the cat like features of their host.

"Bring the food up," ordered Giles, not wishing to come face to face with Alice but even as he spoke he peered through the shadows of the half open buttery door, making out the figure of a woman tucking a child into a crib. His heart sank as Alice stepped into the light. She looked weary, ill and had aged ten years, according to Giles' critical eye. Her once beautiful hair resembled old straw, which she had tied up carelessly with a dirty rag but her face lit up when she recognised him and some of the old sparkle reappeared in her eyes. Instinctively she ran forward, throwing her arms around his neck and kissing him on both cheeks. He struggled not to step back as the smell of baby vomit and milk rose from her upper body, threatening to make him retch but he managed to hold still whilst she clung to him, just long enough to hurriedly search for Mark in the shadows behind him.

"This way sirs," whispered Alice in a hoarse voice, when she realised that he was not with them.

The startled landlord snatched Catesby's wrist as he made to follow Giles and Alice to the staircase.

"You know my wife?" he asked roughly.

"I most certainly do not," replied Catesby and wrestling his arm from Lawton's grip followed the couple upstairs.

"How's Ned," Giles asked, when Alice had opened the door to their chamber.

Her eyes filled with tears. "He's dead sir, over a year since. Mistress Rosy owns all now. It's strange," she added quickly, to intercept the embarrassed apology forming on Giles' lips, "but only yesterday a man came in here asking after you and me not having seen you for five years 'till today."

"What sort of man," asked Catesby, who had been as confounded as the landlord by the personal welcome Alice had afforded his companion.

"A foreigner sir, by the way he spoke.. and a seaman." She covered her brow with the palm of her hand. "I'm sorry sir I forget his name. Roskin or Roscoe. It was foreign. I did not expect to see you, so I didn't think it would matter." She turned to Catesby who had let out a sigh of exasperation. "Really sir I'm sorry, it has been five years…"

"Calm down Alice, it's alright," interrupted Giles, "it was probably Captain Runeskoff. I have business with him and I've been away from the Capital for more than two weeks. Although why he should seek me here I have no idea."

Giles had not considered what would happen to the late King's shipping investments. Presumably the Lord Protector would assume responsibility. Giles would have to consult with Morton regarding the legal implications but tomorrow he would go to the Tower and send for the agents to arrange transport of the cargo and he could leave the profits in the treasury until his uncle arrived and took over.

"It's a long story and it's Mark's to tell, not mine," said Giles, when Alice had left and he sensed the questions bursting in Catesby's head. "Look, you take Mark's supper out to the stables, then I won't have to speak to Alice again and you can tell Mark what happened when we booked in." Catesby was about to protest but Giles continued. "Then, if he wishes to tell you the whole story he can. You'll hear nothing from me."

With that Giles unbuckled his sword belt, pulled off his boots and stretched out on his palliasse. In moments he was snoring gently.

Giles woke with a start, well before dawn and as sleep gave way to consciousness he was aware that the entire hostelry was stirring around him. Catesby was already up and peering out of the open window, trying to discover the nature of the noise that had woken them both.

"There it is again," cried the lawyer, "it sounds like falling masonry."

"More like a war engine of some kind," cried Giles, pulling on his boots and grabbing his sword belt, "The Palace must be under siege."

Both men hurtled downstairs and into the yard where other half dressed men, some holding lanterns and tar-torches high above their heads, were contemplating the nature of the huge booms coming from Westminster, followed by what sounded like falling rocks.

"Look, look, it's the Abbey," screeched a young boy, as a cloud of dust rose high into the sky.

Mark arrived at Giles' side and without further conversation the three men raced the two hundred yards or so to the Abbey precinct. Dawn was breaking in a pink haze behind the towering mass of black stone whilst blankets of mist rolled in from the river, creeping round the Palace walls and drifting across the yard like beckoning ghosts. The huge gates were already open and behind the Chapter house the air was heavy with dust but the booming had stopped and apart from a group of richly dressed lords huddled in deep conversation by the west door, nothing seemed amiss. The group turned to face Giles and his companions as the sound of their footsteps crunched on the gravel path.

"Sir Giles... and Catesby," cried Lord William Hastings extracting himself from the bunch, "is His Grace of Gloucester with you? Where is the young King?"

"Safe in Northampton, my Lord," replied Giles, "we are sent before to discover what sort of reception the Lord Protector and his charge might expect to find in the Capital." Giles coughed discretely and whispered behind his hand so that only Hastings might hear. "The Woodville plot to assassinate his Grace has been foiled and the guilty Lords despatched to Pontefract."

Hastings wound one large arm about Giles' shoulder and the other around Catesby's, hugging them so closely that they could smell the wine fumes from his breath.

"Good, that's very good," slurred Hastings, as he ushered them, a little unsteadily, into the throng of Lords and introduced them like two favoured nephews back from an errand he had sent them to fulfil.

"We heard a noise like cannon-fire and hurried from our beds to investigate," explained Catesby.

"Ah, well, that was a catapult, not a cannon, though I can see why you might think it a cannon," said Lord Hastings, breathing more fumes directly into Catesby's face.

"A catapult," exclaimed Giles, freeing himself from Lord William's right arm, "what in God's name is going on?"

Hastings grinned wickedly and Giles noted the horror and disgust on the faces of others in the group. One of them was Bishop Morton, who made no attempt to acknowledge Giles even though he looked him straight in the face and caught his eye.

"Your news arrived before you sirs," crowed Hastings. "Just before midnight a messenger arrived from Stony Stratford demanding to see the Queen, and bringing news of her kinsmen's treason. She summonsed these noble lords, our late King's council," Hastings gestured towards the group, " and ordered them to close the city gates, call men to arms and declare our Lord Protector a traitor. But they deemed it unwise to antagonise his Grace, knowing as they do, that he is the boy's legal guardian." Hastings emphasised 'legal guardian' and glared round the assembled lords, daring them to contradict him. "And they all know that Gloucester's supporters from the North are a vicious lot when they sense disloyalty to their noble Prince." Hastings winked at Catesby before releasing him with a hefty shove.

"And the catapult?" persisted Giles.

"Ah, yes, well, when the Queen realised that the city of London would welcome Gloucester as well as the King, she and the Marquis of Dorset moved her entire quarters into the Abbot's house and claimed sanctuary. Unfortunately some of her furnishings were too large to go through the doorway and as there was no time to dismantle the pieces, well, she had the walls dismantled instead."

"With a catapult?"

Hastings took a long and noisy swig from the wine skin tied to his belt, wiped his mouth with the back of his hand and laughed raucously.

"It was to hand in the palace yard, so why not use it?" he bellowed, and laughed again.

"I must go," announced Morton curtly, "I've had little sleep and I've a busy day ahead. If you will excuse me my Lords."

"One moment Your Grace, I would speak with you about the

King's shipping," said Giles, stepping forward to block Morton's departure.

Morton looked about him to see who had registered Giles' demand, then taking him by one elbow he manoeuvred him out of earshot.

"Keep your voice down. What is it?"

"Captain Runeskoff has been asking for me at the Rising Sun, which means the Sally Forth must have docked whilst I have been away. I'll send for the merchants' agents to collect their goods and the profits can be housed in the Treasury for the time being but I need you to come to the Tower tomorrow and authorise his payment."

"I'll do no such thing Giles. The Marquis of Dorset has commandeered the Sally Forth and confiscated her cargo. That's why Runeskoff was searching for you."

"Why? She was legal. The King granted Runeskoff her licence himself."

"The *late King*, Giles. Edward is dead."

"The merchants paid large deposits on that cargo, they must be repaid."

Morton walked Giles still further from the group.

"Dorset is, was, deputy constable of the Tower. He allowed Sir Edward Woodville to take half King Edward's treasure when he set sail in pursuit of the supposed pirates in the channel and less than an hour ago I witnessed the other half being carried into sanctuary."

The vein on Giles' temple began to pulsate.

"In manageable size leather bags no doubt?" Giles spat the words through clenched teeth. "Remember Bishop I came to you and asked for your advice when Sir Douglas made a fuss about Dorset repackaging the King's treasure. The poor man was pushed from the parapet for his concern. Well now we know don't we? He *was* murdered. Dorset, Rivers, Grey, they were planning to rob the treasury."

"You can't be sure of that," protested Morton weakly.

"Oh yes I can. And that was *before* King Edward died." screamed Giles, "perhaps they planned his death too?"

All the standers-by had edged forward, listening with amazement to Giles' enraged outburst, but he was spared the embarrassment of having to explain his last remark by the arrival of two men riding at speed through the gateway.

"Archbishop Rotherham," called out Lord Hastings, his disposition becoming less sober with every slurp from his wine skin, "do you come to join your mistress in sanctuary or to enquire after the din that has disturbed your slumbers?"

The thin, harassed looking, older man, pursed his lips and held high a red velvet bag. With sweat dripping from the fine strands of grey hair that fringed his pox marked face, he replied in a shrill, defiant voice.

"I deliver the Great Seal of England into her Majesty's keeping, and may you all rot in Hell for your pathetic weakness in this treason."

The two men abandoned their mounts to a groom who had hurried from the gatehouse as they rode in and without engaging in further banter they entered the Abbey by the west door. The second man was expensively but soberly dressed in fine black wool, trimmed with gold embroidery at the hem. He displayed a full set of ivory teeth which seemed slightly too large for his mouth and gave him the appearance of a snarling dog but he also wore a monk's tonsure which completed his macabre appearance. Mark walked over to Hastings, who was making two finger gestures towards Rotherham's receding figure.

"That was John Alcock, with the Woodville Archbishop, what's he doing sidling up to the Woodvilles?"

"He sidled up, as you so aptly put it, years ago. In fact I think he's related to Anthony Rivers," said Hastings rubbing the stubble on his chin.

The contented Lord Hastings walked back to the Palace supported by his lawyer, William Catesby, who Mark could hear start to relate his part in Gloucester's coup, whilst the other lords dispersed chattering amongst themselves about the uncertainty of the current political scene.

Mark and Giles sauntered down to the river bank and watched the morning sun slowly burn off the mist, revealing the river stage, set with all kinds of craft ready for the opening performance of a new day.

"John Alcock," said Giles slowly, "when did he take holy orders?"

"I've no idea, why?"

"I've been a fool Mark. When I returned from Oxford and discovered John Alcock residing at Clipberry Manor, I assumed that Bishop Robert had invited him to move in. I saw nothing sinister in the arrangement, in fact it seemed to be very desirable that my old guardian should have some company again."

"If you'd have asked me about the arrangement I would have told you differently," said Mark. "According to mother, Alcock is the Bishop's gaoler. He can do nothing and go nowhere without his permission. King Edward established him at Clipberry after he released the Bishop from the Tower."

"It wasn't King Edward who installed Alcock to spy on Bishop Robert, otherwise his duties would have ended with Edward's death and he was busy searching for the Bishop before we left for Middleham – remember?"

"Then who?"

"The day Bishop Robert was released from the Tower I was summoned there myself by Alcock, wearing the attire of a King's herald and over acting the part as I recall. My guess is that when Robert left the Tower, Alcock returned with him to Clipberry and took up his duties for *Earl Rivers.*"

"But King Edward sent for you that day, not Rivers."

"Quite, which is why the cleric was posing as a herald. It would not be difficult if Lord Rivers was behind the charade."

"But why?"

"When King Edward imprisoned Bishop Robert he made a huge mistake, not only because Robert was innocent of betraying his King but also because it signalled a connection between Clarence's public acknowledgement that I was his son and his death in the vat of Malmsey. You and I were confined to Clipberry but Rivers would harvest the endless rumours that would follow Clarence's death. He employed Alcock to ensure that no one made contact with the Bishop until he discovered the real reason for his imprisonment."

"And Matthew's suicide at Clipberry, is that linked to Alcock's spying too?"

Giles shook his head. " I really don't know but tomorrow I want you to travel to Wells and find the Bishop. The poor man has gone into hiding, I'm sure of it but when you do locate him, bring him straight to Gloucester's manor in Bishopgate and try and reassure him that John Alcock will be removed from his household."

"He may not want to return, especially when I break the news of Matthew's death."

"Then stay with him and let me know where you are. Whatever happens Mark once you have found him do not let him out of your sight; understand, I believe he is in mortal danger."

PART 3

"Cry, God save Richard, England's royal king!"
(Richard III – Wm. Shakespeare)

Chapter 25

London 5th May 1483

The journey from Northampton to London was a difficult one. No amount of cajoling from the Dukes of Gloucester and Buckingham could persuade the young King that the Woodville Lords were dangerous men. Perhaps it was to be expected since from the age of three, the boy had been reared exclusively by his Woodville uncle, Earl Rivers and it had been only a matter of days since Gloucester had arrested Rivers and dispatched him to Pontefract along with Lord Grey and Councillor Vaughan. Add to this the rush to sanctuary of his mother, younger brother, sisters and step-brother Dorset, it was understandable that the young King distrusted his uncle Gloucester.

The cavalcade from Northampton entered London on 5th May and made its way to the Bishop of London's Palace to the joyful peel of bells and the adulation of the Capital's citizens and as Giles had predicted, the carts loaded with weapons served as evidence of the aggressive intent of the Woodville Lords, so that Gloucester's coup was judged to be both prudent and legal by the Capital's worthies. The King's council, on the other hand, was less enthusiastic but still managed to confirm Gloucester as Lord Protector and schedule the boy's coronation for 26th June.

News of the foiled assassination attempt at Stony Stratford reached Middleham soon after the offending Woodville Lords were incarcerated in Pontefract Castle and nothing could dissuade Lady Anne, from making the arduous journey south to be with her husband. Gloucester had moved out of Baynard's Castle, his mother's home on the banks of the Thames, in early June and taken up residence in his own manor, Crosby Place where he welcomed his wife, exhausted and distressed after travelling at speed from Yorkshire. Regardless of her need to recover, she insisted that Richard reiterate every detail of the events leading to his coup at Stony Stratford.

"Would you not sooner rest a while?" he soothed, once they were alone in their bedchamber, the obligatory household welcome over.

"How can I rest, when virtual ruin lurks but twenty days away?" Anne slumped onto the cushioned bench at the side of her travel chest.

Richard sighed but inwardly he was glad that he would not have to explain to his wife the precariousness of their situation. He should have known she was alert enough to realise that when the boy was crowned Edward V on 26th of the month his own authority would end and Woodville revenge would take its toll on their little family. With glum resignation he told the story in careful detail, starting with Catesby's message from Hastings and ending with the King's refusal to accept the guilt of his Woodville kin.

"Will Hastings attends the boy daily," said Richard wearily, "and his young Majesty's insistence that Rivers is innocent is causing Hastings to doubt the accuracy of his whore's information."

Anne shook her head in exasperation. "By his own actions, Rivers confirmed what the girl overheard."

"How so?"

"Sweetheart, it's more than two hundred and fifty miles from Middleham to London and less than one hundred and fifty from Ludlow. When Edward died a messenger was despatched immediately to Rivers at Ludlow but Sir Giles set out for Middleham a week later. How could you and Rivers possibly have met at Northampton *if he had not been waiting for you?*"

"St. Georges day; he remained at Ludlow to celebrate St. George's day on 23rd."

"Why did he need to celebrate in Ludlow? He missed the King's funeral for heavens sake! Apart from which, Edward was a fellow devotee of St George and Rivers knew he was to be buried on the 23rd *and* in the very chapel dedicated to the noble Saint. What better acknowledgement of devotion to St. George did Rivers intend?"

"But Will Hastings is no longer sure … "

"No my love. Rivers was waiting to ambush you as Hastings' whore reported. He simply made a hurried excuse about celebrating St George's day at Ludlow when the Queen challenged his tardiness. Which means … ," she paused at the implication in her own words, "which means that neither Elizabeth Woodville nor Dorset, were party to Lord Rivers plan to assassinate you and Buckingham."

"Dorset has to be party to Rivers' plans," insisted Richard, "at least to Edward's murder. Who else could Rivers trust to filled the dates with poison?"

Anne shrugged and held out her arms for him to join her. Richard crossed the room and sat down heavily on the edge of the great bed, closed his eyes and drew his brows together with his forefinger and thumb of his right hand.

"Buckingham would have me take the crown for myself," he said simply and with his eyes still shut. He could hear the sharp intake of Anne's breath and then the rustle of her gown as she dropped to her knees before him. He opened his eyes to meet hers inches from his face. Her perfume reached his nostrils.

"Would you have it so?" she whispered, almost choking on her words as she tried to disguise her enthusiasm but he caught her mood. The vein on Richard's temple threatened to pulsate, as sick anger tore at his heart and his old demon reappeared. Anne would have been England's Queen if Lancaster had prevailed at Tewkesbury. For years after they were married he had tormented himself with the thought that she had gone willingly to Lancaster's bed in order to be crowned his Queen and her restrained eagerness now caused his doubts to resurface.

"Edward has trusted me with his son," he snapped, "would you have me betray that trust to fulfil your ambition to be England's Queen?"

Anne recoiled instantly. His anger was unfair and born of ridiculous jealousy.

"No, of course not," she retaliated sharply, "but what about my trust in you. I need your assurance that you will protect Ned from Woodville retribution."

He stared at her in disbelief. Did she really think he was not aware of the danger they were facing? How dare she use the safety of their son to challenge his loyalties?

"I'm sorry, I'm sorry," she cried, "I'm exhausted from the journey. You are right, I should rest."

She attempted to stand but he held her arm, so she turned her head to hide the tears of frustration threatening to undermine her strength. They had been here so many times before. With his free hand Richard took her chin and turned her face towards him. Dust that had caught in the corners of her eyes was escaping with her tears and causing dirty streaks to run down her face like some fallen child at play.

"I'm sorry too," he whispered, wiping the stains from her face with his finger tips, "let us start again. You asked what I intend to do. Well, I shall tell the young King and his mother, all I know about Edward's murder. Although I still have no idea why Rivers instigated the crime, Sir Giles has uncovered sufficient evidence to show, beyond doubt, how the murder was achieved."

"Tell me, please."

"Not now sweetheart, later." He put his forefinger gently on her lips to stem her protest. "There is a slim chance that Elizabeth will believe the evidence and because of her devotion to Edward, a similarly slim chance that she and I can be reconciled in joint abhorrence of his murder. Of course, Rivers must pay with his life for this treason," he added, "and I must continue as Lord Protector until the lad reaches his majority." He raised her face to his and kissed her forehead. "It may just work."

"And if it doesn't?"

"If it doesn't ? Well then I will listen more closely to Harry's plans."

He pulled her gently onto the bed beside him. "I promise you this my love, I will not put you and Ned at risk without a fight of one kind or another."

That, she never doubted.

***

Giles was astounded by his uncle's suggestion that *he* should tell Queen Elizabeth Woodville everything he had discovered about King Edward's murder, whilst Gloucester himself would recite the story to the young King.

"Elizabeth and I are such bitter enemies," insisted Gloucester, "it is unlikely I will control my temper long enough to tell the tale fully. Whereas you Giles, will last at least as long as she can tolerate the truth of your words."

Giles had not been convinced but he understood the urgency of his uncle's situation and wanted desperately to confide his suspicion as to Rivers' motive but he must speak with Bishop Robert first to confirm his theory. He had done all he could to find his old guardian, dispatching Mark to the cathedral town of Wells, in the hope that he might locate him before Alcock did but so far, there had been no news.

Resigned to his task, Giles returned to his rooms at Westminster for the first time in eight weeks, having lodged with his uncle since their return from Northampton. The entire Palace of Westminster seemed to be suspended in time, awaiting its new master to re-open the royal apartments, shout orders to slumbering servants and reassign idling men-at-arms to their new posts. One or two made a half-hearted attempt to acknowledge Giles but why bother? He was someone who had dealings with the late King: wasn't he?

His chamber was exactly as he had left it. The door-lock responded easily to his key and the shutters, he realised, had remained open since the day he had left. Light flooded through the glass filled fenestralls and Giles removed one to allow the stale air to escape and the dust to rise as air surged in through the open casement. The early June sun was warm but Giles shivered involuntarily in the surroundings he had once considered to be his home. Old friends such as Luke, Margery, John Morton and even Will Hastings all contributed to the atmosphere of 'things past' and Giles knew that in so short a period, his life had move beyond those memories and more disturbingly, beyond those loyalties. He touched the Blanc Sanglier on his sleeve and then shook himself from his reverie, for it was not nostalgia that had diverted him from the Abbey and Elizabeth Woodville's sanctuary.

Giles wanted to collect the drawing he had made of his mother's ring which he had hidden years ago in the worn tapestry and he also needed time alone to organise his thoughts before facing the Queen with the news of her husband's murder. He lit an old tallow-dip with tinder from the side table and pushed aside the leather curtain that opened into his windowless office. A strong reminder of Woof drifted up to his nostrils and disturbed by the sudden light, a small creature scurried from Mark's pallet in the corner and disappeared behind the wooden chest. Giles put the tallow-dip on the table and then surveyed the old arras. There were several fleurs-de-lis on its border but he easily remembered which one covered his sketch and so climbing onto the stool he reached behind the emblem adjacent to his chin, retrieved the scrap of vellum and placed it on the table next to the tallow-dip. Knowing exactly what he was looking for he wafted his hand at the flame to create a draught and as the light danced across the vellum, once again he saw the illusion. Several minutes passed whilst Giles pondered the events that had controlled his life since he received the real ring as a birthday gift from his dead mother, when the tallow-dip dimmed and threatened to burn out. Hurriedly he pushed the drawing into his script and chastising himself for allowing his thoughts to wander from his task, he rummaged in the hide writing box for the emergency candle stump he knew was there. Once it was lit he found a piece of palimpset, ink and a sharpen quill and began to make a few notes.

Giles needed to ensure that Elizabeth Woodville listened to his story, so he organised his tale, leaving the revelation that Rivers was responsible for Edward's murder until the last possible moment. Eventually, satisfied with the order of the facts, Giles snuffed out the candle and with a final lingering look about his old home he locked the door behind him and made his way down the back stairs that led into the kitchen yard below. Some activity persisted in the kitchen block: the mighty Palace was still home to dozens of servants who had to be fed but Giles found the reduced bustle unnerving, confirming his early sensation of a previous era and the unease associated with political uncertainty.

He crossed the Abbey precinct as bells summonsed the faithful to midday Angelus. Giles had deliberately chosen this hour because Abbot Esteney would be leading devotions and unable to attend the Queen during his visit. Esteney was a notorious gossip and Edward's murder must remain a secret for the time being.

A weary, elderly lay-brother ushered Giles into the hall which was stacked from floor to gallery with chests and furniture belonging to Her Majesty. Virtually every room in the Abbot's house had been commandeered by the royal sanctuary seekers, for as well as the Queen and her ten year old son the Duke of York, the house accommodated her brother Lionel, her eldest daughter Beth, her four younger girls and of course, the Marquise of Dorset. Two small children peered at Giles from behind a pile of precariously stacked, arrases. The lay-brother tutted with annoyance at the appearance of the two dishevelled youngsters, who had been hiding and then jumping out of their hidey-holes all morning, startling the poor man out of his wits. Giles knew the boy to be the young Duke of York, the girl, he presumed was one of his sisters. York recognised Giles instantly, as the funny knight who had played under the table with him and his cousin Ned at Yuletide and he bounded up to him like a welcoming puppy but his sister remained half hidden, unsure of their visitor.

The young Duke was small for his age with a face as round and plump as a rosy apple. Slightly over weight for a child of ten, his confident good nature and laughing eyes betrayed his ability to win over most adults, even against their better judgement.

"Sir Giles, Sir Giles it is good to see you again. Is cousin Ned with you?"

"No my Lord, he is not well enough to make the journey from Yorkshire but he sends his good wishes and hopes to see you again next Yuletide." Giles winked at the young Prince to let him know that he had also enjoyed their romp under the tables.

"Have you seen my brother Ed ... , I mean the King?"

"I have my Lord but not since he moved to the Royal Apartments in the Tower. Your uncle Gloucester is with him now."

"I wish I could be with him. There are no other boys here and there's hardly room to spit. Still I'm glad Edward's the eldest," he added quickly, "I wouldn't like to deal with grown ups and all their stuff."

Giles laughed and assured him that his brother had been well trained to deal with adult matters, when the lay-brother who had been hovering behind them, wringing his hands with impatience, coughed discretely.

"Shall I ask Her Majesty if she will she you Sir Giles?"

"I can do that brother," said a cool female voice from the gallery above.

Giles looked up to see the seventeen year old Princess Beth, gracefully descending the polished rosewood stairs and his heart missed a beat. She was stunning. On many occasions Giles had seen her from a distance and once, last Yuletide, she had smiled at him across the table but they had never spoken since that day, five years ago, in the Tower council chamber. She was a child then but now, well now, he could only described her as a goddess. Her golden hair hung loosely about her slim neck and bare shoulders, held in place by a thin gold band around her forehead. She wore a silk gown of forget-me-not blue with the new, fashionable, tightly fitting sleeves which, when she moved, failed to hide the curves of her neat waist and hips unlike the long draping sleeves that fell from the shoulders of most older women. Giles knew he was gaping at the vision before him but could do nothing to gather his composure.

"Not you as well Sir Giles?" scoffed the little prince, "why is it that every man Beth greets, acts like an dim witted idiot?"

The boy's uncompromising words assisted Giles' recovery. "Thank you," he said, a little too spiritedly, "I would be most grateful if you would announce me."

"Can I come too, Beth?" begged the Duke, looking from Giles to his elder sister with his best angelic expression, "Giles is the only visitor I have known since we came to this awful place."

"Of course sweetheart," she purred, "and you too Kate. You should not be playing in here. Her Majesty would be furious if she knew."

"Don't tell then," said the dumpy little six year-old with mousy hair and the same icy blue eyes as the rest of her siblings. She shuffled round the pile of arrases and slipped a chubby hand into her big sister's.

Beth turned and led the way back up the staircase, raising her gown to her ankle with one hand and trailing Kate with the other. The plump little princess struggled manfully with each step, slowing Beth's progress and providing Giles with a riveting back view of his goddess. The Duke of York linked his arm through Giles' and tugging him out of his daydream indicated the way forward with a kick at the bottom step. Beaming up at his captive with a contented grin, he stomped, un-prince like, up the stairs behind his two sisters dragging Giles with him. They were forced to push their way between the packed chests and leather bags, stuffed to bursting with clothes and hangings, that lined every passage way. After taking a short-cut that only the Duke knew, they were obliged to climb over stacked wicker panniers held together with leather straps to restrain the contents but eventually they reached the Abbot's solar. There was no man-at-arms guarding the solar door and Beth took childish delight in entering unannounced.

"Uncle Richard has sent Sir Giles to help you see sense madam," she proclaimed rudely and winked at Giles as she quickly withdrew before the Queen could gather her wits and reprimand her for her insolence. Beth still held Kate's hand and the small girl grabbed at her brother as she was whisked away but the prince moved quickly out of reach whilst still clinging to Giles.

Elizabeth Woodville had been sitting in the window-seat looking out over the Abbey garden, when her daughter had so abruptly announced Giles and her perceived reason for his visit. She looked pale and drawn and Giles suspected she had been crying. To her credit Elizabeth ignored her daughter's attempt to humiliate her and calmly told Giles to 'be gone' as she had no intention of leaving

Sanctuary in the foreseeable future. For a moment he stared speechless at the cluttered solar. Like the passage ways and great hall it was full of chests and heaps of folded wall hangings. A pile of women's shoes spilled from a basket designed for logs and several small tables were crammed with bottles and jars which Giles presumed to be toiletries and scents. For the first time in his life he felt pity for this haughty lady who sat alone amongst her useless finery, the object of her own daughter's scorn.

"I have come to tell you what I have discovered about the late King's death," said Giles with some kindness but before he could elaborate further the door opened behind him and the Marquise of Dorset blustered in and gave Giles an almighty shove in the back.

"Get the hell out of here Butler," he yelled, "I'll have you flogged if you so much as set foot in this place again."

"Run Giles," shouted the Duke of York, who clearly believed every word his half-brother threatened and then with lightening speed darted under Dorset's flailing arms and out of the door. Giles resisted the temptation to draw his sword but once he had recovered his balance he rested his right hand on the hilt of his dagger making it clear to Dorset that he would not suffer another assault.

"Be quiet Thomas," commanded the Queen, with more authority than Giles could have imagined possible from her dejected appearance. "I have warned you before, you will do well not to frighten your brother York so. He will be a man one day and you will live to rue your bulling."

"It's this bastard I'm sending packing madam," protested the Marquise, "have you no more sense than to entertain Gloucester's turd."

Giles gripped his dagger and took a step forward but the Queen intervened.

"Either sit down and listen to what Sir Giles has to say or leave us," she demanded, as much from her determination to control Dorset than from any interest in Giles' mission. Reluctantly he obeyed but sat with his back to Giles who remained standing by the door. Elizabeth Woodville transferred her gaze from her son to Giles, her hard green eyes meeting his, confirming her authority and bidding him speak; now.

"Madam, I have proof that King Edward was murdered," began Giles.

"Bloody nonsense," screeched Dorset without turning to face him. He raised both his arms towards his mother appealing to her to confirm his indignation.

"Be quiet Thomas – or leave," commanded the Queen.

Giles paused to allow Dorset to go but instead he twisted in his seat to face him.

"Well get on with it then," he growled.

In careful detail Giles explained how on two separate occasions, 'someone' had stuffed palm fruits with poison and served them to the King. The first attempt to kill His Majesty had failed but at the second attempt the murderer was successful. Giles and his friend Luke found the remaining contaminated dates thrown from the apartment window and they used them to successfully poison a rat. Giles paused again, waiting for the question he anticipated at this point in his story. It seemed like an age before Dorset obliged.

"The whole thing is preposterous. Who would dare to do such a thing?"

"Not only who, My Lord but why?" said Giles, holding Dorset's startled gaze.

"You don't know? screamed Dorset, "you come here saying the King was murdered and you don't know who or why?"

"I know who planned and instigated the murder," said Giles and noted the tiny beads of perspiration forming on Elizabeth's top lip.

"How do you know?" challenged Dorset.

"Because he kept well away from the scene of Edward's death but arranged for his accomplice to send him a sealed but blank scroll, to signify that Edward was dead. However, the accomplice made the mistake of dispatching the messenger as soon as the King had consumed the first dose of poison on Easter Sunday: the one from which he recovered."

"I don't see how a blank scroll informed you of anything."

Giles explained how he had met Oswald Garvey in York and

how Garvey had been present when the blank scroll had been delivered to Mayor Thorsby in King's Lynn.

"Master Garvey believed the King was dead one week before he actually died. Both he and his wife will testify to who Thorsby's guests were that evening and to whom the message was delivered," concluded Giles, hoping that his references to King's Lynn and Mayor Thorsby would hint at Rivers' identity: his estates covering most of the surrounding area as both Dorset and the Queen were well aware.

"Stop your hellish riddles Butler. Who is this damned associate of the Mayor of King's Lynn?" Dorset's words hung in the air like an endless echo. "He didn't attend the funeral," he whispered under his breath and turned to his mother in the hope that she would explain the coincidence but Elizabeth had covered her face with her hands, confirming his terror. "You lying rouge," he raged inches from Giles' face, "how dare you insinuate that Earl Rivers had Edward murdered. Get out of here and take your.."

"Enough," screamed Elizabeth, "leave us Thomas. I will speak with Sir Giles alone."

"Madam," protested Dorset, but his mother pointed to the door. Angry and swearing violently he roughly pushed passed Giles and left, banging the door behind him.

"Now nephew," began the Queen coldly, her green eyes glistening with some of their old intensity as she prepared to negotiate. "Tell me, why do you suppose Lord Rivers committed this crime? If indeed he did."

She had confused Giles by addressing him as 'nephew'. Furthermore, she had not protested at his implied accusation that Rivers had orchestrated Edward's death. Nor had she pursued the identity of his accomplice and whilst Giles was certain she had been shocked by the revelation, all his senses warned him to be careful.

"The motive for the murder still eludes me, your Majesty, as does the name of the accomplice, but I am certain all will become clear as my investigations progress."

The tiniest of smiles played around Elizabeth's lips.

"Am I correct in assuming that Gloucester will remain silent about the nature of Edward's death if I and my family come out of sanctuary and attend my son's coronation?"

"And that you support the Duke in his bid to extend his protectorship until the young King reaches his majority."

"Of course," she conceded, "York, can return to the Capital with my Lord of Canterbury after he has visited me this afternoon. The boy is desperate to join his brother and I shall be pleased to have the lad from under my feet."

She crossed to where Giles stood near the door and placing her right hand on his shoulder she leaned towards him and whispered into his ear.

"Tell Gloucester from me nephew, if Rivers is guilty as you say then he must pay with his life. But assure him that our love for Edward is the only common ground he and I will ever have."

"And the accomplice Madam? The Lord Protector will not rest until he has the rouge executed for carrying out the Earl's orders."

Elizabeth Woodville nodded her agreement to his caution. Would she have been so happy to comply if she knew that Gloucester had already cast her son Dorset in that particular role?

Giles left her presence with mixed feelings. Closing the door quietly behind him he found a single packing case by an open window and perched on it to collect his thoughts. If she hadn't actually known about the murder then she had certainly suspected it. Maybe she had even considered Rivers to be the murderer? Giles rubbed his eyes with the heels of his hands. There were so many loose ends. As yet he hadn't found the man who took the message to Mayor Thorsby's house and something still niggled him regarding Rivers' ability to persuade anyone, other than Dorset, to commit the crime. Rivers had planned every step with such care, arranging to be miles away when the murder was committed, securing an escape rout via the port of Lynn should the plot fail, so why would he leave his nephew Dorset so exposed? No, difficult though it was to fathom, Giles concluded that Rivers persuaded someone other than his nephew to carry out the murder. Someone who could be silenced afterwards if necessary. Someone he could blackmail perhaps!

"Psst, over here, Giles, over here."

A female arm and beckoning hand, signalled to him from a doorway across the gallery. He jumped down from his perch and pushed his way between the bags and wooden boxes which were stacked down the east side and climbed over a collection of folding leather chairs to reach the partially open door. The disembodied hand grabbed at his sleeve and pulled him into a tiny room that was little more than a long cupboard. There was a small window at the far end of the narrow room but from the door where he stood, Giles faced a tunnel of gowns, cloaks and an assortment of under garments which had been flung over ropes pinned along the walls on either side. Beth shut the door quickly and turned virtually on her heels to face him, their bodies touching at the knees and hips. Instinctively Giles raised his arms above his head to allow some air between her breast and his chest but not for long. Beth giggled and kissed him on both cheeks so he let his arms fall to her waist, her breasts rested tantalisingly on his chest.

"Listen Giles," she whispered into his ear sending incredible sensations throughout his body, "I want you to take a message to uncle Richard for me."

Giles nodded, as his disappointment converted excitement to embarrassment and he tried unsuccessfully to remove his hands from her waist.

"Tell him I want to be out of here. I didn't seek sanctuary and I don't want it."

She cocked her head jerkily to one side as she thought what else she might include in her message which caused her hair to brush against Giles' face and her waist to swing gently in his hands. Beads of perspiration were beginning to form on his brow.

"Ask him if I might stay with him at Crosby Place," she beamed and then instantly frowned, "is my aunt Anne in London?"

"She is my Lady."

"Damn. Well ask him anyway. Please, please." she begged.

All Giles dare do was nod his agreement and once again she kissed him, but this time on the mouth.

"Now I have something for you, to show how grateful I am for your help," she teased, fully aware of the effect her closeness was having on his senses, for she was not entirely immune to the touch of his body, "now close you eyes and turn towards the window."

Hardly able to move without brushing against some part of her anatomy, Giles did as he was bid. Beth gently pushed him in the back to indicate that he should walk forward and whilst he stumbled into the heaps of clothing, she left the cupboard, closing the door gently as she went. Sensing she had gone, Giles opened his eyes to find Margery sat on the floor by the window, her arms wrapped tightly round her knees as if to make herself small enough to fit into the restricted space.

"Where did you come from?" asked Giles, crushed with disappointment.

Margery lifted a red cloak to show that it had been draped over her and that she had been there all the time.

"Come here you silly man," she sighed, "Beth's not for you, apart from anything else she's your cousin."

Giles climbed over the remaining bundles and virtually falling over a leather bag of shoes came to rest with his head in Margery's lap.

"Cousins can marry with dispensation from the Holy Father," he said peevishly, making himself comfortable and then he remembered that she might be his half-sister and added, "but your right, she not for me. Do you think she fancies the Duke of Gloucester? She was disappointed to learn that Lady Anne is at Crosby Place."

"Don't be ridiculous, he's twice her age and he's her uncle."

"So, the Holy Father can grant dispensation just the same – I think."

They both laughed and Giles remembered that he hadn't thanked Margery for her disclosure of Rivers' letter.

"It was very brave of you to try and interpret what Earl Rivers' was hinting at in his letter to Dorset," said Giles, "you may well have saved Gloucester's life."

"It was *you* I was concerned about," she replied coyly and then added with real terror in her voice, "if Dorset discovers that I betrayed his uncle Rivers he will kill me."

"As soon as he sets a foot outside this, so called sanctuary, I will arrest him. I have Gloucester's warrant to take him even now."

Margery hugged Giles' arm and looked up at him like a small child.

"He still tries to take me whenever he sees me. I thought he would have forgotten Edward's promise by now but he hasn't."

"What promise?"

"Being King Edward's mistress was not always easy. He had an awful habit of sharing his ladies with close friends and he promised me to Dorset for a night or two. I never kept the rendezvous but Dorset still considers the debt to be outstanding."

"Oh Margery dearest, I had know idea. You were fortunate that Dorset did not complain to the King about your reluctance to couple with him?"

"Ah well that was the twist in Edward's morality. He never forced himself on any female and considered rape to be a mortal sin. He would never *direct* any of his ladies to comply with his 'gift' of their services. Dorset knew that there was little point in complaining."

During the next hour or so Margery and Giles made love, exchanged news, made love again and finally slept. It was nearly dark when they roused and Margery was eager to be gone for fear of being missed by Lady Stanley.

"I delivered her message to the Queen hours ago," fretted Margery, straightening her gown as best she could, "you go first and if the gallery is clear knock on the door as you leave. If you fail to knock I will wait awhile before leaving."

She was pulling Giles to his feet now and pushing him gently over the cluttered floor towards the cupboard door. He turned and kissed her on the mouth promising to meet her again soon.

Giles closed the door on Margery's hideaway only to be accosted by the abhorrent Marquis bellowing at him from across the gallery, demanding to know why he was still in the Abbot's house.

"What gives him the right to be so aggressive?" hissed Giles under his breath, startled at being discovered and fearful that he might have betrayed the whereabouts of his lover. "I am still here my Lord of Dorset because I have not completed the tasks the Lord Protector set me," he snarled back across the balustrade, "and what are *you* doing, skulking behind your mother's skirts, in this supposed sanctuary?"

Dorset's right hand reached instinctively for his sword, which was not there because he had been forced to relinquish it as part of his sanctuary condition. His face turned a bright red and he all but climbed over the gallery banister to get at his tormentor but Giles used the distance between them wisely.

"I have here a warrant for your arrest in connection with the murder of King Edward," he said, tapping his script. "You see my Lord, Gloucester is convinced that *you* are Lord River's accomplice."

Dorset was less than two strides away, his fist raised and his upper lip curled into a vicious snarl but Giles' words brought him to a dramatic standstill.

"Me?" he barked, in a spray of saliva, "I had nothing to do with Edward's death"

"And we both know you murdered Treasurer Hatton. Perhaps you should retreat to the real sanctuary in the crypt before I call for the guards to enforce this warrant?"

"Hatton? He fell from the parapet in a drunken stupor. Why should I murder him?"

Beads of sweat glistened on Dorset's brow, his bottom lip quivered and his demeanour changed to that other suit of bullies – the coward. Frightened and panicked by Giles' apparent authority to arrest him, he dropped onto a bundle of rolled arrases whining his innocence on both counts.

"Explain yourself," demanded Giles, "what were you doing in the treasury just before Easter?"

Dorset looked up at him like a reprimanded child and sniffed hard.

"Grey and I were packing the King's treasure so that it could be moved to the Chancery as King Edward had instructed."

"You were authorised to move the treasure to the Chancery? I don't believe you."

"Well you can ask Earl Rivers," rallied Dorset but remembering his alibi was interred in Pontefract castle, he sank back into the bundles. "We packed the stuff as Rivers told us, checking the contents of each bag against the inventory, which I handed over to Andrew Dymmock when he called on the last day."

"Rubbish. You had no authorisation to enter the Treasure House and when Hatton suspected you were up to no good and threatened to tell the King, you killed him."

"No we did not," whined Dorset, "I did not need further authorisation. Rivers had transferred his Deputyship of the Tower to *me*. I was acting Constable with authorisation to enter every part of the Tower and that is what I told the idiot Hatton. He could have checked."

"And if he had, he would have discovered that Edward had not ordered the transfer of his treasure to the Chancery." Dorset looked so confused, Giles was inclined to believe his story. "You fool Dorset, surely you can see how convenient your task has proved to be. Half the treasure you packed into 'manageable size bags' is on the high seas with your uncle and the rest in sanctuary with your mother. Why should I believe you did not know what Rivers intended?"

"Maybe Grey knew," suggested Dorset disloyally, "but I swear I did not. I wish Hatton had checked it out now. But he didn't dare after I told him I would beat his brains out if he doubted my word again. But I never touched him. I swear."

"But you told Dymmock that Hatton might check with the King?" suggested Giles' sensing an alternative explanation. Dorset also spotted the possibility and brightened.

"Dymmock could have killed Hatton if he was privy to Earl Rivers' plans. And my actions prove I had nothing to do with King Edward's death either. If I had known what Rivers intended I would never have drawn attention to our packing the treasure by goading Treasurer Hatton. Would I?"

"No," conceded Giles, "but it doesn't mean that you were not told later, when Dymmock reported to Rivers that your childish behaviour had almost wrecked his plans and cost Hatton his life. You certainly expected Edward to die when he was first taken ill on Easter Day. I was there. I witnessed your surprise when Morton announced the King's recovery. *And* I watched you force yourself on Jane Shore. You would not have dared to do that if you had not expected Edward to die."

Dorset's eyes had grown wide with amazement and he opened

his mouth ready to defend himself but closed it again, unable to find the words.

"Well?" persisted Giles, sure he had trapped Dorset into an admission.

"I expected the King to die because I heard his squires and servants announcing his impending death as I was making my way to Edward's chamber," said Dorset weakly.

A shiver ran down Giles' spine and his confidence faltered. He recalled that Sunday evening when Mark had burst into their apartments in search of Doctor Morton. Mark had been screaming that King Edward was dying. Giles grabbed the startled Marquise by the wrist and dragged him to his feet.

"I might just believe you Dorset, but you need to convince me of your innocence by answering my questions honestly and thoroughly."

Dorset nodded vigorously.

"You say you were on your way to the King's chambers when you came across panicking servants claiming Edward was dying?"

"Yes, I told you. I hurried to see for myself."

"Describe the scene when you arrived."

Dorset wet his dry lips with his over large tongue and closed his eyes tightly as proof of his co-operation and then spoke very deliberately.

"The chamber door was open and men-at arms were gossiping amongst themselves. I had to remind them of their duty."

"Yes, yes, get on with it."

"There was nobody in the solar but there was activity in the bedchamber beyond. I could see through the half open door."

"Who was in the bedchamber when you entered?"

"The King was sprawled across his bed, retching and vomiting relentlessly onto the floor on the far side."

"Who attended him?"

"His knights of the body, of course," began Dorset peevishly but concentrated again when Giles tightened his grip.

"Er … Sir Henry Markham, Sir John Westbury, that girly Peter, whatever his name is and Jane Shore."

"And the physicians? you arrived before the physicians?"

"Yes, they arrived like a gaggle of geese later but Sir Matthew Pawson had gone in search of His Majesty's chief physician, Doctor Argentine. Matthew returned with the doctor soon after myself."

"When I arrived Sir Matthew and Mistress Shore were in the solar," mused Giles.

Dorset shrugged. "Matthew escorted Jane out of the death chamber. He insisted women were not allowed to be present."

"But it wasn't a death chamber, was it?"

"Not then but it was a week later," countered Dorset and then swallowed hard as he realised the significance of his own words. "Rivers' accomplice expected the King to die that night didn't he? He had already started the rumour."

"Exactly," said Giles, pushing past Dorset in his urgency to be gone, "and just remember my Lord, I am all that stands between you and Gloucester's belief that *you are Rivers' accomplice*." He turned and glared into the Marquis' sweating face. "And leave Margery Goodman alone Dorset, otherwise I shall be forced to forget that I ever believed your story. Oh and one more thing. Why were you able to rape Jane Shore that night without her crying out?"

"She had promised King Edward that she would move into Westminster Palace as soon as her annulment arrived from the Holy Father. I knew that it had arrived over two months earlier."

"You bastard Dorset. You diabolical bastard."

CHAPTER 26

The Tower of London 12th June 1483

Richard Gloucester, Lord Protector of England, had not been as successful as Sir Giles Butler in relating his tale of murder. The young King was unwell and his physicians were in attendance when his uncle Richard arrived to tell the sad story. Lord Hastings was also in the royal chambers, fussing over his sovereign's health and promising the boy that he would do all he could to secure the release of his uncle Rivers.

"Will, if Rivers is innocent, why is the King not furious with *you* for having convinced me otherwise?" replied Gloucester to Hastings' latest attempt to assure him that he had been mistaken to believe that Rivers had intended assassination at Stony Stratford.

They were in the antechamber of the King's bedchamber, waiting for the physicians to complete their prescribed 'blood letting' in their attempt to restore His Majesty's humours. For all Lord Hastings' experience on the battlefield, he hated to watch slimy leeches take their fill of human blood, swelling up and eventually falling from the patient's veins when fully gorged, so he had retired to the antechamber just as Gloucester had arrived.

"The lad is certain his uncle is blameless Dickon and no-one knows Anthony Rivers better that he. Surely Edward would not have trusted England's heir to a potential traitor? Come on Dickon, let's admit our mistake and release the Woodville Lords – eh. What do you say?"

"I say you are a drunken fool Will. Answer me this. Why did it take Rivers until 29th April to reach Northampton if he wasn't waiting to ambush me?"

"No, no,no," blustered Hastings.

"That child may look like Edward with his winning smile and honeyed words but never forget who his mother is Will. Never forget that!"

Whilst Gloucester and Hastings argued outside the King's bedroom, Henry Duke of Buckingham was pacing the floor of the Tower council chamber. He had ridden from Crosby Place with Gloucester and during the journey the Duke had informed him of King Edward's murder and Giles' belief that Earl Rivers was responsible. The revelation had taken Henry Buckingham by surprise and he had excused himself from accompanying Gloucester into the boy's presence in order to reflect on the news. He hated the late King for arranging his marriage to Elizabeth Woodville's sister, Katherine, when he was barely ten and his loathing had grown to encompass the entire Woodville family. If one of them had been stupid enough to dispose of their benefactor he should be delighted but Buckingham's highly honed sense of distrust of the Woodvilles, suggested that stupidity was not part of the equation.

Through the open casement he could hear Gloucester summonsing a groom and he smiled at the irritation in his voice, something Buckingham had become accustomed to in the short time he had been shadowing His Grace. Henry crossed to the window and hailed the Duke.

"Up here my Lord. I've sent for refreshment. I expected you to be in conference for some time yet."

Gloucester shrugged and shook his head in exasperation and ignoring the groom who was walking his stallion towards him, he climbed the stone stairs to the council chamber. A squire opened the chamber door as he approached and Buckingham bellowed at the lad to bring an additional cup. In a further show of exasperation, Gloucester removed his velvet cap and threw it onto the council table before him. It slid the twelve feet or so on the polished surface to where Buckingham sat with his food and wine. Ceremoniously Buckingham took the cap in both hands and carrying it high above his head, walked solemnly down the full length of the table to where Gloucester had slumped in a chair. Making a tooting noise in imitation of a fanfare, Buckingham dropped the cap onto Gloucester's head.

"Stop the mummery Harry," scolded Gloucester, snatching the mock crown from his head, "both our heads will roll if Lord William sees you fooling about like that."

"Why you tolerate that drunken sot, I'll never understand."

"You know why. He was steadfastly loyal to Edward and has watched both our backs, since Edward died."

"But that was yesteryear my Lord. Now he reckons to have got it all wrong." Buckingham flounced around the table making clumsy drunken gestures and deep unsteady bows as he cleverly mocked Will Hastings. "When those kindly Woodville lords removed the King from Northampton they were only concerned for your comfort and convenience Dickon," he slurred and then leaning across the table and staring into Gloucester's face he added sternly, "I don't think."

"You make light of everything Harry," said Gloucester with a thin smile, "and recently you have been openly mocking the Queen as well. Heaven knows I have no love for her, or any of her kin but if we are to survive as subjects of King Edward V we must find some common ground."

Buckingham snorted in disgust and return to his food at the other end of the table.

"I'm serious Harry, you take enormous risks being so publicly hostile. Sometimes I think you are deliberately causing friction just for your own amusement. You have as much to lose as I. Once the boy is crowned the Woodvilles will demand retribution."

"I'm sorry," said Buckingham faking regret, "but I cannot bear to see you placating the Queen and that bastard son of hers, in the Tower."

Gloucester sat upright in his chair, the vein on his temple being to show.

"As God's my witness my Lord of Buckingham, I have never placated the Queen or any one of her kin. And I would remind you, my Lord, that the young King is my nephew and my brother's son."

Buckingham cut himself a slice of cheese and smiled inwardly. True to form, he thought, get him angry and his attention is diverted. If Gloucester had considered the possibility that he was deliberately causing friction, which of course he was, then he must be more careful in the future. He bit into the cheese.

"I appreciate your loyalty Harry," he heard Gloucester say, as he dragged himself from his reverie, "but the boy is my brother's son, my own blood."

"I understand Dickon, I am truly sorry."

"If Giles manages to convince the Queen that her own brother murdered her beloved Edward, that too will help to save our futures."

"So, our young King knows the truth now, does he?" asked Buckingham, refilling his wine cup, "he understands that his precious uncle Rivers murdered his father and that you and I were to be his next victims at Stony Stratford – yes?"

"No. He is unwell. I could not burden him with the truth just now: tomorrow maybe if he is feeling better. I trust Giles is having more success with the Queen."

The squire returned with a second cup and a pewter plate stacked with apples, imported from France and whilst Gloucester ate nothing and sipped at his wine, Buckingham tucked into his desert smiling to himself. He would be delighted to give the precious boy the bad news about his uncle Rivers and he would have no qualms about the state of his health. In fact, he would make it his first task tomorrow morning and if Gloucester complained then he would fain innocence and claim to have thought he was relieving his friend of an unpleasant task.

The two Dukes returned to Crosby Place early in the afternoon, to discover the erstwhile missing Bishop of Bath and Wells, Robert Stillington, waiting for them in the great hall. He sat in an armed chair on the dais gazing up at the magnificent vaulted wooden ceiling, mesmerised by its intricate symmetry, a jug of wine and an empty platter on the table before him. Dishevelled and travel weary he dragged his lanky body out of the chair as a squire collected the cloaks and hats from the dukes as they entered the hall.

"I apologise for my appearance my Lord but I have only just returned from Wells and Sir Giles Butler insisted I should present myself here at Crosby Place before calling at my own manor in Clerkenwell," explained the Bishop, smoothing down the soiled front of his tunic, "I need to speak with you my Lord, most urgently."

Gloucester rang the tiny silver bell which had been left on the table for the Bishop's convenience and when the squire appeared he ordered more wine to be brought up to his solar. Then he ushered the Bishop up the richly carved wooden staircase leading to the gallery and first floor. Buckingham having no wish to listen to the ramblings of a grubby bishop made to leave.

"I think you should also witness what I have come to say, my Lord of Buckingham," said the Bishop, pausing on the stairway.

"Come Harry. Giles has been looking for the Bishop since we arrived from Stony Stratford," urged Gloucester and then mouthed from behind Robert's back, "the motive !"

When all three were settled in the large comfortable solar with full cups of good claret in their hands, Bishop Robert once again apologised for his grimy appearance and then rummaging in his script, produced a piece of old vellum which had been rolled and tied with fine black silk cord. He handed the scroll to Gloucester as if he was ridding himself of some unwanted odious object.

"I concealed this in Wells Cathedral years ago, at the time of my enthronement. I wasn't certain it would still be there."

Gloucester examined the seal. The impression had not been made by a signet but by a ring or other small object, leaving a reverse imprint. He broke it carefully, unrolled the vellum and read the document, twice, three times and then, fixing his eyes on Robert's anxious face, he handed the scroll to a bemused Buckingham.

"So, it was King Edward who married Eleanor Butler, not George Clarence," spat Gloucester, through clenched teeth. " Is Giles my brother Edward's son?"

"He may well be My Lord."

"Maybe. Maybe," screeched Gloucester, the vein on his temple pulsating alarmingly, "for God's sake man, what is this.. this ... pre-contract?" He waved an impatient hand at the document Buckingham was still trying to fathom. "Answer me man, how did it come into being?"

Robert Stillington had rehearsed his response to that demand so many times over the years, that when he opened his mouth to speak the initial words tumbled out as from a ventriloquist's puppet.

"After King Edward's coronation in '61 I accompanied his majesty on his Royal Progress and whilst we were in Gloucester, Edward was petitioned by a noblewoman called Eleanor Butler. Her manors in Warwickshire had been confiscated by the crown: a wedding gift from her father-in-law I understand but he had failed to obtain a licence to legalise the transfer so ...."

"Spare us the detail," growled Buckingham.

"The lady was most comely," resumed the Bishop squirming in his seat. "You know how His Majesty could never resist a pretty face. Well at nineteen summers my Lords I can assure you his appetite was insatiable."

"So?" snapped Buckingham.

"Well the Lady refused him her bed and he was obliged to promise marriage in order to satisfy his lust for her. *I* married them the following morning but there were no witnesses I'm afraid."

"Then the marriage was not legal," declared Buckingham.

"It didn't need to be," persisted the Bishop, "because that pre-contract certainly is legal. Edward promised marriage for sex and that *was* witnessed. A pre-contract is as binding as marriage itself," he concluded, pointing to the document still in Buckingham's possession.

"And Lady Eleanor, you say she was a noblewoman?" asked Gloucester.

"Yes my Lord, she was the Earl of Shrewsbury's daughter. It was the Earl's sister who persuaded me to come forward when King Edward died but I have been a virtual prisoner in my own home since John Alcock was posted on me after my Lord Clarence died."

Gloucester summonsed a squire and instructed him to 'send in' Sir Giles as soon as he arrived.

"So, Butler was the name of Eleanor's first husband?"

The Bishop nodded.

"Please assure me that she departed this world, one way or the other, when our present Queen so infamously ensnared the late King in a similar manner?" said Buckingham, his sharp mind working out the implications of an undeclared marriage.

The Bishop paused and his hesitation was more than Buckingham could tolerate.

"For God's sake man, tell me she isn't still alive?"

"No my Lord, Eleanor died in '68 but ... "

" ... but Edward married Elizabeth Woodville in '64," interrupted Gloucester, "which means their marriage was bigamous and their offspring illegitimate," and then turning to Buckingham, he added, "you shall have your way Harry. *I* shall be England's next King. And by right of accession."

"Are you sure?" demanded Buckingham, "if all this is true, shouldn't it be King Giles? Is he or isn't he Edward's son by this Eleanor?"

"I er ... believe so," stammered Bishop Robert.

"Then he is the first born son of our late King, Edward. We have King Giles. Giles I of England and France," pronounced Buckingham close to a fit of hysterics.

"May I see that document my Lord?" cried Giles, who had been standing in the doorway long enough to have his worst fears confirmed.

The Bishop shuffled in his seat and Gloucester waved impatiently at the scroll in Buckingham's hand. He seemed reluctant to relinquish it and Giles all but snatched it from the Duke.

"This can't be right," exclaimed Giles without lifting his eyes from the parchment, "this is dated 1461. I was born in 1460."

The Bishop coughed discreetly.

"What does it mean?" begged Giles of the Bishop but Robert averted his gaze.

"That you were conceived out of wedlock," sneered Buckingham unkindly.

"You appear singularly unperturbed by the revelation that your mother married Edward and not George," intervened Gloucester, "how long have you been privy to this vital piece of information?"

Giles flushed with both guilt and anger and the vein on his temple being to react to the underlying accusation.

"My Lord, I swear, I only considered the possibility that King Edward was my father when I discovered that it was impossible for George Clarence to have sired me. There is a tree behind Middleham Castle with initials and birth dates carved into its bark."

"Ah, yes," conceded Gloucester as he vaguely remembered the great oak.

"It was still a huge leap to conclude that Edward was my father simply because I had proof that George Clarence was not. Then there were the matching rings Clarence claimed he had had made as wedding bands for himself and my mother."

"Rings, what rings?" exclaimed Gloucester.

Giles pulled the drawing from his script and handed it to his uncle.

"I drew my mother's ring from memory after King Edward took it from me. I made the drawing in candle light and as the flame danced it distorted the image and I realised that the initials EB, which I assumed stood for Eleanor Butler *could be* EP, Edward Plantagenet. If you follow the vine stem, see," Giles traced the stem with his forefinger demonstrating how it flowed round the base of the second letter and up behind the first, developing the 'P' into a 'B, " but I could not be certain without the actual ring to verify my suspicion."

Gloucester stared in amazement at the drawing whilst Robert Stillington fumbled inside his shirt for a cord which he passed clumsily over his head and handed to Giles. His mother's ring dangled from it like a twinkling star.

"It wasn't buried with George after all," cried Giles, pressing the precious object to his lips and allowing tears to well in his eyes, "and I did mistake the 'P' for a 'B'. Look," he handed the ring to Buckingham.

"Really Sir Giles, you are so gullible," scoffed Buckingham, "who would have a ring made for their lover that bore the initial of a previous husband?"

"Give it here, and the document," commanded Gloucester. He matched the pieces of the broken seal on the pre-contract and pressed the ring into the imprint: it fitted perfectly. " I have a ring like this, bearing my own initials. When my father, York and brother Edmund were killed at the battle of Wakefield in 1460, our mother had gold rings made for her three remaining sons, using a gold brooch our father always wore pinned in his cap. I was eight at the time so it wasn't long before my ring was too small for even my little finger. I had forgotten." He turned the ring round in his fingers as he recalled the past. "This was Edward's and you are correct Giles, EP stands for Edward Plantagenet. Strange how George always wore his, in spite of his lack of loyalty to our House."

"But why did George Clarence acknowledge Giles as *his* son and lie about the origin of the rings?" asked a bewildered Buckingham.

"To buy himself enough time to take his revenge on me," sighed Bishop Robert. "When Clarence saw Eleanor's ring he realised that Edward's marriage was bigamous and that *he* was Edward's heir. He also realised that I had kept that information from him. That I was not his friend. That I was King Edward's spy." The bishop ran his fingers through the wisps of grey hair that framed his anguished face. "By acknowledging Giles to be his son he was able to command Giles not to inform me of their meeting, whilst he arranged an audience with his brother in which he not only claimed to be next in line to the throne but also informed King Edward that it was I who had told him of the earlier marriage to Eleanor."

"Now I understand why Edward had the sentence of death carried out," said Gloucester softly, "George would have been England's next King ... "

"When Edward knew he was dying he sent for me and made me promise to return the ring to Giles if ever it was safe to do so," continued the Bishop, watching Gloucester warily.

Giles' stomach was churning with anxiety. According to his mother's note he was not a bastard but the date of Eleanor's marriage to Edward was a year after his birth. He dare not question the document for fear his uncle would think he was trying to establish himself as Edward's first born, legitimate son and therefore by default, his heir. He desperately needed to speak with the Bishop in private.

Purposefully, Giles crossed the room and knelt before his uncle, his hands steepled in homage. Robert Stillington hurriedly dropped to his knees and finally a confused Buckingham did likewise. The four-man tableau remained motionless for several seconds whilst each considered his new role. Gloucester was the first to break his reverie and taking Giles' hands in his own he raised him to his feet and kissed him on the mouth, as was the custom for a King accepting homage from a kinsman.

"Get up," he whispered, "none of what we have discussed here must be repeated before Robert presents the pre-contract to the council tomorrow. You understand? Not a word to anyone."

A general shuffle and whispers of agreement followed, as the men got to their feet.

"If your Grace will grant me leave to retire," said Buckingham with the smallest of yawns, "I promised to dine with my aunt later. She is already annoyed with me for not having called on her since we returned to the Capital and I would prefer not to upset her further."

Gloucester reminded him that nothing they had discussed must be disclosed until the council met on the following day and with his arm about Giles in a show of kinship he bid Buckingham, good-day.

"You and I need to discuss your meeting with Elizabeth Woodville nephew. Although as events appear to be unfolding it may not matter whether or not she believes your story. Meantime, Robert, Radcliffe will escort you back to your manor and remove John Alcock into the care of Archbishop Rotherham."

"He will not go willingly," whined the Bishop, "God only knows who foisted him on me in the first instance but he has dogged my every step since Clarence died."

"Do not concern yourself," laughed the Duke, "if I instruct Radcliffe to remove the man, he will do so, even if the Holy Father installed him in your house."

Chapter 27

Crosby Place 12th June 1483

Having located Bishop Robert Stillington returning from Wells and having brought him directly to Crosby Place as Giles had instructed, Mark Taylor now stalked the kitchens in search of something to eat. His hose and tunic splattered with mud and his cloak dripping wet from having been dropped it in a puddle, he looked as though he had walked from Wells. It had been raining when Mark and the Bishop had set out that morning, sufficient to turn the surface dust to mud but not enough to soak away into the hard ground, causing the roads to be skimmed with slippery slim and every depression filled with water. However, the inclement weather had not reached the Capital and Mark was receiving curious looks as he sauntered through the kitchen buildings in search of food. A spitted pig was being removed from the irons, the fat hissing and cracking as it spilt over the hard earth floor, whilst a servitor carried a basket full of onions through to the preparation sheds at the back, followed by another lad hauling a basket of cabbages. An agitated cook was considering the consistency of a large stockpot bubbling furiously over a second fire, when a baker's apprentice arrived at the open door with a mule, its panniers loaded with bread. The lad had specific instructions from his master to find out whether the order was to be repeated tomorrow, a question the stockpot cook was unable to answer so the baker's boy walked his beast to the next kitchen along the block. To Mark's untrained eye it did not seem as though they were preparing for a banquet and yet large amounts of provisions were being delivered. He wandered over to the back door where a dark haired slattern of some sixteen years, with large brown cow eyes was gutting fish. Encouraged by her impudent glances and pouting mouth he asked if she could find him a pot of ale and some meat and cheese.

"'Spect so," she replied, noting Gloucester's insignia on the front of his tunic. She put down the fish and wiped her hands on the sack tied round her waist as an apron. "Will that be all then sir?" she asked coyly. "I'll bring the food to the stables if you've a mind."

Mark grinned, "Aye, why not, but rinse off some of that fish from your hands and face first girl. What's your name?"

"Polly sir."

"Right then Polly, bring the food and ale to the stable."

He reached out to pinch her thigh but she moved expertly around the barrel almost colliding with another servant entering through the back door and carrying a large pole on which were tied a dozen or so rabbits.

"What's all the food for Polly? Is the Lord Protector entertaining?"

"No sir, according to Jake," she pointed to the cook filling the stockpot with handfuls of fresh herbs, "The Duke usually stays with his ma at Baynard's when he comes to London, so there's no need for great stores of provisions 'ere. But his Duchess has arrived, 'day afore yesterday, unexpected like, so cook 'as to stock up a bit."

"Lady Anne is here – at Crosby Place?" exclaimed Mark unable to conceal his joy.

"Yes sir she is," replied Polly, astonished at his reaction, " what's it to you sir?" and completely misunderstanding his enthusiasm she made an exaggerated moue and giving him a playful shove, disappeared in search of his meal.

If Lady Anne had journeyed from Middleham then her maid Lucy, would most likely have accompanied her. Mark could hardly restrain the excitement he felt at the thought of seeing Lucy again, but emotional fluttering and the reek of fish began to affect his empty stomach, so he hurried through the back door and into the kitchen yard in search of fresh air. With the first intake of breath he regained his equilibrium and with his mind still full of memories of the delightful hours spent with Lucy at Middleham, he propped himself against a pile of loose stones and basked in the warm afternoon sun.

A mason and his apprentice were using the stones to construct a wall between the kitchens and the stable block, which when completed would screen the busy kitchen yard from view of visitors to the Manor. Mark was about to retreat to the stables to keep his rendezvous with Polly when the great oak door at the top of the flight of stones steps was opened by a footman and the Duke of Buckingham appeared. A squire instantly answered his irritated call and Mark watched from his shielded position whilst the boy scurried into the stables to alert the grooms of his Grace's imminent departure. However, it wasn't a groom that walked Buckingham's restlessly black stallion into the sunlight but the willowy silver headed Sir Humphrey Percivall, Buckingham's trusted retainer. Mark was surprised to see the knight hang close to the stallions neck so that he was hidden from view and his curiosity alerted when Sir Humphrey's intension to stay out of sight was confirmed by the Duke, who uncharacteristically, walked to where the horse was dancing nervously in the shadows, instead of waiting for the beast to brought to his side. Whilst Buckingham held an intense conversation with the knight across the stallion's back, Mark recalled how he had not seen Sir Humphrey since the man had brought Buckingham's offer of support to Nottingham Castle. He was certain the distinctive knight had not been in Buckingham's retinue at Northampton nor had he been around when he and Giles returned to Stony Stratford and why was he keeping out of sight now?

Their conversation over, Humphrey Percivall handed his Lord the reins and then looking furtively about the empty forecourt he pulled his cowl over his silver locks and slipped around the side of the manor and out of view. Mark forgot his hunger, Polly and her promised tumble in the hay and followed Sir Humphrey, first down the south side of the manor house, keeping close to the building itself and then around the fish pond and along the back wall to a postern gate which led into a little used, narrow alley that ran back into Bishopgate Street where it joined Cornehill. Once in the busy streets it was easy for Mark to stay close to Sir Humphrey, mingling with the crowds up Cheap Side and into Holborn, but when the knight turn right beyond the market square, Mark realised he was making for the manor house of John Morton, Bishop of Ely. The lane straightened out as it approached the manor with little cover on either side, so Mark stayed well back until Sir Humphrey had gained admittance. The old bailey wall had long since ceased to act as a defence to this beautiful house with vines and roses assaulting the inner side, whilst moss and ivy covered the outer. Morton had recently completed the building of a new gatehouse that rose eight or so feet above the original height of the wall and from his advantage point the gatekeeper could see approaching visitors long before they turned into the Lane.

"Mark Taylor," hailed Gatekeeper Joby from his look-out above the walls, when he spotted Mark.

Joby reckoned to be a 'warrior churchman' who had served with Morton in the old wars between York and Lancaster. He dressed in the remnants of an ancient, black Benedictine habit, belted with a much worn leather strap and crossed with an old, smooth baldric from which a battered dagger protruded. He wore the tonsure and an incongruous bushy grey beard which combined to give him the appearance of a mad monk rather than a fierce warrior. He sprang down the stone spiral stairs like a man half his age and lifted the weighty wooden bar from the gate which he had only just replaced after admitting Humphrey Percivall. He shook Mark warmly by the hand.

"Been away up North, I hear. Come for your great mutt, have you? His Grace will be disappointed to have to let him go," he said with a grin and then together, they swung the heavy bar back in place.

"Did I see you admit Sir Humphrey Percivall just now?" asked Mark casually.

Joby shrugged and scratched his chin beneath the mass of grey beard.

"Been here once or twice recently," he said carelessly," used to always be calling when the Duke of Buckingham visited regularly.

Haven't seen the Duke lately though, thank goodness – arrogant bastard."

Joby hawked and spat and was about to invite Mark to partake of some of his 'special brew', when a commotion in the lane caused both men to climb the spiral stairs to investigate. The lane followed the bailey wall for another fifty yards and then turned sharply right, back towards West Smithfields. A man leading a heavily laden sumpter pony had just turned the corner and was struggling to halt the beast in order to allow four others, carrying a man on a stretcher, to overtake him. Following the makeshift stretcher was a fifth man, leading a chestnut mare with a distinctive blaze of white on his forehead.

"Lord save us, it's Master Luke," cried Joby as he recognised the horse, "he must have taken a fall."

Mark and Joby clattered down the stone stairs and once again wrested the plank from its housing. Whilst Joby swung the great gate wide, Mark ran to meet the stretcher. He could see from the stillness of Luke's body that he was unconscious and that he had taken a knock on the head for blood was seeping through a cloth wound around it.

"What happened?" he screamed at the boy leading Luke's mare.

"Don't rightly know master," replied the lad, "I found him like what you sees him now, up by the common. I reckon he be dead, or next to. The fellow ahead," he nodded and pointed to the back bearer on the right, "he recognised him as Bishop Morton's man when I raised the hue."

Without waiting for further information Mark turned and ran passed the open gate down the lane into Cheap Side and back up Bishopgate Street to Crosby Manor. All he could contemplate was reaching Giles before Luke's injury proved fatal. As he ran he prayed repeatedly that Luke would survive at least long enough for he and Giles to settle their differences. Mark knew nothing of the cause of the rift between them but was certain that Giles would suffer greatly should Luke die before they were reconciled. He entered Crosby Place through the main gate and hurried straight to the stables to ensure that Giles' horse was still in the stalls but neither Dexter nor Bishop Robert's mount were there.

"How long since they left?" called Mark to a groom who was backing his mare out of her stall.

"Duke of Buckingham just after you left. The Bishop soon after that and Sir Giles just afore you returned sir," said the groom, unsure to whom 'they' referred.

Mark tossed the lad a penny. His mare had been well brushed, fed and watered since he had delivered the Bishop to Crosby Place. He took the reins and set off after Giles as fast as the narrow streets, busy traders and their customers would allow. He assumed that he was returning to Clipberry Manor and arrived at the front of his old home just as Giles was entering the bailey. Bishop Robert and Richard Radcliffe had already surrendered their mounts to Alfred and were climbing the steps to the hall.

"Sir Giles," called Mark, " you are needed at Bishop Morton's manor. Luke has fallen from his horse and is seriously wounded, maybe fatally."

Giles' first instinct was to turn his horse and make for Holborn but to Mark's amazement he checked himself and dismounted. He must speak with the Bishop.

"I'll go as soon as I can Mark. I have business here first."

"Go Sir Giles," insisted Radcliffe, misreading Giles' reason for hesitation, "I can deal with this Alcock toad. Mark can give me a hand."

Giles looked anxiously from the Bishop to Mark but both insisted that he should leave. With a final enquiring look at Bishop Robert, who was waving a dismissive hand towards the gate, Giles remounted and left for Holborn.

Robert climbed the steps to his great hall flanked by Mark and Radcliffe but there were no servants in the hall to greet them and the place seemed strangely uninviting. As the great oak door closed noisily behind them the harsh voice of John Alcock rose from the Bishop's hooded chair by the hearth.

"How dare you burst in here unannounced," he began but then recognising Robert, "I beg your pardon gentlemen. Thank you for returning the good Bishop into my care." Alcock forced a smile and his inordinate number of teeth appeared ominously from his saliva filled mouth. "Come now your Grace," he dribbled, "where have you been wandering? I have been worrying myself sick for lordship's safety."

"Your presence is no longer required at Clipberry," said Radcliffe without ceremony.

Alcock's eyes flashed bright with anger but recognising the Blanc Sanglier on Radcliffe's sleeve he grasped the silver cross which hung around his neck and demanded 'benefit of clergy'.

"We are not here to arrest you," said Mark with disgust, "but you have good reason to fear. Your master, Earl Rivers has been apprehended and imprisoned at Pontefract."

"And the Lord Protector has given Bishop Robert his assurance that you will be removed from this house," added Radcliffe, lifting the priest out of his chair with a handful of the front of his tunic, "you are to report to Archbishop Rotherham."

Alcock's face glistened with sweat. He shook himself when Radcliffe released his grip and ran his finger round the inside of the neck of his shirt in search of relief from the pounding in his head but finding none his nerve collapsed and he simply walked to the door and left without a thought about his belongings.

Almost immediately, servants appeared from their boltholes like birds released from cages. Shutters were opened, food and drink served and the Bishop warmly welcomed home. Mark and his mother hugged and Radcliffe was thanked and congratulated for his effort in ridding the household of the hated Alcock.

"I will stay here tonight and escort you to the council meeting tomorrow," said Mark, helping the Bishop steady his cup of wine.

"Will he be in a fit state to face the council tomorrow?" asked Radcliffe, watching the Bishop's hands shake as he relinquished the cup into Mark's care.

"I'll be fine sir and I'm not a child, I can speak for myself," Robert said stiffly, "it's just the shock. That man has dogged my every movement for the last five years. Watching him dismissed was like removing a cloak of lead from my shoulders. I need a little time to adjust to the lighter load."

Bishop Morton greeted Giles warmly, but the anxiety in his aging face made him look tired and vulnerable.

"Luke has recovered consciousness and although he is still weak, the prognosis is good," said Morton resting his hand on Giles' arm in a gesture of comfort.

"Do you think he had one of his old seizures whilst out riding?"

"I don't know. He has hardly spoken and cannot be questioned yet. Brother Jordan, from the community of Black Friars is with him now. I trust him implicitly but he has no real idea what ails Luke. Like most churchmen he is inclined to leave too much in the hands of the Almighty."

Giles smiled to himself. That was something Morton could never be accused of. They were climbing the outside steps to reach the recently constructed single chamber above a much older wing. It was part of Bishop Morton's renovation work and provided Luke with his own quarters.

"If he doesn't make a full recovery quickly, I shall send to Italy for Dr. Antonio Benivieni," declared Morton, stopping to catch his breath.

Giles took the older man's arm and helped him gently up the remaining three steps. He was touched by the aging cleric's devotion to this nameless man he had rescued from the battlefield so long ago. Opening the door quietly for fear Luke was sleeping, they stepped into the large new chamber where Brother Jordan indicated with a hushing finger to his lips that the patient was asleep.

"I'll sit with him for a while if I may?" whispered Giles and nodding his agreement, the friar picked up his satchel, collected Morton with an encircling arm and led the weary Bishop back down the stairs.

The chamber was long and narrow with three windows down one side, each filled with expensive glass that allowed the late afternoon sun to flood the room. A large new arras hung on the longest wall, the gold and silver threads sparkling in the bright light, whilst hung on the far wall were two smaller tapestries, both depicting Ruth; one 'gleaning' and the other 'at the well'. A writing table, two chests and several stools beside an unlit brazier, furnished the lower living area, whilst the luxurious bed and a prie-dieu were raised on a low dais at the far end. Woollen rugs were scattered about the two levels in abundance and bees wax candles set in silver candlesticks flanked the crucifix on the table before the prie-dieu.

Luke stirred and Giles crossed silently from the doorway and mounted the dais but his friend was not awake. The limbs beneath the covers were jerking involuntarily and his head thrashed from side to side on the pillows as if he were enduring a nightmare from which he could not wake. Drops of sweat were forming on Luke's handsome olive face, his breathing was becoming laboured but still he did not wake. Giles reached for a linen cloth that lay in a bowl of lavender water on the floor by the bed and after squeezing out the excess, dabbed at the rivulets of sweat running down Luke's head and neck. After a while the fitting ceased, his breathing eased and he slipped into a much deeper slumber. Satisfied that there was nothing to be gained from alerting the friar, Giles poured himself a cup of wine from a jug which had been left on the table and in doing so noticed a small blue velvet cushion to the left of the crucifix, on which rested the brooch Luke believed he had been given by the Lancastrian Prince of Wales. Lifting the beautiful object from its velvet cushion, Giles gazed at it in awe. Why had the Prince of Lancaster entrusted such a precious jewel to Luke? Was it as Morton believed, a means of identifying the Prince to a third party or was it a gift?

Giles felt sleepy, perhaps it was the wine, the heat or just exhaustion? He pulled two of the woollen rugs to the side of Luke's bed and settled down to wait for his friend to wake. Within moments Giles was also sleeping soundly.

It was still light when he woke some hours later and even though the sun no longer streamed through the windows, the room was stiflingly hot. He clambered to his knees and flinging the woollen rug to one side leaned across the bed to check on his friend. Luke was still sleeping peacefully so Giles tip-toed to the casements and removed one of the three glazed fenestralls that had attracted the heat and caused the room to heat up like a bake-house. Someone on the lower floor had also been suffering from the heat, for the three corresponding windows below were open to the air and through them drifted familiar, raised voices. Morton and Lord Hastings, Giles recognized easily but in order to identify the other he leaned over the sill and listened intently. Yes – Lord Stanley was the third voice and then he remembered. They would be holding their pre-council get-together to ensure that all were in one accord, before voting at the full council meeting tomorrow.

Giles chuckled to himself, "wait till they hear what Bishop Robert has to reveal."

He was about to leave his listening post when he clearly heard Morton say that if they hadn't the courage to take matters into their own hands, Richard Gloucester, would be crowned by the end of the month. Giles froze and prayed he had misheard the treason. It was the voice of Lord Stanley that confirmed his horror.

"Have you seen this 'pre-contract' Bishop Robert purports to have hidden away all these years? I mean, it does actually exist, does it?"

"Robert presented it to the two Dukes this afternoon," replied Morton impatiently.

"What does it matter if Edward's marriage to the Woodville bitch was bigamous," slurred Hastings, "as far as I'm concerned, Edward was King, so his son is our next King. Who he married first, is irreverent er … irrelevant."

"I'm sure King Edward would applaud your devotion, however illegal the sentiment," soothed Morton, "but your friend and comrade-in-arms, Richard Gloucester, is not of the same mind, my Lord."

"Then bugger Gloucester," countered Hastings, "if we all stand together and tell him to shove this 'pre-contract' where the sun don't shine, that'll be an end to it, I guarantee it."

"Don't be so stupid," snapped Lord Stanley, and Giles heard Hastings' chair scrape on the floor as he rose to defend himself against the insult.

"Apologise for that last remark … and quickly," demanded Morton.

"Forgive me Lord Hastings: please."

"Come now Will," Morton continued hurriedly, "Lord Stanley does not know the Lord Protector as well as you. I'm sure Richard Gloucester would defer to your reasoning, if only you were dealing with him alone."

"Meaning?"

"That he is much influenced by Henry Buckingham. Has he not prevented Gloucester from promoting your good self to new posts of responsibility in his Protectorship?"

"Perhaps."

"And then there is Sir Giles Butler. He will encourage his uncle to take the crown, if only to ensure his own rise to power."

"Giles loves him well, that's for certain," conceded Hastings, "so what's to be done?"

"Bring some more wine over here, Catesby," commanded Morton and Giles strained his ears whilst he presumed that wine cups were being filled and Hastings was being encouraged to slip still further into an alcoholic stupor.

"We will be guided by you," Morton dissembled, "you are the senior man here."

"We could arrest Gloucester during the council session," declared Hastings, his sense of self-importance overcoming the effect of the wine, "that's when he'll have fewest men around him."

"But we can't make the arrest ourselves," wailed Stanley, "there will be Buckingham and Sir Giles to deal with as well."

"No problem," slurred Hastings, "I can take a dozen armed men into the Tower on the pretext of collecting newly minted coins for the coronation. I'm still Master of the Mint, despite Buckingham's attempt to secure the post for himself."

"Excellent," said a genuinely impressed Morton, "but can your men be near enough to the council chamber and in place before Gloucester can summons his own guards?"

There was a pause whilst this problem was considered.

"Here's the plan," began Morton, reclaiming control. "We will all arrive at the Tower early tomorrow. Hastings, you can secrete your men in the Royal Mint as you suggest and then join us in the council chamber. When Gloucester and his party arrive we will act as normal until the meeting is about to commence formally. Then, I will suddenly remember that I promised the Duke of Buckingham some strawberries from the garden here in Holborn and without waiting for permission, I will excuse myself and leave the chamber to send for them."

"What does that achieve?" asked Stanley.

"Two things. Firstly, I can see exactly where the Dukes' bodyguards are positioned and secondly, I can collect Hastings' men from the Mint and bring them to the council chamber for Will to conduct the arrests."

"There'll be a scuffle," warned Hastings, "Dickon won't go quietly, he's as fierce as the White Boar on his standard once challenged."

"Then you must bring as many men as it will take," snapped Morton impatiently.

"Aye and some besides. Who knows Butler's worth with the sword?" said Stanley and then added nervously, "what happens once they are all under lock and key?"

"We shall crown the young King the day after tomorrow," began Morton.

"And we shall release the dukes the day after that," concluded Hastings.

"So soon?" asked Stanley, "Gloucester will be after our blood."

Hastings roared with laughter. "Little good it will do him once the lad is crowned. Courage man, his authority will be over. Take it from me, Gloucester will be too concerned about his own safety to be chasing after us."

"I wonder?" mused Morton, "he may feel he has nothing to loose once the boy is King. He could launch an all out attack using his hordes of loyal Northerners and try and take the crown by force."

"Then I shall stick him like the hog he is, for such treason against the royal line," proclaimed Hastings and to Giles' horror he heard Morton uncompromisingly reply that *'that might be altogether a better solution.'*

"Giles, is that you? What are you doing leaning out of the window?"

Luke was awake and he had rolled over onto his side staring at Giles' legs and backside hanging precariously from the sill. His friend hauled himself back into the room and closed the windows slowly to give himself time to gather his thoughts.

"It's good to see you are back with us," said Giles with a smile, "you really must curb this habit of falling from your horse and banging your head."

"That isn't funny; I feel terrible."

"I'm sorry Luke. I'll tell Morton that you are awake but then I must go. I have an urgent message to take to Richard Gloucester but I will return early tomorrow morning before the council meeting. Is there anything you want before I leave?"

Luke wasn't listening. His mind was beginning to clear and fleeting glimpses of the past were flashing through his brain.

"Whatever is the matter," cried Giles, as he watched his friend struggle to sit up; his face flushed, eyes bulging and his mouth opening and closing like a landed cod, "hold on, I'll call for Brother Jordan."

"No Giles, I'm fine, really I'm fine. My memory is beginning to return."

"What?" Giles retraced his steps from the doorway to sit on the edge of the bed. "What do you recall Luke?"

"Not much yet … The battle at Tewkesbury, but it doesn't make sense. I can remember being struck from behind and stumbling forward … and then … or maybe later, I'm not sure but I can remember looking up into an assailant's face and rolling to one side as his mace missed its mark and.. and a fallen man beside me, taking the full weight of the blow in his face. God what an awful sight."

"Can you remember the assailants tabard: his lord's arms?"

Luke smiled thinly and reminded his friend that he had an urgent message to deliver. Giles hesitated but Luke insisted that he should not keep Gloucester waiting, so he bid Luke farewell, promising again to return tomorrow before the council meeting.

Relaxing back into his pillows, Luke tried to encourage sleep by counting imaginary rabbits as they popped out of their burrow but snippets of memory interrupted the flow of rabbits causing him to loose count time and again. The only flash backs he could make sense of were from Tewkesbury and even these seemed out of sequence. He could remember men leaving the battlefield, many dropping their weapons and fleeing despite horrific injuries. He could recall the victor's cry for blood as the rout began but was he with the chase or being chased? He couldn't tell. A few rabbits later he recalled the thunder of hooves so close that he had panicked for fear of being trampled and later still, he remembered the cry of, 'Wenlock, Wenlock' and turning to see the Prince of Lancaster bearing down from behind their lines.

Eventually, Luke drifted into a fitful sleep, only to be abruptly woken by a dream that he knew was in essence a memory but one that terrified him so much he prayed it was only a dream.

He was still on his horse, virtually uninjured and surrounded by other mounted knights all engaged in one to one combat. He turned sharply from one kill to engage the next when he saw a knight, wearing the plumes of Wales, riding straight at him. Luke did not think for one moment that the knight *was* the Prince of Wales as it was common practise for experienced champions to protect the mighty ones by wearing their colours. So he was surprised to see his opponent rashly raise his sword as if to slash at his horse's head, thus exposing the minute gap beneath his arm pit, where the breast-plate joined the back-plate. He waited until the knight's sword was about to descend and then moving instinctively, Luke thrust his own sword into the exposed gap, savouring the lack of resistance to his weapon as it seared through the thin leather under-jerkin and into the man's flesh. His would-be assailant slumped forward and within seconds other knights surrounded the injured man in an attempt to escort him from the field but Luke's associates charged after them, felling most and leaving the remainder to flee. The injured knight had fallen to the ground, blood pumping from his armpit at an amazing rate and without recollection of how or when he had dismounted, Luke turned the body and raised the visor. To his astonishment the agonised face was that of a boy, no-more than twenty summers.

"Mercy, mercy," he begged in French but no physician could have saved the lad's life. Luke ripped the mail from the boy's neck and with one swift movement, slashed the tender throat with his misericorde.

In sheer panic Luke sat up in bed, the sweat pouring from his brow as he recalled the sequel to his dream. The boy he had slain *was the Prince of Wales* and Luke had been searching for him throughout the battle. *But why* had he been so intent on finding the Prince of Lancaster? Oh no, no: now he could remember the Duke of Clarence presenting him with that brooch as a trophy! Mother of God, it had been pinned to the boy's tunic when the body was stripped. His stomach churned as he recalled how Morton had found the brooch in his closed hand and had completely misinterpreted his possession of the jewel.

Chapter 28

Crosby Place 12th June 1483

At the gatehouse Joby wanted to know how Master Luke was faring and Giles was pleased to be able to report his improvement.

"Has Lord Hastings returned to the city," asked Giles, needing to be on his way.

"Yes Sir Giles, both my Lords, Hastings and Stanley left only minutes ago."

Giles thanked Joby and kicked the reluctant Dexter into a trot down the lane that opened onto Holborn's market square. The summer evenings were lengthening and local people were taking advantage of the cooler air but Giles rode on oblivious to the sights and sounds of their pleasures, entering Newgate well before curfew.

Throughout the journey to Crosby Place he replayed in his head the exact words that Morton, Hastings and Stanley had used in their conspiracy and although he had not been able to see their faces and observe those tell-tale signs that reveal disguised truths, he was of the opinion that Morton had manoeuvred Hastings into treason. He was also concerned as to how Bishop Morton had acquired such accurate information about the pre-contract. It was only a matter of hours since Bishop Robert had related his story to Gloucester in the presence of Buckingham and Giles himself and Bishop Robert could not have informed Morton, Giles had left him with Radcliffe and Mark at Clipberry. It simply had to be Buckingham but why? Buckingham had been present when his uncle insisted that the news remain a secret until tomorrow's meeting in the Tower. Perhaps he had let the information slip inadvertently? He had left Crosby Place to visit his aunt and presumably the aunt in question was Lady Stanley? Yes that must be it, concluded Giles to himself whilst handing his reins to a groom at Crosby Place, Buckingham has told Lady Stanley and she has relayed the news to her husband, who in turn told Bishop Morton at their pre-council meeting this evening. Giles winced as he thought of his uncle's reaction to the news he must now deliver.

At the top of the stone steps that led into the great hall a footman hovered, agitation written all over his usually passive face.

"Perhaps you might choose to delay your visit," whispered the squire, "Master Catesby arrived a little while since and His Grace is in someway displeased."

Giles grinned at the man's understatement but much relieved that Catesby had chosen to speak out, he nodded towards the door, at the same time assuring the nervous squire that he would announce himself on this occasion. The servant opened it cautiously and Giles stepped into the hall, bracing himself against the torrent of angry words he expected to flow in his direction. But there were none. His uncle stood with his back to the door, his hands on the chimney surround, gazing into the fireless grate. Catesby was fidgeting by the table, undecided as to whether he should leave without being dismissed. Giles read the sequence of events accurately. At first Gloucester would have been infuriated by the news, as the footman had doubtless heard but now he was considering the issue of disloyalty and Giles knew that he would show little compassion towards those who had betrayed his trust. Never-the-less, Giles felt compelled to offer his own version of what had taken place in Morton's solar that evening and tentatively he moved to his uncle's side. Gloucester did not stir.

"My Lord, I have been visiting my sick friend Luke Lazarus, at Bishop Morton's home in Holborn." He had Gloucester's attention now. "His room is above Morton's solar and with the weather being so warm all the windows were open. I heard all that was said."

"Catesby attended Will Hastings at that meeting," said Gloucester harshly, "so what did you make of this treason nephew?"

"I believe that John Morton, Bishop of Ely, persuaded the

drunken Lord Hastings to plot treason. I think Hastings' blind love for the boy King and too much wine clouded his judgement."

"Do you now? Hastings is not a child, to make allowances for, Giles. He has made the decision to champion Edward's bastard at all cost."

"Possibly; but if you leave his arrest until tomorrow's meeting you will know for certain. I mean, if he fails to conceal armed men in the Mint then presumably all his angry words this evening can be accredited to his drunkenness and not to treason."

"I hear what you say Giles but I do not share your optimism." He rang the small silver bell on the side table and ordered more wine and another cup for his nephew.

"My Lord, there is the secondary matter of how Morton became privy to the pre-contract and your intention to present it to the council tomorrow."

"Indeed, when Catesby and Hastings arrived, Morton and Stanley were already discussing the document."

Catesby nodded glumly and Giles cleared his throat.

"My Lord, only His Grace of Buckingham could have spoken of the matter. I know I did not and I left Bishop Robert in the care of Radcliffe and my own squire, before leaving to visit Luke."

"Christ man, of what do you accuse Henry Buckingham?"

"Nothing more than careless talk uncle. He announced this afternoon that he intended visiting his aunt, Lady Stanley and Lord Stanley was the third conspirator."

"No Giles, he would not have been so reckless. But since I have already sent for him so that we might discuss this treason, we can asked him directly."

The three men fell silent as they listened to Buckingham haranguing the stable men in the court yard below and within seconds the door flung wide and Buckingham flounced into the hall, annoyed at being disturbed and red faced with the large quantity of strong wine he had recently consumed. Without preamble Gloucester explained the necessity for his presence, concluding with Giles' assertion that he must have let slip the Bishop's revelations to his aunt during their dinner this evening.

"Christ Almighty you wretched son of a bitch, how dare you

accuse *me* of treason," screamed Buckingham, drawing his sword and striding across the hall to where Giles had moved aside to allow the flamboyant Duke space to stage his usual entrance. Giles could see the Duke was drunk but his challenge was no idle jest so unwilling he drew his own sword.

"Sheath your blades," demanded Gloucester his hand twitching nervously about his own dagger, "nothing can be gained by fighting amongst ourselves."

Buckingham ignored the order and continued to advance on Giles who had no option but to stand his ground. However, as Buckingham moved forward he passed close to Catesby and the lawyer could smell the wine on the Duke's breath. Reckoning that he was sufficiently drunk not to notice, Catesby kicked a footstool into the Duke's path and the noble Lord obligingly sprawled across the floor like a felled tree, dropping his sword and sending it clanking across the tiles and into the hearth where Catesby rushed to retrieve it.

"Get up Harry, nobody here is accusing you of treason and if you say you are not responsible for the broken confidence then so be it," cried Gloucester.

Buckingham clambered to his feet spitting and snarling like a cornered wild cat. In an attempt at reconciliation Giles brought the Duke a cup of wine from the tray on the table and before Buckingham could swipe it from Giles' hand, Gloucester stepped between them and taking the cup from Giles he ushered the humiliated Duke into his own high backed armed chair and placed the cup in his hands.

Buckingham's embarrassment was short lived. Gloucester had also ordered Radcliffe to return from Clipberry and his timely appearance necessitated yet another telling of the events that had taken place at Holborn, thus diverting attention from the Duke of Buckingham and the blow to his dignity. As soon as Catesby and Giles had retold their tale, Buckingham was eager to leave, insisting that his aunt expected his return. However, Gloucester was adamant that he should remain, demanding that the Duke give his opinion as to whether the conspirators should be arrested tonight, as he himself preferred or wait until tomorrow, giving

Hastings time to reconsider, as Giles had suggested. After some discussion, Radcliffe and Catesby agreed with Gloucester, arguing that Hastings had already demonstrated his unconditional support for the young King by trying to secure the release of the Woodville traitors. Then to everyone's surprise Henry Buckingham agreed with Giles, graciously calling attention to his own impetuous reaction to Giles' earlier assertion which, as he pointed out, could have resulted in disastrous consequences. Therefore he proposed that the arrest of Lord William should be delayed until tomorrow because like Giles, he was convinced that Hastings would shun an attack on Gloucester once he was sober. Accordingly, Radcliffe was charged with arranging for armed men to be stationed in the Mint throughout the night so that, should Hasting not change his mind when his head cleared and attempt to secrete his own force there tomorrow, they could be apprehended without fuss.

Although his uncle seemed to accept Buckingham's astonishing humility on face value, Giles felt uncomfortable. Weeks later, he would come to realise that it was at this point that Henry Buckingham made the first of two amendments to his own ambitions but for now the warning bells were only tinkling and so Giles found himself a stool in the shadows and settled down to observe Buckingham in his newly donned sack-cloth and ashes.

With the timing of Hastings' possible arrest settled, the Duke could have returned to his aunt's party but his earlier urgency was forgotten and now fully immersed in his new conciliatory role, he refilled the wine cups and toasted the health of 'Our rightful Sovereign Lord, King Richard'. Other toasts quickly followed; to the memory of the Duke of York, to our late King Edward, to the health of Richard's son and heir, soon to be the new Prince of Wales and to his Grace, Robert Stillington, Bishop of Bath and Wells.

"Until now, I was of the opinion that Stillington's revelation to the council tomorrow would be sufficient to secure the crown for you Dickon," began Buckingham, pouring himself some more wine, "but this amazing reaction of Will Hastings to the news, all-be-it a drunken one of course, gives me cause to wonder."

"You think others will be prepared to over-look Edward's bigamy?"

Roses are White

"Possibly. We know we can rely on the support of your Northern friends and I am equally sure that the merchants and traders in the capital will prefer a mature King with a proven record for justice over a boy King, being led by the nose by avaricious Woodvilles, however ... " he paused for effect.

"Who would not support the Duke of Gloucester when we can show that he is the late King Edward's legal heir?" demanded Catesby, ever the lawyer.

"Latent adherents to the house of Lancaster?" volunteered Giles mischievously. He fixed his gaze firmly on Buckingham who, sure enough, shot him an angry glance which melted instantly.

"Well yes, there may still be some," he conceded.

"Bishop Morton for example," snapped Gloucester, "according to Giles he nudged Hastings into this treason."

"And as you rightly said Dickon, Hastings must stand by his own decisions."

"Yes, yes, so to whom do you refer Harry?"

"Firstly, all the Woodvilles and their hangers on. We should not underestimate their number. Since the crowning of Elizabeth Woodville every Woodville priest is now a Bishop, every Woodville apprentice, a guild master, every Woodville lawyer a King's Justice, every Woodville bailiff ... "

" ... a Lord Mayor. We get the picture Harry. You have not answered my question. Who might choose to ignore Edward's bigamy?"

"Yorkist my Lord."

"Ridiculous," spat Radcliffe, who could not imagine any decent man rejecting his master's claim to the throne.

"No Radcliffe, my Lord of Buckingham is right," sighed Gloucester, "all adherents to the White Rose have a choice between the *son* of the Duke of York, myself, and the *grandson* of the Duke of York, my brother's son."

"But there is a solution," offered Buckingham knowingly.

"Which is?"

"Well, you may not like it much Dickon but the Duke of Clarence always maintained that Edward was not his father's son and ... "

"No Harry I will not have my mother's virtue brought into question."

"But my Lord if we can show that King Edward was not your father's son then supporters of the House of York will follow you to a man."

"No Harry, I will not present my mother as an adulteress."

"It was she who first raised the matter," Buckingham declared reasonably. "When Edward married the Woodville woman your mother was so infuriated by his disregard for her lowly birth that she begged his council to allow her to go before parliament and denounce him as a bastard. Do you not know the story My Lord?"

"I do not and I am surprised that you are acquainted with such irresponsible gossip."

"Dickon, Dickon, you have been protected from the truth by your time in the North. Your brother George Clarence, believed Edward to be a bastard. He never stopped denouncing him until the day he died. At least speak to the Lady about it. To her credit she was prepared to accuse herself once in an attempt to keep the Woodvilles from power. She may well be prepared to do so again."

Impetuous as ever, Richard summonsed a squire and gave orders for his horse to be made ready and six men-at-arms to assemble in the courtyard to escort him to Baynard's Castle.

"I didn't mean you should challenge Her Grace tonight Dickon," cried Buckingham, "its but an hour from midnight."

"Exactly, my mother will rise from her bed at midnight for prayers in the chapel. I will speak with her then."

"But there is no hurry ... "

"Of course there is Harry. Tomorrow Bishop Robert will tell the council that Edward's sons are illegitimate. If what you say is true and their father is also illegitimate, then that too must be brought to their attention," so saying he signalled to Radcliffe and the two of them left the hall.

Catesby mumbled something about making an early start and followed closely behind, leaving Giles and Buckingham alone in the quickly darkening hall. A manservant entered from the screened passage and after bowing courteously, firstly to Buckingham and then a little less fully to Giles, began to light the wall sconces and candelabras. Giles left his seat in the shadows and came to the hearth intending to bid the Duke goodnight, when

Buckingham bade him stay a while longer. They waited in silence until the servant had completed his task and then the Duke launched once more into profuse apologise for his earlier outburst.

"How can I possibly make amends for drawing my sword on you tonight Sir Giles. I do earnestly beg your forgiveness."

"Let it rest my Lord. The matter is closed as far as I am concerned."

"I trust your uncle will see it as you do Giles, an honest, if misguided reaction to being accused of treason. I just didn't look at it form your point of view. Now I can quite see how my dinner with Lady Stanley, tonight of all nights, might appeared to implicate me in this leak." He poured himself some more wine. "There must be a ghost with Woodville sympathies lurking in this very household, listening behind the screens," he declared, acting the part of a scary story teller.

Giles laughed politely at his mummery and then pointed out that they were in the Gloucester's solar when Bishop Robert delivered his news and well out of earshot of listening servants, if not of ghosts.

"Well then, you must be the ghost," continued Buckingham in the same silly spooky voice, "were you not at Holborn yourself this evening?"

"*I told no one*," countered Giles hotly, "I wouldn't have gone to Holborn if Luke's injuries hadn't been life threatening. We both agreed months ago that our friendship was untenable, Richard Gloucester being my uncle and Luke owing his life to Bishop Morton."

As soon as the words left Giles' mouth he realised his mistake. Until the discovery of Morton's plotting this evening there was no reason for Luke and Giles not to be friends, unless of course Giles was already privy to the old pact between Luke, Morton, Buckingham and Lady Stanley. Had the Duke noticed his faux pas? perhaps not. The arrogant lord hardly ever listened to what anyone else had to say, which was why his current demeanour was so unreal.

"I think we should wait for your uncle to return from Baynard's," continued Buckingham smoothly, "if his mother concedes to the delicate question of King Edward's illegitimacy then he may need our support. Our new Sovereign has a misplaced sense of loyalty towards his late brother. Don't you agree?"

Giles did not agree but before he could open his mouth to reply the Duke continued.

"We will await His Highness together Giles but first I need to check that my stallion is being properly cared for."

Now why did Giles not believe him? He followed Buckingham across the hall and watched from the top of the stone stairway whilst he descended and crossed the yard, disappearing into the darkness of the stables. By the time he returned the night watchman had lit the four large torches extending outwards from masonry pillars at each corner of the courtyard, flooding the area with dancing light. It was in these deceptive swirls of light and shadow that Giles thought he saw the figure of a man slide from behind the cover of Buckingham's billowing cloak and slip down the south side of the manor. He mentioned his concern to the Duke when he eventually returned to the great hall but Buckingham laughed and said, that no-one could creep about behind him without his knowledge. That was exactly what Giles was thinking when he took the wine cup Buckingham offered and drank deeply. It tasted bitter and no sooner did Giles feel the dryness at the back of his throat than his legs crumbled beneath him. Believing that death would follow, he feverishly grasped at the cord around his neck in search of his mother's ring and then in a vain attempt to raise the household he tried to scream, BUCKINGHAM and TRAITOR but he couldn't form the words. His mouth was ridged, there was no sensation in his tongue and unconsciousness was closing fast.

Chapter 29

Road to Wales 13th June 1483

The first time Giles recovered consciousness he found himself strapped to the saddle of a horse. His hands were tied behind him and round a plank rammed down his tunic which had chaffed his back until blood had dribbled into the seat of his hose. A cloth bag was over his head but the saddle had the comfort of his own and the beast's gait felt familiar. Someone must have been leading his mount and Giles sensed that at least one rider was behind him. He raised his head and tried to cry out only to find a gag in his mouth but his movements had alerted his captors and his steed was halted; no one spoke. Giles felt the straps removed from his legs before being dragged from the saddle, the bag roughly pulled from his head and the gag slackened. It was daylight and at first Giles had to screw up his eyes against the glare of the sun but when he became accustomed to the light he was surprised to see only one man, wearing a mask and offering a wine skin. Without the use of his hands Giles was obliged to part his lips and allow the liquid to be poured into his mouth but as soon as he tasted the bitterness, he realised his error, remaining conscious just long enough to note that they were no longer in London but somewhere in the country, the sweet smell of Woodbine filling his senses as once again it was dark and then – nothing.

The next time Giles regained consciousness he was sitting, propped against a tumbled wall, the stones jutting into his sore back and thighs. He was still bound but the gag, hood and plank had been removed. It was pitch dark and for a moment he thought he had been abandoned but as his senses gathered he could hear horses breathing as they slept, presumably tethered on the other side of the wall. His head was throbbing, as if he had been on the ale for a week and his stomach repeatedly turned, causing him to retch and vomit until every trace of its contents were arrayed on the grass beside him. The sound of his vomiting did not waken his captors and shout as he might nobody came either to silence him or to relieve his thirst. Eventually he drifted into a fitful sleep, waking at first light by the dawn chorus of summer birds. His thirst was painful and he could no longer hear any of the sounds he associated with tethered horses.

The landscape before him was of tree covered hills, rocky outcrops and a deep ravine below. Carefully he rolled onto his side and pushing himself off with one foot on a boulder he managed to roll over a couple of times coming to rest on what was no more than a mound of tufted grass but from his new position he could look down into the ravine. He could see two men watering three horses in the beck that ran in the valley and desperate for water himself, he shouted as loudly as his parched throat would allow. The masked man climbed back up the hillside leading two of the horses whilst the other remained by the beck, wrapped in a long cloak with the cowl pulled over his head but even from this distance Giles could see that he was much taller than his companion and something about him was familiar.

The masked man hobbled the horses and then roughly pulled Giles into a sitting position. He drank deeply from the dripping wineskin he carried over his shoulder and then held it out to his captive. Once again Giles was forced to open his mouth and allow the brackish water to be poured down his throat. This time it was drug free and he greedily slurped as much of the precious liquid as he could manage before the man retrieved the skin and sank down on the grass besides him. Without the gag in his mouth Giles was able to demand where they were? where they were bound? and who had abducted him? but the masked man steadfastly ignored him. It was as if he was stone deaf or Giles spoke a different language, his questions being a string of unintelligible words falling on untutored ears. A glance down into the valley told Giles that the second man had left the beck and hearing a slight rustle behind in the longer grass, he struggled to turn and see if the tall man had returned. As soon as the masked man noticed his movement he grabbed Giles by the throat and thrust the gag back into his mouth. Then he pulled the bag over his head and with one swift movement two sets of hands deftly lifted him onto his horse, strapping his legs securely around the beast's girth. No words passed between the owners of the pairs of hands and within minutes Giles' dark journey continued.

His head was still throbbing but the lethargy caused by the drugs was beginning to wear off and Giles was considering what opportunities, if any, he had of escaping. He reckoned they would stop before mid-day to eat and if so, his hands would probably be untied for the first time since his abduction but until then, all he could do was sit astride Dexter and wait in the dark. To pass the time he tried to work out why Henry Buckingham was having him transported so far away from the Capital, when it would have been easier to murder him and hide the body. Perhaps Buckingham considered the disposal of a body in London to be risky, the Thames certainly had a reputation for giving up its dead within twenty four hours and he could be sure that his uncle would mount a thorough search for him. Giles shivered, he had just argued himself into a lonely death miles away from home but further deliberation told him it wasn't the answer. They had already travelled deep into the countryside and last night's camp was a suitable spot for his murder had that been the plan. No, Buckingham was removing him out of Gloucester's reach, maybe only temporarily, for his captors were going to extraordinary lengths not to be recognised. That thought raised Giles' spirits and he began dredging his memory for identification of the tall man he had seen watering the horses and who kept out of sight at the rear of their little caravan but he could not unlock his memory, so he tackled another question. Where was he being taken? It was difficult for Giles to assess how long he had been unconscious but he calculated that if they had set out from Crosby Place at midnight on the 12th June and they slept in the open last night, then this must be at least day two of their journey. They had camped on a wooded hill side and Dexter had been climbing steadily since they broke camp and he could hear water falling much of the time but there must be hills within two days ride in almost every direction from London.

The sun had been beating down on his head for some time and Giles reckoned it must be mid-day and if his captors were as tired and thirsty as he was then the journey break he was anticipating must be soon. When it came Giles was surprised to discover that they had ridden into some inhabited place because he could hear voices, albeit in a strange tongue. Dexter was led into a stable before Giles was pulled from the saddle, his hood and gag removed and then pushed to the ground by his masked abductor who spoke for the first time to hail the ostler. The words he used were not English or French but as the stable-hand understood what was said to him and replied in the same tongue, Giles decided they must be in Wales. Of course, it made perfect sense, why had he not thought of it before? He was being taken to Buckingham's castle deep in the Welsh hills at Brecknock.

All three horses were tended by young boys taking orders from a pox faced ostler whose belly drooped so far over his cods that Giles doubted he could see his feet. His huge girth necessitated a rolling gait which he measured with a puff and a blow as he swayed rhythmically from side to side. There was no sign of the tall man and Giles assumed he must have gone straight into the tavern as further discussion between the ostler and the masked man resulted in money changing hands and Giles being left tethered to the front of Dexter's stall. It was not long before the ostler was hailed by another traveller but before leaving Giles alone, he gave him a swift swipe across the face with the back of his hand and then wagging his fat forefinger, as if daring him to move, he left puffing and blowing like a pair of bellows. Before his return, a pot boy in a greasy apron with hands and hair to match, poked his cheeky face round the door and yelled something in Welsh. Giles could smell the onions or leaks in the hot soup he carried and yelled back hopefully. The boy grinned when he saw Giles tied to the post and dumped the soup and dry bread at his feet together with a pot of ale. Giles held up his bound hands for release but the lad only grinned, shook his head and disappeared back into the tavern. When the ostler returned, Giles held up his tied hands again. Breathing foul breath into Giles' face, the fat man leaned precariously forward and untied the bindings on his wrists but he left Giles bound to the post and stood over him whilst he ate his food. Giles contemplated throwing the bowl of hot broth into the man's face but he knew he would not have sufficient time to grapple with the ropes that bound him to the stall so he drank his watered ail and then signed to the man that he needed to relieve himself. It was a reasonable request and without hesitation the fat ostler unwound the ropes that tethered Giles to the stall. As soon as he felt himself loose, Giles picked up the ale pot and swung it with all his strength at the ostler's head. The huge man swayed and toppled forward towards his assailant, who side stepped the crashing body and climbed into Dexter's stall. Feverishly Giles tried to back the animal out but by now the floored fat man was screaming at the top of his voice and before he could mount Dexter the stable was full of men from the tavern, all eager for a brawl and an excuse to beat up an English felon.

Meanwhile, that same morning, the King's Councillors were due to assemble in the Tower, where a very nervous Bishop Robert was to present their lordships with the evidence of King Edward's bigamy. As Giles had not returned to Clipberry the previous evening and the Duke of Gloucester had recalled his man, Radcliffe, that left only Mark Taylor to escort the Bishop to the Council Chamber. So a very agitated Bishop Robert had left well before dawn for Gloucester's manor house in Bishopgate, determined to travel to the Tower under the Duke's personal protection. Mark and the Bishop had arrived at Crosby Place before Gloucester and Buckingham were ready to leave and whilst the Bishop was invited to break his fast with the Dukes, Mark hung around the kitchens watching the great fires being revived and considering how he might contact Lady Anne's maid, Lucy.

"You again, what are you doing here at this hour?" scolded Polly, the slattern he had abandoned only yesterday. She had entered the kitchen from the back door carrying fire wood in a large canvas sling across her chest.

"Here, let me take that," cried Mark, seeing how the wood had scratched her face.

Polly laughed and dropping her load at his feet, she pointed to where a sweating cook was stoking one of the fires. To her amusement Mark piled the logs by the cook and then carried several more loads from the stock pile in the yard. Eventually she took pity on him and signalled him to stop and join her by the buttery door, where a tapster had just finished breaching a new barrel of ale. Polly reached for two quart pots from the shelf above the stacked barrels and filled them to the brim and then raising the pots in the air she called to Mark to follow her out into the kitchen yard.

"Ave you come looking for your master?" she asked, after drinking deeply.

"Sir Giles? No, why should I?" replied Mark, wiping the froth from his mouth with the back of his hand.

"Cos he's been kidnapped."

"Don't be ridiculous. Whatever makes you think that?"

Polly shrugged her pretty shoulders and made a moue but it was enough to send a cold shiver down Mark's spine. Giles *should* have returned to Clipberry last night.

"Tell me what you know Polly – please. Sir Giles did not return home last night but I assumed he was here, with his uncle Gloucester."

Polly's eyes widened and her mouth dropped open.

"His Grace is your master's uncle? God save us."

She grabbed Mark by the sleeve and dragged him across the yard into the stables and holding tight to his arm, trudged from stall to stall yelling, 'Benjamin'. At last a lad raised himself from a pile of hay and rubbed the sleep from his eyes with a grubby hand. Mark looked from Polly to the lad and back to Polly in astonishment, they were two peas from the same pod.

"We're twins," sighed Polly, who unlike most identical siblings was unimpressed with having to share her identity with another. "Come here Ben and tell master Mark what you told me first thing this morning."

Ben looked doubtful, Mark was scowling and Gloucester's 'White Boar' on the front of Mark's tunic warned him from 'making mischief', which was Ben's term for repeating information that would definitely lead to trouble.

"Ben, did you or didn't you see Sir Giles last evening?" persisted Polly. Her brother nodded his assent. "Telling what you know is not making mischief. Tell, or I will."

Ben climbed down from his bed of hay and beckoned Mark and his sister to follow him into the next stable. He climbed a small loft ladder and bid Mark and Polly, follow. It was no more that a hayrack and the three of them had to squeeze together to fit onto the small platform that supported the roof between two stables. It was too low to stand but from his kneeling position Mark could see directly down into the adjoining stable where grooms were leading Gloucester's white stallion and Buckingham's black one, out into the yard.

"Duke Henry's great black beast was in there last night," said Ben, "and that tall man with silver hair was with him as usual."

"What man?"

"The one you followed the other day when our Polly was looking for you."

"Go on," pressed Mark not wanting to be side tracked.

"Well first off, the Duke of Buckingham came down to the stables himself and took Silver Head back into the manor. Then Silver Head and another man appeared with your Sir Giles propped between them as if he were in his cups."

"Perhaps he was."

"Aye, well, I'm sure if anyone saw 'em that's what they was meant to reckon but when they got him down there they strapped him onto 'is horse and stuck a plank a wood down his jacket so as to make him look sat up. Come to think on, 'e could well 'av been dead."

"What?"

"Well he never moved and even though Dexter's reins were in his hands, Silver Head had a leading rein and led him out the gate bold as you like and … "

The noise in the court yard stopped Ben in mid sentence. All three crouched in the hay loft straining to hear what was being said. Odd words drifted their way and they could see Gloucester, Buckingham and the Bishop mounted and ready to leave. Servants were rushing about and assuring the three Lords that Sir Giles was nowhere to be found and that his horse was not in the stables.

"Hadn't you best tell the Duke of Gloucester what our Ben saw?" whispered Polly.

"Shush ... keep quiet," warned Mark, "I can't tell him in front of the Duke of Buckingham. I need to find help."

As soon as Gloucester's party had left for the Tower, Mark took his leave of Polly and Ben and made for Morton's manor in Holborn. He was sure that Sir Humphrey Percivall and Ben's tall, silver haired man were one and the same *and* that somehow Buckingham was responsible for Giles' disappearance. The thought that his young master might be dead made his blood run cold and the only man he dare trust with his fear was fighting for his own life in Bishop Morton's manor. Mark planned to gain entry to the manor house on the pretext of collecting Woof, something he should have done days ago, trusting that Bishop Morton would have already left for the Tower. He did not want to come face to face with the Bishop for he would feel obliged to explain that he had followed Sir Humphrey to Holborn on the previous day. Luke's fall had erased the incident from Mark's mind but now he fretted over whatever business the knight might have had with Bishop Morton for if Ben was correct, it was Sir Humphrey, Buckingham had trusted with the Giles' unconscious or worse, dead body.

Joby welcomed Mark and grumbled good humouredly about 'early risers'. Bishop Morton had knocked him up long before dawn and now here was another caller before he had managed to break his fast. Mark pretended to be sorry to have missed the Bishop, explaining that he had returned for Woof, having left in such a hurry yesterday. Red faced at how easily he had lied to Joby he made his way across the bailey and round to the front of the Manor where a young squire recognised him and agreed to show him to Luke's quarters. When they reached the bottom of the outside stone staircase Mark thanked the lad for his help and started up the steps.

"Could you find Woof for me and bring him here," called Mark from half way up the stairs. He rummaged in his purse for a coin which he tossed to the lad below.

"I don't think I can do that," said the boy, catching the coin deftly, "His Grace will be mad with me if I hand him over without his permission."

"Damn it lad, he's *my* dog. Oh alright, just find out where he is and let me know. I'll collect him myself before I leave."

The boy pocketed the coin and scurried off before Mark changed his mind

At the top of the steps an old Friar roused himself as he approached Luke's quarters.

"Master Luke seems to have taken a turn for the worse," said the friar, "I doubt he will want to talk to you. But if you would sit with him whilst I fetch brother Jordan, you would be doing both myself and Master Luke a favour."

"Of course brother," agreed Mark, disappointed that Luke was not well enough to assist in his search for Giles.

He pushed open the heavy door as quietly as possible and tiptoed across to the dais where Luke lay motionless in the great bed. Mark hesitated, uncertain whether to wake him, when suddenly the covers were pushed back and using his one good arm, Luke scrambled to sit up, causing Mark to cry out in alarm.

"Quiet Mark," he warned, "I'm pretending to be at death's door."

"Good God man, why?"

"Because, little by little my memory is returning and I need time to come to terms with what I am remembering before I tell Bishop Morton." He patted the bed for Mark to sit. "Where is Giles, I need to speak with him?"

Momentarily Mark was tongue tied, he was unsure whether to inquire about Luke's recovering memory or to launch into the details of Giles' abduction.

"Who are you then?" asked Mark, deciding the former to be the more courteous.

"I haven't got that far yet but I know that I fought for York at Tewkesbury."

"Hell's teeth Luke, that will upset Bishop Morton."

"Upset him? Wait till he learns it was I who killed his precious Prince of Lancaster."

"You can't mean it?"

"I most certainly do. That brooch the Bishop believes to be a present from Lancaster was in fact a trophy, awarded me by the Duke of Clarence for slaying the Prince."

"Oh Luke, what will you do?"

"Feign illness until I have the whole picture. That's why I need to speak with Giles urgently. You see, we put our friendship on hold because I owed my life to Morton and even though I suspected him of anti-Yorkist activities, I had come to believe that my own loyalties were to Lancaster."

"I don't understand, Bishop Morton was one of the late King's closes friends."

"And one of Richard Gloucester's fiercest opponents. Where is Giles?"

Mark swallowed hard and reiterated the story of the kidnapping according to Ben. Luke became agitated.

"If Buckingham has abducted Giles he is in serious danger," he whispered, "and you say Bishop Robert is to deliver some information to the Council this morning, which necessitated his protection last night.?"

Mark nodded. "Giles and Radcliffe were supposed to escort him to the Tower this morning to attend the council meeting."

"You must go to the Tower at once Mark. Find the Duke of Gloucester and tell him Buckingham has kidnapped his nephew?"

"I can't do that Luke. Gloucester may have ordered his abduction."

"What? Of course he didn't. Why should he?"

"Giles now believes that King Edward was his father, not George Clarence," said Mark and then told Luke about the tree at Middleham carved with dates and initials.

"Hell's teeth but even so, why should Gloucester arrange for Giles to be abducted?"

"Because if Edward married Elizabeth Woodville *before* Eleanor Butler died then Giles is our late King's first born son and heir."

A commotion in the courtyard below took Mark to the window where he saw men rushing about like wasps in a disturbed nest. Luke swung his legs over the edge of the bed but found he was unable to stand as the ceiling rolled before his eyes, turning the room on its side and sending him crashing back onto the pillows, clutching at his head as he fell. Running steps could be heard climbing the outside staircase and before Luke could pull the covers over his naked body, the door swung wide and the lad who was supposed to be locating Woof, stood framed in the incoming flood of sunlight.

"Bishop Morton has been arrested and Lord Hastings is to be executed before noon," screamed the lad at the top of his voice.

Mark ran to the door but the vision had fled to deliver his message to other members of the household. Mark turned and stared helplessly at Luke who was trying once again to stand upright.

Chapter 30

Brecknock Castle 1st July 1483

The first sensation to register in Giles' throbbing head was the sound of gushing water. In those initial moments of consciousness he believed he was back in his old childhood bedchamber at Clipberry Manor, the rain streaming down the roof and falling in sheets passed his horn filled window but this was a heavier deluge, more akin to a high waterfall, hurling the full force of a flooded river into a bottomless cavern. He tried to open his eyes but it was too painful, his lids were puffed and swollen both above and below the sockets. The back of his throat was dry and when he parted his lips they cracked and smarted as if the frost had slit them with cold. Someone pressed a damp sponge to the soreness and tiny drops of soothing wetness trickled to the back of his parched throat and painful though it was, Giles coughed and sputtered with the sensation. He heard a voice whisper urgently and his heart sank as he recognised the gentle lilt of that foreign tongue, the language of the attackers who had kicked and punched him and left him for dead.

He may have slipped back into unconsciousness or he may have dreamt his anguish but the next words Giles heard were English and the voice was familiar.

"God be praised Giles, you are alive. Can you hear me?"

"Doctor Morton?" breathed Giles, reverting to the first title by which he had known the Bishop, "how did you find me?"

"Rest now Giles, we can talk later when you are feeling better."

Giles relaxed. If Morton was here everything must be well but he could still hear the falling water and the other voices in the room were unintelligible.

"Where am I? Doctor where am I?"

There was no reply but the wet sponge was still being gently pressed to his lips, its healing moisture quenching his thirst, so what were his instincts warning him against?

Days past before Giles felt able to rouse himself sufficiently to take serious notice of his surroundings but when he sat up for the first time it was dark and he was alone in the small room, dominated by the sound of falling of water. There was no candle or lamp light but a full moon in a cloudless sky entered though a single, unshuttered window. Giles turned on one elbow and stared at the crude wooden walls that contain his box-bed. There were no drapes and no rugs and the only other furniture was a low stool on one side of the bed and an old chest on the other. A smelly night jar was beside the stool and a pitcher and wooden basin, containing a sponge, had been left on the top of the chest. As Giles pushed back the sheepskin cover he could see that strips of linen were bound tightly around his chest and he knew that he must remain still. Mary had bound Woof's chest in the same way when, as a pup, Mark had rescued him from the middenstead with a suspected crushed rib cage. If a splintered rib were to pierce his lung, death would shortly follow. Without more movement he could see that his belly was a mass of purple bruising and large areas of broken skin were setting in scars amongst more bruises on all his limbs. Fearful of his broken ribs, Giles retrieved the sheepskin and gently lay back against his pillows. Most of his body was throbbing with pain but his head was by far the worst. Every tiny movement felt as though the contents of his scull were been swung about, causing dizziness, nausea and a vice like tightening above his eyes that threatened to burst and release his brains through every aperture in his head.

As if somewhere a great tocsin tolled Giles suddenly recalled all the events that had led to his present dilemma and the vein on his temple quickly became enlarged and pulsated vigorously as he cursed Henry Buckingham under his breath. The throbbing in his head intensified and momentarily Giles lost consciousness but when he gathered his senses again he swore to remain calm. Head injuries often led to brain damage, as Luke bore witness and Giles thank God that his memory was still intact. Laying as still as he possible could, he forced the image of Henry Buckingham out of his mind and concentrated instead on the sound of falling water, eventually drifting into a fitful shallow sleep.

Hours later he woke again to the incessant sound of water but it was day light and a gruff looking woman in her middle-age was leaning over him with a wooden spoon and bowl of thin broth that smelt of garlic. His nausea resurfaced and Giles turned his head away from the offered bowl causing the pain in his head to strike with such renewed intensity that he cried out in agony.

"Be careful woman," bellowed Bishop Morton from the open doorway, "leave that slop and bring me some brandy-wine."

The woman put the bowl and wooden spoon down on the stool and without a word left the chamber.

"I'm sorry Giles, hardly any of these people understand a word of English, it's driving me mad." He took the sponge from the bowl and poured water from the jug over it and then, holding it to Giles' mouth, squeezed gently. "I have looked in on you several times. How are you feeling now?"

"Lucky to be alive, after being beaten to a pulp?" replied Giles grumpily, "I was drugged the night before the council met and I have only been half conscious since."

Giles felt the vein on his temple begin to swell and the room to sway. He grabbed Morton's hand and pulled the sponge to his mouth to calm himself.

"Ah yes, the council meeting, what a calamity," sighed Morton, "that drunken fool, Lord Hastings brought armed men to the Tower, intending to arrest the Dukes of Buckingham and Gloucester and imprison them until the young Prince of Wales was crowned. Fortunately, Gloucester discovered his treason but he sent Hastings to the block with unseemly haste. There was no trial or opportunity for me to plead for him. It was a disgrace after his loyal service to our late King."

"Oh no," sighed Giles, genuinely distressed by the news.

"The poor lord had no time even to make his peace with God and more to the point, no time to exonerate myself and Stanley from complicity."

"I don't understand," said Giles truthfully.

"Based on nothing more than the fact that Hastings and Stanley had dined at Holborn with me on the previous evening, Stanley and I were arrested as his accomplices, would you believe?"

Of course Giles believed it and had he been at the council meeting himself he would have defended Hastings and suggested Bishop Morton should die a traitor's death.

"So, Your Grace and Lord Stanley knew nothing of Hastings intentions?" mumbled Giles with a hint of sarcasm.

"Of course not. I have no love for Gloucester as you well know but had I even an inkling of what Lord William intended, I would have done all in my power to have restrained him. That lawyer Catesby wrongly accused us. Poor old Stanley was dispatched to the Tower and I was sent here to Brecknock."

The middle-aged woman returned with Morton's brandy-wine and whilst the Bishop poured them both a cup of his favourite tipple, Giles considered how to respond to Morton's duplicity. He was very tempted to call the Bishop a liar and swear to inform Gloucester of his true part in the plot but he was dependent on Morton to help him recover and hopefully escape, so he decided to play along with the Bishop's version of events for the time being. Giles hauled himself carefully into a semi sitting position and trying not to move his head, he took the cup of brandy-wine Morton offered. What he was struggling to work out, was the link between Morton and Buckingham. Had they reactivated their old covin after all? He believed that Buckingham had abducted him because he had let slip his own knowledge of that old conspiracy, which would certainly damage the Duke's standing with Gloucester but it did not necessarily mean that he was *actively* plotting to make Henry Tudor England's King. However, Buckingham had apparently rescued Morton from the ugly situation in the council chamber by bringing him to Wales. So, if it was Buckingham who had informed Morton of Bishop Robert's secret in the first instance, why hadn't he also warned him that Catesby had told Gloucester of their plans to arrest the Dukes?

"Who told Hastings about the announcement Bishop Robert was to make at the council meeting?" asked Giles sipping the glorious liquor.

"What?" snapped Morton chocking on his, " what announcement?"

"I assumed that it was Robert's revelation that had angered Hastings and caused him to undertake such drastic action against my uncle," said Giles, feigning innocence.

"I know nothing about any 'revelation'," lied Morton, "Hastings thought Gloucester was delaying the crowning of the young King and decided to take matters into his own hands."

"Ah, well, that explains it then."

"Explains what?"

"Well, I know that Robert Stillington had proof that Edward's marriage to Elizabeth Woodville was bigamous."

"Rubbish."

"When Bishop Robert made his announcement at Crosby Place, Gloucester swore those of us present to secrecy and I assumed that someone betrayed his trust and told Hastings. What I still cannot fathom is why the traitor did not send a second message to warn Hastings that his plot had been discovered."

"Presumably because the informant wasn't present when Catesby betrayed Hastings' to Gloucester," Morton said with just a hint of failing confidence in his voice.

"Oh but he was. All who were privy to Bishop Robert's revelation were also told of the plot to arrest the Dukes. I know. I was there on *both* occasions."

Morton's face drained of colour, his eyes flitted from side to side as he tried to rationalise his panic. His small fat fingers gripped his cup until his knuckles turn white. Surely Buckingham had not betrayed him? He began to pant as he recalled how Buckingham had hurried Hastings to the block and bundled his own person from the council chamber before he could open his mouth in his own defence.

Giles tried not to smile; at least there was some satisfaction in seeing Morton squirm.

"But it is of no consequence Your Grace, is it? I mean, I was mistaken in thinking that there had been an informant in the first place, wasn't I?"

It was a day or so longer before Giles could get out of bed but he was healing fast now, his ribs had been badly bruised but not broken and although his head still hurt when he forgot to move carefully, non of his other injuries seemed life threatening. He stood by the window, at last able to see the torrent of water that had dominated his conscious hours. The craggy outcrop from which it fell was directly opposite and the swollen river, which dropped so dramatically, was at eye level across a ravine. Below the window for as far as he could see, the tree canopy spread like a swaying green carpet, linking his side of the ravine to where the fall of water disappeared into its foliage. The only hint as to the depth it plunged, being the harrowing echo that boomed around the steep sided gorge, endlessly repeating the constant thunder below. Beyond the trees he could see another, broader river, into which the torrent must ultimately feed, providing natural defence for at least two sides of Buckingham's fortress. By stretching as far out of the window as his injuries would allow, Giles could see that the castle walls followed one side of the ravine and that his wooden chamber appeared to be perched on the wall itself.

"For the love of God Giles, what are you doing?" Giles retreated from the sill. "Clearly you are feeling much better," continued Bishop Morton, puffing and blowing from the effort of the stairs.

He was followed into the chamber by a short, stocky man carrying a tray of assorted blades and razors. His right eye was missing and the socket and side of his face were horribly scared with a long wound caused by either a knife or a sword. A boy of about ten years with a cheeky grin, trailed behind cradling a bowl of hot steaming towels.

"I have instructed my barber here to shave you Giles and then, if you are feeling strong enough, you can join me in my quarters for the midday meal. There are two fellows down stairs instructed to help you make your way to the central keep."

Giles' instinct was to snub the Bishop but if he was to escape, he must discover the layout of the castle and besides, good wine and a change of surroundings would be a tonic to his spirit. So he thanked Morton stiffly and agreed to join him later.

Whilst the barber worked on his beard, Giles tried to ignore the man's disfigured eye socket by contemplating the nature of Bishop Morton's imprisonment. He seemed to roam about the fortress at will and his reference to, 'my barber' and 'my quarters', were hardly consistent with a prison sentence. He appeared to order the servants about as if he was in his own manor and he was determining Giles' treatment too.

When the barber spread the last of the hot towels over his face, Giles relaxed, relishing the tingling sensation that the heat drew from his raw skin and closing his eyes he dozed for a luxurious moment only to be jolted back to the present by the door being banged open wide. The now unmistakeable Welsh tones of the middle-age woman, who had ungraciously attended him throughout his illness, crashed on his ears once again so he removed the towel and gingerly turned his head to face her onslaught. She dumped his freshly laundered clothes on the bed and dropped his cleaned boots and sword belt, without weapon, on the floor beside him. Slapping her hands to show she was well rid of the items, she turned and flounced out, still ranting in her own tongue. Giles looked to the barber for an interpretation but it was the young boy who spoke.

"Gwyneth expected your clothes and boots in payment for her care of you."

"I will pay her for her trouble," said Giles but his script and purse were not amongst his returned belongings. "Someone has had payment enough already."

The barber waited until Giles had changed and then summoned the two guards who had been waiting at the bottom of the steps. They were rough looking men with bare arms and sacking bound to their legs. They wore beards and moustaches and their hair was cut short to show their ears. They walked forward and considered Giles as if they were assessing the suitability of a horse or hunting dog and after conferring in their own tongue, each man grabbed one of Giles' arms at the elbow and lifting him until his feet barley touched the ground, they marched him out of his cell and down the flight of wooden steps into the castle bailey below. Here they put down their load, cursing in Welsh at their underestimation of his weight. Giles was annoyed too, his sudden transportation from his chamber-on-the-wall to the busy bailey like a sack of flour was demeaning but his humiliation was not yet over. Grabbing his arms for a second time and ignoring his protestations, the rough Welshmen marched him straight across the bailey to the external steps of the central keep, once again raising him so that his feet scraped the ground, they carried him up the steps and into the great hall. Here he was unceremoniously dropped before another man-at-arms wearing a tunic emblazoned with Buckingham's insignia and who Giles believed to be his masked captor because for a moment, he thought he recognised his scent. Speaking in Welsh, the man dismissed the escort and then smiling thinly, indicated that Giles should make his way to the door left of the dais. Giles crossed the cold, drab hall to the echo of his own footsteps to where a squire opened the chamber door and then abandoned him to enter unannounced.

"Ah Giles. Please come and join me."

The chamber in which Morton sat presiding over a table full of food was an amazing contrast to the dingy hall. Tapestries hung from all four walls, the red and white tiled floor was covered in Persian rugs and silk cushions were liberally strewn over two Roman style couches, placed either side of a long low iron table. The table was stacked with dishes of fruit and sweetmeats, cheeses and wine, whilst gold plates and goblets glistened in the light dispensed by five, six-branch standing candelabras.

"My Lord of Buckingham uses this chamber himself, so I am told," said Morton "it's more comfortable than the draughty hall."

"Forgive my asking," said Giles coldly, "but what exactly is your status here?"

Morton hesitated and passed Giles his own, gold handled knife so that he might cut a slice of cheese, when the door open and a very agitated Katherine Woodville, Duchess of Buckingham flounced into the chamber.

Instinctively, Giles rose from his seat surprised to learn that Buckingham's wife had not joined her Lord in London. He stared impolitely at the woman who hovered impatiently beside Morton, pulling at the lace edged cloth in her hands. She was not as beautiful as her sister the queen, although she shared the same hair and eye colour. She was plumper and less groomed, even shabby, thought Giles unkindly but most noticeable was the pain etched into Katherine's face.

"A local man has just returned from London with the news that Richard Gloucester was crowned King of England *more than a week ago*. Why was I not informed and what in God's name has become of my sister and her sons?"

Morton was on his feet shaking from head to toe as he tried to absorb the horror of her news. He made no attempt to comfort the distraught Duchess, it was all he could do to control his own panic but Giles felt a surge of joy he could not restrain.

"Madam there is nothing to fear. King Edward married your sister bigamously, her sons are illegitimate. I promise you, Richard is England's rightful King."

Lady Katherine spun round almost falling amidst the tangle of her own gown.

"What do you know of that lie?" she spat, "is it common knowledge now?"

"Bishop Robert Stillington told the Dukes of Gloucester and Buckingham the night I was abducted. It is not a lie my lady, of that I am certain."

"And what of my treacherous husband, surely he cannot support this abomination?" She fixed her gaze on Morton. "My Lord Bishop, has he betrayed us both?"

Morton avoided her question by rebuking Giles for his euphoria.

"Your obvious pleasure at this news is insensitive and unwelcome Giles. The Duchess has saved your life and made you welcome in her home. The least you can do is respected the distress, so unfairly inflicted on her by the crisis now facing her family."

"Saved my life? How?"

Morton assisted Lady Katherine to sit and poured her a cup of bandy-wine, then taking Giles to one side he pushed his face so close to Giles' that he could smell the garlic on his breath.

"Your captors dumped you in the dungeons beneath this keep, sir," he said tersely, "you would have been dead within days if Lady Katherine had not had you moved."

Giles shoved Morton away and knelt at Lady Katherine's feet.

"Thank you madam for your kindness," he said softly, "I meant no insult. My uncle will treat you kindly. I am certain you have nothing to fear."

She smiled down at him and shook her head.

"It is *Buckingham* I fear Sir Giles. King Edward arranged my marriage when Henry was too young to understand the implications of our union and he has hated me ever since for being a Woodville."

Giles said nothing but she could see the sympathy in his eyes and she smiled sadly at his upturned face.

"I felt secure whilst my sister the Queen held sway, but now she, like the rest of the Woodvilles, are powerless. Buckingham will not rest until he has disposed of me."

"No madam, that's a wicked thing to say," said Morton chiding her gently. But even as the words were leaving his mouth, the reason for Buckingham joining the conspiracy in the first instance flashed across his mind: 'The total destruction of the Woodville family'. Why had he missed the obvious?

Buckingham had already achieved his goal.

Chapter 31

Brecknock Castle 14th July 1483

A harbinger arrived the following morning, announcing the home coming of the Duke of Buckingham, so Giles was confined once again to his wall-top prison and Bishop Morton rehearsed his newly conceived plan. If he had read the situation correctly, Buckingham had abandoned the conspirators in favour of being King Richard's chief councillor because the destruction of the Woodville family had been achieved by Bishop Robert's revelation. Besides, King Richard would have rewarded Buckingham handsomely for his assistance in gaining the crown, dwarfing any promises Henry Tudor might insinuate. The Bishop also reasoned that Buckingham would arrive with Luke Lazereth who would ride willingly to Brecknock to be with Morton, unaware of the trap Buckingham had baited. Luke, Giles and Morton, all knew of Buckingham's involvement in the original plot to bring Henry Tudor to England and they all three posed a danger to the Duke's change of loyalty and so he was drawing them into his own castle, here at Brecknock away from King Richard's immediate reach. There remained the Stanleys of course but whereas Luke, Giles and Morton were motivated by loyalties of one kind or another, Lord Stanley had no such baggage. If Buckingham promised to personally sponsor him, then that mercenary Lord would conveniently forget their joint involvement in the plot, as all he sort from any venture was material gain and anyway neither he nor Lady Stanley could denounce the Duke of Buckingham without implicating themselves.

Morton wiped the sweat from his brow with the back of his hand. He was getting too old for this kind of intrigue. In his younger days he would have relished pitting his wits against the conceited assurance of the likes of Henry Buckingham but what he planned on this occasion was rash, even by his earlier exploits. Not only was his own life in danger but so were Luke's and Giles'. He sighed, in the long term he and Giles could not both survive, unless he could convince the lad to relinquish his loyalty to the House of York and he doubted that was possible. In a perverse way that was the aspect of Giles' character that Bishop Morton admired most, for he himself would never forsake his need to avenge the death of Margaret's son.

Stretched out on his bed in the wooden chamber, Giles had also made sense of the situation. He could see now that Luke had severed their friendship after Edward's death because Morton had resurrected the old conspiracy and that Buckingham played his part faithfully until Giles accused him of betraying Bishop Robert Stillington's secret. The Duke's uncharacteristic change of mood on that evening was the very point at which he shifted his allegiance to genuinely supporting Richard, his mission to destroy the Woodvilles being accomplished. However, after a careless slip by Giles, the Duke realised that Luke had told Giles about his involvement in the old plot and he had arranged Giles' abduction to prevent him repeating what he knew to his uncle. By the same reasoning Giles concluded that one way or another, Luke and possibly Mark, would be joining Morton and Giles at Brecknock, if Buckingham intended to silence all potential tale tellers.

The thought that Luke might appear with Buckingham raised Giles' spirits. He was sure Mark Taylor would be looking for him and he believed his uncle the King would be searching too but whereas it would not occur to King Richard that Buckingham was hiding him, Luke just might make the connection, especially if Mark had enlisted his help.

Henry Buckingham rode into his favourite castle at Brecknock two days later than he had intended because Luke had not really been fit to travel and they had made slow progress. Buckingham had easily convinced Luke that Bishop Morton had need of him at Brecknock and he had thought it fortuitous that Mark Taylor had offered to ride with them in order to take care of Luke. However, the Duke would have felt more secure if Mark had not slipped away on the previous evening but they had been deep in the heart of Wales when he had disappeared and Buckingham was confident that he would be found and brought to Brecknock within hours of his own arrival there. He had also inveigled Reginald Bray into riding with them, for he too was privy to the Duke's role in the old conspiracy and Buckingham could not afford for Bray's silly chatter to reach King Richard's ears. Lady Stanley had been easily deceived as she was eager for Bray to ride to Brecknock with information for Bishop Morton regarding her son Henry Tudor and Lord Stanley posed no threat, he had readily seen the financial advantage of abandoning the plot to bring Tudor to England, now that Richard had been crowned.

Sir Humphrey Percivall attended the Duke as he, Luke and Reginald Bray entered the great hall. Speaking in the local tongue, he ordered grooms and servants, to quicken their step and sharpen their responses now their Lord had returned home. The entire household had crowded into the hall to welcome the Duke and Lady Katherine curtsied low as her husband swept past her, grabbing the eldest of his sons tightly by the shoulder and pulling him roughly from his mother's side. The frail ten year old shrieked with fright at his rough handling and stumbled into his father's path, causing the Duke to halt abruptly before Morton, where he waited impatiently until the Bishop deigned to acknowledge his Grace by bending his head.

"I will speak with you when I have rested," he said, without looking at the Bishop and retaining his grip on the terrified child he forced him forward.

Once the pair had disappeared into the Duke's solar, Morton hurried across the hall to where Luke had draped his feeble body against a heavy double fronted cupboard.

"You should never have made this journey, Luke. You have barely recovered from your fall."

"I had little option, Your Grace, Giles is missing and I have good reason to believe that arrogant Lord abducted him and brought him here," said Luke, inclining his head towards the door that had just closed, "have *you* seen Giles?"

"Shush Luke. We can talk later," warned Morton, conscious that Sir Reginald Bray was listening from behind the large cup of wine he was sipping.

Lady Katherine joined them, taking Luke by his good arm she assured him that she would attend to his needs personally. Gently she ushered him towards the guest wing whilst Morton also tried to support Luke with an extended arm but he refused the assistance, leaving the Bishop stunned by the rejection. Bray diverted his attention.

"My Lord Bishop, Lady Stanley sends her greetings and trusts that her nephew has provided well for you during your confinement here," he simpered, sidling up to Morton with a smirk on his face that was supposed to indicate that he knew his imprisonment to be a sham.

"Hold your tongue Sir, I beg you, everything is not as you suppose," snapped Morton, "take your things to your chamber and meet me in Luke's quarters within the hour."

Bray nodded and swiftly left the great hall. Morton eased his considerable bulk onto the first step of the dais and resigned himself to waiting there until the Duke had rested from his journey. Clearly Buckingham had intended to unnerve Morton by his casual treatment of him but the Bishop was one step ahead and he chuckled to himself as he considered the clever trap he was waiting to spring on the treacherous Lord.

After the hour candle on the side table had burned down a full notch Morton abandoned his vigil and summonsing a servant to be his guide, he made his way to Luke's chamber. Reginald Bray was already there, seated at the window, away from the sumptuous bed, on top of which Luke lay fully clothed, surrounded by plump pillows and attended by Lady Katherine. Sir Reginald appeared relived to see Morton and closed the shutters on the activity in the tilt yard below, which until then he had been watching without seeing. Morton was surprised to find himself irritated by the Lady Katherine's presence. She was dabbing Luke's brow with a cloth soaked in lavender water from a silver bowl, the scent of which filled the room with a heady fragrance. She looked up as Morton entered and smiled sweetly. Somehow she seemed younger, more feminine and wearing that low cut gown of pale green silk; dare he think it? Yes, she was attractive. Why had he not noticed before?

"Luke will be fine Your Grace," she said, conscious that he was staring at her, "he needs rest now and I have made up a tisane of mint and sorrel to prevent further dizziness."

Morton shook himself out of his reverie and shuffled his plump body onto the edge of Luke's bed.

"Please excuse me Lady Katherine but I need to speak to Luke and Sir Reginald alone," began Morton, only to be interrupted by the knight.

"My message from Lady Stanley is for both yourself Bishop and the Lady Katherine."

"Then speak first man."

Bray coughed discretely, bowed slightly to the Bishop and then to Lady Katherine.

"Your sister, the Queen has admitted to my mistress that her marriage to King Edward was bigamous and that since Bishop Robert Stillington has presented his proof of her disgrace to parliament, her son will never be accepted as England's rightful King." Morton, Luke and Katherine all expressed astonishment at his revelation but there was more. "She has agreed, therefore, to cooperate with my Lady Stanley and give her support to Henry Tudor, Prince of Lancaster, with the proviso that Tudor will marry her eldest daughter, Elizabeth of York."

"The crafty witch," declared Luke,

For once Bishop Morton was speechless. A combined Woodville Tudor attack on King Richard might just prove workable but the promise of marriage between Tudor and Edward IV's daughter was unthinkable. If the princes were illegitimate then so was their sister Beth. Tudor could pronounce Beth legitimate by calling Stillington a liar but by the same token he would be reinstating the eldest boy as Edward's heir: *unless they were dead* ... Oh no that was too much to contemplate. Was it? Maybe not ...

"Even now, members of the Woodville family are calling men to arms in the south of the country, intent on releasing the Prince of Wales and his brother from the Tower," continued Bray, "Lady Stanley is assured that their support will be transferred to Tudor the moment he lands on English soil. I am to make my way to France and give Henry Tudor the good news as soon as I have informed yourselves of these developments."

"Is Buckingham privy to this?" asked Morton.

Sir Reginald shuffled uneasily. "To be honest Your Grace, I'm not sure. Her Ladyship gave no specific order to inform the Duke of Buckingham."

"I'm not surprised," sobbed Katherine, "she must be as disappointed with his defection to Richard as we are."

"What do you mean?" demanded Reginald.

"I'm afraid Duke Henry Buckingham has forsaken our cause and now supports King Richard in earnest," explained Morton, "we four face extreme danger."

Only Reginald Bray expressed disbelief. Lady Katherine let her gaze fall to her lap with just the faintest sigh, acknowledging the truth of Morton's words.

"You and I were lured here because of what we know of the plot to bring Tudor to these shores and more specifically, Buckingham's role in that conspiracy," said Luke, in reply to Bray's continued protestations.

"Lady Stanley may have suspected," conceded Bray, "she was highly critical of her nephew's speeches in Richard's favour and she tried unsuccessfully to seek him out before the King's coronation. Are we the only ones who knew of his earlier alliance?"

"No: Giles Butler knew. *Is* Giles here?" demanded Luke.

"He is and safe for now," said Morton quietly, "he would have died weeks ago but for Lady Katherine removing him from the cells beneath the keep."

"Then I thank you madam, Giles is very dear to me," said Luke staring up into Katherine's face. To Morton's astonishment the Lady blushed and tenderly touched the back of Luke's limp hand.

The Bishop blustered on.

"When Buckingham brought me here, he didn't mention the fact that Giles was also his prisoner, so I think it better if we pretend we are unaware of his presence. His life and ours may depend on that continued deceit," warned Morton.

"But why?"

"Because Giles is the one person Buckingham cannot allow to survive."

"Dear God, you are right: as always," sneered Luke, "given the opportunity, Giles will definitely tell King Richard about the old conspiracy. The rest of us will remain quiet because we are as guilty as the Duke himself."

"Perhaps he will attempt to blackmail us into silence," suggested Reginald hopefully.

"Perhaps, but only if we are ignorant of the abduction of Sir Giles Butler," insisted Morton.

"Then we must get him out of here without delay," cried Luke, trying to raise himself on his good elbow.

"I have a plan to help us *all* escape" lied Morton, " but if it is to succeed, the Duke must believe we have no knowledge of his change of loyalty *or* of Giles being here."

"He is bound to discover that I persuaded Sir Humphrey to move Giles from the dungeon," sighed Lady Katherine, "but it is of no consequence as I am the last of his Woodville victims anyway."

Luke swung his long elegant legs to the floor and clumsily fell on one knee.

"I swear to you, on my honour as a knight of this realm, that you will *not suffer* for your kindness to Sir Giles."

A knock on the door and the appearance of the English speaking imp with the sing-song voice, prevented Morton from enquiring about Luke's assumed knighthood.

"His Grace the Duke says the Bishop has to go to his solar. Right now."

"Yes, yes, I'm on my way," said Morton irritably. He was keen to set his plan in motion. The sooner he compromised this treacherous Lord the better but he disliked being summonsed by an unruly child.

Chapter 32

Abergavenny 14th July 1483

Earlier that day Mark and Luke had agreed that they must not both ride into the castle at Brecknock with Buckingham. If the Duke's invitation was indeed a trap, as they suspected, then it was a sensible precaution for one or other to remain on the outside. They knew for certain that Bishop Morton was being held at Brecknock and believed that Giles was also Buckingham's involuntary guest but for the time being, Luke and Mark pretended that they were unaware of the potential danger, giving the Duke no cause to guard them closely. Luke had not recovered from his fall and the journey had exhausted him, so it was Mark who took it upon himself to slip away from their final overnight stop in Abergavenny. With so little distance still to travel, he was convinced that he could make it alone to Brecknock, even though he knew not a word of the local language and was acutely aware that Englishmen were generally unwelcome in these hills.

As Buckingham's men were making for their beds, Mark called out to Luke, saying that he was going to check on his mare before retiring. It was their pre-arranged signal for his departure and also gave Mark a legitimate reason to go to the stables to collect Old Sal. They had arrived at the Abergavenny Tavern before dark and Mark had noticed that a back exit from the stables led into an open field, where beasts who were stabled for longer periods could graze. A brook ran through a thicket at the south corner of this paddock and he had gambled on being able to cross this and ride unseen onto the hillside beyond.

Mark was already taking a serious risk setting out after dark and he had to coax Old Sal over the brook in the blackness but when the drizzle suddenly turned into a violent thunder storm he struggled to control his mare who was spooked by the repeating flashes of lightening. It was not long before he was lost and disorientated and as the storm was getting closer and the thunder louder, he sort shelter, in what appeared in a flash of lightening, to be a derelict shepherd's hut. Persuading Old Sal to leave the track and make her way up the overgrown path in the pitch dark was not easy but he persisted. A collapsed turf roof straddled the remains of two walls of the hut providing sufficient room for Mark to lead his nervous mount out of the wet and tether her to a wooden plank protruding from the back wall. Unfortunately, the refuge wasn't as deserted as Mark had anticipated, for no sooner had he secured his horse when two men, built like Goliath and smelling of garlic, grabbed him from behind and pulled him backwards through an animal skin curtain that covered a gap in the second wall and which opened into a larger but filthy hovel. Kicking wildly, Mark freed himself sufficiently to dive back through the flapping skin and make the three strides necessary to reach his horse, but the giants were upon him, tackling his ankles and pulling him to the ground as he desperately tried to mount Old Sal. The startled animal reared and shied away from the scuffle catching Mark's left shin with her hoof. With a shriek of pain he slumped in a heap, gripping his leg with both hands, whilst his assailants grabbed the back of his tunic for a second time and hauled him back into the hovel. Bound, gagged and dumped alongside a dead sheep and a couple of game birds, identifiable only by the sensation of oily wool and feathers against his soaking skin, Mark squeezed back his tears of pain. He was convinced that at least one bone in his injured leg must have broken but he could see nothing in the pitch black not even his captors, although he knew there were two of them, disgruntled and in disagreement as to what to do with their victim.

"If we leave him here to be found, dead or alive the locals will blame us, they always do," whinged one man.

"But if we take him to the camp they will come looking for him there, once they find him missing," argued the second man.

The rain eased by the time the two giants finally agreed to take Mark with them. They threw him across Old Sal's back like a sack of grain with little care for his injured leg, affording the same indignity to the dead sheep and four rabbits poached from some poor fellows warren. The birds were tied to the saddle and although Mark could not see any fish his nose told him that a priory fish pond had also been raided.

Despite his pain and fear, Mark begrudgingly conceded that the two travelling men were accomplished horsemen, gently coaxing Old Sal to walk through uneven and wet terrain in the pitch dark but the journey to the camp site was agony for Mark, slipping in and out of consciousness as the momentum of the horse's gait exacerbated his pain.

It was almost light when he first smelt smoke and Old Sal was brought to a halt and tethered to a thorn bush. His captives lay him on the ground whilst they unloaded their night's work and Mark rolled onto his good leg to keep the pressure of his body away from his injury. From where he lay he was able to make out the outline of several wagons, the remains of a fire and men and women immerging from the shadows as news of the poacher's return was relayed around the camp. Mark's leg was still throbbing but not so painfully now he was still, but it would not be for long. The onlookers were converging on the unloaded bounty only to halt suddenly and catch their breath when an old woman used her foot to turn over the trussed bundle that was Mark. Tears of pain welled his eyes, the injured leg hitting the ground as he rolled. Through the dampness he could just make out the heads of children peering round taller bodies as they all looked down in amazement at the human heap. A third giant of a man, with so much facial hair it was impossible to determine his features or his mood, pushed to the front of the spectators and stared down at Mark's soiled tunic.

"In the name of God what have you done?" he roared at the poachers, "you'll have the King's men on our backs for this."

He took a knife from his belt and sliced through Mark's gag

and bindings. Mark rubbed furiously at his wrists before inspecting his damaged leg which was leaking blood into his soggy boot. Dawn was providing a weak light now and he realised why the hairy man was so fearful, for emblazoned on his tunic and smeared with filth and blood was King Richard's White Boar.

"They were not to know Sir," began Mark seizing the initiative, "they were as frightened as I when we stumbled on each other in the pitch dark. They believed I was a local poacher and about to attack them."

"Is this true?" demanded the man.

Mark's captors stood open mouthed at his defence and nodded vigorously.

"Hob, Nob, carry him to the wagon and Ailish, see to his injury."

With care close to reverence, the two poachers lifted Mark between them and transported him gently to a small covered wagon into which the old woman climbed after them. Mark could see now that they were twins, probably the hag's grandsons for they all three had red golden hair, the men's receding prematurely for their age and forming a low tonsure just above their necks, their bald pates compensated by bushy red beards and heavy moustaches. Wisps of the same red hair escaped Ailish's wimple but it was the sparkling blue eyes and freckled foreheads that confirmed her kinship to the two giants. She lit a small candle stump, setting it first in a guard and then hustled the poachers out of her wagon whilst she inspected Mark's injured leg but they were fascinated by this strange fellow who had saved them a from a certain whipping and remained in Mark's view: two huge disembodied faces peering over the weather board at the entrance of the wagon.

"A horse did this?" asked Ailish, after stripping away what remained of Mark's hose and washing the wound in something that smelt like strong ale.

Mark nodded and tried not to wince as the liquid stung the broken flesh.

"The bone isn't broken through but it could well be cracked. You'll be abed for sometime lad."

"He can't travel like that Nan, can he?" ask one head in the wagon entrance.

"No Hob he can't. You must take him back to where you found him."

"I'm on my way to Brecknock Castle," said Mark, trying not to flinch as Ailish pocked around his shin in search of protruding splints of bone. He sensed that she froze for a brief moment and was convinced of it when the two heads exchanged glances and Hob, or the one on the right, disappeared to reappear moments later with the man Mark assumed to be in charge. Now three heads peered over the weather board of the wagon entrance.

"What is the nature of your business at Brecknock?" asked the third head.

Mark sensed distrust in his tone and decided to tell the truth. It was a risk but these folk spoke English and instinct persuaded him that they had a problem with Buckingham and if so, they might be prepared to help him. They listen in silence whilst Mark explained that he had proof and a witness to verify that the Duke of Buckingham had abducted his master, Sir Giles Butler, the King's nephew.

"Buckingham," growled the dark face and all three faces hawked and spat in unison.

"I'm Watcyn Vaughan," continued the dark face, after wiping his mouth on the back of his hand, "my kinsman, Sir Thomas Vaughan is Buckingham's tenant. I had land and a manor once myself but it's a long and useless tale," he grimaced, "Come on lads we make for Tretower Court."

The faces were gone.

Henry, Duke of Buckingham, sprawled across one of the Roman style couches dressed in a purple silk gown, lined with fine woollen cloth dyed to match and tied around his waist with a gold fringed silk cord. He had been soaking in a hot tub and his damp hair still dripped from beneath the cowl which was pulled forward over his brow, turning his fleshy face and popping eyes into a terrifying gargoyle. He sipped from a jewel encrusted cup and with his free hand waved towards the couch opposite. Morton nodded deferentially then dropped heavily into its plumped cushions. A servant poured wine into a second cup for the Bishop, then refilled Buckingham's before being dismissed by the recumbent Duke.

"John, it's good to see you," purred Buckingham, insincerely. Morton grunted a none decipherable reply. "Much has happened my lord, since I sent you here in disgrace."

"The 'disgrace,' *my lord*," echoed Morton, "I believe is yours, for failing to inform me that our plot to arrest Richard Gloucester was discovered."

"Watch your tongue Bishop, your situation has changed considerably since you saw fit to entertain Sir Giles Butler in this castle."

Morton caught his breath. The Duke already knew that he had been in contact with Giles. Ah well, keeping it a secret was always going to be difficult.

"I no longer intend to be part of your sordid little treason," continued the Duke, "and I need to ensure that Sir Giles cannot inform the King of my previous involvement with your plotting." He tutted as if Morton were an errant child and the Bishop had to resist the temptation to wipe away the specs of spittle that reached the rim of his cup. "I expected gratitude for rescuing you from King Richard's fury but you repay my kindness by resuscitating Sir Giles. Perhaps I should have left you to be executed like the old toper Hastings."

"Come now my lord, we both know I would have screamed your duplicity from the scaffold if you had dared deny me the Right of Clergy."

"Well none of that nonsense applies here at Brecknock," said Buckingham, banging the table with his fist.

Morton wriggled back onto the couch until his short legs barley touched the thick rug beneath his feet.

"I don't altogether blame you for shifting your loyalties. I mean, you committed yourself to our cause simply as a method of destroying the Woodvilles and their ruin is already achieved. And I'd wager King Richard has rewarded you handsomely for your efforts on his behalf."

"I have been of great service to the King and he has rewarded me accordingly," pronounced the Duke arrogantly, "amongst other honours I have at last been granted the Lancastrian half of the Bohun estates which the late King Edward steadfastly refused to acknowledge was part of my inheritance."

"Indeed, that will cost the royal coffers some ten thousand a year," marvelled Morton, who had been instrumental in reviving King Edward's personal fortune and privy to the details of his income.

"It should never had been held by the crown in the first place," continued the Duke, "and I have no intention of allowing Giles Butler, yourself or any of your pathetic conspirators to whisper old treasons in King Richard's ear. He believes loyalties are for life, not convenience." Buckingham tutted again and Morton moved his cup out of range. "He can be most tiresome about such issues, he really can."

"Perhaps I can still be of service my Lord," said Morton slowly, pretending an idea was forming in his brain.

"Really?" smirked Buckingham, convinced that he had the Bishop on the back foot, "surely *you* are not prepared to renege on your own loyalties to Lancaster?"

"Oh no, you misunderstand me. I would never relinquish my loyalty to Lancaster but I have no such qualms about relinquishing my loyalty to Tudor."

"Are they not one of the same?"

"Certainly not. Tudor is an upstart, born of illegitimate forebears. His grandfather was a common soldier that bedded a queen and even his mother is a direct descendant of Katherine Swinford, mistress to John of Gaunt."

"True enough, although Gaunt bribed the Pope to legitimise her bastards."

"Supposedly, but many would argue that being born out of wedlock is not something even the Holy Father cannot rectify. But let me speak plainly. I am prepared to support Henry Tudor in order to avenge the death of Queen Margaret's son. As you well know, Edward IV became a personal friend and so I postponed my vengeance but now he is dead, Margaret and her boy need wait no longer." He coughed discretely behind his hand. "I will defend with my life, the Lancastrian Prince who destroys King Richard III. Tudor has nominated himself for the task but his credentials are flimsy *compared to your own.*"

Buckingham sat upright and planted his cup firmly on the low table.

"Be more specific," he said harshly.

"My Lord of Buckingham, Henry Stafford, *direct* descendant of Edward III," simpered Morton, " your father and grandfather died fighting for Lancaster and you hated the late King Edward because he shackled you to York through a Woodville marriage. Break free my Lord and take up your sword against the usurpers. Are you not the heir to Lancaster and the throne of England?"

Morton dared not look into Buckingham's face for fear he should smirk. He could hear the Duke draw short excited breaths as the possibility of supreme power teased his greed and courted his vanity. He was taking the bait, Morton knew he would. He rubbed the sweat from his palms on either side of his tunic.

"How might I gather support for such a dangerous venture?" Buckingham said at last, forcing himself to face some of the difficulties which would precede such glory.

"I understand that even now, Woodville supporters are raising men to rescue the Queen's sons from the Tower and that she has pledged their support to Henry Tudor now that she accepts her own children are illegitimate."

"How does that benefit me?"

"Well," continued Morton trying to level his voice and avoid the disgust that threatened to surface in his tone, "if you were to announce your *own* support for Tudor and rally all the remaining Lancastrians to your banner, then as senior magnet you would be in command of those waiting for Tudor to land. Let him confront King Richard with his French mercenaries on one hand and yourself in command of a considerable army on the other. We simply ensure that Tudor falls in battle and the crown will be yours."

"Defeating King Richard will be no simple task, however large an army we muster. He has massive support from the North. His men are well armed and fiercely loyal. Even now, he is on his progress to those parts of his realm where he is less well known and believe me, reports tell only of the hearts he is winning with his promise of justice, particularly amongst the poor."

"Well *that* can only alienate him from the nobility. Most crimes against the poor are committed by the rich, who expect support from their King not justice. Little good it will do King Richard if he finds against an overlord in law, that he subsequently needs to call to arms."

Buckingham laughed nervously. "Seriously man, he is making a good impression, I should know, I receive the letters of adulation."

"There *is* a way to discredit him but it would test your nerve to the limit."

"Go on."

"If you could persuade the King that his crown cannot possibly be secure whilst ever the Princes in the Tower are alive ... " began Morton.

"Persuade him to have the boys put to death? Are you crazy man? Richard is not a fool. It would be political suicide. His Majesty would question my sanity were I to make such an irresponsible suggestion."

"But if he *could* be persuaded to put the bastards to death he would be accused of murder and that would crush his popularity and leave the way open for you my lord."

"Even if they posed some threat, which they do not, he would never harm his brother's sons, the man is too principled."

"Could *you* dispose of them and then inform His Majesty that you did so on his behalf, knowing it had to be done and that he would find the task too difficult?"

"Possibly. But I would be taking an enormous risk. Richard acts on impulse when his temper is charged. There would be a real chance he would have my head for such presumption."

Pity you worked that out, thought Morton to himself, that would have been the ideal solution. "Ah well," he said aloud, "we shall have to rely on his popularity being short lived. That is, if you are still willing to take on the burden of being Lancaster's champion?"

Both men sat in silence, pondering their next move. Morton was fearful that if he continued to persist with his 'solution' to

Richard's popularity, the Duke may realise that the only true beneficiary of the death of Edward IV's sons would be Henry Tudor. Suddenly Buckingham rose from his couch and dragging Morton to his feet, hugged him like a small child, before releasing him just as suddenly, leaving the Bishop tottering and grabbing the back of the couch to steady himself.

"I have the perfect plan," cried Buckingham, swaggering around the room like an actor in some Greek drama. He stopped by the side table and poured wine into fresh cups. Passing one to the Bishop, he invited Morton to drink to his brilliance.

As dawn broke on the following morning, John Morton watched from his bedchamber window as the Duke of Buckingham, escorted by some twenty or so well armed men, left the castle via the gatehouse. The man riding at his side was Sir Humphrey Percivall, his long silver locks straggling beneath his cap. Behind the Duke, rode Sir Reginald Bray.

"Damn," swore Morton aloud, "I would have preferred to have acquainted Bray with what I have put in motion before he left but if he is on his way to Brittany with a letter from Buckingham offering his support to Henry Tudor then I will settle for that, for now."

The bishop smiled contentedly and rubbed his hands together as he savoured the audacity of his deceit. Absentmindedly, he picked up and rang the bell that summonsed his servant whilst considering what culinary delights he might choose with which to break his fast. He settled on some of the delicious cheese produced locally and two or three slices of the cold beef he had enjoyed at midday yesterday when it had been freshly roasted and piping hot. The local ale was not to his taste and although he professed never to drink wine before noon, he would make an exception today and celebrate his considerable cunning with a fresh cask of Buckingham's best Burgundy. He was salivating with anticipation when he realised his servant had not responded to the bell so he rang again more vigorously but there was still no response. Huffing and puffing, partially in temper and partially from the effort of heaving himself out of the chair by the window, he crossed to the door. Morton tugged at its handle but it remained firmly shut. Convinced that the thing was stuck, he banged on the door and shouted for assistance through the empty key hole but no one came and try as he might the door remained jammed. Resigned to having to wait until his servant reappeared, Morton returned to his seat by the window and quickly slipped into a second sleep.

An hour or so later the rattle of the key in the lock roused the Bishop from his dozing and to his astonishment the door was opened smoothly by a man-at arms. The servant who had attended him since his arrival entered with a tray of food and a pot of ale which he placed on the sideboard and then raising both hands in the air to indicate that 'this arrangement' was not his fault, he shook his head apologetically and scurried away pushing passed the man-at-arms as he escaped. Before the Bishop could gather his wits the man-at-arms closed the door, turned the key and removed it from the lock.

Morton was furious, clearly he was no longer free to roam the fortress at will. Had Buckingham rumbled his deception? Was it just a matter of time before he was marched to an execution block? Sweat began to pour from his brow as he assessed the possibility of escaping from the window. That was ridiculous, even if he found some means of climbing down the forty feet of sheer wall, he would not be able to get out of the bailey unchallenged. He walked round and round the chamber allowing his panic to rise until a sharp stabbing pain in his chest reminded him of his physician's warning. The pain was brought about by his red humours being dangerously out of balance. Such serious imbalance often preceded death and although Morton scorned the physician's remedies, he knew from the experience of previous attacks, if he calmed down and breathed deeply the pain would cease. With tremendous effort he controlled his panic and after a while the tightness across his chest relented and the period of time between the stabbing pains increased until eventually he was sure they had ceased altogether.

The priory bells were sounding for Nones and weary and frightened, he forced himself to walk to the sideboard and swallow some of the weak ale from the quart pot. He managed a smile when he saw the slices of cold beef and local cheese which he had intended ordering but his stomach rejected even the smell of food. The Bishop lay down on his bed, chastising himself for instantly panicking and damaging his health at a time when he may need all the strength he could muster. He tried to pray but he was exhausted. Sleep was his only escape and within seconds he had succumbed.

Henry Buckingham's single night in his favourite castle at Brecknock had been a disturbed one. After the initial thrill and excitement of John Morton's suggestion that he should claim the throne for himself, doubts about the feasibility of the plot flooded his mind. He had already made one dramatic about-turn when he had decided to support King Richard but that had accrued more difficulties than he had anticipated. Firstly he must dispose of Giles Butler or leave him to rot in the Brecknock dungeons, a secret he would need to guard for the rest of his life. Then there was John Morton. He had intended persuading the King that Morton had been the instigator of Hastings' treason, which after all was the truth, and then dispatch the Bishop from Brecknock, where any final speech he might make about Buckingham's past would be heard only by Welsh speakers. It had seemed the perfect solution that night at Crosby Place when he had quickly made the decision to stand by the King but later he had realized that King Richard would grant Bishop Morton the right to be tried by the Church. Then he had remembered the lesser mortals, Morton's adopted son, Luke, Sir Giles' squire, Mark Taylor and Lady Stanley's champion, Reginald Bray, they too would all have to be silenced. It had been easy to corral them at Brecknock but could he really *execute all of them*? It would be a significant blood letting, a horror that would surely be repeated across Wales and ultimately translated into English. There would be a real danger that the story would eventually reach the ear's of the King. Now if *he, Henry Buckingham* were King, there would be nothing to fear, nobody to answer to, his past dalliance with treason would be irrelevant. Was this the perfect solution? Was he up to the challenge?

Well before dawn Buckingham had come to at least one conclusion, his role as the King's chief advisor and England's mightiest magnet would be an uneasy existence. He would be constantly looking over his shoulder, waiting for that surreptitious whisper of murder in the Welsh Marshes that would herald his downfall. Whilst breaking his fast with cheese, fish and watered ale he made the only decision possible; abandon King Richard. So Henry Stafford, Duke of Buckingham had penned a letter to Henry Tudor offering his support. Whether the contents were sincere or the means by which to raise an army for his own purpose, that decision could wait. He had summonsed Sir Reginald Bray and told him he was free to travel to Brittany, giving into his care his own letter for Henry Tudor. He had placed his arm around Bray's shoulders and bid him return quickly as he was keen for his aunt, Lady Stanley to realize she had been mistaken in her judgement of him and that he had confirmed his allegiance to her son. Buckingham knew this news would quickly find its way to Lord Thomas Stanley and there was a chance that he too would desert King Richard.

That done he had two remaining options. One was to aim for the crown for himself, which he favoured and the second, was to throw his weight behind Henry Tudor as he had first intended. The latter would be the safer option but during the last few months he had become accustomed to his new wealth and power and he knew that Morton would assume the position closest to Tudor. Buckingham had long suspected that it was Morton who had convinced Edward IV not to hand over the Bohun estates because of the cost to the crown and with Morton keeping a watch on Tudor's purse strings, Buckingham could not expect Henry's gratitude to match the magnitude of Richard's generosity. More and more he was favouring his own anointment but he was wary of Morton's motives. It wasn't difficult to work out the Bishop's reason for suggesting he took the crown for himself. Clearly it eliminated the need to execute Morton and his beloved Luke and maybe he hoped to save Giles' neck too but was it just a trap, a sop to his vanity which simply released his captives or was the crafty Bishop in earnest? Buckingham smiled to himself as he thought of Morton trying to open his chamber door. He was not so gullible as to ignore the man's insidious political ability and ensuring that each one of his prisoners remained isolated until he had time to judge the workability of the proposal, was a justifiable and amusing precaution.

Chapter 33

The Tower 24th July 1483

By the time they reached the Tower of London, Buckingham had convinced himself he was Lancaster's rightful heir. He could not contemplate a reduction in his power and influence and the very thought of paying homage to the son of a common soldier's bastard was abhorrent to him. During the past two days he had repeatedly described Henry Tudor thus to his faithful kinsman, Sir Humphrey Percivall, who was at a loss to know what his master was obsessing about.

"It is all the more intolerable Humphrey, because Bishop Morton is correct, I am without question, Lancaster's rightful heir."

Not that Sir Humphrey would have dared question his Lord, he was far too experienced in dealing with him to contradict his logic but he was never-the-less nervous about where all this righteous indignation was leading. They entered the Tower by the Lion Gate, guards snapping to attention as they recognised the Duke of Buckingham and during the short ride between the Gate and the Middle Tower, the Duke gave Sir Humphrey orders to billet the men and see to the horses before joining him in the council chamber.

"But take a saunter about the inner bailey first Humphrey, familiarise yourself with the place and look for any means by which we might effect the removal of the two bastard princes without being observed."

"My Lord?"

The Duke held up his hand to silence the knight as guards at the Middle Tower stood to attention. The crooked backed keeper appeared at the doorway and struggling to look up into the face of the mounted Duke, asked if he wished him to inform the Constable of the Tower of his arrival.

"Tell him to attend me in the Council chamber," snapped Buckingham, then spurred his stallion forward.

"There is no hurry Humphrey, we can stay for as long as it takes," said Buckingham continuing his earlier theme, "next week or the week after will be fine, so long as we leave with the boys before the King returns from his Progress."

Eventually, the narrow alleys and pathways of the ancient fortress opened upon the central green where grooms came forward to take their horses and Sir Humphrey took his leave of the Duke.

When Sir Robert Brackenbury, constable of the Tower, received the news of the arrival of his mighty visitor, he made his way to the council chamber to find the Duke already there and ordering refreshment. A square faced, thick set man in his early forties and a seasoned campaigner from the old wars, Sir Robert was not impressed with Buckingham's rise to power. He considered the Duke's honour to be suspect, he had failed to fight for York at Tewkesbury and more significantly, his forebears had fought for Lancaster. Brackenbury was convinced that Buckingham, rather than his beloved King, was responsible for the execution of Lord Hastings, a manoeuvre he believed the Duke had conceived to eliminate his rival for Richard's favour. Furthermore, Brackenbury had been in attendance when Buckingham had insisted that Richard had ordered a log be used as a makeshift block so that the execution could be immediate. According to Buckingham, Hastings was to die before dinner and Richard was hungry and ready to dine. Brackenbury knew this to be a lie and it served only to intensify his loathing of the Duke.

"Sir Robert, I am here at the request of His Majesty," began the Duke, extending his arms as if he were about to bow graciously but didn't, "our most sovereign Lord is naturally concerned about the safety of his illegitimate nephews."

"I'm sure he has no need to be," bristled Brackenbury, " they are both safe and well cared for, although Prince Edward is suffering from some ailment his physician appears unable to stem."

"*Prince* Edward is it?" said the Duke making a moue and raising his eyebrows.

Brackenbury wasn't phased by insinuations made by this flamboyant idiot. He had fought alongside King Richard and King Edward in the wars against Lancaster and Richard had appointed him Constable of the Tower.

"Take a look for yourself if you like," he said bluntly, "the youngster is in the gardens and the older lad is with his physician. I'll show you."

Brackenbury turned on his heels and without either waiting for Buckingham to reply, or for him to take refreshment from the Claret jug which had just been set before him by a squire, he trundled back down the stairs that led to the open green and crossed to the Garden Tower on the other side. Never once did he look back to check that the Duke was following him but he paused by the door of the rectangular tower and pointed to the patch of grass surrounded by cultivated shrubs. Here, the youngest boy was shooting arrows at a target, without much success. The Duke had followed, infuriated by Brackenbury's rudeness but seeing his quarry, swallowed his anger and opened the wicket gate that led into the garden. He strolled over to the young boy, beaming broadly and bowing ever so slightly as he approach. The Duke of York, who had been named Richard after his father's youngest brother, dropped his shoulders in exasperation.

"Good day my Lord of Buckingham," he called politely, "I don't seem able to hit the butt let alone the centre of the darned target."

Buckingham laughed and feigning fear of being struck by an arrow, bid the youngster put down his bow.

"The target is too far away for a boy of your tender years," said the Duke taking the lad's arm and guiding him several paces nearer the butt, "try now."

York selected an arrow from his quiver but before he could pull back the bowstring Buckingham grasped his hand.

"Pretend I am helping you to hold it correctly," he whispered in York's ear, at the same time moving his body so that both their faces were obscured from Brackenbury's view. York's, questioning eyes stared up into Buckingham's face.

"There is a move a foot to rescue you from this place, my Lord. Your mother's family have sent me to tell you to be ready to leave without notice."

"What? Are you not my uncle Richard's man?"

"I was my Lord, until he seized your brother's crown. You forget my wife is your mother's sister, I am your loyal kinsman," lied the Duke smoothly, "I need you to inform your brother. Can you do that?"

York nodded vigorously.

"Good lad. Now pull back the string and release the arrow."

The Duke stood back as York set the arrow and drew back the string with all his strength. He had considerable difficulty holding it steady but once released it whizzed through the air and embedded itself in the outer ring of the target. The boy's instinctive shout of genuine joy completed Buckingham's little charade.

He followed Brackenbury up to the first floor of the adjacent tower where the elder boy, named Edward after his father, sat in a window seat, dishevelled and unwashed. His physician, Doctor Argentine was unsuccessfully encouraging him to eat from a dish of roast rabbit. The doctor was a cleric of small stature with angular bones that protruded from his face and neck suggesting that he could well have done with the food himself.

"Is the lad ill or just melancholy?" asked Buckingham tactlessly from the shadow of the doorway.

Argentine looked askance. "Probably both," he sighed, "look at his face, the poor child is burning with fever but that aside, I fear he has lost much of his will to live since his uncle, King Richard ... "

Argentine's words faded away as he recognised the man now standing next to him. Buckingham ignored him.

"Have you everything you need, my Lord?" he asked briskly, making his way to the window seat, "this chamber seems light and well furnished."

Prince Edward turned his head away from the Duke and gazed out of the window.

"This chamber is one of the best in all the royal apartments,"

Brackenbury said, answering Buckingham's enquiry, "the bed was brought in from the King's chamber. It had to be dismantled to get it up the stairs."

"The King's chamber?" mocked the prince, "if that bed belongs to my traitorous uncle Richard, I will never lie on it again."

"Your uncle can not be held responsible for your father's bigamy," snapped Buckingham, irritated by the insolence he perceived Edward to be exhibiting.

He stalked out of the Garden Tower and past the wicket gate, failing to acknowledge the wave from the youngest boy in his rush to return to the council chamber where Sir Humphrey Percivall was tucking into the abandoned meal.

Conscious of his master's bad temper, Sir Humphrey rose from his own seat and pulled back the chair at the top of the table, into which Buckingham slumped, annoyed at having to tolerate his Woodville nephews. Sir Humphrey filled the Duke's cup with claret and passed the dishes of fast cooling roast rabbit and boiled onions down the table.

"Shall I ring for some fresh food, my Lord? Most of this is cold."

Buckingham shook his head "I'm not hungry. Now listen Humphrey, what I have to say is for your ears only."

Sir Humphrey sat back and waited for his master to finish his wine.

"I intend to take the crown for myself," Buckingham announced quietly, "I am convinced of my entitlement to the throne and Bishop Morton assures me that it will be an easy matter to turn the Woodville rebels to my own advantage." Buckingham looked into the inscrutable face of Humphrey Percivall and thumped the table. "God's bollocks man, did you hear what I said?"

"Indeed my Lord. You can be assured of my continued loyalty in your quest."

"I *own* your loyalty man. Its your opinion I seek."

Humphrey licked this thin lips and although his face betrayed nothing of his fear, his hands shook beneath the table.

"King Richard is enjoying much popularity and … "

"*I* made him popular and *I* can reverse his fortunes," said Buckingham hotly.

What Humphrey referred to was Richard's refusal to accept the usual gifts of money offered him by the elders of the towns and cities he visited. Word had spread rapidly that the King required only the loyalty of his subjects and it was this that was causing the crowds to receive him with such acclaim but Humphrey was not prepared to anger his Lord by enlightening him, so he just nodded his accent.

"I intend to discredit our *popular* new King by secretly removing his bastard nephews from the Tower and then accusing his *popular* majesty of murdering them."

"You have a plan my Lord, ... to secretly remove them?"

"Come to the window and I will show you," purred Buckingham. "They are being held there, in that rectangular Tower but they have a free run of the gardens below. You cannot see from here but the round tower beyond is being repaired: there is scaffolding covering the walls."

"Indeed my lord, I have walked around the base of that Tower and spoken to the men working there."

"Good, that may be useful, because when they have completed the repairs and removed the scaffolding, they will need several wagons to cart it away and *you* are going to offer the strong arms of our men to assist with the loading and moving of those wagons out of the Tower," declared Buckingham, "and the two princes will be hidden in one of those carts when they leave." He beamed at Sir Humphrey and awaited his congratulations but Humphrey only cleared his throat.

"What is it man? Spit it out. You see a problem with my plan?"

"The scaffolding is being dismantled this evening," stammered Humphrey, " it is kept within the Tower work sheds and the workmen live here in the garrison."

"What, they can't all be retained by the Crown?"

"There is one specialist mason and he has a hand cart. He will be leaving the Tower before curfew."

"We can hardly pack up and leave tonight," whined Buckingham as if it were Sir Humphrey's fault, "we have only just arrived and anyway it would be obvious to even that birdbrain Brackenbury, that we had something to do with the princes' disappearance if they were found missing tomorrow, even if we could secrete them both in the mason's hand cart, which I doubt."

"If you intend accusing the King of their murder, why take the trouble to remove them from the Tower?" ventured Humphrey, "wouldn't it be easier to kill them here and leave the bodies as evidence of your accusation?"

"Easier, yes but King Richard would soon discover that I had been here prior to their deaths, and then when I make my own bid for the crown he would display the bodies and accuse me of their murder."

"But if the boys are only missing," reasoned Humphrey, "then the King is more likely to assume that the Woodvilles have staged a successful rescue."

"That is the idea Humphrey, to deflect the responsibility for their disappearance away from myself. Then I shall start the rumour that the King has had the brats murdered."

"And he won't be able to *disprove* your rumour because he'll be unable to produce them alive. Brilliant my Lord," concluded Sir Humphrey, genuinely impressed.

"It would be, if the workmen did not live-in and were leaving in a day or so."

"There may be a way my Lord and perhaps a better one," said Humphrey pulling at his pointed chin and closing his mouth so tightly that his lips disappeared altogether.

"How?"

"Well, our reason for being here in the Tower is to assess the security arrangements for holding the Princes?"

"Ostensively, yes."

"And what have we found? The boys roaming freely and one single guard on the door to their apartments."

"Get to the point Humphrey."

"Well security is so lax you could justifiably take it over yourself."

"To what purpose, if we have to leave tonight?"

"*We won't.* Only the princes will leave tonight. But first you must insist that our men guard the Garden Tower and the surrounding gardens and that *they* take in the boy's food and laundry from the servants at the door. If you make sufficient fuss about lax security your takeover will seem like a natural reaction. Then tomorrow, you announce that you have just received information that the Woodville's attempt to rescue the princes is imminent and therefore, all but your own men will be denied access to the gardens and the Garden Tower until the threat is over."

"You mean get the boys out tonight but stay here ourselves for several days longer, pretending the princes are deep in the Tower for their own protection?" said Buckingham slowly.

"Exactly my Lord. I will instruct two of our best men to help the mason when he prepares to leave. They will ensure that the hand cart is unfit for use, a buckled wheel perhaps or a broken shaft. Then they will offer the use of one of our own horse drawn carts, already loaded of course, with our human cargo but with ample room to accommodate the mason's tools and broken hand cart."

The Duke was getting excited, his eyes shining and popping like an animated jester.

"We'll do it Humphrey," he said, drumming all his fingers on the table before him, "we may not get a better chance."

"Nobody will look for the boys until *we* say they are missing my Lord and we can still blame the Woodvilles and discipline our own guards for the sake of the charade."

"By which time the princes will be well on their way to Brecknock. Now be gone Humphrey, I have already warned the younger boy to be ready at a moments notice. Tell him to get his brother into the garden at once. Go man."

Chapter 34

Brecknock 12th August 1483

Although he was the least confused and isolated of the Brecknock prisoners, Luke's bed was his jail. Unable to stand without loosing his balance and suffering from blurred vision, he had resigned himself to laying fully clothed on his bed during the day and allowing a servant to wash and change him each night. Before sleeping, Luke lay shaking for hours beneath the coverlets, the effort of disrobing and moving resulting in the most awful disorientation. During daylight hours, Lady Katherine was constantly at his bedside and he often woke at night to find her kneeling in prayer at the side of his bed. Luke used his illness as an excuse not to have to talk because his memory had returned almost completely now but his past would not impress Lady Katherine Woodville.

    He had been retained by the King's errant brother George, Duke of Clarence, who the Woodvilles had considered a threat to their family. Luke or Sir Henry Pierrepoint as he now knew himself to be, had fought alongside the Duke of Clarence and the great Earl of Warwick and had fled to France with the Duke and the Earl's family when George's bid for the crown had failed. He could recall trying to comfort Lady Anne, the Earl's daughter and now Richard's Queen, when her parents had insisted she marry the Lancastrian Prince of Wales and he remembered the horror of discovering that Clarence had changed his allegiance for a second time but most vividly he recalled fighting for York at Tewkesbury and slaying the

Prince of Lancaster, Queen Margaret's son and the boy mourned so piteously by Bishop Morton. His sickly brain played over and over the simple ceremony when Clarence had honoured him by ripping the brooch from the dismembered torso of the Prince and presenting him with the jewel. George Clarence's pleasure at the death of the seventeen year old prince had been unseemly and Luke remembered leaving the victory celebrations and riding over Tewkesbury's field searching amongst the dead for the mortally wounded and relieving their suffering with one swift slice across the throat with the misericorde which had once been his father's. One thing that was not yet clear in his mind, was how his horse had been slain prior to John Morton discovering him in the brook.

"I really need to speak to Giles, my Lady," pleaded Luke, one night just before dawn when he was unable to sleep and Katherine had moved silently into his room and knelt at the prie dieu.

"I'm sorry Luke, I cannot help you to see either of your friends. My Lord has given strict instructions that they must stay locked in their rooms and without visitors until he returns."

She raised herself gracefully from her prayers and sat on the edge of his bed.

"But you rescued Giles from the dungeon?"

"Ah yes, but Sir Humphrey Percivall was here then." She smiled coquettishly from beneath her lowered lids. "He is susceptible to my wishes, where-as these Welsh guards … "

Luke turned his head in the pillow and looked away from her. She read his response accurately and surprised him with a swift and intense reprimand.

"So Luke, you have been deceived by a lady who preyed on your lust to further her own ends. Well that does not give you the right to judge me. Sir Giles Butler is alive because I wooed the dull, reliable Humphrey Percivall. Would you prefer that I remained unsullied and Giles were dead?"

"I would not have you debase yourself for me," replied Luke gallantly, "I would willing die first."

Lady Katherine smiled sweetly.

"That was not what I asked. Would you prefer that I left your friend to die in the dungeons or bought his life with my body?"

Roses are White

"I'm sorry," said Luke, smiling thinly, "it just isn't right."

There was an awkward pause whilst each considered a retreat but in the end Luke changed the subject.

"Do you really believe that Elizabeth Woodville has accepted that her marriage to Edward was bigamous?" he asked.

"She probably knew it was," sighed Katherine, "I did. My brother told me last Yuletide when he came to visit his nephews."

"Indeed, how did Anthony Rivers know?"

Katherine shrugged but there was no time to answer. Torches were being lit in the bailey below, sending dancing shadows across the chamber as the huge flames were fanned by the night air. Men called to one another in Welsh and a teeth gritting grinding noise echoed round the bailey as the massive iron grill of the portcullis was raised.

"It's my Lord of Buckingham. He has returned," cried Katherine, from the window, "Holy Mother, he has a child with him and another being lifted from the wagon."

She turned and fled from the chamber, leaving Luke motionless and wishing for the first time in years for the sight and touch of Margery Goodman.

Henry Buckingham sat alone at the head of his tabled, raised on the dais in the great hall whilst servants hurried back and forth from the kitchens, serving him food and wine with which to break his fast. The sun was up by the time he dispatched Sir Humphrey to escort Bishop Morton into his presence but the Bishop had taken his time, insisting that he must be shaved and dressed in fresh attire before joining his Grace for breakfast. Not even the tiresome wait for Morton could thwart the Duke's exuberance today for he had just pulled off the most daring feat of cunning and the reward for his brilliance would be the Crown itself.

"Where in God's name is Bishop Morton?" he cried out good humouredly to nobody in particular. He was bursting with the tale he had to tell and only Morton could fully appreciate the beauty of his guile.

"I'm here my gracious Lord and pleased to see you in such an ebullient mood," soothed Morton, as he appeared on the gallery above the stairs.

"John my friend, come and breakfast with me. It's good to see you," cried Buckingham, rising from his seat to greet the Bishop and guiding him gently by the elbow the Duke indicated the stool opposite for him to be seated. "Bring his Grace a cup boy and another plate, quickly now, then leave us, all of you."

Whilst the servants completed their tasks, Buckingham stuffed his mouth with slices of ham cut from a roasted leg and pushing the heavy platter across to Morton he spluttered words, spittle and shreds of meat, in praise of the quality of the joint. Morton took his own knife from his pouch and cut himself a modest slice, his usual interest in food being somewhat diminished by the queasy feeling in his stomach for he had learned over the years to be wary of the Duke's apparent good humour. When all the servants had retreated, Buckingham wiped his mouth and swilled the remains of his chewed ham down his throat with several gulps of wine.

"Guess what I have brought to Brecknock?" he said with a broad smile, followed by an exaggerated wink."

"The Princes? My God, you've abducted the Princes. Have you my Lord? Have you really managed to rescue them without being observed?"

It was just the reaction Buckingham craved and he nodded vigorously. Of course, he had misread Morton's jubilation as admiration for his achievement, where-as in fact Morton was celebrating his own success in having duped the Duke into helping Tudor's cause.

With much drama and taking all the credit for the plan, Buckingham explained how he and Sir Humphrey, had remain in charge of the Garden tower for two days after the boys had escaped in the stone mason's cart.

"We all met up at Gloucester and whilst my men camped with the boys outside the city, I joined King Richard, who was already billeted there on his Royal Progress. You should have seen the King's face John, when I told him the sad news of how the Woodville's plan to rescue the Princes from the Tower had succeeded."

"Christ man, that was brave of you," said Morton honestly.

Buckingham preened himself. "Oh believe me, His Majesty raged at me for hours. Like Plantagenets before him, he has a temper that the devil himself would be proud to exhibit but that's Dickon's Achilles' heel, John. Once his temper begins to cool, he turns his anger on himself for loosing control and those who thought they had offended him find their roles reversed and pardon being asked instead of given," he laughed heartily, providing Morton with a view of his tonsils and shards of the ham that still clung to his yellowing teeth.

"Umm, well we both know of one man he sent to the block *before* he cooled down," said the Bishop warily.

"No matter John. He dispatched a fellow by the name of Tyrell, James Tyrell I believe, back to London to question Brackenbury as to how the Princes could have been smuggled out of the Tower," again Buckingham threw back his head and laughed, "the mighty fortress, the Tower of bloody London."

"Will Tyrell be able to discover the truth?"

"Never John, I warrant you, never. I employed only my own men and they are all here in this castle now. No one else was privy to the escape, not even the stone mason knew what was hidden beneath his broken handcart and bag of tools."

"You have exceeded all expectations my Lord but we must now build on this fine beginning. The next task is to spread the rumour that our worthy King has done away with his brother's children to secure his own state."

"I have already made a start by spreading that very rumour on my return journey and now I propose to write immediately to my noble aunt Margaret, giving her the good news. She will most certainly inform Elizabeth Woodville that her precious chicks are gone, slaughtered by Richard's order, so leaving the Woodville rebels ready for combat but without a cause."

"Excellent. When will you muster your own men and gather the Woodville rebels to your standard?"

"Not until I have sent messages to as many ex-Lancastrian nobles and gentry as I can recall. Perhaps you can help me compile a list. You see, I intend to present my Lancastrian credentials to these men *before* we join Henry Tudor. It will ensure the smooth transfer of their allegiance to myself, once Tudor has fallen. This conflict may rage for some time, maybe months, so those who oppose King Richard must pin their hopes on the revival of the House of Lancaster not the bastard House of Tudor."

It was a fair point. Bishop Morton wondered at the Duke's political awareness and for a brief moment it occurred to him that Buckingham might prove to be a better investment than Henry Tudor but it was a very brief moment. Tudor would be exceedingly grateful to those who made him King. He had already promised Morton the mitre of Canterbury and he would pledge more for those closes to him and the Bishop intended to be very close indeed. No such obligation or recognition would be forthcoming from Buckingham, even now he considered the Crown to be his of right. No, by supporting Henry Tudor, Bishop Morton could take revenge for the loss of his loved ones and increase his own fortune at the same time.

"Many Yorkist will also defect when they learn of the King's disgraceful murder and they too will look to you for leadership, my Lord," continued Morton aloud, "but there must be no hint that the boys are still alive, otherwise you will loose both their support and that of the Woodvilles."

"You would have me snuff out their young lives Bishop?"

"It would be for the best, my Lord."

"For Tudor maybe but not for me John," replied Buckingham, searching the Bishop's face for signs of duplicity, "mud sticks in the strangest places and there may come a time when I, like Richard now, might need to prove that I did not murder the royal bastards."

"You intend to keep them alive as insurance against future allegations?" declared the astonished Bishop. Once again he had underestimated the Duke and he must proceed with care. "I applaud your shrewdness my Lord, of course the boys pose no more of a threat to you than they ever did to King Richard."

"But?"

"Well if the truth escapes before you secure the crown, then you loose everything."

"Then it is in both our interests that the fewer people who know they are here, the better and never forget John, my safety is your safety and my failure is also yours."

"Indeed it is Your Grace and may I respectfully remind *you* that we must both pretend to support Henry Tudor until he defeats King Richard. To do otherwise would split our forces and we would be faced with fighting both King Richard and Henry Tudor."

"I know your game John," smirked Buckingham and Morton's heart missed a beat, "if King Richard defeats Henry Tudor and there is every chance he will, then you and I can slip away without having declared our hand. I'm right, aren't I? You're a crafty old bugger John but I have the measure of you."

Buckingham landed a heavy slap on Morton's back, causing him to lurch forward and then laughing raucously the Duke, once again provided the Bishop with a magnificent display of his tonsils.

After delivering Bishop Morton into Buckingham's presence, Sir Humphrey Percivall slipped away to the apartments in the guest wing, where the Princes were resting in the care of their aunt, Lady Katherine. On arriving at Brecknock, Humphrey had expressed his concern for the health of the older boy and Katherine had announced her intention to accommodate them in the chamber adjacent to Luke's so that she could tend both her charges with more ease. However, it was not his concerned for the well being of the princes that inspired him to wander the galleries of the guest wing but rather his wish to be reacquainted with the Duchess of Buckingham. Some weeks earlier she had rewarded him 'in kind' for relocating Giles Butler in the wooden tower on the ravine wall and he had fantasised endless about their relationship ever since. Now in his fifty-fifth year, Humphrey had abandoned all hope of experiencing genuine romance. Even as a young man he had never been attractive to the opposite sex and had struggled, often unsuccessfully, to requite his need for sexual activity. So he had been taken by surprise by Lady Katherine's attention which had awoken in him an intensity of desire that he had not believed possible. He was not a licentious man, he had been more or less faithful to his plain and frighteningly devout wife for nigh on thirty five years but neither fear of her wroth nor the sullying of his hither-too unquestionable loyalty to the Duke was sufficient to dissuade him from approaching the beautiful Lady Katherine with the hope of further coupling.

He found his heart's desire sat on the edge of Luke's bed cradling the invalid's lifeless hand in hers'.

"Sir Humphrey, what are you doing here?" she asked with a broad smile as Humphrey tentatively entered the chamber.

"His Lordship commanded me to enquire after the health of his nephews," lied Humphrey.

Lady Katherine's beautiful green eyes opened wide in disbelief. "Edward has a high fever and is exhausted after the journey," she said, "York is tired but well and at this moment, reading to his elder brother."

Humphrey nodded but made no attempt to leave.

"Close the door Humphrey, why don't you stay for a while and cheer up Sir Henry," continued Katherine, "no, please don't struggle to sit up dearest, Humphrey understands that you are unable to move without pain."

Humphrey stared in horror at the tenderness Katherine was showing the sick man and his response betrayed his jealousy.

"He's Luke Lazarus. What's all this, Sir Henry nonsense?" spat Humphrey.

"It isn't nonsense," said Luke, "I lost my memory and now it's back. I *am* Sir Henry, Sir Henry Pierrepoint of Holbeck and Woodhouse, a manor south-west of York."

Lady Katherine placed Luke's hand gently on the coverlet and walked over to Humphrey, who was stood at the foot of the bed glowering at his perceived rival. She laid her hand on his arm and guided him to a stool at the other side of the bed. Humphrey sat like an obedient child and looked up into her adorable face with such appeal that even Katherine was taken aback by his apparent devotion.

"Why has my Lord of Buckingham brought Prince Edward and Prince Richard to Brecknock Humphrey," she asked softly.

There was no reply from the love sick Humphrey but Katherine realised the potential of his unguarded state of mind and knelt beside him revealing extensive cleavage as she pressed her breasts against his knee.

"Humphrey, tell me, please my love, why are the Princes here at Brecknock?"

Without taking his eyes from her breasts and with the words 'my love' soothing his jealousy, Humphrey explained how the Duke, encouraged by Bishop Morton, intended to take the crown for himself. To win the support of the Woodvilles and erode Richard's Yorkist support, he had kidnapped the Princes and spread the rumour that the King had murdered them.

Katherine slumped back on her heels unable to immediately comprehend the significance of Humphrey's words.

"What will become of them: and of me?" she asked, as she gathered her wits, "he will never allow me to be crowned his queen?"

"He'll not win the crown from King Richard," sneered Luke, "you'll be free of him via the block once the news of his ambition reaches King Richard's ears."

Humphrey was not so confident, the Duke was making audacious plans and so far had been successful. Never-the-less, he could not allow lady Katherine to be compromised and he would willingly give his own life to save hers. As chivalry gripped the soul of this aging and slightly ridiculous knight, somewhere in the back of his brain, Luke's words, 'you'll be free of him via the block,' were pricking his subconscious like a flurry of Cupid's finest arrows.

Over the next weeks Buckingham and Bishop Morton worked tirelessly, contacting Woodville and Yorkist nobles across the South, inviting them to take up arms against the child murderer, King Richard III and support the ambitions of England's rightful sovereign and Lancaster's heir. To Morton this meant Henry Tudor but Buckingham was confident that most would believe that only he, Henry Stafford, could rightly claim that title. However, the cautious Bishop left nothing to chance, adding a post script to his communications explaining that the marriage of King Edward's daughter to Henry Tudor had been agreed by both parties which would unit the Houses of York and Lancaster for ever, putting an end to the years of bloodshed that many families had endured.

Each evening Bishop Morton visited his sick, adopted son Luke but as the days passed into weeks Morton began to realise that Luke was unlikely to recover his health in time to join the rebellion being planned. For his part, Luke had decided not to tell his Grace that his memory had returned and pretended to be sicker than he was, in order to distract the Bishop from involving him in his treason. It was not cowardice that prevented Luke from telling the Bishop his memory had returned but the genuine desire not to destroy the man who had saved his life. Morton believed that the Almighty had entrusted Luke into his care that day on Tewkesbury field and to inform the Bishop that he had unwittingly reared the killer of his beloved Prince of Lancaster, was to tell him that God had played a cruel joke on him. In fact Luke's health *was* deteriorating slowly and towards the end he began to wonder whether his own deceit had so displeased God that he must pay for Morton's protection with his own life.

On the eve of October 18th, the night before Buckingham and Morton unfurled their banners and set out to muster the Duke's tenants from the surrounding manors, Morton called on Luke earlier than usual and was surprised to find him propped on pillows, surrounded by four children. Three were Katherine's brood but the fourth child was their cousin, the younger Prince, Richard Duke of York. He was reading from a book that was far too difficult for him and Luke and his companions were laughing good humouredly as he struggled manfully with the Latin text. But the book dropped to the floor and the laughter ceased abruptly when Morton entered unannounced. Four sets of small feet jumped down from the bed and four sets of frightened eyes gazed longingly into the darkness behind the man that filled the doorway. Morton stepped into the chamber leaving the door open and through which the four children scampered away.

"We leave tomorrow morning, at first light," said Morton sadly, "I'm truly sorry you will not be with us but I promise as soon as this business is over I will send for you."

Luke managed a weak smile.

"Is there anything you need? Can I arrange for anything to be brought in?" continued Morton, genuinely distressed that he must leave Luke behind.

"Giles, you can find Giles and bring him to me, please my lord I beg of you."

The Bishop's contorted face expressed his pain.

"Luke, you *must* forget about Giles. I know it's difficult, I loved him too but he has made his choice and I can do nothing for him."

"You think he's dead?" screamed Luke, trying to raise himself on his good arm, "you do, don't you? Oh God no. In the name of Christ, tell me, is Giles dead?"

"Calm yourself Luke, calm yourself. The truth is that I have no idea whether Giles is still alive. The last time I saw him he was recovering well but he was confined again to the chamber on the eastern wall almost three months ago when Buckingham first returned from King Richard's coronation."

"You haven't seen him since? Have you enquired after him at all since then?"

Morton shook his head.

"I thought it best not to remind the Duke. He had intended executing Giles immediately but as soon as I suggested he reach for the crown himself, he just forgot about him."

"So who is caring for him?"

"I have tried to ensure that food and water are sent daily to the cell on the walls and providing my orders are being carried out he will be well enough."

Luke relaxed a little but sweat was streaming from his brow. Morton wrung out the flannel laying in the bowl of lavender water on the stool by the bed and dabbed at his forehead. Luke felt the muscles in his face and neck tense involuntarily and he tried not to wince. Since his memory had returned he found himself repulsed by this man who had provided and cared for him throughout his years of darkness but he was determined to repay the debt by not letting his feelings show.

"So are you for Tudor or for Buckingham or are you keeping your options open?" asked Luke, deliberately trying to provoke the Bishop. He had started to wipe Luke's neck and he could stand the man's touch no longer. It worked. Morton threw the flannel into the bowl and water slopped onto the floor.

"My loyalties are as they have always been," snapped Morton, hurt by Luke's cutting remarks but unwilling to argue when they were to be parted for an indeterminate period of time.

"You have exceeded your undoubted gift for cunning to have convinced the Duke that you will support his bid for the crown," jibed Luke, "how did you achieve that?"

"Never mind Buckingham," countered Morton, forcing himself to believe that Luke's hostility was linked to his ill health and inability to fight for their cause, "you still have a very important part to play in this saga. One for which Henry Tudor will repay you handsomely."

Morton delved into the sleeve of his gown and produced a small silk bag containing sweetmeats. Holding them carefully by the drawstring the Bishop dangled them in front of Luke's face but as he reached for the bag, Morton pulled it away.

"Careful, these sweetmeat are covered in poison. They are a small present for the two Woodville boys."

"What?" Luke could not find the words to express his horror but a smiling Morton continued anyway.

"Those bastards must not be alive when Henry Tudor lands in Devon next week. He has promised to wed their elder sister and unite the Houses of York and Lancaster. It was a rash promise and can only be fulfilled if the lads are dead."

"Why?"

"Because if the boys are illegitimate so is their sister. Tudor has enough problems with his own lineage without confounding it by marrying a bastard."

"And if the boys are dead then Tudor can claim that King Richard made up the story about Edward's bigamy and marry a legitimate Princess of York."

"Exactly," concluded Morton, "so you understand the importance of our little gift to the Woodville boys?"

Luke dare not refuse for fear Morton would find another recruit, willing to carry out this abomination.

"Very well," he croaked, "for the sake of Queen Margaret and her son." Then he remembered; poisoned sweets had been the method by which King Edward had been murdered. "How did you acquire the poison?"

"Lady Katherine is an accomplished herbalist. She has a special herb garden separate from the kitchen plot, with a well equipped workshop at the far end. She produces all her own tisanes, salves, tinctures and the like."

"But she didn't just provide you with poison on demand," pressed Luke.

"N-no, Buckingham showed Sir Humphrey and myself around the plot and workshop yesterday. The shelves above the workbench were full of labelled jars and so I slipped a small phial of Laudanum into my sleeve whilst inspecting the stock."

"Why did the Duke show you around the workshop in the first place?"

"I have no idea," replied Morton firmly and Luke sensed that nothing useful would result from pressing the Bishop further.

Some hours later the grind of the rising portcullis roused Luke from his fitful slumber. His pillow was soaking wet and the chamber swayed even with the rise and fall of his chest as he gasped for breath. After a few minutes his eyes steadied enough for him to see the now familiar outline of Lady Katherine knelt at his side.

"Are they gone?" he rasped, concluding that the trundling noise of feet and hooves was not in his head but outside in the bailey. Another figure came into focus as he struggled to look over the cup of watered wine Katherine was holding to his lips.

"It won't be long now, Sir Henry," replied Humphrey. He had stepped forward to take the wine cup from Katherine's hand whilst passing her a bundle of towels which she wrapped round Luke's shoulders, absorbing the sweat and providing dry support for his head and neck.

"Bishop Morton visited you earlier," began Humphrey tentatively, "can you remember what he had to say?"

"I'm ill man, not senile, of course I can remember. But first you tell me what Buckingham, Morton and you were doing in Lady Katherine's workshop yesterday?"

Luke could not make out the expressions on his visitors' faces but he was certain they exchanged glances. Humphrey collected two stools from beneath the window and placed them either side of the bed. Lady Katherine pulled her stool up close and took Luke's lifeless hand in her own. Humphrey cleared his throat, dragged his stool as close as possible to Luke's right side and leaned even closer.

"The Duke has left me behind to guard the Princes. They are his insurance against future accusations," whispered Humphrey, his protruding eyes darting from side to side, fearful of eaves droppers. He took in a sharp breath. "He also instructed me to poison Lady Katherine and Sir Giles Butler and dispose of their bodies before he and the Bishop return."

Luke heard Katherine sniff and although he could not make out her face clearly, he knew she was crying. Humphrey reached out across the bed, but it was too far for the pair to make physical contact.

"If you so much as touch a hair of Giles' head … ," croaked Luke but then stopped, realizing he was in no position to threaten Sir Humphrey.

"Don't be ridiculous man, would I tell you if I had any intention of carrying out the order? You asked what we were doing in the workshop."

"I'm sorry, please continue."

"The Duke took me to the workshop to provide me with the means of murder."

"Poison," said Luke flatly.

"So the Bishop did inform you ?"

"Not exactly," said Luke shuffling his shoulder away from the pillows, "look under the bolster, here."

Humphrey pushed his hand under the pillows beneath Luke's right shoulder and pulled out the silken bag containing the poisoned sweetmeats. He released the drawstring and peered into the bag.

"Be careful," warned Luke, "the good Bishop has smeared them with poison and has instructed *me* to ensure that King Edward's sons consume them."

Katherine let out a cry of horror and Humphrey dropped the offensive morsels onto the floor.

"I knew he was up to something," spat the knight.

"How long will they be gone?" asked Luke.

"For ever," cried Katherine, "if God be just."

"They have set out to muster the Duke's tenants and retainers from the Black Mountains before marching south to rendezvous with the rebels from Exeter," said Humphrey, "but they will make slow progress in this atrocious weather."

Even as he spoke lightening flashed and down the valley the ominous roll of thunder heralded the deluge that was to soak the land for the next ten days.

"I know you hate King Richard madam," began Luke, "but he may well rid you of your murderous husband and I'm sure he will reward you for taking such care of his brother's sons."

Lady Katherine let Luke's limp hand drop on the bed.

"None of this would have come to pass if he had not usurped Prince Edward's throne in the first instance." She burst into tears and Humphrey rushed round the bed to comfort her.

"Prince Edward died in the early hours this morning," said Sir Humphrey flatly, "my lady sat up all night with the child but to no avail." Gently he brushed the tears from her cheeks. "We have not informed Buckingham of his death lest he decide to dispose of the younger boy. If he did, then I would be ordered to accompany the Duke and Bishop on this muster and leave my lady unprotected."

Luke could sense the terror in Lady Katherine's wails and desperately tried to ignore the pain increasing alarmingly in his own head.

"What will you do?" he asked but the drumming in his brain drowned out Sir Humphrey's reply and Lady Katherine's sobs were becoming strangely distorted. Panicked by the fear of his own pending death, Luke grabbed at the shape he believed to be Katherine. "Can I see Giles?" he begged

"I have already sent hot water and the barber across to his chamber," cut in Sir Humphrey, "he will be with you as soon as he has bathed and changed."

"Thank you."

Luke sank back into his pain, vaguely aware of two warped human forms drawing away from his bedside. Maybe he lost consciousness or perhaps he was dreaming. He had no measure of the time that had past since the apparitions had left but the next sensation to register in his failing awareness was the sound of incessant rain driving against the shutters together with a strange certainty that he was alone in a vast stone tomb. He could neither move nor cry out but then the sound of approaching footsteps enabled his hopeless brain to sort the reality from the illusion.

"He's in here sir," said the barber's boy, pushing wide the door to Luke's chamber. Giles stepped into the room cautiously for fear his friend was sleeping.

"Giles is that you, come close my eyes are failing." Giles dropped to his knees at Luke's side and reached for his friend's hand. "Listen carefully to what I have to tell you Giles. I may not have long. Come closer."

Giles leaned across the bed and gasped in horror as he looked into Luke's sightless eyes.

The midday meal of roast mutton and boiled leaks remained untouched on the stool beside Luke's bed when the servant returned for the dishes. Giles shook his head in response to the man's raised eyebrows as he surveyed the cold food.

"Bring some watered wine in a shallow cup," whispered Giles to the departing servant and then turned to his friend. "You have exhausted yourself with so much talking. You should rest now."

A rye smile played on Luke's face and he reached for Giles' hand but suddenly started to wheeze like an old man with the winter ague. Giles tried to support his friend's head as the coughing caused it to jerk and inflict such agony upon Luke that Giles was frightened by the sight of his suffering. When the coughing fit eased Luke relaxed back against the pillows and signed to Giles to lean closer.

"A priest Giles, I haven't long now."

Startled by the request and feeling helpless in the face of his friend's certainty, Giles wiped away the tiny stream of blood that was oozing from the corner of Luke's mouth and then hurried out into the corridor. Calling for assistance as he ran, Giles began to panic. Where were all the servants, the men-at-arms, the squires, cooks, stable hands, anybody? He had reached the buttery now and there, perched on a table next to a freshly breached cask of ale, sat the cheeky barber's boy who together with another lad of about the same age was helping himself to successive pots of ale from the cask.

"I need a priest, my friend is dying, please help me," begged Giles.

The boy put down his pot and held out his hand for payment whilst his drinking companion grinned inanely at him from his seat on the floor. Giles screamed at the lad that he would be well paid on his return and dragging him off the table, pushed him roughly in the direction of the door. As soon as Giles was sure the boy had gone he picked up the unfinished quart pot and hurried back to Luke's chamber, where he slowed his pace, struggled to control his panting and crept into the room. Luke was either asleep or unconscious. His eyes were shut and his breath was coming in short spasms. Giles stared at Luke's translucent skin, all the more ghastly for having once been a rich olive colour but now yellowing, it stretched over his nose and cheek bones, falling into hollows around his eyes and mouth where once flesh had padded and supported his handsome Mediterranean face.

How long Giles waited for the man of God to arrive was to be a torment that stayed with him for the rest of his life. All he could recall was kneeling at Luke's bedside and praying for his friend to survive. Maybe he even slept for a few minutes, God knows he was exhausted from living with the constant sound of falling water for the last twelve weeks. Although he was unsure of the exact sequence of events, he later remembered straightening the pillows, wiping Luke's brow and draining the contents of the quart pot; and whatever the passage of time, when he next looked at the knight, the rise and fall of his chest had ceased, his lips were slightly parted and his eyes were open but unseeing.

The noise outside in the bailey was deafening and before Giles could even close Luke's dead eyes the repeated twang of arrows sinking deep into the shutters caused him to instinctively throw himself to the floor. The smell of burning was followed by a burst of flame at the window and within seconds the arrased walls either side of the opening were ablaze, dancing with orange light. Giles threw the top coverlet over Luke's body and tried to drag the corpse off the bed and towards the door but before he had travelled two or three paces the room was full of dense smoke. Fumbling for the latch, he managed to pull it open only to collapse into the arms of someone who knew his name.

He regained conscious also to the sound of his name and the trickle of soothing white wine being poured down his sore throat. Gratefully he gulped at the liquid, gradually becoming aware that his eyes were stinging and then the smell of smoke brought him quickly to his senses.

"Luke," he croaked, "Luke, I must get his body out of that chamber." He tried to get up but found himself restrained by a stronger arm than his own.

"There is nothing more you can do for Luke," said Mark gently.

"I must find what remains of him," insisted Giles, "the least I can do is ensure that he is buried with some dignity."

"His body was pulled clear of the flames and transferred to the Priory up the valley."

"Mark? Mark, oh thank God. You can help me, we must get Luke's body out of here."

"Luke's body is being cared for at the Priory. You can see for yourself later."

Finally the words registered in Giles' confused brain, allowing him to relax and permit his tears to fall. Mark tended his grieving master with wine and soothing words but it would be many years before Giles forgave himself for not finding a priest in time. The castle too was calmer now, with only intermittent shouts of triumphant and fierce dispute as pillaging men fought over their booty.

"What is happening Mark? Are we in danger? How did you get here? How did the fire start? Have you heard anything about Buckingham's rebels ... and Bishop Morton he left with the Duke. Are the children safe?"

"Slow down Sir Giles, drink some more wine and save your voice."

Mark refilled Giles' cup and sat himself on the opposite couch. They were in Buckingham's luxurious solar, although the smoke had penetrated the fine woollen rugs and silken drapes it was still comfortable and unburned.

"My these are comfy," Mark said, shuffling back into the cushions. Giles said nothing but stared at his squire impatiently.

"Luke and I travelled to Wales as guests of the Duke of Buckingham," began Mark, "we knew that he had abducted you, so we did not trust him and decided to split up at Abergavenny. To cut a long story short, I nearly broke my leg and ... "

"You *nearly* broke your leg?"

"I cracked the bone and some travellers took me to Tretower Court, the home of Sir Thomas Vaughan, so that I could recover. Vaughan is a fiercely loyal Yorkist with a passionate dislike for Jasper Tudor."

"Who is *Jasper* Tudor?"

"Henry Tudor's uncle, the idiot who has instilled ideas of sovereignty into Henry's head. Apparently, after the battle of Tewkesbury Jasper executed Sir Thomas Vaughan's father. King Edward had dispatched Vaughan the elder to search for the Tudors and he followed them to Chepstow, but the Tudors were made welcome in the town and Sir Thomas' father rode into a trap and was put to the sword. Anyway, when the rumours reached Tretower Court that Buckingham was supporting Tudor's proposed invasion, Sir Thomas flew into a rage and we ended up here and laid siege to the castle. The fire was started by our burning arrow heads but we soon doused it ourselves as there was hardly any resistance, all the fighting men have ridden out with the Duke. The rest you know."

"I wonder whether the King knows about Buckingham's treachery?"

"Oh he knows about it. Sir Thomas Vaughan sent a messenger to York as long ago as the middle of September. There were just rumours then and maybe his Majesty didn't believe them but he will now that the Duke of Norfolk has crushed the Kentish men's uprising and their leaders have squealed."

"Dear God he'll be devastated. I wouldn't like to be in Buckingham's shoes if he ever catches up with him."

The solar door opened and the huge hairy faced giant that was Sir Thomas Vaughan lumbered in.

"Christ's teeth this room is like a whore's bedchamber," swore Sir Thomas, picking up a silk cushion. "Was Duke Henry really a man or is there a chest of ladies' gowns stowed away in his closet?" Vaughan started to laugh but stopped abruptly. "You alright lad?" he asked of Giles, after noticing the tear stains on his face.

"I'm fine thank you. Is there any news of Lady Katherine and the children?"

"Aye lad, they were seen leaving through the postern gate before we arrived. I understand Sir Humphrey Percivall was with them. They can't have gone far. My brother Watcyn has set out after them."

"Luke told me that Buckingham brought the son's of Edward IV here and that the elder boy died of some awful infection in his jaw. His body was taken to the Prior further up the valley."

Giles coughed violently and so Mark held the cup of wine to his lips and gradually the fit ceased.

"What happened to York, the younger prince?" asked Vaughan.

"I am sure Lady Katherine will have taken him with her own brood," said Giles hoarsely, "but we should search and make sure he isn't here before we leave, then I must find the King, I have important information for him. Can you help me reach him?"

Chapter 35

Weobley 28th October 1483

The weather was unrelenting and as the days passed, Bishop Morton was becoming more frustrated by his temporary role as Buckingham's champion. It wasn't the Duke's fault that they were stranded at Weobley, the constant storms had swollen the rivers and flooded the ground, making it impossible to tramp the tracks and roadways let alone cross the River Severn, which had burst its banks. Even so, Morton held Buckingham responsible for the moral of his men, most of whom were unpaid, unwilling conscripts and whilst Duke Henry idled away his time in the dry and relative comfort of Lord Ferrers' Manor, his men were left to fend for themselves, scrounging food and shelter wherever they could. It was impossible to fish the swollen rivers or to hunt in the soggy forests but the Duke had dismissed Morton's concern as irrelevant and had made no attempt to deal with the crisis. So it was not surprising that as the Bishop predicted, exhausted, sodden and hungry, men deserted Buckingham's sorry little troop daily.

For Bishop Morton, the final frustration came on their ninth day at Weobley when a messenger arrived with the news that the Duke of Norfolk had successfully cut of their supporters from Kent and London had held firm for King Richard. The Bishop sighed and made his decision to abandon the Duke at the first opportunity. The charade had virtually served its purpose now anyway. It would have been an additional accolade for the Bishop if his stooge had managed to muster a substantial army as well as abduct the princes from the Tower but Morton would have to be satisfied with using the Duke to discredit the King. After all, that in itself was an enormous achievement and Henry Tudor would be well pleased. He chuckled and started to collect his belongings and stuff them into his saddlebags. This uprising may never get off the mark, he thought to himself, but banners have been unfurled and allegiances sworn, I'm not hanging around to be executed for treason.

On the tenth day the morning sun rose temporarily in a blue sky and the Duke of Buckingham rang for his breakfast an hour earlier than he had done on previous mornings. Perhaps today would be the start of the reversing of his fortunes, the sun was shining and he could hear the sound of horses being walked into the yard below his chamber window. If the weather holds, perhaps he could finally set out for the Severn? Maybe the river would be crossable by the time he reached its banks? Some minutes later he was startled from his reverie by the sound of urgent banging on his chamber door and he shouted angrily for his squire to, 'attend and open the door.'

"My Lord of Buckingham," stammered Lord Ferrers, taking only one step beyond the doorway, "I think you should know at once that the good Bishop has ridden out of Weobley, never to return, or so he said as he departed and there are but three men left in the stables attending your stallion."

Buckingham rose to his feet shaking with anger and humiliation.

"Explain yourself," he screamed at the top of his voice, "John Morton cannot have gone he is my ... my ... Get the hell out of here and ... and ... "

"This is my manor your Grace," replied Ferrers hotly, "and it is *I* who wish *you* to be gone: before midday preferably."

"How dare you, how dare you speak to your future king so. I'll have you ... have you ... " Words failed the frightened Duke as slowly the reality of his predicament pressured his brain.

Lord Ferrers retreated from the bedchamber leaving the door open and calling to a servant as he crossed his hall, to send the three men still in the stables, up to the Duke's chamber. Minutes later two scruffy wet individuals hovered outside the open door.

"I thought there were three of you," called Buckingham resentfully.

The two fellows shrugged their shoulders and fiddled with their soaking wet hats.

Buckingham untied his purse and took out two silver coins, which he threw to the bedraggled pair.

"Feed my stallion and be gone," he said mournfully.

The two needed no second telling. After briefly fumbling on the floor for the coins, the only evidence of their being there was a whiff of unwashed wet clothing and two small pools of water.

The rain clouds were gathering again as His Royal Highness, Henry Stafford, Duke of Buckingham set out alone, dressed in the humble clothing of a servant, a disguise he hoped would enable him to ride undetected into the Forest of Dean. His aim was to cross the Severn and search for any of Henry Tudor's supporters who could offer him protection. Initially, he had considered returning to Brecknock but for how long would he be safe even there? The King was already aware of his defection and would instruct Sir Thomas Vaughan of Tretower Court to besiege Brecknock Castle, if he hadn't already done so and then the Princes would be discovered alive and well and King Richard would be able to prove his innocence.

Chapter 36

Salisbury 1st November 1483

On the first day of November, a small band of assorted Welshmen accompanied Sir Giles Butler and his squire Mark Taylor as they rode into the Cathedral Close in the ancient market town of Salisbury. Bells were tolling for midday Angelus and the precinct was busy with clerically garbed cannons and their vicars, responding to the call to payers. Four squires wearing the King's livery forced their way into the precinct from the market area and hailed Sir Giles to follow them to the aptly named, White Boar on the north side of the market place. Mark chuckled and nudged Giles as they approached, pointing to the recently painted sign where the wet paint had streaked and run in the inclement weather so that the rampant beast had six legs and an additional drooping tusk.

"I wonder how many tavern signs have been repainted since Richard became king?" mused Mark, "remember that place at Northampton, the taverner there had repainted his sign too."

The square was busy with soldiers, harbingers and intelligence gatherers, rushing about on the King's business and although some traders were hawking their goods from booths and shop fronts around the square, normal business was subdued. The hurried exit of men who had mustered under the fleeing Woodville Bishop of Salisbury had left some traders short of sons and apprentices and when the news of the collapse of Buckingham's muster reached the town, local gentry had also fled, leaving town's folk to withstand the impact of any Royal disapproval. People here had yet to learn that it was not in Richard's nature to appease his anger by inflicting pain on the guiltless, however, security in Salisbury was in evidence throughout the town.

It was a full hour before Giles was shown into King Richard's presence. Things had certainly changed. At Crosby Place he was able to walk straight into the great hall and expect to be greeted personally by his uncle but now he was King, procedure and etiquette surrounded him. So many officials, even when they were mustering for war and Giles, who was suffering bouts of nausea since his inhalation of smoke, was flustered and annoyed by the questions and assurances these minions insisted upon. Eventually, two men-at-arms escorted him upstairs and opened the door to the room serving as the King's council chamber. To Giles' amazement he was announced formally by a herald. It was only a chamber above the local hostelry for heavens sake and Giles was about to ask why the fan-fare of trumpets had been omitted, when he realised his uncle was oblivious to all the fuss that had enveloped him now that he was King Richard III.

"Sir Giles," cried the King sternly, "where in God's name have you been these past months?"

"Imprisoned at Brecknock," responded Giles, just as sternly.

Ignoring the curtness of his nephew's reply, King Richard rose from the chair at the head of the table where documents and maps were spread before him. Radcliffe and a bird like man, Giles did not recognise, were sat either side of the King and both rose immediately he left his seat.

Giles abandoned his sarcasm, sank to one knee before his Sovereign and kissed the Royal hand. Relieved there was no substance to Buckingham's allegations regarding Giles' own claim to the crown, the King grabbed his nephew by the shoulders and raising him to his feet hugged him and then called for more wine and another cup.

"I have much to report Sire and some is for your ears only."

Without further ado the King dismissed Radcliffe and the bird like man and ushered Giles to the window seat.

"Now nephew, what is so urgent you cannot join us first in a cup of claret?" asked the King gravely.

"I was abducted by the Duke of Buckingham before your coronation and have only now been rescued by Sir Thomas Vaughan of Tretower Court."

Richard looked away, even the mention of the traitor's name offended him. He stared out of the window at some imaginary distraction in the distance.

"Sir Thomas Vaughan is pursuing the Duke now, his men are combing Shropshire where he is believed to be hiding," continued Giles.

"He's already taken. He took refuge with a servant he thought he could trust but the man betrayed him to the sheriff of Shropshire. They will be here by tomorrow."

Giles acknowledged the news with a nod. He could not find the appropriate words.

"Why did ... why were you abducted?" asked the King his eyes still fixed somewhere beyond the Cathedral spire.

"Because he suspected I knew of his duplicity."

"And did you?" demanded Richard, turning and facing his nephew. The vein on his forehead already threatening to enlarge.

"In a way, yes."

"What kind of answer is that?"

Giles was terrified but the truth had to be told and there would never be a right moment to tell his uncle that he had known all along that Buckingham was involved with Morton's plotting.

"When Luke and I discovered that King Edward had been murdered we could not imagine who might have been responsible. It was the lack of suspects that prompted Luke to tell me about an old plot to help Henry Tudor invade England."

"God's teeth man and you failed to tell us?"

"Please hear me out Sire. I will submit to your judgement willingly but please hear what I have to say first."

The King bristled and Giles could see he was fighting his instinct to rage but thankfully he managed to control himself sufficiently to nod his assent. Choosing his words carefully Giles explained how Morton and Luke had escaped to Chepstow after the battle of Tewkesbury, from there being sent by Henry Tudor to Brecknock with a message for his mother Lady Stanley. How at Brecknock

Morton had planned for each of them to ingratiated themselves into the House of York and wait for an opportunity to raise Lancaster's standards against their conquerors.

"It was a pathetic rallying of the defeated," explained Giles, "an attempt to boost their moral and knowing Morton an excuse not to flee the country; and according to Luke, only Henry's mother took the conspiracy seriously. She managed to find herself a Yorkist husband under whose protection she could infiltrate the new regime. She became one of Elizabeth Woodvilles ladies and later, godmother to her youngest."

"The cursed woman carried Anne's train at our coronation." spat Richard.

"However, the Duke of Buckingham made no attempt to wheedle his way into Edward's favour. Apart from Lady Stanley being his aunt and the plans being made at his castle at Brecknock, his reason for participation in the plot was based on his hatred of the Woodvilles. Luke was convinced that Buckingham spared not another thought to the conspiracy after he and Morton left for London."

King Richard seemed to relax a little and Giles felt he was exonerating himself. The fresh cup was brought in by a wary servant and both King and nephew took a break before the next round of revelations.

"Bishop Morton, *Doctor* Morton as he was then, threw himself on Edward's mercy and offered his services as an able administrator, "resumed Giles, feeling braver after a quart of fine wine.

The King's mouth dropped open as he remembered Edward's affection for the rotund and aging priest.

"Oh don't misunderstand me, I would swear on the Holy Book that Morton truly loved King Edward and never conspired to raise Lancaster's banners whilst he lived. He was twenty years older than King Edward and could reasonably have expected to meet his maker long before the King."

"So, you dismissed the idea that Morton was responsible for our brother's murder but failed to consider that his death released the Bishop from his loyalty to York."

"Exactly," agreed Giles, "Luke had warned me earlier that Morton would support the Woodville's against your Protectorship and when he ended our friendship he claimed he was doing so because to remain friends compromised our respective loyalties. But that was all I thought there was to it: an open difference in loyalties."

"You never suspected that Luke dissolved your friendship because Morton had reactivated the old plot?"

Giles shook his head as he tried to recall the exact events surround his break up with Luke.

"It was the day I was leaving for Middleham. I was really angry, I had just learned that Elizabeth Woodville had not informed you of King Edward's death. My temper was as bad as I have ever had to contend with. I just wasn't concentrating."

"Quite," sighed the King, who was used to his own temper over shadowing reason.

"But I still didn't suspected that Morton had reactivated his conspiracy even when I spotted Luke in Buckingham's entourage at Northampton. Later he warned me about Lord Rivers' plot to assassinate you."

"Why warn you, if Morton was against our becoming Lord Protector?"

"Because the aim of the reactivated conspirators was to cause as much friction between the Woodvilles and the Protectorship as possible in order to present Tudor as the solution to endless bitterness. Had we not been warned of Rivers' intention to assassinate you and had he been successful, the Woodvilles would have won control of the boy King and the dispute ended."

"So Morton sent Luke to warn Buckingham simply to keep the power struggle alive but he reported to you instead of the Duke."

"That's correct. Even after the boy was crowned they intended to continue playing one party off against the other, until parliament and the people were so frustrated by the bickering that they would welcome Henry Tudor and the peace his reign would promise."

"But Bishop Robert Stillington put an end to the contest when he announced the precontract between your mother and King Edward."

"Yes, your right of accession meant that England was about to have an adult monarch, rendering Henry Tudor instantly redundant."

"So Morton contrived to force through the coronation of the boy king by persuading poor drunken Hastings to arrest and hold us captive until after the lad was crowned."

"Yes Sire. And it was Buckingham who informed Morton of the Bishop's revelation but when he realised that Catesby and I were privy to Morton's plans to arrest you at the council meeting on the following day, he reassessed his position. Buckingham's reason for being part of the conspiracy in the first instance was accomplished. With you as King, the Woodvilles were finished and he could not expect more gratitude from Henry Tudor than he had already received from you."

"He had no motive to continue his part in their conspiracy."

"Quite, so he let Hastings walk into our trap and whisked Morton away to Brecknock for fear he might be implicated should Morton confess all when interrogated."

"So why wasn't that the end to it; why did he muster against us?"

"Ah well that was down to Bishop Morton. Left alone at Brecknock to consider his own situation, Morton realised that the Duke had benefited enormously from his role as your chief advisor and that once you were King there was no advantage to Buckingham risking what he had gained by aiding Tudor."

"So clever Morton upped the stakes and lured Harry Buckingham into treason for a second time by suggesting he should claim the crown for himself," reasoned the King. He left his cup on the table and returned to gaze out of the window.

"Morton also convinced Buckingham that you would be credited with the murder of the Princes if *he* disposed of them and spread rumours blaming you for their demise."

The King spun round, his face so close to Giles' that the knight was obliged to lean back in order to focus on his uncle's expression.

"Our brother's boys are murdered?"

"No, no my Lord. The Duke kept them alive as insurance against the possibility that similar accusations might be levied at him once he had won the crown."

"They are at Brecknock? For pity's sake Giles, why did you not say so at once?"

"They were Sire but no longer. When the Duke stole them from the Tower, the eldest, Prince Edward was sick and the journey to Wales further damaged his humours. I'm afraid he died just days before the Duke unfurled his banners in support of Tudor."

"Dear Christ have mercy on us. Are you sure of this?"

"I am your Majesty. Luke also died at Brecknock some days ago and I attended his funeral at Brecknock Priory where the Prior informed me that the eldest son of King Edward IV had also been interned there during the previous week."

"And what of our nephew, York?"

"Sir Humphrey Percivall and Lady Katherine left Brecknock with the young Duke of York and Buckingham's children only hours before Sir Thomas Vaughan stormed the castle. Vaughan's brothers, Watkin and Roger, are fast on the heels and hopefully will restore him to your care shortly."

After pouring himself another cup from the jug of claret and drinking deeply, King Richard sat down heavily in his chair at the top of the table and pushed the documents and maps away from him as if they were now of little use. He sat with his head cradled in his hands for some minutes and Giles waited in silence until his uncle had composed himself.

"But York is well ?" asked the King simply, raising this head to meet Giles' eyes.

"He is my liege and I'm sure will soon be found."

Giles hesitated, unsure whether it was appropriate to continue as the King was so clearly distressed with the news of the elder boy's death but Richard sensed his indecision and bid him continue.

"My friend that died, Luke Lazarus, well, he lost his memory after the battle of Tewkesbury but in recent weeks it had returned," began Giles, "he asked me to deliver a message to your Majesty but I need to explain the circumstances first."

"You have our attention nephew, get on with it."

"Luke's real name is Sir Henry Pierrepoint of Holbeck and Woodhouse."

"Sir Henry Pierrepoint? Goodness, he was one of George

Clarence's men."

"I believe so Sire. Sir Henry attended the Duke when he fled to France with his father-in-law, the Earl of Warwick and the Earl's er.. er.. family."

"Family? Do you refer to our Queen, Warwick's youngest daughter?"

"Yes Sire, I mean … "

"Deliver your message," demanded Richard amidst rising panic.

Giles took a deep breath, he knew his uncle was exceedingly touchy about Anne's first marriage to the Prince of Lancaster and he wasn't convinced that reopening the wound at this point in time was wise.

"Clarence, his family and retinue were billeted some distance from King Louis' residence, because the French King and John Morton were plotting to split the Earl from his son-in-law with the intention of gaining Warwick's support for Queen Margaret and the Prince of Lancaster."

"We know all this," said Richard tersely.

"Indeed Sire, but when Warwick and his wife informed their daughter Anne of her part in the alliance, she fled to Clarence and his wife, her sister Isobel and begged for their assistance. She did not wish to marry the Prince of Lancaster."

The King had once again turned to gaze out of the window, he did not want to concede how little he knew of Anne's reaction to the proposed marriage. His concern had been with its taking place, not with the preamble.

"The Duke of Clarence appointed Luke, Sir Henry, to help Anne escape her unwanted union and return to England. They would have succeeded but for the Countess looking in on her daughter late the very night they had set out to cross the channel."

"The bitch raised the alarm?"

"Yes my Lord. Sir Henry was condemned to death for his part in the planned escape and the Earl of Warwick swore that he would drag Anne to the alter bound and gagged whether she would or no and repeat her marriage vows for her if necessary."

"And did he? ask King Richard the vein on his temple beginning to pulsate"

"No Sire, Anne bought Sir Henry's life with her acceptance of her fate. She married the Prince of Lancaster of her own free will and saved Sir Henry, Luke, from the executioner's axe, which is why he repaid the debt on the field at Tewkesbury."

"How do you mean?"

"Sir Henry spent his battle searching for the Prince of Lancaster and when he finally came upon him he managed to fell and fatally wound the boy, thus freeing Lady Anne from the loveless marriage she had undertaken to save his life."

As the words tumbled from Giles' mouth he could not help wondering if the Lady had nurtured feelings for Luke. He must have been exceedingly handsome before he lost his memory and the use of his left arm. Fortunately no such thought crossed the King's mind.

"He asked me to give you this." Giles drew Luke's brooch from his script and handed it to his uncle. "Luke, I mean Sir Henry was presented with this as a trophy by the Duke of Clarence when Lancaster's body was discovered after the battle. The Duke of Clarence claimed that the Earl of Warwick first presented it to the Lancastrian Prince as a wedding gift on Anne's behalf."

King Richard let the brooch drop to the floor as if it had burned his fingers. It bounced and turning, lodged in a crack between the bare boards, the diamonds in the protruding coronet sparkling defiantly. Richard crushed it with his heel, forcing the jewel further between the planks until it disappeared from view.

"Later Sir Henry was to receive a blow to the head which took his memory for the next twelve years," continued Giles hurriedly.

"Luke, Luke Lazarus, isn't he Bishop Morton's adopted son?" queried the King, "and is this the same Luke who is actually Sir Henry Pierrepoint?"

"It is my Lord. The irony of the story is that John Morton misread the significance of the brooch and believed that Almighty God had delivered the knight into his care."

Giles risked a sideways glance at his uncle to see if the vein on his temple was still visible but he could not make it out.

"A very deserved cuckoo in Bishop Morton's nest," observed the King.

CHAPTER 37

Salisbury 1st November 1483

Giles woke the next morning with a stiff neck. He and Mark had squeezed into the overcrowded tap room of the White Boar and spent an uncomfortable night propped against a stack of ale casks. The King had commandeered the entire hostelry for his immediate associates but there was hardly enough room for those billeted there to sit, let alone lie down and sleep. It was useless trying to find alternative accommodation, the town was full of the King's men, their horses, servants and provisions. Many men would normally have slept in the open but after days of incessant rain they had sort shelter in every covered corner of the town.

"It's still raining," whispered Mark, once he realised his master was awake, "I went for a piss ages ago and I haven't been able to sleep since."

A cock crowed somewhere in the distance and even the shrillness of his call seemed to creek with the damp. It was barley light, the heavy rain clouds delaying the natural dawn and men and women who would normally have been up and bustling even in the winter cold, were tarrying indoors to delay yet another soaking.

"I'm out of here," whispered Giles, "it stinks like hell's worst cesspit," and clambering to his feet he picked his way carefully over the heaps of wet and sweaty sleepers until he found the door. Mark followed, managing to disturb most of those Giles had carefully avoided, standing on one man's hand and tripping over another's foot and sprawling across several other disgruntled sleepers who shifted and cursed at his ungainly exit.

"At least the air is fart free out here," whinged Giles, fastening his points after relieving himself against the wall.

"Look Sir Giles, over there by the Guildhall, a group of riders and yes, that is Sir Thomas Vaughan. See the hairy faced man in front."

Giles and Mark strode across the deserted market place, splashing through potholes and puddles as they approached the Guildhall. There were six horsemen in all and Giles recognised Sir James Tyrell amongst them, a knight in his forties, for many years retained by the late King Edward. Tyrell acknowledged Giles with a raised hand but it was the tall bedraggled man, his wrists bound and his legs tied to the belly of the black stallion that spoke first.

"Good God Sir Giles what are you doing here? Hurry now and tell the King that I am arrived and wish to speak with him urgently."

Giles stared in disbelief at the Duke of Buckingham. Dressed in the poor, ill fitting attire of a woodman, perched upon his magnificent stallion and bound like a hind ready for the spit, he was *still* giving orders.

"The arrogance of the man," scoffed Tyrell, his dark eyes flashing angrily "ignore him Sir Giles, Vaughan and I will inform King Richard of our arrival *as soon as His Majesty has broken his fast and not before.*" Tyrell shouted his last remark at their prisoner. "It's good to see you again Giles," he continued, sidestepping the rear of the black beast, as Buckingham shuffled in the saddle in an attempt to manoeuvre his rump into Tyrell's chest. "Vaughan tells me this traitor held you at Brecknock these last weeks."

Tyrell slapped the rear of Buckingham's stallion sharply and the horse short forward almost unseating the Duke who hurled abuse back at Tyrell when the animal finally pulled up some yards further down the market place. A florid faced man with expensive, if wet clothing pulled his mount about and kicked it forward to follow the prisoner. He was the arresting officer and sheriff of Shropshire.

"I need somewhere secure to hold him," said the sheriff over his shoulder to Tyrell, "I'll find the Mayor whilst you speak with the King."

"I doubt King Richard will speak with the Duke," said Giles, watching them go, "he could hardly bear to hear his name spoken yesterday. He'll go straight to the block."

Mark and Giles walked with Tyrell to the bottom of the stone steps that led to the King's chamber and took their leave.

"Let's find something to eat before the entire muster wants breakfast," said Mark.

Giles following his squire around the side of the hostelry in search of the kitchen, a brick building across a small yard from the buttery. The fire must have been alight for some time, as the cook, a frail woman well past her allotted three score and ten years, stirred a huge vat of thickening oats that smelt much better than Giles remembered porridge ever tasting. Pot boys and slatterns were about their tasks like a drove of steaming ghosts, their thin bodies barely disguised by their wet bedraggled clothing, releasing moisture in the heat. The cook took one look at the insignia on Giles' sleeve and without a word ladled ample helpings of hot oatmeal into two wooden bowls and placed them noisily on a bench close to the door. A boy of about six or seven summers heaved a heavy clay pot of goats milk onto the bench besides them and a shy little girl of the same age with the most beguiling smile offered honey from a pot she cradled in her arms like a new baby. Mark and Giles sat on the bench and tucked into the welcome, if simple feast.

"For once mother, this oatmeal tastes as good as it smells," announced Giles with genuine appreciation in his voice.

The old woman turned and thanked him with a toothless grin, at the same time using a long bony finger to prod the young lad who was dawdling over the return to his duties. When they had finished their food the seven year old returned with quart pots of ale but a sleepy eyed, almost dressed squire, appeared in the kitchen doorway and hailed Sir Giles by his name.

"You're to come at once to the royal presence," called the dishevelled lad.

Giles hurried to the front of the inn and mounted the stairs two at a time, unsure of the nature of the urgent summons. The guard on the heavy outer door snapped to attention and the squire escorted Giles into the inner room and announced his arrival.

King Richard was sat alone in the window seat wearing a heavy velvet dressing gown over his night attire. He signalled for the squire to leave and when the door latch clicked into its housing he bid Giles sit beside him on the cushioned sill.

"You know Tyrell and Vaughan have returned with ... with the traitor?" said the King, gazing out of the window beyond the square, to where the spire of the Cathedral reached for the low clouds that were just allowing daylight to creep into the sodden town. It was Sunday and bells were already tolling across the landscape for the first mass of the day.

"Yes Sire, I have spoken with them and with ... "

The King turned to face his nephew and the pain in his uncle's face caused Giles' words to fade. Richard's eyes were rimmed with red. Had he been crying? His skin was sallow and he had chewed his lower lip until the blood had run down his chin.

"We will not see him Giles. How can he ask, let alone *demand* to speak with us?"

Was the question rhetorical? Giles was unsure. The King was wringing his hands and he bit open the small wound on his lip. It dripped blood onto his nightshirt.

"I guess he must have lost his mind along with his honour," ventured Giles.

"You think he may be mad?" echoed the King, seizing on the idea like the proverbial straw within the reach of a drowning man, "George Clarence was mad. He was so jealous of Edward's crown that he became consumed with envy and it turned his mind. Could it be the same with Harry?"

What a question: Giles had no way of knowing if Buckingham's arrogance and resentfulness had somehow eaten into his brain and destroyed his mind but instinct told him this was about preserving his uncle's sanity.

"Since he was ten years old, he has complained about his enforced, lowly marriage to Katherine Woodville," Giles said tentatively, "and even now the Woodvilles have lost their power, he is still bound by his marriage vows."

"Twenty years is a long time to bear a grudge," admitted the King, "he may be mad."

"Mad or not Sire, dispatch him immediately," urged Giles. "Why agonise over what cannot be changed? There need only be a perfunctory trial. I understand you have created Assheton, Vice Constable of England as a result of the Duke's treason. Let him read the indictment, find the man guilty and pass sentence. His head can be on the block by noon."

"Aye, you're right lad," sighed the King without much conviction. "Let the Almighty ponder over the state of his mind, we need to confront that surviving menace, Tudor."

King Richard left the window and returned to the long table. Absentmindedly he shuffled through the papers strewn there and then, as if he had come to a decision, he wiped the blood from his chin with one hand and placed the other purposefully on the Great Seal.

"Leave us Giles but send in our secretary, Kendall and the lawyer Catesby, that we might get this unpleasant business underway."

"It isn't like you to be disturbed by these occasions," said a concerned Mark, as he and Giles waited at the back of the assembled crowd for the Duke of Buckingham to appear.

His master had been sick twice since breakfast and his face was still tinged with a green hue. Giles shrugged and tried to edge his way nearer the Guildhall.

Salisbury market place was full of spectators, and an excited buzz was started by those closest to the Guildhall when the Duke of Buckingham appeared on the steps. It quickly swelled into a fevered call for blood as the news of his appearance carried round the crowd. Held firmly by two hefty guards, their tabards emblazoned with the royal coat of arms, the Duke struggled as he desperately tried to free himself from their grip, at the same time screaming for assistance from anyone who might take pity on his plight. The once arrogant, mighty Duke looked remarkably ordinary wearing only an open necked shirt and hose, his head bare and his hands tied behind his back. Giles winced as one of the guards kneed him viciously in the groin so that he dropped forward in agony, which enabled the soldiers to force him forward without further protest. A priest led the way, reading from the Holy Book and making the sign of the cross as they stepped down into the square to make the short journey to the newly erected scaffold before the market cross. The hooded executioner followed, carrying his axe across his arms like a royal sceptre.

"I've seen enough," said Giles, turning his back on the scene and retreating hurriedly down the alley that ran between the Guildhall and the adjacent candle makers. To Mark's amazement his master was immediately sick, retching several times until the contents of his stomach stretched yards down the snicket.

"Hell's teeth Giles, his head is still attached," exclaimed Mark, "at least it was."

Oos and ahs and finally deafening cheers, carried from the square into the alley.

"Maybe it's the tallow," whimpered Giles, pointing to the candle makers.

"Oh yer," said Mark with a grin, "lets get you back to the Boar and cleaned up."

Exhausted, Giles allowed his squire to guide him through the alleyways that skirted vegetable plots and workshops at the rear of the properties to find the hostelry strangely quiet. The taverner and his customers were temporarily occupied watching the gruesome last moments of Buckingham's life and a miserable lanky youth had been left in charge. He loped over to Giles and after wiping the back of his hand under his nose he pointed to a figure huddled by the fire.

"He was asking after you, Sir Giles," said the lad and then raising his voice he hailed the bundle by the fire. "He's here as I said Sir."

The huddled figure unwound himself from his outer garb and noticing both the stains and odour of Giles' clothing he presented himself to Mark.

"John Hatton. My colleague, William Catesby, tells me you wish to speak with me."

Giles sighed, corrected Hatton's mistake and sent Mark to fetch watered wine.

"I have been unwell, you understand," began Giles but lack of strength made him impatient and without further preamble he asked Hatton why he had allowed a verdict of 'accidental death' to go unchallenged at the inquest on Douglas Hatton. "You were there. I saw you," accused Giles. "Everyone at the inquest was familiar with the White Tower and yet no one explained the difficulty an aging man would have climbing into the crenulations."

John Hatton dropped back into his seat and rubbed his eyes with the heels of his hands. Mark returned with two cups of watered wine and before setting them down, kicked a couple of stools towards the fire for Giles and himself.

"You are correct Sir Giles. The clerk to the court, Sir Douglas, myself and the jury all work at the Tower," sighed Hatton, "Sir Douglas is ... was my uncle. He had been ill for years with a hereditary shaking sickness." John Hatton held out his own left hand to demonstrate and then grasped it with his right in order to control the involuntary quivering. "The tisane he took contained a small amount of opiate but unfortunately, over the years he became dependant on larger and larger quantities of the drug until he eventually purchased it separately from a back street apothecary." Hatton drank the remains of his wine. "Douglas used to shut himself in his chamber to take the neat opium because he claimed it induced vivid dreams whilst he was fully awake."

"I have heard of the strange effect opiates can have on the mind," said Giles.

"The night he died he must have forgotten to lock his door, because he was seen climbing onto the parapet with the aid of a stool, flapping his arms and crowing."

"Crowing?"

"The truth is Sir Giles, Douglas Hatton launched himself from the parapet believing himself to be cockerel."

"Why was this not revealed at the inquest?"

"Those who work at the Tower are like a family. We see little of the wider world. It was wrong, I know but we agreed upon the story of the broken wine jug for fear the Coroner would bring in a verdict of suicide if he discovered Douglas had used a stool to climb onto the wall. He deserved better than to have his body thrown into the city ditch. I'm sure you know that suicides are denied burial in consecrated ground?"

Giles sipped his wine and felt his stomach turn over. He was about to assure John that his secret was safe when Mark asked how Sir Andrew Dymmock came to deliver the news of Sir Douglas' death to Westminster?

"What? I have no idea," stammered Hatton.

"Dymmock was Earl Rivers' agent and *you* were in Rivers' party at Stony Stratford," accused Mark, "what is the connection?"

Hatton covered his face with his hands and rocked in his seat. Giles forgot his churning innards and grabbed Hatton's arm, pulling his hands from his face.

"I have been threatened with my life if I tell," whimpered Hatton.

"You have a choice John," said Giles sternly, "either you tell me of your own free will or King Richard will sanction whatever force is necessary to extract the truth."

Hatton looked from Giles to Mark in horror, swallowed hard and shook his head.

"I do not understand why it is so important to you or to Dymmock." He sniffed hard and wiped his face with two shaking hands. "Andrew Dymmock was in the Treasury that evening looking for Sir Douglas. Unfortunately he found him just in time to witness Sir Douglas jumping from the parapet. As the stool was still in view we were obliged to include him in our deceit."

"I am surprised he agreed," said Giles.

"At first he did refuse but then he had an idea. He said he would keep quiet about what he had seen *and* inform the King of the Hatton's 'accident', if I would deliver a message for a friend of his. Not right away but when the friend sent for me. It seemed innocent enough but he threatened me, saying that if I told anyone about the message before or after I had delivered it, I could expect my throat to be cut." Hatton was shaking from head to toe. Clearly he believed his life was in danger if he reneged on his promise. "I beg you Sir Giles not to insist on more detail. I have already told you more than I should."

"I know the rest," said Giles, his eyes shinning and his sickness abandoned. "Sir Matthew Pawson sent for you on Easter Sunday evening. He gave you a small scroll, sealed but without a signet impression. You delivered it to Earl Anthony Rivers at the home of the Mayor of King's Lynn. Am I correct?"

John Hatton stared in confusion at Giles and nodded indiscernibly.

The rain had stopped by the afternoon and the second day in November promised to be bright, if chilly. The drinkers in the White Boar were mainly King Richard's men, snatching their ale when they could as they made preparation to leave the next day. The mood was good humoured but Giles was obliged to leave the roaring fire and make his way out into the square as the lurid tales of Buckingham's execution, embellished with detailed accounts of other gruesome decapitations, began to affect his stomach again. He signalled to Mark to stay put and enjoy himself with the local lass who had attached herself to his arm, or his purse, and was matching him, jar for jar with the taverner's strongest ale.

He felt better as soon as the cold air reached his lungs and decided to take a walk and check on the fitness of his horse, stabled at the far end of the square. As he crossed the front of the hostelry he met Sir James Tyrell about to ascend the stone stairway that led up to the King's accommodation. Sir James smiled, displaying a near complete set of exceedingly white teeth.

"There you are Sir Giles. The King was asking for you earlier. Let the herald know where you can be found when you leave his Majesty's presence in future. You are a retainer sir."

Giles sighed and dropped down onto the bottom step, his head in his hands.

"I'm sorry. All those weeks imprisoned at Brecknock with the constant sound of falling water have affected my concentration and my stomach is weaker than ever."

"And the death of your friend Luke. You must still be grieving for him?"

Giles lifted his head and nodded his assent.

"And Bishop Morton's defection must have been a terrible shock for you as well," added Tyrell, "the old King would turn in his grave if he knew how his dear friend had betrayed the House of York."

"Would he?" queried Giles, "he was aware of Morton's Lancastrian past"

"Yes, he was and better than Morton ever suspected," agreed Tyrell, his beady black eyes twinkling as he recalled the story that king Edward used to tell at the Bishop's expense. "John Morton must be in his sixties now but he was only a young man and clerk to mad King Henry's council when Edward's father first encountered him."

"I suppose he was young once," said Giles grudgingly, "but it's difficult to imagine."

"Oh he was young and madly in love with Henry's Queen, Margaret of Anjou. *And* when Margaret presented her husband with a new born baby boy, mad Henry declared the child to be 'a miracle' which the Yorkist contingent instantly interpreted to mean that Henry had not fathered the child." Tyrell made a moue and nodded knowingly.

"Oh no, I don't believe they thought Morton was the father," cried Giles.

"No, not the Yorkist Lords. They pointed the finger at the Duke of Somerset but King Edward liked to tease John Morton by insisting that *he* was the real father."

"Well perhaps it isn't so preposterous," said Giles after a moment's thought, " he escaped to France with Margaret and her baby son after the battle of Towton, leaving King Henry to face Edward alone. And Morton tutored the Prince into adulthood *and* help arrange his marriage to Anne Neville."

"Are you sure?" asked an astonished Tyrell.

"Oh yes I'm certain. I suppose you know he arranged for the Spider King, Louis of France to ransom Margaret from the Tower of London?"

"Yes," said Tyrell grinning broadly, "that was when King Edward started the rumour about him fathering her son." They both laughed and Giles began to feel much better.

"Come up and sit with your uncle," suggested Tyrell, "truth be known, he is distraught. Buckingham was his kinsman and he is taking his defection hard."

Giles hesitated, his nausea could return at any time.

"His Majesty has been asking for you," persisted Tyrell, "and for no particular reason other than he wants you close."

Sir James Tyrell and Sir Giles Butler were both ushered into the King's presence to find much excitement amongst those attending His Majesty. Sir Thomas Vaughan and Sir Richard Radcliffe were there, as was William Catesby and the King's Secretary, Kendall. The latter was the bird like man Giles had seen earlier. Now he bobbed up and down on his stool by the window, his over large, black habit flapping like wings when he moved and his long scrawny arms reaching out of voluminous sleeves, picking at this scroll and that, with bony, claw like hands.

"They are here now, my liege," cried Kendall scraping back his stool and peering out of the window like a perched crow, "they are here, below in the square."

Both Tyrell and Giles turned on their heels to discover who was following behind them and causing such excitement. The first to appear was Watkin Vaughan, his beard shaved and his fresh pink face glistening raw with recent exposure to the elements. He stood at the bottom of the table and bowed to the King, seated at the other end.

"Your Majesty my brother and I have brought the young Prince, Richard of York into your keeping."

Murmurings of anticipation were followed by gasps of disbelief as Roger Vaughan, similarly shaven, entered with a small girl at his side. The King jumped to his feet.

"What in God's name are you ... ?" He stopped speechless as the lass ripped off her small wimple and ran to greet him.

"It's me uncle Dickon, it is me, see," screamed the child, but the King could only stare at the shaven head and dirty buddle in female attire.

"I had to pretend to be a maid, so that nobody would guess who I really am. My head had to be shaved too and these two knights shaved their beards so that no-one would recognise them either. *And* I had to ride like a maid with both legs over one side of my horse. It is most difficult. Uncle, why do ladies ride so?"

The astonished silence of those watching snapped like a dry

crust at the boy's innocence and the room was filled with joyous laughter. King Richard picked up his nephew and hugged him close but when he eventually set him down he could see tears in the lads eyes. Before he could ask, the boy blurted out the cause of his pain.

"My brother is dead uncle Dickon. He was too ill to make the journey from the Tower into Wales. Aunt Kate nursed him well but he never left his bed." York wiped his face with his hand and sniffed hard. "Before he died he told me *I* must be King but I don't want to be. Please don't make me be King uncle Dickon. Please don't make me."

It was as if the music had stopped in a game of statues. Everyone froze. Nobody dared to speak, even if they had known what to say but York had spotted Giles at the back of the room, his question forgotten, he bounded over to him, oblivious of the consternation his plea had engendered.

"Sir Giles you are here too, how wonderful. Look, can you find me some proper clothes?"

"You shall have the finest cloths you can possibly imagine," said the King, "Master Kendall will attend to it immediately."

King Richard dined alone that evening but sent for Giles and Tyrell before he retired. When summonsed, Giles was recovering from another bout of vomiting and wanted only to curl up on the bed Mark had secured for him in a baker's shop. It was dark and an icy wind heralded the first of the winter's snow, causing Giles to feel dizzy as the sharpness of its bite cut into his sallow flesh and dried lips. Both men were huddled in their cloaks as they were shown into the King's bedchamber, a small room adjacent to the upper hall and barely large enough to house Richard's bed, which had travelled with him from Crosby Place. Apart from a series of chests stacked along the far wall, three strategically placed braziers and a floor standing candelabra, the room was bare. A couple of stools were carried in for the comfort of the two knights and with the King himself perched above them on the edge of his bed, dressed in his night attire, the scene reminded Tyrell of 'story time in the nursery'.

"I have just received intelligence that thirteen of Tudor's fleet of fifteen ships have been destroyed by heavy seas and that he has decided not to land off the Dorset coast after all," announced Richard, "pity really, we had a substantial reception waiting."

"The weather in the channel has been no kinder to Tudor than to Buckingham," smirked Tyrell, his fierce eyes burning with contempt, "God willing the rebels that fled to Flanders will also be bedding down with the fishes tonight."

"There is no news of them," said the King, "but tomorrow we set out for Bridport and then on to Exeter. If Tudor dares to land at Plymouth we will be ready for him."

Giles was shivering, not from the cold but from the weakness his vomiting had caused. King Richard moved the candelabra so that the light danced across his nephew's face. He scowled at his pinched features and sniffed a couple of times, curious to determine the smell which emanated from the damp patch on the front of Giles' tunic.

"Are you unwell nephew?"

"I fear so my Liege, I find it impossible to retain my food."

"Then that settles it," said the King firmly, "*you* will take our brother's son north for his own safety. If we engage any rebels tomorrow, you will be less than alert in your present state of health."

"No, please Your Majesty it will pass," begged Giles, hoping he sounded convincing. Like all young men in his position Giles had trained regularly in the tilt yard, proving himself skilful with most weapons but as yet his prowess had not been tested.

"Why take the boy north?" asked Tyrell, "why not take him to my home near Stowmarket? Nobody will think of looking for him at Gipping Hall and it's near enough to the coast should he need to escape from England."

"It will not come to that," said the King sternly, "but it's a sensible precaution. You can settle the boy at Gipping Hall Giles and join us later, if you feel well enough."

"The lad's mother might be persuaded to join him, if the location is kept secret?" suggested Tyrell.

"Indeed, yes," said the King, warming to the proposal, "send a messenger to London to inform Elizabeth Woodville of the arrangements for her son before you leave." King Richard grinned at the expression on Tyrell's face. "Go on with you man, you're dismissed. Go write a letter to your wife. Sir Giles can deliver it along with our instructions for the safe-keeping of the Duke of York."

Sir James Tyrell backed out of the King's presence offering thanks and promising not to be long composing his letter. The King climbed off the bed and signalled to Giles to remain seated. Opening a small trunk, Richard searched amongst its contents until he found a tiny ring which he passed to his nephew.

"See, it is like the one Edward gave your mother, except that the initials are RP; Richard Plantagenet."

Giles turned the ring between his forefinger and thumb, continuing to gaze at it whilst the tears welled uncontrollably in his eyes. Meanwhile the King rang the small silver bell on the floor by his bed which was answered by a bleary eyed squire.

"Bring Bishop Robert Stillington to our chamber at once," demanded Richard, and then perched on a stool next to a surprised Giles.

"Bishop Robert is here?"

"We've kept him close, since our coronation. There are those who blame the Bishop for the bloodless coup." The King warmed his hands over the nearest brazier. "Giles, the Bishop tells me that you and he still have much to sort out and as we leave for different destinations tomorrow, perhaps you should clear the air this evening."

Giles thought his uncle inferred 'whilst you have the chance' and when the door opened and the squire announced 'Bishop Stillington', he understood the need for haste. The once tall, proud man had aged amazingly since Giles had seen him last. The poor Bishop had been called from his bed, his night shirt billowing from beneath a hurriedly donned, cowled cloak. His fleshless frame tottered to the stool offered by the King and he perched precariously on its rim. The Bishop nodded to Giles and extended a bony hand covered in protruding veins but it was his yellowing skin and watery eyes that told of the precarious state of his health. Giles knelt at the Bishop's feet and kissed his ring.

"Say what needs to be said Robert," said King Richard softly, sitting on the stool furthest away from the pair.

The Bishop gazed into the face of his ward and being so close was able to read the concern in his eyes.

"I'm well enough Giles," he said by way of explanation, "His Majesty has taken good care of me but Matthew's death haunts my every living hour." He paused and smiled, "but it is not my demons we are here to slay, is it?"

"How old am I?" asked Giles, eager to make the most of the opportunity.

"Ah you've guessed," said the Bishop with a wry smile, "I thought you might. You were born in January 1462 as a result of King Edward's union with Eleanor Butler *after* their marriage in '61."

"So why the deceit?"

"It was for your protection Giles. When Edward married his queen in '64 Clarence must have heard some rumour because his men were asking questions in Norwich for months afterwards. Their enquiries came to nought but Eleanor was concerned that Edward's bigamy might become public knowledge in the near future and by claiming you were born in 1460 she hoped that Edward would not consider you his issue."

"You say George Clarence suspected Edward was hiding something in '64 and sent men to Norwich. Did they find the convent where my mother was living?"

The Bishop nodded.

"So why did my mother warn you about George Clarence in a note you were not going to read until my eighteenth birthday ten years later?"

"What note ? What warning?"

Giles flushed crimson. Of course, after all these years, the Bishop had never seen the note. Giles rummaged in his script and withdrew the copies he had made and passed them to the bewildered Bishop but quickly came to his aid as the old man fumbled awkwardly with the parchment.

"This one was for me, explaining that I was not illegitimate and that you married my parents and this one," Giles smoothed the parchment and placed it between Robert's shaking fingers, "was for you. I'm truly sorry I opened it."

Bishop Robert held the note close to his face and read the words aloud. *"Dearest Robert. Never allow my son Giles to meet the Duke of Clarence. Tell the King."* Slowly he lowered his hands whilst his mind reached back deep into the past.

"This note is why you believed the Duke of Clarence was your father?"

"Yes, together with my note and the ring. What is it?"

"You've misunderstood Giles," said the Bishop, wiping the sweat from his brow with his sleeve. "On the day of your mothers funeral, the old nun who had nursed Eleanor gave me your box and the key. She explained that you were to be given the box on your eighteenth birthday but she also gave *me* a tiny scroll with my name scratched into the wax seal. She told me that Clarence's men had been to the Convent asking questions just before Eleanor died and that your mother had made her promise to inform me of anyone who came asking questions in the future. Not satisfied that she had done all she could to warn me, Eleanor penned me a note which *I* slipped into your box for safe keeping, fully intending to remove it when we returned."

Giles dropped onto his stool, his brain whizzing like a spinning top.

"I simply forgot about the note," continued the Bishop, "you were so distressed when we left that I locked the box and gave it to you to hold as a comfort and after that you would not part with it. I kept the key for the next ten years. The rest you know."

Giles was speechless and taking pity on his nephew, Richard poured him wine and carried it over to where Giles sat dumbfounded on his stool.

"The note should have been read on the day of my mother's funeral and referred to Clarence's snooping around in '64"

"A cautionary tale," said the King with mock severity, "now, *we* have a question for you Robert. Why did you continue to lie about Giles' age after you delivered the pre-contract into our hands?"

Bishop Robert licked his dry lips and stared without sight

towards the blurred shape he knew to be the King.

"Sir Giles had a genuine claim to the throne Your Majesty and with so much instability and struggle for power, I took it upon myself to continue to protect him with the lie."

"There was no need," cried Giles, the vein on his temple beginning to pulsate, "I would not have challenged King Richard's right to the crown."

"Steady lad," calmed the King, "Robert was only carrying out your mother's wishes. The threat she perceived was just as real then, as it would have been if Edward's bigamy had been discovered when he was alive."

"BUT THERE IS NO THREAT NOW" said Giles, rising slowly from his seat and emphasising each word separately, "there is no threat to me *now* because Your Majesty, you have been anointed England's King. I may still have a *claim* to your throne but I have no *right* to it. It is yours. God has acknowledged you as his representative on English soil."

"So?"

Giles clasped his hands over his ears as if to shut out all thoughts but those which had just entered his brain.

"My God, that *is* the motive," he cried, "it is so mundane it went unnoticed."

"Motive?" cried King Richard, grabbing Giles by the arm and spinning him round, "Have you discovered *why* Edward was murdered?"

"Bear with me Your Majesty, I need to ask one more question of the Bishop."

Richard released Giles' arm and he bowed away from his uncle and faced Bishop Robert who sat in a terrified heap on his stool.

"Eleanor gave you instructions that if anyone approached the Convent with questions that would endanger King Edward or myself, they were to inform you." The Bishop swallowed hard and nodded. He knew Giles' next question. "Your Grace, did you receive any recent message from the Convent?"

"Just after the Christmas festivities, last year," stammered the Bishop, "the Prioress wrote saying that Anthony Earl Rivers had sort an audience with the old nun who had tended Eleanor Butler and that after Rivers departed, the confused woman had been distraught for fear she had unwittingly divulged Eleanor's secret."

"Your Majesty, once Rivers *knew for certain* that the princes were illegitimate, that in itself was the motive for murdering their father," exclaimed Giles triumphantly.

"Why?"

"Because if the secret broke before Edward died, his children would be pronounced bastards and you would become Edward's rightful heir."

"That has always been the situation since Edward married bigamously in 1464."

"Yes but it was a secure secret until five years ago when Clarence was put to death. It was only then that rumours of bigamy began to leak. Rivers heard the whispers and eventually tracked Eleanor Butler to the Convent in Norwich where he confronted the old nun and learned the whole truth. King Edward was in good health and likely to live for twenty or so years and Rivers believed the entire story would be public knowledge long before his natural death. You would be declared 'heir apparent' and unless King Edward re-married Elizabeth Woodville and she bore him another son, the reign of Woodville was ended."

"Rivers murdered Edward so that the boy could be crowed before the secret broke." cried Richard. "Now I follow your argument nephew. Once a monarch has been anointed he is accepted by God. If the boy was pronounced a bastard after his coronation then as you so aptly demonstrated, I would have had a *claim* to his crown but no *right* to it. Well done Giles. Well done."

Both uncle and nephew sat in silence for some minutes when Giles suddenly jumped to his feet like a released spring. Anthony Rivers visited his sister Lady Katherine Buckingham last Christmas. That is how she knew her nephews were illegitimate. But who else did he tell?"

"All the Woodvilles close to Edward," spat King Richard, "Elizabeth, Dorset and Grey. Even Lionel Woodville, Bishop of Salisbury. Christ save us! were they all party to Edward's murder?"

"No, no, not the murder," insisted Giles, Rivers informed his family of Edward's bigamy and promised them *he* would deal with it. Clearly the fewer people knew the nature of his remedy the better."

"Can you be certain?" persisted King Richard, "all those involved must be punished."

"Queen Elizabeth Woodville may have suspected after your coup at Stony Stratford but not before," said Giles, recalling how she had appeared nervous when he had hinted at Rivers' guilt. "However, when Edward died she recognised the advantage of crowning the Prince immediately, not only did it make your claim to the throne more difficult should the boy's illegitimacy become public knowledge but it also alleviated the need for your Protectorship."

"Which is why she deliberately failed to inform us of Edward's death."

"Yes, she needed time to make the arrangements for the coronation and to send for the Prince from Ludlow. If she had been party to the murder she would have informed you of Edward's death immediately."

"Because the sequel to Rivers' murder of King Edward was our assassination and by delaying our coming to London she unwittingly also delayed Rivers and the Prince," said the King, recalling that his wife had drawn that particular conclusion weeks ago.

"When I informed Elizabeth that her brother had murdered King Edward, she agreed he must pay for the deed with his life."

"He did," said the King coldly, "at Pontefract, before our coronation. Officially he died for attempting to assassinate myself and Buckingham at Stony Stratford but which of the Woodvilles was Rivers' accomplice Giles? Who actually poisoned our brother King Edward?"

"It was not a Woodville Your Majesty. I am certain Sir Matthew Pawson stuffed the fruits with arsenic. Lord Rivers somehow managed to blackmail the knight. I have found the man who delivered the blank parchment to Lord Rivers at King's Lynn and he has confirmed that it was Sir Matthew Pawson who employed him."

"No, no" wailed the Bishop rocking precariously on his stool, "that's a wicked lie."

"You have proof Giles? Of blackmail?" demanded the King.

"Not exactly. The accomplice had to be someone very close to Edward. Someone who knew of his dislike for marchpane and Jane Shore's love of the sweet so that the harmless, marchpane stuffed dates could be placed on the same plate as the plain ones filled with arsenic."

"But that could have been one of several individuals."

"Not really my Lord. Only Matthew had control of the serving dish. If anyone else had tampered with the dates it would have been pure chance as to when the sweetmeats were placed on the table. Without careful management other diners besides the King may have been poisoned and then the food and drink would have been rigorously scrutinised. No, for Rivers' plan to succeed, Edward must appear to die from natural causes. To ensure this deceit, Jane Shore had to eat from the same dishes without ill effect and to guarantee that the dates were served to only Jane and Edward the accomplice needed to be in attendance in the supper chamber."

"But you suspected the palm fruits almost immediately nephew?"

"Yes but only as a source of natural food poisoning. By simple coincidence I was present at the Tower five years ago when Matthew served two separate plates of dates, one stuffed with marchpane as they are normally prepared and one without, prepared exclusively for King Edward. I remembered because I dislike marchpane myself and Edward commented at the time. So, when Edward was first taken ill I pointed out to Matthew that whilst Jane and Edward had chosen dates from the same dish they had eaten separately prepared and identifiable pieces of fruit."

"Sir Matthew must have been terrified," mused King Richard.

"He was utterly confused my Lord but his flamboyant nature and love of drama formed a natural cover for his guilty panic and as Edward recovered, foul play was never suspected."

"Until the second attempt to murder him was successful."

"Even then I failed to identify Matthew as the culprit because he was escorting Jane Shore to Westminster when Edward consumed the poisoned fruits, innocently brought to him by the knight deputising for Sir Matthew. I quickly proved the method of murder by feeding the discarded dates to the sewer rats but I failed to recognize the poisoner because the only real evidence of his identity was to be found after the first attempt on Edward's life a week earlier. You see, in his panic Matthew had announced the King's impending death as soon as he collapsed. How could he have come to such a dramatic conclusion if he had no knowledge of what had caused his vomiting? He even escorted Jane out of the King's bedroom saying that women were not allowed in the death chamber, *before* the physicians had given their opinion and then he sent the prearranged blank note to Rivers at Thorsby's manor in Lynn."

"Only to have to do it all over again a week later," concluded the King with a shudder, "but how could Rivers blackmail the wretch into such atrocious action?"

"I have no idea," sighed Giles, "the poor man could not live with what he had done. His suicide is evidence of that."

"What is it Giles, are you feeling ill again?" asked the King. Giles had gasped suddenly and covered his face with his hands.

"Ill? No, no, I have just remembered. The day I left Hatton at the Tower grumbling about Dorset re-packaging King Edward's treasure, I returned to Westminster and was about to knock on Sir Matthew's door. I intended consulting him regarding Douglas Hatton's dilemma when I heard raised voices. I recognised Matthew's shrill protests but could not place the other voice but now I realise it was Lord Rivers. He must have been appraising Matthew of the part he was to play in the murder. I failed to recognise his voice because he was supposedly in Ludlow at the time."

In the pause that followed, King Richard and Giles became aware of the Bishop whimpering and rocking on his stool like a miserable child.

"It has been a terrible shock for him. He did not know until now that Edward was murdered, let alone that his friend Matthew administered the poison," whispered Giles. "My Lord it has been too much for His Grace to assimilate."

Servants were summonsed and ordered to take the Bishop to his bed and a watch to be placed outside his door. Giles pulled

Robert's cloak tightly around the old man's shoulders and fastened it with the clasp at his neck. The Bishop made no attempt to move and Giles gently guided him to the door, pulling the cowl down over his vacant face against the chill night air.

"The Vaughan brothers will escort you to Stowmarket tomorrow," said the King soberly, as the door closed behind the broken Bishop, "Take good care of your cousin, York ... your stepbrother York." Giles waited to be dismissed but the King hesitated, chewing his bottom lip whilst making his decision. Minutes appeared to pass before his uncle spoke again. "Sit down Giles."

Giles perched on the nearest stool and King Richard dragged a second one and sat so close to him that their knees touched.

"Your loyalty has earned you the right to be told another family secret but you must guard it with your life. Those involved have suffered enough but it has implications that you should be aware of."

Giles braced himself. He dreaded every undeclared detail of his family history and a secret that required such close protection could only cause more distress.

"Have you never wondered why Clarence was so adamant that Edward was illegitimate?" began the King.

"Not really. Most folk believe the Duke lost his mind."

"That may well be true but ... " Richard took a deep breath. "When our brother King Edward announced he had secretly married Elizabeth Woodville, he publicly humiliated the Earl of Warwick who had just returned from Europe with a politically suitable bride for his licentious young majesty. Our mother, Warwick's aunt, was also humiliated, embarrassed and very, very angry." The King left his stool and paced the floor whilst he composed the words for his revelation. "Few people are aware Giles that our mother summonsed her kinsman Warwick and told him that she was prepared to go before parliament and say that Edward was *not* the son of her husband, the Duke of York." The King returned to his stool and stared earnestly at Giles. "Understand nephew, those privy to her offer believed she was prepared to falsely accuse herself out of loyalty to Warwick. You see, it was well known that our mother and father were devoted to one another and as Edward was the eldest, it seemed unlikely that she would have committed adultery so soon after her marriage."

"But George Clarence chose to believe the story?" ventured Giles.

"George was fifteen at the time and we were both living at Middleham Castle, wards of the Earl. We never heard a word of the story because Warwick refused his aunt's generosity, insisting that he could rise above the humiliation but when he and Edward fell out he told George of our mother's claim of adultery and George chose to believe it, henceforth claiming that *he* was York's rightful heir."

"How dishonourable of the Earl of Warwick," said Giles stiffly, "since his aunt had invented her story of adultery to save him from embarrassment."

The King ignored Giles' observation.

"On the night of your abduction last July, we sort an audience with our mother just before midnight. Perhaps you remember?"

"I do. Buckingham suggested that if King Edward was not the Duke of York's issue, as George Clarence had always claimed, then that would further support your claim to the throne."

"It did. Our mother conceded that Edward was not the son of our father York but she did not commit adultery. The Duchess had travelled to Rouen in France to be with the Duke of York, where she stayed whilst he joined the fighting men some sixty miles away. She was in France in hostile times Giles and was ravished by a French soldier. When York returned and discovered the newly born Edward, he knew the child was not his because he had not lain with her for many weeks longer than a child can reasonably remain in the womb."

Giles left his stool and began to pace the room in an attempt to contain his panic.

"So York is not my grandfather, and your Majesty is only my step-uncle."

"Indeed Giles. But more significantly you have no claim what-so-ever to the crown."

"I don't care," said Giles petulantly, "I'm sick of this family and its secrets. Just when I think I know who I am another revelation destroys me again." The pulse on his temple was throbbing painfully and pacing the floor was not enough to control his anger which burst through and raged unfettered. "If York is not my grandfather then who is? I have a right to know his identity so do not tell me others have suffered and need the protection of silence. I swear I will not rest until I know his name."

On hearing the commotion two guards burst into the chamber to defend their King but Richard screamed at them to retire and they disappeared just as swiftly. Their abrupt appearance shocked Giles out of his tantrum leaving him deflated, exhausted and sobbing in a helpless heap on the floor.

To his credit, King Richard neither chided him for his rudeness nor patronised him with sympathy and comfort. He simply waited in silence until Giles had recovered his composure and lamely apologised for his outburst.

"No matter nephew," sighed the King, "your display of tantrum was like watching myself in some mummery. We should both try harder to restrain our anger."

"Did King Edward know he was not York's son?" ask Giles meekly.

"On the night Clarence was to die, Edward travelled to Baynard's Castle, knowing that our mother would rise from her bed for Matins. Little Ned told me he had seen the King with his grandma in the great hall but I dismissed his childish chatter as a dream but he was not dreaming. In the small hours of that dreadful day, Edward had had the grace to inform our mother of his intension to execute George, citing his bigamy as justification for the deed and in return she confided that he was not York's son."

CHAPTER 38
Salisbury 2nd November 1483

An hour later Giles left the King's chamber still humiliated by his outburst, but the cold night air swept in from beyond the opened door, stinging his face and jolting him sharply out of his embarrassment. A dusting of snow had fallen and a gentle scrunch of flakes compressed beneath his feet. There were no lights in any of the buildings around the square but a hunter's moon illuminated the night scene with eerie light, merging shape with shadow and substance with silhouette.

"Come on Giles, its freezing out here," called Mark from the bottom of the steps, "watch yourself its slippery."

"How long have you been waiting?" called Giles, as he slithered down the last two steps and grabbed at Mark's sleeve to regain his balance.

"I've found you a bed for the night, remember? Well you don't know where to go, do you? and since it's paid for, I'm just making sure you sleep in the darn thing."

Mark, stamped his feet and rubbed his arms to ward off the increasing cold before ploughing across the square in the direction of the bakery. Giles dawdled behind, making incomprehensible tracks in the snow. He was contemplating his own woeful temper and his growing fondness for his step-uncle, King Richard.

"Stop arsing about," whinged Mark, and waited by the market cross for Giles to catch up.

The scaffold had been dismantled and removed, leaving no sign of the execution that had take place only hours before. If the ground had been disturbed by the construction, the grass flattened by the feet of the crowd or if blood had splattered the base of the cross, this gentle snowfall had obliterated the evidence.

"So mighty a man," whispered Giles, sobered by the scene.

"Come on Giles. Let it be," and taking his master by the elbow, Mark guided him towards the shop. "We can bed down in front of the hearth. The baker and his wife have the back room and the apprentice sleeps by the ovens out back."

The door was not locked so Giles and Mark crept into the darkness. As they gained their night eyes they could just make out the leather curtain that covered the entrance leading to the backroom and the board that served as a counter, leaning against the trestles on the side wall. Two blankets had been left on a stool well away from the hearth as the embers were still glowing but not for much longer. A quart of ale, a basket of shrivelled apples and some cheese were on a shelf above the trestles and Mark brought them to the hearth and tried to persuade Giles to eat. Mark tucked in but Giles picked at the cheese fearful that his stomach would reject it.

"Try and eat something Giles, we have a long ride tomorrow."

It was not cold in the shop but Giles was shivering again so Mark wrapped the blankets around his master like a shroud and using two small sacks of grain for bolsters, they huddled in front of the fire. Before either had settled, the leather curtain swung silently to one side and a large hairy dog padded in and pushed his wet nose into Mark's face. The animal must have satisfied himself that he was a dog lover because without investigating Giles' odour the hound stretched out between the two men with his head resting on Mark's chest.

"I suspect the baker has rented you this mutt's bed," whispered Giles, "but he'll keep us both warm if he stays still."

He had stopped shivering now, the ale had warmed him and the blankets wound tightly around his body felt reassuring and comfortable.

"Do you remember, years ago when we slept with Woof for warmth, on the floor in front of the hearth at Clipberry Manor?"

asked Mark, "it was snowing that night too. The night before your birthday and the momentous opening of the casket your mother left you. Do you remember?"

"Of course I remember," replied Giles with such a cracked voice that Mark turned to face him and was startled to see the tears running down Giles' face.

"What is it? For God's sake Giles, whatever is the matter?"

"I also remember the following morning. If I hadn't opened the note addressed to the Bishop I would never have revealed my identity to the Duke of Clarence. He would not have challenged King Edward and the King would not have executed him."

"You can't be sure of that," countered Mark.

"Can't I ? Well, at the very least Earl Rivers would not have been alerted to Edward's bigamy and would not have murdered the King or blackmailed poor Matthew so that he committed suicide. Richard Gloucester would have remained at Middleham, where both he and his wife would rather be and Lord Hastings would still be alive."

"Well yes," conceded Mark, "but you cannot blame yourself for other people's actions, even if you did start the ball rolling."

"No? Think about it Mark. Bishop Morton's plot to bring Tudor to England would never have been revived if Edward had not been murdered and the Duke of Buckingham would still be alive."

"This is ridiculous Giles. Stop it"

"Why should I?" sniffed Giles, "I would not have been kidnapped so Luke would not have made the journey to Brecknock and may well have survived his fall. Buckingham would not have forced Edward's sons to travel to Wales and the elder boy may also have lived. *It's all my fault*. If only I hadn't opened the note addressed to Bishop Robert Stillington."

"You are being pathetic Giles. Twelve weeks imprisoned at Brecknock has unhinged your mind. You might just as well say that it is all your mother's fault."

"How dare you!"

"Face it Giles, if Eleanor had not included a note for Bishop Robert in your confounded box then it would not have been there for you to open in the first place."

"She didn't," wailed Giles, "on the day of Eleanor's funeral the Bishop was handed that note separately from my box. He had the key to the box and just placed his note inside for safe keeping but he forgot about it and the next time it saw light of day was when I opened the casket on my birthday."

Mark stared in disbelief at Giles who wiped his face on the rough blanket and sniffed.

"Well that makes more sense," said Mark, after quickly running though the implications in his head.

"Of course it does," sighed Giles, "the only thing I still don't understand is why Earl Rivers was able to blackmail Sir Mathew Pawson?"

Again Mark stared at Giles with wide eyes. "You really don't know? You didn't even suspect?"

It was Giles' turn to be surprised. "Suspect what ? What are you on about Mark?"

"Bishop Robert and Sir Matthew were lovers. How could you not have guessed? All those Sunday afternoons when they, ' played chess' in Robert's chamber?"

"I knew that Matthew was a Piers Gaveston," stammered Giles, "but Bishop Robert ... no, I had no idea."

"Rivers installed John Alcock at Clipberry to find out what the Bishop knew of King Edward's secret but he must have stumbled on the Bishop's relationship with Matthew and informed his master."

"That would certainly be sufficient ammunition for Rivers to blackmail poor Matthew," whispered Giles, as he tried to assimilate the new information. "If Alcock had reported the Bishop to the church authorities and made sufficient fuss, King Edward would have been powerless to prevent his being boiled alive. That is still the punishment for proven sodomy, even in these modern times."

Mark winced and reached across the floor to where he had dropped his sword belt and script. Pulling his script into the blankets he began to search through the contents.

"The Bishop was at Wells Cathedral recovering Eleanor's precontract when Matthew committed suicide," explained Mark, "it was Arthur who discovered the hanging body and informed Alcock but not before he had removed Matthew's suicide note, which he later handed to my mother."

Giles snatched the rolled parchment that Mark was dragging from his script.

"It is unopened!"

"And it's addressed to the Bishop," warned Mark, watching Giles fingering the seal, "Arthur and Mary concealed the note from Alcock's prying eyes and gave it to me to hand to Bishop Robert. It is sure to be Matthew's confession. Bishop Robert may guess that Matthew succumbed to Rivers' blackmail to save him from being boiled alive but to see the truth written in Matthew's own hand may be too much for his sanity."

"You can be sure of that," sighed Giles, "tonight I witnessed him crumble when he learned of Matthew's treason. Fortunately I was telling the truth when I told the King I had no idea how Rivers managed to blackmail poor Mathew."

"Need King Richard be told the truth now?"

By way of an answer Giles threw the unopened note onto the dying fire. It smouldered and charred slowly but then burst into flames and burned brightly for a few seconds before shrinking back and disintegrating into blackened fragments.

Giles woke early on the third day of November, disturbed by the apprentice raking out the ovens in preparation for their relighting. It had stopped snowing and whilst the pink sky threatened more bad weather, it enhanced the magic of the spotless white stretching across the square.

He had not been sick during the night and the sound of water in his head was not so deafening this morning. Taking two apples from the shelf, Giles tiptoed out into the street to relieve himself and after kicking snow over the melted trail where his urine had soiled the path, he turned and faced the snow covered square. Munching hungrily on an apple, he relived the childhood thrill of being the first to walk across the virgin blanket and absorbed in renewed wonderment he gazed into the glistening softness, trying to distinguish the individual flakes that winked up at him. Less than a dozen stride into the blaze of white he discovered an earlier riser had had the temerity to tread before him. The vein on his temple began to pulsate as he following the trespassing foot prints which brought him to the steps of the market cross.

"What are you so angry about this morning nephew," asked the King, as Giles halted less than two strides away from the offending feet.

He lifted his head in surprise, considered the ludicrous situation and burst into laughter.

"I was lost in my own childish world Sire. Believing myself to be the only one up at this hour, your footprints irritated me."

"Now that is serious," laughed Richard, pushing the cowl from his head and forcing his cloak behind his shoulders, "our sleep was disturbed by a messenger from Plymouth. Tudor has sailed back to Brittany, the Bishops Morton and Woodville are in Flanders."

"Is that good?"

"Maybe. Since Tudor has made such poor use of Duke Francis' investment, the Duke may now be prepared to consider our request to extradite the bastard from Brittany. What it does mean, is that there will be no more bloodshed for the time being, other than those traitors we apprehend before they can make it across the channel."

"What about the little Prince My Lord, will you show him to parliament and retrieve your good name?"

"By Christmas perhaps but for now we will endure the slur," said the King with a rye smile, "the lad's life is in danger until we have mopped up all Tudor's support. But Giles, ensure his mother knows he is safe at Gipping Hall."

"My squire, Mark Taylor will return to London immediately to inform Elizabeth. I know that he is smitten by Queen Anne's maid and will be overjoyed to return to Westminster."

"Lucy? That's good news. It's high time the lass was wed," said the King seriously.

Giles doubted Mark's intention to *wed* Lucy. He thought a tumble in the laundry room was all his squire had in mind but he dare not joke about such things with his uncle who was well known for his strange sense of morality.

"And you Giles," continued the King, "have you a sweetheart hidden in the Capital?"

"Er, no, Your Majesty" replied Giles rather too firmly so that the King smiled and put his arm about his nephew's shoulders.

"It's alright Giles, it's allowed," he said kindly.

Giles stared helplessly into the snow. He dare not meet his uncle's eyes for fear he could read his thoughts. The only woman Giles craved was Margery and she had whored for King Edward, Lord Hastings and dozens of other nobles as well as once being promised to Luke. Even Mark had enjoyed her bed. Giles knew the King would recoil at such wantonness, though he failed to see why.

"There will be time enough for such pleasures now that Tudor is thwarted. And once the Woodvilles discover that we have not murdered our brother's sons they will retract their support for Tudor, leaving the Welsh bastard confined to Brittany for the foreseeable future."

"I think not uncle," said Giles seriously.

"Oh, and why not?"

"Because Bishop Morton is now openly committed to Tudor and the Bishop has no longer the luxury of time."

"What has Bishop Morton got to do with anything?"

"John Morton is the real enemy my Liege. Since the death of Queen Margaret's son, Morton's loyalties have been only to himself.

"Rubbish, that fat priest was devoted to our brother. You said so yourself."

Giles shook his head.

"Only in so far as it suited him. After the rout at Tewkesbury, Tudor bought Morton's support with the promise of his becoming Archbishop of Canterbury and when King Edward died he turned his energies towards Tudor's cause. He was merciless in leading Lord Hastings into treason and when Buckingham was looking to put his own treason behind him and support you in earnest, it was Morton who suggested the Duke should aim for the crown for himself, so that he could walk free from Brecknock."

"I'm sure you are correct Giles but you cannot blame Bishop Morton for treason committed by Will Hastings and Harry Buckingham. They, like us, are judged by what they *do*. We cannot pass the responsibility for our actions on to those who advise and encourage us, however skilfully they deceive. And there's an end to it."

Across the square, concerned knights and squires were spilling out of the Boar in search of the King. He had been missed from his lodgings and had left no message as to his whereabouts. Richard sighed, there were some aspects of his exalted royal status he could do without and being constantly surrounded and fussed over by attendants and advisors was one of them.

"Granted that Morton will dedicate himself to Tudor from now on, why does that mean a second attempt to invade these shores will be sooner rather than later?" asked King Richard, holding up his hand to signal his whereabouts to Radcliffe, as the knight hurried from the stables with a column of guards, intent on widening the search.

"Morton is only a few months from his seventieth birthday Sire. If he intends to become Archbishop of Canterbury he needs Tudor to make a move quickly, before the aging Bishop is summonsed by his Maker."

"I doubt Tudor will be concerned about Bishop Morton's ambitions, or his age," laughed the King, turning to walk back to the Boar and his anxious attendants. "Come and take your leave of us before you set out for Stowmarket. We wish to see both you and York before you go."

You're so wrong, thought Giles to himself as he watched his uncle climb the steps to the upper chamber. With Bishop Morton behind the scenes, Tudor will be back sooner than you think. Morton can ensnare and persuade even the most powerful men and at the same time convince them that they are thinking for themselves. After-all, it was John Morton who convinced the King of France to support Warwick and it was Morton who inveigled Warwick into abandoning York and marrying his daughter to the Lancastrian Prince. It was John Morton who prevailed on the Spider King to buy off King Edward with an annual pension when he invaded France, despite Richard's efforts to convince his brother that it was dishonourable to accept the bribe.

Giles sighed and began to retrace his steps back to the bakery, the shutters were open and the trestles bearing the board, laden with bread and hot meat pies.

"Morton's influence is greater than you imagine," whispered Giles to himself, "he works though other people, deliberately keeping himself in the shadows but pulling all the stings like an accomplished puppeteer. I warrant that even history will not record the true extent of his influence in our time."

Author's Notes

'Roses are White' is a story based on the secret known only to Edward IV and Bishop Robert Stillington.

In truth, the marriage pre-contract between Edward IV and Lady Eleanor Butler is dismissed by many historians as a lie concocted by Richard III to support his claim to the throne. Undoubtedly, Bishop Robert Stillington's disclosure was convenient but that in itself does not render it untrue.

The disputed details of Edward's first marriage and subsequent bigamous marriage are recorded in the *Titulus Regius*, Richard III's official claim to the throne which was set before parliament in 1484. The Act has survived despite Henry Tudor's (Henry VII) efforts to destroy every copy.

The account of Stillington being the source of this information is recorded by Tudor historians but the name of Eleanor Butler is replaced by that of Elizabeth Lucy, a courtesan and known mistress of Edward IV. Clearly this was done deliberately in order to discredit the story as Edward was unlikely to have married a prostitute, suggesting that the Tudors had reason to believe Stillington's disclosure. The accurate version was not published until the end of the eighteenth century.

Assuming the story to be true, it is impossible to say whether the pre-contract took the form of a written document or was simply Stillington's recollection of having witnessed the vows. Never-the-less, one of Henry Tudor's first actions as England's king was to arrest and imprison Bishop Robert Stillington. Parliament requested permission to re-examine the Bishop but Tudor refused and Robert Stillington died in prison some years later.

Many documents from this period are missing and there is good reason to believe most were burned during the reigns of Henry VII and his son Henry VIII. If Stillington's evidence took the form of a written contract it would certainly have been the first to be thrown on the fire.

Giles Butler

Eleanor Butler was the daughter of the Earl of Shrewsbury and she is known to have given birth to a son prior to entering a nunnery in Norwich. I am indebted to *Alison Weir* for discovering that the child was named Giles. Little is known of his life but if Edward IV took Eleanor to his bed, pre-contracted or not, then it is most likely that Giles was his son.

The Death of Edward IV

The cause of Edward IV's premature death was a mystery to his doctors and several contemporary commentators suggest that he was poisoned. However, most modern historians do not subscribe to the murder theory, believing instead that he had a stroke or a heart attack. I am indebted to R. C. Collins for his essay, "The Death of Edward IV" in which he applies his own medical expertise as well as that of his colleagues to Edward's illness, concluding that the king was in fact poisoned and that it took two attempts for the murderer to succeed.